MW01174825

Desires Unleashed

Knights of the Darkness Chronicles

by

D.N. Simmons

authorHOUSE™

1663 LIBERTY DRIVE, SUITE 200
BLOOMINGTON, INDIANA 47403
(800) 839-8640
WWW.AUTHORHOUSE.COM

This book is a work of fiction. Places, events, and situations in this story are purely fictional and any resemblance to actual persons, living or dead, is coincidental.

© 2004 D.N. Simmons
All Rights Reserved.

No part of this book may be reproduced, stored in a retrieval system, or transmitted by any means without the written permission of the author.

First published by AuthorHouse 10/04/04

ISBN: 1-4184-8115-7 (sc)
ISBN: 1-4184-8116-5 (dj)

Printed in the United States of America
Bloomington, Indiana

This book is printed on acid-free paper.

Dedication and Acknowledgments

This is dedicated to my beautiful mother, Marian Simmons, who believed in me, when it was difficult for me to believe in myself. Mother, you are truly the "Wind beneath my Wings." God blessed me the day I was born to you, Thank You.

I would like to thank the following people with all of my heart: Anisi Bath and Beauty, Adele Stadeker, Michelle Barta(hellkat), Christine Savage(Megalo), Crystal Savage(Peppermintstix), Krista Herrington(Dark Destiny), Alia Savage(S. Joisan), Richard Moss(Alucard), Stephanie Polukis(Danika Valin), Shondolyn J Gibson(Synthesia), Steven M. Ciecko(Dino) Nicky Sims(Batty) Raven(Mystress Bathory), Caitlin Johnston (DragonGirl), Ladyprye, and all of the members of the Knights of the Darkness Discussion Forum for all of your support and encouragement, I love you all

Prologue

"You should never have betrayed me, Anthony," Darian was saying as he beckoned for Xavier to come closer. "Goodbye, Anthony." The horrifying truth finally dawned on Anthony. His death was inevitable. He mentally cursed himself for not booking town. He should have never tried to wait for her. He should have hightailed it out of the city on the fastest plane to Timbuktu. He should have never opened the door, he should have known they'd come for him. Now he was going to die. A spark in his brain told him to try to escape.

"NO!!!!" Anthony screamed and tried to rise up from the floor, but John's strong hands held him in an iron grip. He could not move an inch, not even to struggle. He watched in horror as Xavier stood in front of him, then kneeled down. He cringed when Xavier caressed his face, softly with both hands. Tears rolled down his cheeks and Xavier leaned forward and caught a tear drop on his tongue, savoring his fear. A low groan rumbled through Xavier's chest that was a mingle of pure hunger and lust.

"Shhhh, quiet," Xavier cooed. "You die tonight, but you die as the chosen. Fear not, you are lucky to die tonight by a vampire's kiss." Xavier whispered into Anthony's ears. Xavier extended his silent command-coaxing Anthony to relax. Once Xavier felt the other man's muscles relax, he leaned closer to the pulsating artery underneath the smooth soft skin of Anthony's neck. Xavier's mouth opened, fangs extending for the feeding. Anthony gasped, his back arching as Xavier's fangs broke through the skin. As Xavier began to feed, audible sucking noises filled the room. Low moans were coming from the two men, both enwrapped in pleasure, both sharing this special union. Darian watched closely, he enjoyed watching the vampire's kiss in motion. He delighted in watching other people enjoying pleasure in all forms.

Anthony let out a long shivering moan, his body twitched once, twice and then, fell limp in Xavier's arms. Xavier continue to feed, draining the body completely. He savored the warm delicious, thick fluid as it filled his mouth and flowed down his throat. He could not, would not give this sensation up for anything in the world. He tilted his head slightly, to widen his mouth and capture more of the blood that warmed him. It excited him, he could feel it spread throughout all of his limbs. His body tingled as though little electric shocks where bursting over his body. He had grown hard during the feeding as all vampires do, and he felt his passions rise to the crest.

Xavier had to contain his disappointment when the blood stopped flowing. He forced himself away and let Anthony's corpse slip from his hands. His head rolled back, eyes half open, mouth parted slightly, blood stained his full shaped lips. He ran his hands down the length of this torso, past his stomach, to caress his groin. His body twitched as he massaged his organ. Darian smiled and waved John out of his office. John nodded and bent down to retrieved the lifeless body of Anthony, he threw the body over his shoulder and exited the room. Darian walked up behind Xavier and he peered into Xavier's grey eyes and smiled. He squatted beside Xavier, his arm encircling the other man's chest. He held Xavier against his torso with his left arm, while his right hand slid up Xavier's chest to caress his throat. He grabbed Xavier's chin held his face up to his. Darian's tongue darted out to lick up the spilt blood from Xavier's lips. Their tongues met and the two embraced in a passionate kiss. A low groan escaped from Xavier. Darian began to caress Xavier's chest, he slid a hand inside his shirt, his fingers sought the firm nipples and gently rolled the delicate flesh between his fingertips, sending shivers through Xavier's form. Darian's other hand, slid further down to caress Xavier's crotch, massaging the hardness through the denim material. Ragged panting moans filled the room and Xavier begin to feel his climax. Then all the sensation stopped, when Darian released Xavier and rose from the floor.

Chapter 1

Detective Warren Davis shuffled through the messy stack of files on his desk. He was searching desperately for his desk key. He had hidden a box of *Crunchy Cream* glazed donuts in his side drawer and wanted to indulge selfishly in the delicious sugery taste of-in his opinion, "*the best damn donuts to hit the 21st century.*" Finally after turning his desk into a disaster area he located the tiny metal key. He glanced slyly over one shoulder then the other to make sure no one was watching, he knew how irresistible *Crunchy Creams* could be, he would hate to have to share. He slowly turned the key and unlocked the drawer.

There they lay, the sweets of gods! Slowly Warren opened the box and pulled one glazed donut from the container and stuffed the donut in its' entirety, into his mouth. He savored the gigantic burst of sweetness that followed "*mmm delicious,*" he thought to himself as he closed the drawer and settled back in his battered leather chair, chewing the donut slowly so that he could savor every bite.

"What are you eating?" His Partner Det. Matthew Eric asked as he approached him and stood beside Warren's relaxing figure, noting the huge bulges in the insides of his partners' cheeks. Matthew Eric stood six-feet-three, very muscular and extremely handsome. His mop of dark brown curls fell over his light brown eyes, his skin was tanned a perfect soft -golden shade. His physique reminded Warren of a light weight wrestler.

Warren swallowed, forcing one huge piece of donut down his throat then another, which he was thankful for, because it gave him time to think of a believable lie. Matthew looked down at his partner, a smile spreading across his face as he watched Warren nearly choking to rid himself of the evidence. He waited patiently for the lie that would sure enough come spilling from

1

those glazed covered lips. He thought Warren should know better than to open a box of *Crunchy Cremes,* and not think anyone would not want some.

"Oh" Warren managed to say swallowing the last of his donut. "This? It's nothing," He followed up with a huge gulp of his decaffeinated coffee. Then he smiled innocently up at his partner. The expression on Matthew's face told Warren the gig was up and he had better share the wealth. "What?" Warren asked, shrugging his shoulders.

"If you don't cough it up, there's going to be repercussions" Matthew threatened playfully.

"Are you sure?" Warren asked, smiling slyly.

"Un-hmm." Matthew nodded.

"Okay." Warren began coughing and gagging playfully, attempting to bring up what he had swallowed.

Matthew grimaced in mock disgust. "Oh god, man stop it!"

Warren laughing, reached into his drawer and offered the box up. "I was going to give you some anyway." He stated.

"Yeah, sure you were." Matthew teased jokingly as he all but snatched a donut from the box.

He sat back into his chair and took a bite out of the donut. After savoring the first bite, he looked at Warren.

"Remember when we first shared a box of these donuts?" Matthew asked.

"Yeah. That was when you first discovered my secret." The two men sat at their desk enjoying their tasty treats.

Twelve years ago, when Matthew was twenty-one, and fresh out of college, he had joined the Police force. After Matthew had been on the force for seven years, already a seasoned detective, he was partnered up with Warren, who had been on the force for five years. They hit it off instantly and have been partners and friends ever since. But they never dreamt they would become crime fighters against supernatural criminals. When the supernatural race(the politically correct phrase) was exposed, the government was forced to create a nationwide policing unit to monitor and arrest certain individuals with supernatural abilities who broke the law. So they began by recruiting one hundred thousand of the nations top cops and military personnel who were physically fit and mentally astute to began the arduous training in paramilitary tactics, and weaponry specially designed to deal with those who possessed supernatural abilities. The training had been created to improve motor skills and heighten senses of sight, smell, and hearing, extremely necessary to combat and apprehend the unique criminal element in the supernatural world. Only five hundred out of the first one hundred thousand recruited made it through the demanding process, but more were needed. And then the call went out for more volunteers, which, in the end gave the government an additional thousand officers needed to complete the fifteen hundred armed member force. And two thousand civilian force, specializing in the fields of forensics, chemistry, character profiling, social behaviorists and weaponry. Because of their impeccable record of being among the best of the best on the police force, Warren and Matthew were drafted by the Superintendent of Police via the Mayor of Chicago for the recruitment. Mainly due to their unique partnership, and believing it would be very beneficial to the local Supernatural Unit Investigation Team, they were reassigned as partners to the Chicago division.

As Matthew took another bite of his donut, he remembered their captain wanted to see the two of them in her office-pronto. After he swallowed, he then decided to inform his partner.

"Hey I forgot, the Captain wanted us in her office 'ASAP!'" Matthew said calmly, as he munched on more of the donut.

"Oh really? Well I guest we better hurry!" Det. Davis smiled as he reached in his drawer for a third donut. The two were still enjoying their donuts when officer Brown walked by. He was a tall good looking black man, clean shaven, well built, the health conscience/athletic type.

"Hey, the Captain is looking for you two, If I were you, I'd hustle in there, on the double." Officer Brown said, then he grimaced in disgust at the two men fattening themselves on the two hundred calories per serving donuts. "Damn shame" he said, then he walked away, leaving the two Detectives to smile at each other before rising to head into their Captain's office.

They passed a few officers teasing them by making throat slitting motions. Everyone suspected the Captain was going to have another difficult case for the two detectives to work on, they were right.

"What took you two so long to get in here!?" Captain Michelle Lawrence asked as she sat at her desk. The two detectives were disappointed that they could not get a glimpse of her long shapely legs hidden behind the desk. Her long blonde hair fell in waves past her shoulders onto her shirt front, denying them a peek of her 'famous cleavage; that the majority of the male; and some female cops admired.

"Well, you know, Det. Eric, I didn't expect to be waiting this long when I called both of you in here about fifteen minutes ago." She said, both eyebrows raised, a finger lightly tapping the desk.

"Sorry, Capt., but Warren here, he was in the little boy's room!" Det. Eric fibbed quickly. Warren tried hard to force back the chuckles that threatened to erupt from him at any second. Captain Lawrence looked at the two men, and shook her head, restraining her own laughter. '*These two…*' She thought to herself.

"Look gentlemen, It's time to get right down to business, we have a report of a body found in an alley off 79th and Cottage Grove Avenue. The preliminary report stated the body appeared to be drained of blood and the head was…well…missing. Furthermore, there are no witnesses I'm assigning this case to you. It's right up your alley, she said smiling. The coroner's on the scene. Detectives Weinstein and Johnson are there right now, questioning the employee of a bakery store who discovered the body." She handed Warren the address of the crime scene. "Now get the hell out of here."

"Hey Capt, feel like cutting us some slack, we just got off doing the Joliet case?" Warren asked, as he glance at the little white sheet of paper with the location of the crime scene on it.

"Oh geez, guys," she shrugged and smiled, enjoying the moment. "I'd love to let you both sit back and eat your "donuts" but you know this damn government…" She smacked her lips together and shrugged her shoulders as if to ask, '*what can you do?*' "If only they'd put more than one division per state, I wouldn't have to spread your asses so thin, but being as it is, get out there, make me proud."

"Geez, Capt, you can spread my ass thin anytime." Matthew joked. Warren laughed.

"Get out." Captain Lawrence said flatly, as she fought the urge to laugh. Both men gave each other a playful look and pouted like children as they headed for the door.

"Great, a body drained of blood and the head is missing. Let's just chuck this one up to a vampire and head on over to Calvin's for some ribs." Warren suggested as he closed the office door behind them.

"Yeah, I know it is a pain in the ass, let's go." Matthew said as both men grabbed their coats and headed for the parking lot.

"I'll drive!" Det. Warren said eagerly as he made a mad dash for the drivers' side of Matthew's car.

"Like hell you will! You have a little too much of the speed demon in you. If you want to drag race, then do it in your own shit, not mine. Now saddle yourself into the spectators seat." Matthew said as he pushed his partner in the direction of the passenger side of his 2004 Python Triton. One of the new foreign cars from Asia, that everyone was buying, it was an economy car, great on gas and looked like a sports car. Warren admired the car and mentally noted to put the automobile on his wish list for Christmas.

"You know" Warren started as he looked around his partners new car "You should give this car to me as a Christmas present." He smiled at his partner as he waited for an answer.

"Sure…if you give me your Diamond Back SUV. You know that I love that truck."

"Point taken, now let's drop the subject." Warren said, smiling coyly. Matthew smiled broadly, he had gotten the last word, which was hard to do with Warren. He reached for his emergency light and placed it on the top of the car, and clicked on the portable siren as they sped through the morning rush hour traffic on the urban streets of Chicago.

The location of the crime scene, an alley at 79ᵗʰ and Cottage Grove was packed with onlookers. Uniformed officers struggled desparetly to keep the onlookers away from the crime scene. Cars were backed up for blocks as more and more police vehicles and media trucks pulled up. Matthew had to carefully navigate his car through the helter skelter of parked patrol cars finally parking in a spot that was not too close to the other patrol cars. The two detectives emerged from the car and made their way pass the bevy of excited reporters and curious onlookers. An ambitious reporter who was desperate to get the "scoop" cut in front of them as they tried to make their way to the crime scene. Before they could get one step further the reporter thrust a microphone in Warren's face and began to bombard him with questions.

"Detective, detective! Is it true that the body is headless? Do you think a supernatural did this!?" The blonde female reporter in the tight blue pants suit asked as she struggled to keep pace with the two detectives' long strides.

"No comments." Warren said as he approached the uniformed officer that was guarding the crime scene. The answer given did not seem to satisfy the pushy reporter and she continued to asked the same questions in a different manner.

"Detectives, are you from the S.U.I.T. Precinct? This must have been a supernatural killing. What kind of supernatural did this? Was it a vampire or a shape shifter?" She asked in succession. The two detectives ignored the line of questioning and continued to the yellow and black police tape that had blocked off the crime scene. Both men decided to do a little limbo under the tape. The cops on duty only shook their heads and smiled, everyone knew these two were the "Riggs and Murtough" of the Special Unit Investigation Team, better known as the SUITS.

"Hey, Barry, look who's graced us with their presence! If it isn't the *Dynamic Duo*" Detective Gabriel Johnson joked to his partner Barry Weinstein who was kneeling by the body. "Heya boys!" He greeted the approaching officers.

Barry rose from his kneeling position and walked over and stood by his partner. "Warren...Matthew" Barry said, giving a little 'hello' nod to the two detectives. "Gabe and I were the first on the scene. The guy who discovered the body is over there away from the media sharks." He pointed to a young black male appearing to be in his early twenties, five-feet-eight inches tall, wearing a brown uniform, standing against the side of a building. "You know how hungry the media is for a story when they get a whiff of fresh blood" Barry joked. All four detectives chuckled and nodded in agreement.

"Yeah, but the guy won't be able to tell you much, he was dumping the trash that should have been dumped the night before when he came across the body. He said 'he saw the legs protruding from behind the dumpster and knew something wasn't right.' That's when he called the police, who in turned called us. That's about it." Gabriel said.

"Captain must really like you two, she gives you guys all the coveted cases." Barry chuckled as he spoke jokingly.

"Yeah, remind me to send her one of those famous *Anisi gift baskets* as a 'Thank You'." Matthew retorted sarcastically, laughing.

"Well, as much as we would liked to stay here, and chit chat with the two of you, we've just received a page, Captain wants us. Maybe she'll bestow upon us the same generosity she's shone you two." Gabriel teased as he gazed at the number on his beeper.

"Ha! Don't bet on it, she wants the two of us, cause we're hot!" Warren joked.

"Yeah, I heard she like guys with young firm balls," Matthew added.

"Exactly, not old shriveled wrinkled balls, like yours, so you're both out of luck." Warren finished.

"Well, I guess I have to settle for your mother then, hey Matthew?" Gabriel shot back, smiling slyly.

"Shit, be my guest! If she has a little *Romeo* on the side maybe she'll stop bugging me about making her a grandmother!" Matthew joked, and the four detectives laughed. Gabriel and Barry said their "goodbyes" wrapping up their friendly banter and began walking away towards their detectives car as Warren and Matthew headed towards the body.

Matthew and Warren looked at the white sheet that covered the body. The body lay partially behind a dumpster in back of the *Dark Night Travel Agency*. It was an agency that catered to the supernatural. After the supernatural race was exposed, all types of businesses saw it as another way to make a profit. This particular agency helped vampires travel during the day. Both detectives stood over the corpse. They noted the small drops of blood that spotted the sheet where the head should have been. Matthew squatted down beside the corpse and lifted the sheet to peek under. The corpse looked to be the body of a black male and on a closer inspection, he appeared to be middle-aged. Matthew threw a glance at Warren who seemed to be having a dilemma of his own. Matthew noticed Warren's breathing had increased and his jaw muscles had tightened. He also noticed the tiny beads of sweat forming on Warren's forehead.

"Hey, keep it together, man! You don't want to attract attention to yourself!" Matthew encouraged his partner in a hushed voice. Matthew began to think back to the time when he discovered Warren's secret. It was almost three years ago, when he discovered his partner was a supernatural himself. They'd been on a stakeout, tracking down a murdering child molester, who strangle his child victims dress them up as life size dolls, and rape their lifeless bodies. The stakeout had gone wrong when their suspect noticed their plain black van parked across the street from his house. Matthew and Warren hated the idea of trying to conduct an "inconspicuous stakeout", using the black van, but they had no other choice. They had sat in the van for eight hours, their butt cheeks numb and their bellies begging for refueling, when the nut came bursting through the front door of his house blasting his twelve gage shotgun at their van.

Matthew would have caught a blast straight to the head had Warren not threw himself in front of him taking the blast of the shotgun pellets in his upper right shoulder. Never losing their composure, they returned fire, taking down their suspect. After disarming the man and confirming his death, Matthew had returned to the van to check on his friend and partner, the one he trusted and now owed his life to. He remembered running back to the van to find his partner looking worried. Warren had covered his wound with his jacket not wanting to show it to his partner who urged him to let him see it. Matthew had wanted to apply pressure to stop the bleeding. He remembered trying to snatch the jacket away from Warren who seemed to be behaving as children sometimes do, hiding their wounds from their mothers, so that they wouldn't go dabbing alcohol into the wound. He joked with Warren telling him not to worry, he promised it wouldn't sting. Warren however, was most adamant about keeping the wound hidden until Matthew pulled at the jacket with all his might and Warren relented, exposing a partially healed scar. Matthew watched in amazement as the wound began to heal. He watched as the torn muscles began to reattached themselves, he looked on in awe and disbelief as the skin reformed over it, leaving nothing but the blood around the area where the wound had been. He was speechless, he looked at Warren for an explanation.

Matthew listened as Warren, his partner of nearly two years confessed that he was a werewolf, Warren had decided to use the mortal terminology for his species. Shape-shifters, like himself, never used terms like 'werewolf' or 'werecheetah' He did not like having his secret out because the law itself, did not shine on those who were not of the mortal/human race. Even if he was a cop. Even if his intentions were good, he would be fired and probably prosecuted for lying and providing false information during exams and testings. The human race did not trust those of the supernatural race. "Birds of a feather," he supposed. He trusted his partner enough to give Matthew the choice of keeping his secret or revealing it. In the beginning, Matthew had felt leery about such a revelation. He wasn't sure how he felt about having a flesh-eating beast as his partner.

In the end, Matthew believed he knew his partner well enough to know that he would never eat him…he hoped. He decided to keep the secret and their bond became stronger. It wasn't until after Matthew knew the truth about Warren that he started to understand his strange behavior's of the past. Such as; the constant eating of high-fat high-protein foods. He had never seen anyone who could put away two-20 ounce porterhouse steaks the way Warren could and this was with side dishes! He also begin to recognize the look of bloodlust in Warrens' eyes whenever they went to a bloody crime scene, he wondered how the hell it slipped his radar in the first damn place. He was amazed at how well Warren could endure the strong scent and sight of blood and flesh at these crime scenes. He had chalked it up to Warren's own personal high level of discipline, determination and dedication to the job.

Matthew remembered the times when Warren had broken the handle of his car door not once, but twice trying to hop out of the car in a rush, he also remembered the time they had to chase down a suspect, he decided to cut the suspect off in the car and Warren took to chasing the perpetrator on foot. He found it amazing when Warren had beat him to the punch and had the suspect apprehended. Now that he knew the truth, everything that did not make sense in the past, all fell into place.

Now, as Matthew looked at Warren, he could tell by the way Warren's breathing was returning to normal that he had gotten control over his bloodlust and hunger, and was ready to get his mind on the job at hand. Matthew pulled the white sheet back revealing the entire corpse. He reached into his right breast pocket and produced a retractable metal rod he used to further examine the corpse without actually touching the body. A uniformed officer walked over to them and gave them each a pair of latex gloves. Matthew put on his gloves without hesitation. Warren always hated wearing these gloves. The scent from the latex and the powder substance inside the gloves always agitated the sensory glands of his nose and mouth. Nevertheless, he slowly slid his hands into the gloves.

"Hey, look at this here, come closer!" Matthew said curiously as he gestured for his partner to take a closer look at the open wound where the victim's head used to be. As both men peered into the gaping hole, Warren's breathing had begun to increase but he kept his mind focused. He looked at the broken spinal cord, and torn muscles and sinew that were left behind. The remaining flesh looked jagged as though the head had been ripped away from the body.

Both men gave each other a guarded look. The conclusion was not one they wanted to embrace, but the evidence left them no other choice. Whatever it was they were going to be dealing with was strong...and vicious, never a good combination. So far, they had been lucky. The last case they were on had been the most grueling case since they joined the new division or rather, they were "appointed" to the new division. They had to track down a werewolf in Joliet, IL. The werewolf had ran amok in the suburban neighborhoods and had killed and mutilated four people. They had cornered the werewolf on a farm right outside Joliet, it had slaughtered two cows. The family had heard the ruckus and alerted the local police, who in turn notified the S.U.I.T. authorities. The suspect was not negotiable and they had to take him down. At that point, Matthew was more than happy that his partner was a supernatural, they would not have survived otherwise.

"It looks as though the fucking head was snatched off!" Matthew said as he inspected more of the corpse noting that the body was fully clothed. Relief spread through his mind that if there was anything else to find, that it would be Marshall Galen's job as coroner to find it. Then as soon as that thought came into this head, so did the dread that whatever Marshall found would just add more drama to an already-becoming-dramatic case.

"Yeah, that's what it looks like, the spinal cord was just snapped like a twig. And the flesh of the neck is all torn, the edges, see look here" Warren pointed and made a circular motion around the neck area. "Looks a little stretched doesn't it. Like someone or something pulled and pulled until the skin gave way. They could have done it in a fast motion but I think...at least I feel in my gut that this killer wanted to feel and savor the sensation of slowly ripping off someone's head." Warren rose quickly and shook his head from side to side as he walked a few paces away from the corpse.

He had to regain his composure. The thought of someone so sick and twisted that they would derive pleasure out of such a macabre act of violence disgusted him. But what unnerved him even more was that the remains of that violent act made him want to get down on all fours and crawl over to the headless corpse and pig out like ninety-going- north. Matthew looked at him, he knew how hard it was for Warren, he knew his secret.

"Hey, Detective Davis, you ain't gonna puke are you!?" A uniformed officer called out as he noticed Warren with his back towards the corpse. "Awe, don't tell me a little blood gets you two boys all green."

"Fuck you, asshole! Don't you have some tickets to write!?" Matthew said as he took the gloves off and tossed them in a disposal unit. He walked to his partner and patted him on the shoulder. "Are you okay?" Warren nodded. "Good. Are you ready to talk to the one lead we have?" Matthew asked. Warren took a deep breath, he looked at Matthew and nodded.

In retrospect, Warren was relieved he had confided in his partner when he did. He trusted in their relationship now enough to let it all hang out. Matthew knew his friend's "condition" even though it still shook him up, especially if Warren became glassy eyed over spilt blood. Warren wished he had the control of the older ones. The pride of the pack, those who can walk into a slaughterhouse and never even blink once. He marveled at the amount of self-control that one must have to resist such a temptation. He admired his pack leader Xander for his superior self-control, However, Xander was controlling of his pack which sometimes got on Warren's nerves. But by the same token, Xander was equally protective of the pack and Warren respected and loved him for that.

Xander never really approved of Warren joining the police force. He was strict to the traditional ways, old traditions had wisdom. In Xander's opinion, it just was not wise to take up a profession that might expose your secret. Being a police officer was high on his 'hell no' list. But ever since Warren's parents were murdered in front of him when he was a child, he wanted to be a cop so that he could catch the bad guys. Xander acknowledged the benefits one could gain from working within and beside the law, he was not blind to that fact, but he feared Warren would be exposed, then hunted down because he was what he was and Xander would not stand for that. Warren remembered the heated argument he had with Xander when he informed him that his secret had been exposed to his partner. Xander had threatened to kill Matthew, said he knew too much, but Warren had convinced Xander that this exposure was a move in the right direction.

Xander had scoffed at that statement. It did not ease his suspicions nor his hidden thoughts of killing all who knew about them. It was one thing for the whole supernatural race existence to be exposed, and it was another to paste a sign on your head that said, ' here I am, come and get me." Warren had been the orphaned son of his pack mates. Warren's mother and father had been murdered by a renegade group of deranged mortals. They shot both of his parents in their heads with silver bullets while they were tending to their farm. Warren barely escaped with his life, he had ran into the woods and stayed hidden until nightfall. He then went to the one place his parents told him would be safe if anything ever went wrong. He ended up on Xander's doorstep in the middle of the night, a scared six year old boy. Xander had taken Warren under his wing and raised him as his own. Warren was raised in the traditional way of the pack, but in spite of all Xander's teachings, Warren had embraced the "mortal" lifestyle.

Warren thought Xander should loosen up a bit, He knew because of Xander's old age, change was always difficult. Warren knew that Xander was one who believed wholeheartedly in tradition and after being alive for two centuries, Xander was pretty much hell bent on keeping with tradition and was most reluctant to change the old rules.

Warren reminisced on the day when he was at home watching TV, when his favorite family cartoon show was interrupted for a special news bulletin. He remembered thinking it *better be pretty fucking important to interrupt my favorite cartoon family*. He sat there and watched history in the making as the report commenced to prove supernatural existence beyond what the human mind could comprehend. It was all over the radio and even worked it's way into the cable network channels. So even if you were watching *QueerPeople* you were going to catch this news bulletin!

Warren watched along with billions of people worldwide, as the supernatural world was exposed for all to see, for all to know. An overambitious reporter had scooped the story, revealing a corrupted politician who had been bitten and turned by a tiger. This politician, along with several others were secretly keeping an abandoned military base in Death Valley. A facility specially designed to perform experiments on vampires and shape-shifters and study the results. His mouth dropped open as he watched that report. He felt grateful that he had been skilled enough at deceiving the mortals about his true identity thus far. He had learned how to control his hungers and lust, well enough to remain unnoticed, and unchallenged (outside of Matthew).

Xander had resented everything about the outing. It angered him that shape-shifters were tortured and killed at the military base. He knew that mortals would react badly after finding out. "Mortals always hunt down and destroy what they can not control, or understand, or fear" Xander had said as he made numerous phone calls to other Pack leaders arranging an emergency meeting. Xander had been right. In the months that followed, after the human world got over the shock of supernatural beings existing in their world, mass paranoia began, people began to panic and there had been pure chaos. Humans started looking over their shoulders, people started killing each other over the slightest suspicions.

Warren remembered getting a call from a hysterical woman who said her husband had just shot and killed their neighbor with a sniper rifle. Her husband was convinced his neighbor was a vampire, because he only saw him up and about at night. Turns out the now dead neighbor liked to take nightly walks because he suffered from insomnia. The madness did not stop there. The crime rate increased, it was the highest in years, and the ironic part of it was this; it was not the supernatural creatures that were committing all the crimes, but the human race itself- killing other humans!

It was not until some bills were passed a year later that the madness subsided. Angry and fed up family members were tired of fending for their lives and the lives of their loved ones who had been turned. Those people made their voices heard loud and clear and the government had to acknowledge that the worldwide fear-induced bloodshed had to be dealt with and fast! Marshall law was enforced and it gave the government time to think of a plan.

Some supernaturals fearing they would be hunted down, and slain, decided to form a council in an attempt to gain positive exposer and establish themselves. They joined with the American government to share information and develop laws equal to humans. The human race was trying to restore order from the madness they had caused. The human race was trying to get control over what they could not comprehend. Many supernaturals believed that the human race was foolish and vain to think that they could be the overlords of all the supernatural's power and wisdom. The human race had been underestimated. America was the first country to form a "Law of Co-existence" with the supernaturals, successfully. Most of Europe followed then Canada and Asia, making the "Law of Co-existence" partially universal.

The first bill that was passed into law, clearly stated, supernatural creatures were now required to obey the same law as every mortal was. If they committed a murder they were arrested and were to have their day in court. If a supernatural was suspected of a crime, once tracked down if they turned themselves in willingly, they would await their trial date up to a period of seven days. They would then be tried by a mixed jury of humans and supernaturals. If found innocent they were set free but monitored. If found guilty, they were to be executed immediately. However, if a supernatural refused to be taken into custody, they were executed on the spot. Due to their supernatural abilities, their right to "Due Process" was not equal to humans.

Law number two, this was more for the vampires than shape-shifters. No bloodsucking on mortals who were not willing. It was understood, that a bite from a vampire was equivalent to sex. You could not arrest and charge two adults for having consensual sex, therefore, you could not charge a vampire for getting down right bloody with someone who consented to the bloodletting. However, the union could not be fatal, it also had to be with an adult. Anyone under the tender age of eighteen was jail bait and anyone who did not consent was considered raped. In addition to this law, the willing conversion of a mortal was prohibited. It was considered suicide if a mortal consented to conversion. Of course, vampires did not really adhere to this portion of the law.

The vampires had taken to that law rather harshly. Some of the young ones retaliated. They had no idea what mortals had in store for them. If found in the act of "raping," "murdering" or "child molesting," if that supernatural could not be apprehended in a "peaceful" manner, they were to be shot and killed on the spot. This was stated in the news bulletin when they announced the new laws. What they did not say was that they had gathered a great deal of information on the supernaturals. Due in part to all the materials and documentation gathered from the secret facility in Death Valley. For instance, a trained mortal knew what to look for in appearance, physical attributes, etc. The government was better prepared and were well equipped to deal with the supernaturals. The S.U.I.T. Organization was armed with ultraviolet gel ammunition for the bloodsucking undead and liquid sliver-nitrate bullets for shape-shifters. these specially designed bullets would exploded upon impact as it entered the body of a supernatural and work it's way through the blood stream making it virtually impossible for any to survive. Regular silver bullets hurt and took longer to heal, but the bullets did not kill the shifter, unless the bullet struck in a vital area. But liquid silver that entered the blood stream meant an inevitable death.

Warren wondered if Xander would be able to survive a vital hit from a regular silver bullet, he suspected that maybe because of his age he may be able to heal, if he drank the blood of the pack healer. However, he doubted Xander would be able to survive being shot by a liquid silver-nitrate bullet.

The humans had been prepared. After a few vampires were made examples of law number two the vampires were "less inclined to exhibit any 'rash' behavior." Or so, that's what the Secretary of State said during his speech when he announced the decrease in supernatural crime. Warren had to admit the thought of a combustible silver nitrate bullet going through his chest *would* make *him* feel a little more law abiding. His other pack mates had been outraged and felt helpless against the change. Warren wondered in amazement if this was the first time the supernatural race felt truly vulnerable. He suspected Xander was not worried, but cautious...always cautious.

Law number three, this one was pretty much directed at shape-shifters. Shape-shifters were to go to a government protected and sanctioned hunting ground on the nights when there would be a full moon. Some of the Pack leaders had disputed this bill. Many said they had they're own private property, and would not take too kindly to being monitored while they changed, mated and hunted. After three months of deliberation. The government relented, only to revise the bill to state that; if you did not have a "designated" hunting ground, you were required to go to a government sanctioned one, provided in each state. Once finalized, there were no exceptions to this law. If found off hunting grounds the shape-shifter would be contained and charged and most likely deemed dangerous, then executed.

In the beginning, there were a lot of unexplained "accidents" when a supernatural was taken into custody for suspicion of committing a crime. They were often tortured or murdered by spiteful officers wanting revenge. It was during this time when the supernatruals protested and their council spoke out against the cruel and illegal tactics of the government supernatural police force. The entire S.U.I.T. organization went under investigation, and the offending officers were arrested and sentenced.

The last bill to be added became law number four to establish equal protection for supernaturals. For the individuals and radical humanist groups who decided to turn their Thursday night poker club into outlandish cults, that would chase down members of the supernatural race and destroy what they could and maimed and killed who they could. This new law, which was much needed, prohibited any type of random vigilante acts of violence upon a member of the supernatural race. Many outraged groups felt that the human race should not have to share the world with "freaks". They vowed to continue their "fight against the forsaken," as they called it. Warren had arrested a few of these fanatics, satisfied to have finally rid the streets of them, though he knew where there was one, there were several thousand.

However, there were enough intelligent civilians, including politicians who knew that to start a war with the supernaturals, would incite the destruction of the human race. These individuals lobbied ceaselessly to pass law number four, they knew that the government had to offer protection to the supernaturals in order to guarantee protection for human existence.

The laws left little for mischief and seemed to keep things under control. Supernaturals were U.S. citizens rightfully. All humans now knew they could not destroy the supernatural race, some humans did not want to destroy supernaturals at all. Many historians baffled and marveled at the whole idea of immortal creatures. Beings that have seen empires rise and fall, wars begun and ended. They knew who shot Kennedy, they knew what it was like to watch Rome burn and hear the psychotic tunes from Nero's violin. Then you had the medical scientist that wanted blood samples, urine samples, sperm and egg samples. They wanted to know what was in the supernatural's blood that was different from their own, and how to make that blood work for them. Just think how much a serum made from vampire blood would cost healthcare! Many other business, including restaurants, bars, clubs, stores, and airports open their markets to the supernaturals. However there were some businesses that reinstated the segregation law, barring supernatuals from "human only" establishments. Even though mankind was learning to co exist, the two races were far from equal in all that the world had to offer. There were other bills being brought before the legislature that wanted to incorporate supernatrual studies in schools as well as cultural awareness courses. This caused great debates within the ranks and the bills have yet to be voted on.

Chapter 2

"Girl, get up already, your ass needs to get downtown for that damn job interview! You know you can't live off of me forever!" Annette said playfully with her southern accent as she pulled the satin sheets from the stubborn fingers of her best friend Natasha. "Come on, Tasha, get up girl! I *let* your ass sleep through exercise time! So now you don't have any excuse to be tired, get up!" With one final tug, Annette freed the sheets from her friends grip and tossed them aside, she flopped down on the bed beside the grumpy woman and begin tickling her. Natasha could no longer pretend to be asleep and begin to wiggle and laugh outright as the other woman's fingers traced over her ticklish areas.

"Okay, okay already, damn I'm up! I'm awake! Breathe back and let me up, I'm getting out of the bed right this minute, happy?" She glared at her friend playfully. "You know, sometimes I hate you." She joked. Annette only smiled and crawled off of the bed and headed for the kitchen to flip over the bacon. This was her week to cook breakfast and she was accustomed to a true down home southern style breakfast with all the trimmings. Sizzling maple glazed bacon, scrambled eggs with cheddar cheese. Not to ever be without a few slices of honey glazed ham, thick slices of french toast sprinkled with cinnamon and powdered sugar, slow cooked grits, (cheese is optional) and hash browns mixed with green and red peppers and onions. All this was to be topped off with a tall glass of freshly squeezed orange juice.

Natasha always wondered how Annette could eat like a bear and still retain her slim, curvy figure that always seemed to get her the big bucks at *Desires Unleashed*, the super popular dance and strip nightclub where Annette worked, stripping five nights out of the week. She herself hated her figure, well maybe hate was too strong a word to describe her personal feelings

16

about her own figure. One thing she knew for certain, if she continued to eat Annette's southern style meals, she would no doubt end up looking like a beached whale. She could smell the tantalizing aroma coming from the kitchen and felt her mouth water. She would have drooled had she not closed her mouth in time. It was always embarrassing to catch yourself drooling. She remembered once when she fell asleep on the red line train coming home from work, and woke up just in time to feel a drop of drool hit her hand. She had been as embarrassed as she was disgusted. *Everyone knows that drooling is for babies and drunks.*

She finished handling her necessities and reached for her battery operated OralSmart toothbrush. The advertising guaranteed that the toothbrush would reach the back molars and remove plaque and debris that would have otherwise been left to damage your teeth by the competition. Annette had accused her of being a "lazy ass" when she first caught her using the motorized toothbrush. Natasha did not care, she loved the way the brussels massaged her gums as the toothpastes provided a cool foam. After gargling, she hit the shower and hoped that Annette was too preoccupied in the kitchen cooking her high-fat, high calorie, high-blood pressure, quick heart-attack breakfast to come running into the bathroom to flush the toilet like she did that one time last week. She could have killed her for that.

That little act of cruelty would not go unpunished, Natasha had to keep score so that she could get even. She finished bathing and climbed out of the shower. She rummaged through her closet for something to wear that was not to small or out of date. Natasha silently noted that she needed to go shopping. She had been avoiding going shopping because she would have to face the fact that she had gained a few pounds. No longer was she the size four she had been. But thanks to Annette cattle prodding her out of the door at five o'clock in the morning four days out of the week, she had worked her weight down to a size eight. She knew the reason for her weight gain. Her mom had always warned her to never take comfort in food, but when her boyfriend of four years left her for a size two slut with silicone tits and collagen lips, and her dog of twelve years passed away of old age, then the sudden promotion on her job, only to be caught up in the downsizing struck her all in the same month, she took it pretty hard.

But instead of diving *onto* the jagged rocks of Lake Michigan, she decided to dive *into* a gallon of double fudge cookies and ice-cream, which was followed up by endless amounts of ribs, chicken and candy bars. Now looking at her reflection in the mirror, she regretted going into her depression. She had noted the thin stretch marks on her stomach and the underside of her arm had began to appear. Her mom always told her vitamin E and cocoa butter would get rid of any small blemish over time and she was putting that to the test. The results were better than she expected, the thin stretch marks were virtually invisible.

She held her arm outstretched and was thankful the flesh did not jiggle, there was still hope. Natasha finally settled on a pair of black front pleated slacks and a satin smoke grey button up shirt with fake *mother-of-pearl* buttons. She searched her shoe rack for the perfect footwear and spotted a pair of black leather ankle boots with a two and a half inch heel. Two inch heels were a challenge enough for her to walk in. She could not see how Annette managed to walk in six inch spikes every day let alone dance in them five nights out of the week. Leaning over the vanity, Natasha applied her make up. Because of her caramel complexion, she chose flesh toned cosmetics by Anisi, She preferred the more "natural" look. She appreciated cosmetic companies that acknowledged other flesh tones in the world.

"Well, look at you, don't you look gorgeous! I like how you did your hair, it turned out nicely, I was doubtful, but it's all good." Annette said smiling at her friends crinkly long locks. "I like that whole ethnic look, remind me to try that style."

Natasha looked at her friend with raised eyebrows. "I think if you were to try this look out, you may end up looking like a tumbleweed. I think your hair would look so cute with spiral rods or braids, you should do that Annette, it would look so cute! Ain't you tired of the 'Haile Barrymore' look?"

"Shit girl, not if I still look good I'm not!" Annette said with a swivel of her hips and a shake of her well rounded derriere.

Natasha giggled at her friend "So you're working tonight?" Natasha asked "I thought you were off this Friday?" She sat down at the table and began preparing her plate. She added small servings of everything. She thought twice about adding bacon and the ham, or grits, toasts and the hash browns all together, but then decided you only live once and taking small portions of everything, settle back into her chair and started stuffing her mouth.

"Yeah, I have to be there at seven o' clock. I wasn't going to work tonight, but then Sara wanted to switch nights with me so that she and her asshole boyfriend could patch up their sinking relationship. They're planning on going to a hotel or some sleazy motel, for a passionate night of three two-minutes interval of sexacapdes.." So I'm on the night shift. The only good thing about it is that it's a Friday night so the place will be super crowded and the tips will be oh, so lovely.! This body's going to get mama that new car, ain't that right!" She exclaimed, then proceeded to lap dance in the chair she was sitting in.

"Your ass is disgusting." Natasha said with a mock grimace.

"On the contrary, my ass is firm, round and bodacious! Do I need to demonstrate?"

"Oh god, no! I don't know how much more of your ass fetish I can take!" The two women laughed and finished breakfast.

The time was 10:42am, and Natasha had every thing she needed. She had her resume, references, portfolio and confidence. She headed down to the *Chicago Word* for her appointment. She had heard through a friend of a friend, who's cousin worked at the popular and well credited newspaper, that there was a position available for a photographer. It was a longshot but a shot nonetheless, she hoped the position was not already filled. She hated looking for a new job, it always made her think of prostitution. You get dressed in your most attractive attire, the kind of outfit that states you mean business. Then you leave the comfort of your home to go from interview to interview, trying to sell yourself to just about anyone who would give you a chance to prove your worth. If you were really good at what you did, then you can name your price while you recited your skills.

"Miss, you may go in now." Said the little snooty secretary. Natasha did not like this woman. She did not appreciate the little sideways glances she kept getting from the woman. Besides she thought her cleavage bearing red blouse and just-below-crotch length black skirt was inappropriate for the work place. Then again, maybe she did not like her because she reminded her of her ex-boyfriends new flame. One thing was for certain, she would continue to not like her until the woman proved herself likeable. She knew she was being judgmental and unfair, but it made her feel better.

Once inside the office, she sat nervously as the interviewer went through her portfolio and resume`. Every once in a while darting expressionless glances at her. Natasha couldn't decided whether it was this man's three piece charcoal-black suit, complete with buttoned up vest, the big office, or his own masculine aura, whatever the case, she could feel her confidence melting away with every passing minute.

"It says here," and he pointed at a spot on her resume. "that you graduated from Gibson College here in Chicago. You majored in photography and…" he cocked his head sideways, "psychology. What interested you in those two fields?" He looked up at Natasha, anticipating her response.

Natasha sat up straight, she had not realized she was slouching, she hoped to god the interviewer did not notice either. "Well, I've always been

19

entertained by the idea of capturing beauty or freeze framing the special events of time in a photograph. As a child, I would take pictures of random things with my instant camera and make collages. I loved how a person could capture motion or emotion in an instant. With a picture, that one moment would last forever, even if the memory faded." She paused to catch her breath. The interviewer seemed pleased with her answer and genuinely impressed by her obvious passion.

"And what about the psychology?" He asked. It really didn't matter to him what her answer was for that question. He was just intrigued by her choice of the double majors. He decided immediately after reviewing her portfolio that it was the best work he had seen in a long time. He was pleased with the way she worked with light and shadows. She had an eye for beauty as well as freezing the "moment." Whether it was a roaring waterfall or an elderly lady celebrating a birthday, her photographs came to life to tell their own story.

"Well that's a more boring story, I had to take a psychology-credited class for one of my general electives and I just became intrigued by the human psyche. I found it interesting that there were classifications for the various behaviors that people exhibited. And as equally interesting were the various scientific reasoning for these behaviors. Not to mention the various methods used for treatments, only to discover there's still so much for us to learn." She finished with a slight shrug of her shoulders.

The interviewer seemed to ponder that for a moment, the answer was even more simple than he expected. Then he gathered himself and clapped his hands together as if he was breaking a spell and rose from his seat.

"Well, Miss. Hemingway, you will be pleased to know that you have the job. Congratulations! We expect to see you bright and early, Monday morning. And the good new is you'll start working at the beginning of the pay period." He said as he shook her hand. Natasha couldn't believe her luck. She finally got a job and only after six months of being jobless. Well she did have to admit that for the first three months, she had spent that valuable time perfecting her couch potato skills.

Her best friend Annette had tried to convince her to apply at one of the many new, hot spots popping up all over the city being run by bloodsuckers and flesh eaters. However that was a little too close for comfort. She never saw the vampire owned club that Annette worked in. She did not even want see a vampire or shape shifter if she didn't have to.

Annette had laughed at her, saying that she'd probably had already seen vampires and shape shifters time and time again and did not know it. She said that the differences between the supernatural and human race were so subtle, normally people overlooked the difference either by refusing to believe what their eyes see, or by sheer ignorance. Still, Natasha decided to not tempt the wolf with a steak, the steak being her. She just stayed clear of establishments that were known to be owned or patronized by supernaturals. She was glad the government made those particular business owners register their businesses. Of course she couldn't decide whether or not they did it to keep track of the supernatural businesses for the safety of the people, or just to charge such businesses an outrageous tax fee. In the end she decided to leave it alone.

There was a celebration to be had! She finally landed a job and it was the kind of job she had wanted for a long time. It was true that good things come to those who wait, and lord knows she had waited. She pulled out her little cell phone to call Annette. She waited impatiently while the phone rang several times. She hoped Annette was home, *there was nothing worse than having something to say, and no one to say it to.* Finally after what seemed like an eternity, Annette answered the phone just in time. Natasha was *just* about to hang up.

"Hello!?" The voice was breathless as if the person ran the hundred meter dash or just had some really wild sex. She wasn't sure which one would be Annette's excuse. It would not be the first time that Annette answered the phone in the middle of an unmentionable activity.

"Annette?" Natasha asked to make sure.

"Yeah, Natasha!? Girl, you had me running from the shower like I was going for the gold! What's up? It better be some good news!" Annette said as she returned to a normal breathing pace.

"Guess what?"

"What? Please tell me you got the job!!!?"

"I got the job!!!" Both women screamed over the telephone so loudly, they both had to pull the phones away from their ears.

"Oh my God! Girl I"m so happy for you! I knew if you got off your lazy ass, you could accomplish anything, even getting a job." So now, does this mean I can start borrowing back all the money your ass has borrowed from me?" Annette asked jokingly.

"Yeah, for sure! You've been the greatest letting me move in with you and taking care of me. I'll never forget it, Annette." Natasha said with the upmost sincerity. She silently vowed she would return the favor one day.

"Oh girl, don't mention it, you would have done the same for me." Annette stated matter-of-factly. And Natasha would have done the same for her and probably anyone else who was down on their luck and who did not pose a threat. Everyone who knew her called her a "bleeding heart". She believed wholeheartedly in the golden rule. She always treated people the way she herself wanted to be treated. She also believed that if you do good on this earth, then you are bound to be granted numerous blessings. You just had to recognized the blessings when they came. She knew that getting this job at this time in her life was a blessing, just like meeting Annette at a laundry mat three years ago had been a blessing.

"Okay look, we have to celebrate! I'll be getting off tonight at 1am. I don't care if you don't drink, tonight your punk ass is going to have at least one Long Island with me. Say, why don't you meet me at-" Annette thought about her friend's reluctance to delve in the underworld, and decided to choose a meeting place where Natasha could feel comfortable. "Let's hook up at the *Slayer's Lair*. Cool?" The two women set their plan for that night. Natasha was content with celebrating at the *Slayer's Lair*. It was one of the few establishments that did not let their greed blind them. They tried not to cater to "scum," *Scum* meaning vampires, shape-shifters, supernatural groupies and whatever else fairytales are made of.

There was even a plaque on the wall outside of the popular dance club that stated the requirements for entry. The dress code alone was strict enough to scare off the groupies...All patrons who wanted to party the night away would have to be human and adhere to the dress code of brightly colored clothes of considerable taste. To wear all black was to be denied entry, the right was reserved. Natasha decided to go shopping for a brand new outfit for later that night. The outfit had to reflect her ecstatic mood, she was thinking along the lines of a white jean skirt and matching halter top. She hit Michigan Ave to see what she could fine. She walked up and down the crowded Michigan Ave shopping district searching for her outfit. There were so many stores. Some of them carried high priced designer fashions and others were more reasonable and definitely affordable for Natasha, she entered these stores first.

She enjoyed shopping on Michigan Ave, especially in the winter time like now. The streetlights were all decorated with yellow Christmas lights and green, red and sliver tinsel. The department stores' windows all had festive displays or decorations, either displaying the nativity or Santa Clause out making his rounds. People were friendlier in the winter time, she figured it was because December was the most giving holiday in the year. She passed a Salvation Army steward, dressed in an old and worn looking Santa suit, rattling his bell somewhat lazily. She assumed they had been out there for hours and were probably cold. She believed wholeheartedly that it was always better to give than to receive and now that she had a new job, it was time to spread the blessings. She walked over to the man and gave him a five dollar bill so that he could get something to eat and put another five dollars in the little red metal pail as a donation.

She then continued down the street until she saw what she wanted to wear in a store window. She knew it was cold outside, *but that is why you have a down coat*, she thought. Tonight she wanted to show off her new slimmer figure. She paid for her outfit, had something to eat and caught a movie. She looked at her watch and was surprised at how fast time flew. The sun had already set, it was past five o'clock. The nights were coming faster and lasting longer now. She had to get back home and catch a "disco nap" before she got dressed to go out to celebrate her knew job.

Chapter 3

"Master, I've counted the bank from last night five times and I still come up with the same total, we're short from last nights profits one thousand, five hundred and sixty dollars. You want me to call Anthony and tell him to come in tonight so that you can speak with him?" Asked the slender vampire as he kneeled on one knee in the middle of the office. His blue eyes hidden behind the veil of his long blonde bangs. He was apprehensive about the outcome. He was hoping that he would not be blamed for this blunder, he *was* the night manager at *Desires Unleashed*, but he could not see all.

Darian laid stretched out on his back on the black suede sofa. His fingers lay interlocked on his chest. His legs crossed at the ankles allowing his feet to rest elevated on the armrest of the sofa. An expression of sheer amusement spread across his face as he gazed at the dimmed lights in the ceiling of his office. His second in command and lover, Xavier sat on the armrest nearest his head. One leg crossed over the other and both hands resting in his lap. He shifted his body position a bit to glance down at Darian and smiled. He knew what this powerful master vampire clad in a black silk shirt and pants was going to do to this individual, this fool who dared to steal from him. Xavier reflected on Anthony's predicament, not only was Anthony a moron for trying to steal from his boss, but he was beyond the norm of idiocy for trying to steal a measly $1,560 from a master vampire, especially one with Darian's reputation. *What the hell was with the sixty bucks for anyway?*

Xavier reached over to Darian's face and removed a wavy lock of jet-black hair that blocked his view of those gorgeous forest green eyes, which was accented by his thick, perfectly-arched, black eyebrows. Darian's eyes held a depth, that could be both dramatic and sensual. Xavier had never seen eyes that shade of green before. In the beginning, when Xavier first became a vampire, it had freaked him out, but then as time moved on he began to notice a lot of vampires' features were extraordinary compared to mortals. Some vampires, especially powerful ones, were well known for having rare and exotic eye color. In addition to a set of knock-out eyes, powerful vampires had hair as soft as a new born baby and skin just as smooth and silky. Xavier relished the feel of Darian's skin against his. The sensation of their fingers caressing each others most sensitive zones, the very thought of it sent goose bumps to the surface of his skin.

He broke his gaze from Darian eyes, though no spell was cast, just one look into those eyes, one glance at those full luscious lips and double dimpled smile sent a rush of desire through his body. It made his mouth water, and the bloodlust rise to a boiling point. At this point, he would want nothing more than to be thrown to the floor, his black leather jacket ripped from his back, followed by his grey ribbed sweater and boot cut blue jeans. His underwear would be last, his lover would take those off slowly to feed his lust, to add anticipation for the indescribable pleasure that would soon follow.

No, he had to get back on track, back to the seriousness of the situation at hand. Sometimes he resented moments where just one look at Darian or just to hear Darian's voice could make him feel like a new born fledgling, consumed with desire for his master's touch. Well one thing was for sure, he was no longer a new born fledgling. Darian smiled at Xavier as if he just read his mind, which he could easily do.

There are two bonds vampires shared, a mental and blood bond. The mental bond between master and fledgling varied in a matter of stages. When a fledgling is first reborn the master can mentally manipulate the fledgling to help train and guide them. Over time, the strength of that bond fades out completely as the master ceases to control the fledgling. However the ability to read each others' thoughts is shared between all vampires, unless the more powerful vampire blocks the connection. However, the blood bond is forever. It is a bond that can be manipulated to increase a vampires strength or to heal and nourish. Vampires of the same bloodline can share blood for the healing power and to increase strength, depending upon the strength of the vampires, but any vampire can share blood for nourishment and pleasure. Pleasure was to be shared by all bloodsuckers. The taking and giving of blood from one vampire to another was orgasmic and the stronger the vampire sharing the union, the more pleasurable the entire experience.

But only the blood of a direct line can work a certain magic. Darian was extremely particular when it came to sharing his blood. For he would make certain that whom ever he would share with would be his lover in both flesh and blood. He also demanded a certain allegiance for such an offer which he did not take lightly. He laid there on his expensive sofa, never moving from his comfortable position and then began to speak.

"John, please do call in our little Anthony, tell him that Richard took the day off and he is needed to fill the time slot. Inform him that he will be paid time-and-a-half for the double shift." He turned his head slightly to set his gaze on the kneeling vampire "Then when he arrives bring him to me. Do not allow him to escape. Do I make myself clear." His voice was low and deep, you could hear the vibrations of each syllable, each word laced with a trace of his Greek accent.

"Yes Master, crystal." John bowed slightly, rose and left the room. Xavier watched John Fallon leave and then he rose from the armrest. He walked over to the three hundred gallon fish tank filled with piranhas, that was built into the wall behind a huge desk. He had admitted to Darian, that he loved this office. The floors were black and red marble, a thick black, grey and blood red art decor area rug covered the middle of the floor. The rug itself was a pleasure to walk on with or without shoes.

There was a three section black marble desk with carvings of ancient Greek mythological gods on each leg. It reminded Xavier of carved pillars. The black leather chair behind the desk, reclined and was temperature controlled. One side of the wall had a painted mural of an ancient city being burned to the ground of what he was told was the last hours of Troy. The other wall was made up of twenty-five fifteen inch television screens. Each screen could work individually as a security monitor or all screens could work collectively as a computer monitor or an extra large screen television.

Darian had spared no expense when it came to the state of the art sound system. He hired a contractor to rig up his office and install a 5.0 Digitex digital surround sound speaker system. The system was compatible with the television screens and computer as well as a stand alone audio system. Not only was his office a technical and electronic paradise, but everything was voice controlled all the way down to the lighting system, but it was done tastefully. There was also a remote control on stand by, just in case fifty-five thousand dollars went wrong.

"I think I will feed the fish now." Xavier said, he knew Darian would not care, both men delighted in watching the piranhas tear chunks of flesh to bits and pieces then devour them. Xavier walked through the doorway that led to the feeding compartment of the tank. He located the cooler and pulled out a ten pound chunk of meat, still dripping with blood. Climbing on the ladder, he open the top of the tank, then dangled the meat over the tank, letting the blood drops tempt the fish. He dodged the lunging predators as they gathered for the prize. After a while, he dropped the meat into the tank and watched with perverse fascination. He enjoyed the feeding frenzy. There was a certain respect he had for anything that enjoyed the taste of fresh blood.

Nature did not have to worry about the laws of man. Darian had been most sour when the bills were passed concerning vampires. Darian felt that vampires were the superior beings to both mankind and shape-shifters. He was resentful of the supernatural council for siding with the US government and creating laws that only supernaturals had to abide by. He, along with other vampires did not like being monitored. He did not appreciate that vampires were being forced to abide by laws that discriminate. Xavier remembered hearing Darian complaining about how foolish mankind was, how utterly naive to believe that they really had the supernatural race under control. He would play along with their fantasy as long as it didn't interfere with him. Xavier came back into the room and looked at Darian, who was still in the same position as before. Only his eyes were closed and he looked content.

"Are you going to lie there all night! No pun intended, but you look like a corpse." He watched Darian's shoulders shake slightly from laughter. Xavier walked over to his lover and pounced on his lap. He received the reaction he wanted when Darians' lips parted in a beautiful dimpled smile. Xavier was always fascinated that Darian could look utterly harmless and dangerous at the same time. His dimples always made him look like a mischievous boy. He placed his hands on the sides of his lover and master's head and peered into his green eyes. A dangerous thing to do unless your goal was to get sweaty fast.

Darian rested his hands on Xavier's thighs. "You are quite beautiful, my little *inamorato*.(male lover)" He said as he ran his fingers through Xavier's long dark brown locks and peered into his grey eyes. "You have not fed. I think you will have a treat tonight. That is, if our little rat doesn't scamper away. Then your treat will have to be postponed until tomorrow night." Darian found the whole situation comical. Every once in a while he would run into a mortal that would surprise him with their bravado or stupidity, either way, he found it entertaining.

"Aren't you worried about the law that prohibits vampires from killing innocent mortals?" Xavier asked jokingly. He knew full well that Darian would work inside the law when and only when he chose to do so. He knew that Darian preferred to handle his personal affairs…well…personally.

"A thief is not innocent and the word innocent is always taken out of context where mortals are concerned. Everything for them is taken to the

27

extreme. Good fortune, used to be an act of god, now it's just a *lucky shot*. The meaning of *hero* meant someone who sacrificed their own life for the lives of others, now it means someone who just happen to survive no matter the manner of that survival."

Xavier seemed to ponder this, sometimes Darian could be so cynical in his reasoning, that often he wrote off his rants as just rants of a man that had seen too many years. But then there were times like these, when he actually made sense. Xavier supposed Darian made sense most of the time in his rantings, he just never paid enough attention to notice. The room was silent and now it was Darian's turn to wonder what was on the mind of his lover.

"What are you thinking about?" He cocked his head to the side slightly as he gazed at him. His fingers tightened on Xavier's thighs.

"I'm thinking I should get off of you right now." He said with a chuckle as he playfully tugged at Darian's grip and rose off of his lap. It was evident that Xavier was enjoying where he had been sitting. He marveled at how Darian could control himself so well, he simply wrote it off to Darian being an older vampire.

Darian sat up and rose from the sofa in one fluid movement and glided across the room to his desk to finger through his employee files. He was going to have to call the next in line of mortal employees to maintain the club during the day. He found the name of Annette Balfour, quickly he scanned his mind to see if it was a name of a person he would recognize. He did, he smiled. Annette was indeed a beautiful, sexy woman of color. He wondered why he had not yet seduced her, *he would have to correct that*. He thought it would be interesting to have a female as a day time assistant manager, it was definitely a change from the mortal men who thought they could always pull one over the resting eyes of the boss and high tail it out of town before nightfall. He leaned over his desk and buzzed his secretary.

"Yes master?" Asked a soft feminine voice

"I want you to contact a Miss. Annette Balfour, I want to meet with her tomorrow night."

"Miss Balfour was scheduled to work tomorrow night master, but that has been switched to tonight. She should be in by seven. Shall I send her to your office when she arrives?" Asked the voice. Darian contemplated if he would still be occupied with eliminating the soon-to-be ex-assistant manager when she arrived, then decided the dirty work might be done by that time.

"Yes."

"As you wish Master." Both ended the connection. He looked at Xavier and smiled.

"So is that your choice, what if she doesn't have accounting skills?" Xavier asked playfully.

Darian made an offhand gesture. "Doesn't matter, if she can count, then it won't be a problem." His gaze trailed Xavier from head to toe, taking him in, savoring the vision of him like a groom on his wedding night looking at his bride in her lacy undies. "We need to attend to matters before the opening of the club and I want you to arrange for the truck to deliver the blood." Darian said. Xavier nodded and left the room to head to his office to make arrangements for the synthetic blood delivery.

According to most vampires, synthetic blood was mortals way of saying "look what we've done for you, now you can stop eating us!" What they fail to understand is the differences between synthetic blood and human blood is the taste as well as the pleasure, not to mention the strength one gained through feeding. Only another vampire can understand the pure joy of feeding. One feels the pleasure of the blood flowing through their veins while they feed from a mortal who's heart pumps the blood to their hunger, their need. Many vampires refused to drink the synthetic blood and opted to feed on willing mortals. These mortals were known as vampire groupies, they hung out at vampire owned establishments, waiting to be picked. They gave the vampires an endless supply of blood. Other vampires, like those who resented being turned, rejoiced in the drinking of synthetic blood, even if it meant enduring the loss of pleasure and strength gained in the traditional manner of feeding.

Darian felt that these were the kind of vampires that should never have been chosen for such a gift. They were weak, and still clinging to their lost mortal existence. For them, the synthetic blood was the last string that tied them to humanity. Some vampires, like Darian and Xavier chose the more traditional way of feeding. They hunted still, but their hunting nights were few and far between. Their main food source came from the vampire groupies. One good thing came from the *Exposure* and that was the predictability of mortals. Thousands of mortals lined up to feel the vampire's kiss. But even more of a treat than a willing mortal, was a willing shape shifter, it appeared that the bite from a vampire was pure ecstasy to both humans and shape-shifters. Shape shifters were considered the true delicacy, they were stronger, more resilient and it was needless to say, they tasted better.

Chapter 4

Elise lay sprawled on her bed, the head of one of her pack mates rested in her lap. They laid naked together as most shape-shifters do. To lay in that fashion proved that one was comfortable and trusting, it strengthened their bonds. She ran her fingers through his hair, twirling her fingers around the dark silky curls. He looked up at her with his grey eyes and smiled.

"What are you thinking about?" Sergio asked. "I see that far off gaze in your eyes and I know you're not even here." Sergio said, his Italian accent threaded through each word. His own hand raising to cup her chin in his palm.

"Nothing, just random thoughts." She sighed "I want to go down to the club tonight." Elise said almost dreamily. Sergio frowned and sat up straight on the bed. He was annoyed that a perfect moment was ruined by her lust for Darian. He knew that was the only reason she wanted to go to the club. His feelings towards Darian were as cold as the arctic winds. He felt that Darian used her to feed his own lust and hungers. He believed that Darian was the type of man you didn't get attached to. Elise noted Sergio's frown-at the mention of Darian's club and had correctly assumed his emotions were based on jealousy and she did not want to hear his ranting. She controlled the pride, and she did not have to answer to anyone.

Elise looked at the sour expression on Sergio's face. She knew the numerous phrases that often followed that expression. 'He's not right for you', 'he's just using you', 'he's a vampire, you're a shape shifter, he'll never respect you, vampires only respect other vampires,' she'd heard it all before, but they didn't know Darian, he was different. He made her feel like a woman all the while taming the leopard inside. Many of the other leopards were against her fornicating with a non pride member, let alone a vampire. She paid them no mind, Darian would protect them, he would protect her. Not to mention, Darian saved their pride member, Daniel from possibly being sentenced to death six months ago; after he'd been caught in the woods hunting on non-sanctioned grounds. To Elise, Darian had proved himself to be a worthy lover.

"I know what you're going to say and I don't want to hear it, you can save it, Sergio." Elise climbed out of the bed with a smoothness that only a feline can accomplish.

"The only reason you don't want to hear it is because you know it's true!" Sergio retorted. "You belong with your own kind Elise. This affair you have with Darian is wrong, it isn't proper!" Elise flashed him a look that nearly stopped him, but he continued. "Look, I'm sorry, but you know I'm right Elise. Elise…" He rose from the bed, his tall naked body glowing in the moonlight. Elise watched as the muscles in his thighs flexed to aid him in movement. He walked over to her and gently cupped her cheeks, he tilted her head upwards, so that their eyes met.

"Elise, you don't need him. Yes it's true that he saved Daniel but it's no reason for you to keep repaying him. Your place is here with us, with me. He can not offer you true companionship, not like I can. I am your true mate." He leaned closer to her, his lips brushed hers lightly. Their eyes closed as the heat of the kiss grew more passionate. Then as soon as it begun, Elise broke away, she moved from Sergio's grasp. Anger flared in his eyes and he turned away, not wanting to say anything that might hurt her feelings. That, he did not want to do. He only wanted her to see that Darian was not what he seemed. He wanted her to see the truth that was right in front of her eyes. The truth that *he* was there, *and* had been there for over twenty-five years, waiting for her to except him as her mate. He was second to care for the pride, but he longed to be her equal within the pride and above all else-her mate. He watched her as she walked into the bathroom, he heard the shower and knew she was bathing her soft, creamy delicate skin. Sergio walked into the bath room and leaned against the door frame crossing his powerful arms over his thick muscular chest. He was six-foot-four-inches tall, olive complexion, grey eyes and short curly black hair. His chin was clean shaven, his long dark lashes curled at the very ends. Sergio knew Elise desired him, not only could he see her desire but he could smell it.

"Do you want me to go with you? You know what! Better yet! I think I will go with you." Without waiting for an answer or permission, he turn and started for his bedroom. He knew he was pushing it but he always felt that Elise was worth it and then some. He hated that she was so enthralled with a vampire. Especially Darian, who's reputation spoke for itself. Many who knew him, compared him to a mob boss. He always seemed to be so well connected. The S.U.I.T.'s never seemed to hang around and monitor his popular establishment. *Desires Unleashed* did not seem to get any undercover investigations the way other supernatural owned businesses did. Sergio was quite certain that *Desires Unleashed* was more than just a dance and strip club.

When their pride member Daniel found himself in trouble with the law six months ago, Sergio urged Elise to take himself as her mate and protector of the pride, he felt confident that he could handle the situation himself. But instead, she decided to go to Darian and with his political connections, he arranged to have Daniel released in their care. The whole act angered Sergio, not only had she sought outside help.But in doing so, made him appear incompetent. He was more than prepared and he had earned his place as the dominate male in the pride. Sergio took at quick shower, making sure he used a shampoo that was not too strong, but just the right scent to entice Elise. If he had to woo her away from Darian, then he would do so. He opened his closet and fished through his extensive wardrobe. He had not realized how many articles of clothing he had. Some things inside his closet he had not worn since the 80's. He pulled out a checkered pink and orange shirt and wondered what the hell he was thinking when he brought it, let alone wore it.

Further more, why had he kept it?

There was a knock at his door, he threw the ghastly shirt back into the closet and walked to the door to unlock it. He opened the door and saw Devin standing there with and sly smile on his face. Devin was a black male about five feet eight inches and natural born leopard. He had close cropped hair and hazel eyes, his caramel skin complexion was smooth and blemish free. He was currently twenty-one years old, though at times he acted as if he were younger. Devin was the pride prankster. Sergio loved all of his pride members but wasn't necessarily in the mood for visitors right now. Sergio walked away from the door to continued fishing through his clothes. He wanted to wear something that was going to show the *best* he had to offer without revealing *all* he had to offer, which meant no sheer net shirts or spandex pants. Though he was not opposed to spandex and sheer clothing, goodness knows he was well endowed, never had a complaint in the bedroom department. And his chiseled torso and tight firm abs was what most mortal men dreamed of.

He looked at the pride mate who just sprawled himself across his bed and was watching him as he searched for something to wear. Sergio wondered why Devin had come to visit him, he was just curious to know if this visit had a reason. He finally found a pair of black leather pants then he searched harder until he found a black satin button up shirt with metal buttons. He looked across the room and located his black motorcycle boots. He returned his attention to Devin and decided to ask him if there was a particular reason he was there.

"So, what's up? Do you have anything that you want to tell me? Or are you here just to keep me company?" Sergio asked as he tossed the towel he had wrapped around his waste and started pulling on the tight black leather pants.

"No, I just wanted to keep you company, I heard you and Elise talking earlier, did you two have a fight or something? I mean, I know how pissed you are that she hasn't chosen you as mate yet or even named you as pride king. I also know how pissed you are that she's with Darian. So now, are you going to go with her to *Desires Unleashed*?" Devin asked as he began to jump up and down on the mattress.

Sergio did not want to answer. He wanted to keep that to himself. "Well as for the other stuff you mentioned, that's none of your business. But to answer the latter of your questions, yes, I will be accompanying Elise to that retched club." Sergio said as he pulled on his shirt and began buttoning it up.

"Well, do us all a favor..." Devin started.

"What's that?"

"When you get there, get laid. You've been so damn uptight. I reckon it has been a while since the last time you fucked someone, you're starting to get on everyone nerves. So do us all a favor and get laid or something, because we're all tired of getting our heads bitten off." Devin said as he hopped off the bed and smiled at Sergio.

"You little asshole" Sergio smiled and chuckled. The sound of his laughter was sensuous. "Go, go on, bugger off, tell everyone that I'll lighted up, but only a little, if I start slacking on you guys you'll just get worse." Both men laughed and Devin left Sergio alone to finish dressing. Sergio had splashed on a little cologne, the same scent as his shampoo and body wash, he did not want to smell of several different things. People who used several different scents of their cosmetics gave him headaches whenever he was caught upwind of them. He then applied a little styling gel to his hair and raked his fingers through, allowing some locks to hang over his forehead. He gave himself a look over, once he was satisfied with his appearance, he headed down to Elise's room to see if she was ready.

"Are you ready to go?" Sergio asked as he cracked Elise's door open and peeked inside. His eyes focused on her and what she was wearing. She was beautiful. He looked at her tight fitting black leather mini skirt that barely covered her crotch. Her thigh high black heeled boots added another six inches to her height, she resembled a dominatrix. To add to that effect was a black leather bra covered by a black sheer nylon shirt with black satin collar and cuffs.

At first glance, Sergio wanted to slowly peel every piece of clothing off her body. He wanted to lay her down on the satin covers and kiss her all over and savor her scent, he found her intoxicating. Then it all came rushing back to him like a freight train, all of this, this complete ensemble was picked by Elise, to please Darian. Sergio wanted to know what Darian had that he did not. He wanted to know his competition. He opened the door wider and leaned across the oak frame.

"Is all that for him?" He asked.

"What does it matter to you?" Elise answered defensively.

"What does it matter to me? Well, it should matter to you, Do you think he can love you as I do, as a matter of fact, do you think he loves you at all?" Elise did not want to answer that question, she did not want to think about such a thing. *Of course Darian loved her, he had helped her, helped all of them, and he made love to her, better than anyone else ever had, of that she'd been certain. Sergio would just have to get over his jealousy, she'd chosen her lover and it was not up for discussion.*

"I'm not going to stand here Sergio and play these games with you. You simply have to get over this jealousy you have towards Darian, and my relationship with him. Now, you should direct your interest to the other females in the pride, you need to settle with one of them, and stop this constant badgering, I grow tired of it!" Elise said, confident she would put an end to Sergio's protest of whom she chose to sleep with.

Sergio watched Elise closely. He could sense her apprehension. He believed she was aware that she was not the apple of Darian's eye. He could not understand her obsession with him. Tonight, he would see for himself, firsthand the two of them together. He wanted to see the manipulation in the act. He wanted to be able to bring it up to her later, and say, 'see, I told you, he doesn't love you, but I do!' He wondered if even that would be enough to convince her just how serious he was. Only time would tell.

Chapter 5

Darian sat back comfortably in his black leather chair. He had turned the chair's temperature up to eighty-five degrees. He enjoyed the sensation of the heat over his skin. Not that he was cold, his skin would only be cold until he fed, but naturally he liked heat inside his body and out. Heat was sensual, heat was sexy... heat was lust. He read through the gambling profits he made the week before in his hidden underground arena. "*The Coliseum*" is what he called it. The arena was the pride and joy of his club. The large arena was hidden three stories underground. He charged the rich and wealthy an outrageous amount of money to gain access to the arena and then he made additional profits on the gambling. Rich, self indulgent mortals would place tons of money on a chosen fighter in the twelve men, three day tournament. These mortals shared Darian's blood lust and though he set the stage for the violence, they hungered for it more than he had. They never really cared about the fighter personally, only that he or she was strong and could fight.

Every week, Friday through Sunday there would be a new elimination tournament held with a total of twelve fighters. One fighter would be pitted against another for combat and for each match one would win, there was a prize of ten thousand dollars added to his or her purse. In the event that a fighter did not survive, which was often, the money they earned would be sent to the designated person stated in their contracts. On the third night, the last remaining fighters would face off in a three-way, every-person-for-themselves-battle. if he or she survived then they would receive five million dollars and could live a nice life in the tropics. But the real appeal of the arena was that the loser's fate was always at the mercy of the crowd. Darian had found it amusing that for all the preaching about kindness, compassion and good will towards your fellow man that the human race barked out, he very rarely witnessed a merciful audience. Darian believed that mortals were just as monstrous as the next being. His club proved his theory-nightly. The hidden arena and bordello, both were very profitable. His club was a place where both human and supernaturals could go to indulge in the pleasures of sin.

The idea to register the popular club as a supernatural owned business, came to him one night as he watched the news. The anchorwoman was relating to the public all the crime that had taken place right after the *Exposure*. He watched the human race kill each other out of sheer panic. It did not surprise him. He knew that humans would automatically convince themselves that the supernaturals were of the purest evil and needed to be destroyed. But what they failed to realize was that just about every supernatural creature that walked the earth, the majority of them used to be human. They still had human desires and goals. Human ambition and lust *and* above all, the desire to survive. He witnessed over the centuries of his long life families torn apart out of greed. Spouses murdering each other for insurance money or the lust of a new lover. So Darian did not see a line that separated supernatural evil to that of the human race. If humans considered them evil, it was because the supernaturals were higher on the food chain.

He waited impatiently for Annette Balfour to arrive. Just when he was about to buzz his secretary to find out if Annette had arrived, he heard the high pitched beep from his telephone on his desk. He pressed the little square green button that allowed him to answer.

"Yes?" He asked, then waited for the response.

"Mast-Mr. Alexander, Miss. Annette Balfour has just arrived. Shall I send her in, sir?" The soft female voice asked. Darian smiled, he liked hearing his subordinates call him master, but not when he was handling business in front of a mortal, unless of course that mortal was the business at hand.

"Yes, please do so Miss. Baker." Darian released the little green button and settled comfortably into his chair. When he heard the door open and then close he knew it was Miss. Balfour. He could smell the blood underneath her skin, he could feel her pulse beating fast, making her body heat rise. Ah yes, Darian loved the heat. Slowly he turned around in his chair to face her. He thought she was beautiful indeed. He could not understand why he had not met her personally before. He would have to have a small talk with Xavier.

He entrusted all of the hiring of the staff to Xavier. He knew Xavier would have the right eye for such beauty. He was sure that Xavier had already bedded Miss. Balfour and if he had not then it was his loss and Darian's gain. It was one of the aspects of their relationship Darian enjoyed most of all, he would not have it any other way, they had to have an open sexual relationship. Sex was one of Darian's favorite pastimes. He enjoyed the feel of hot, sweaty bodies underneath him or behind him. The sensation of the heat as it increased until it spilled over their bodies in that one final moment when time would freeze.

He gazed at her caramel colored skin, he admired the smoothness of it. He wanted to feel that smoothness underneath his fingertips. He liked her permed straight hair, how it framed her slender oval shaped face. Her lips attracted him as well, he loved how full and luscious they were. He was a lover of both male and female and cherished all of the individual qualities each offered. His mind raced to what he wanted to do with her before the night was out and a wicked smile spread across his lips, exposing his dimples, making him look both innocent and guilty.

He looked at her entire appearance, mentally calculating the quickest way to remove her clothing based on hooks, zippers, snaps, etc. She was dressed in a leopard print bra top and a black satin skirt with a leopard print hem and wearing a pair of black heels. Darian, admired the way the outfit enveloped her. It was one of the reasons he decided to have a strip club, bordello and arena in addition to his dance club-the seduction! *Desires Unleashed* was exactly what the name stated, and that was what Darian wanted.

"Miss, Balfour I called you into my office tonight because I have some good news. You see, I have been going through my employee records and reviewing some of my best staff." He looked in her direction and smiled. He rose from his chair, and glided around the desk. All of his movements were as smooth as satin. His body never looked clumsy, never once. He leaned against the corner of his desk in front of Annette. He held her open file in his hand as he looked down at her over the edge of the file and smiled. His eyes sparkled as his smiled warmed her. He slid half-way onto the corner of his desk and pretended to look over her information. He had already memorized her file before she came into his office but now, he was putting up appearances.

"It says here, that you've never been late and only absent one time since you started working here." He paused and leaned in closer to her. "Most impressive," he whispered seductively. His forest green eyes peered into the chocolate brown of her own. She felt his aura pelting her making a heat rise from between her legs, she fought the urge to squirm in her seat. She could smell his cologne, as if he needed any. She was willing to bet he was just as good in bed as he looked *and that was saying a lot!* She had the desire to press her hand to her chest and comment in a exaggerated southern bell accent, and say 'Why sir, I'm just a southern bell and we southern gals don't do things like-ooooohh, Oh My!' She mentally shook her head, she wanted to focus on what he was saying to her, even though it was proving to be more difficult with each passing second.

"Did you hear what I said?" Darian asked, humor hidden in his smile. He knew damn well that she had not heard a word he said and it was just how he planned it. She did not need to hear what he saying, only that he was paying her attention and that she had his favor for the evening. She should be so blessed.

"Oh, yeah...um..." she took a deep breath and let it out. *This was bad.* "No. I'm sorry, I didn't catch the...um..last thing you said." She was hoping he would not think lowly of her. *Nothing was worse than being condemned as an airhead.* Well, there were worse things, but at this point airhead was the one she was worried about. He obviously called her into his luxurious office for a reason, and from the rumors she heard circulating around the club. No one got to see the owner's office unless they were getting fired or a special promotion. She was hoping it was the latter.

Darian's chuckle vibrated deep in his throat. He decided to cut-to-the-chase. "What I said was- congratulations, Miss. Balfour. If you decide to take the job, you will be the new assistant day manager of *Desires Unleashed.* So what do you say; Yay or nay?" He gazed at her thrilled expression for a moment, then he placed her file on his desk and move to kneel down in front of her. Her breath was caught in her throat. It was true what she heard about how beautiful the owner was supposed to be. She knew that all of the vampires she saw on a nightly basis were obviously picked by another vampire for their lovely features. Even though she had sexual thoughts about those vampires that worked at the club, something always held her back. She continued to stare at Darian, she had never seen a man so gorgeous he left her speechless. Annette wanted to run her fingers through his long black flowing waves, she wanted to see if his hair was as silky and soft as it looked. She wanted to trace her fingertips along his jaw line and feel the tight muscles there. She wanted to lean forward and take hold of his face and tilt it up to hers, look deeply into his deep forest green eyes and press her lips to the soft warm flesh of his lips. Annette wanted to feel him inside her-she wanted all of him! She could feel a burning from deep inside of her, feeling it rush to her head like lava!

Darian smiled. He should be ashamed of himself, he thought. But he can not help that he was born with a gift and what the affect that gift had on others. Without waiting for her consent, he trailed his fingertips in a wavy motion up her calves working his way slowly to her thighs. Never taking his gaze from hers, he caressed her thighs messaging the firm flesh. He leaned forward as he parted her legs and began kissing very softly on the inside of her thighs from one side to the other working his way up. His hand slid under her skirt and found her lace thong panties and grabbing a hold of them, he began to slowly slide them down past her thighs and calves.

She raised her feet so that Darian could pull the panties off. He tossed the panties on his desk and began his tender kisses again on her inner thighs. He could smell her passion rising from her pleasure zone. He could feel the heat pulsating from between her legs. He inched forward and blew a long slow breath over her quivering vagina. She felt it constrict as his breath tickled her delicate soft flesh. Darian's face inched closer until he heard Xavier's soft footstep approaching. He withdrew as his door opened.

"Ah, I see you're interviewing the new assistant manager! Should I leave you alone to finish going over her...um...credentials?" Xavier asked as he stood in the open doorway. Darian was slightly disappointed that he had been interrupted during a sexual conquest.

"Give me a minute." Darian said to Xavier as he rose to his feet. Darian settled his gaze on Annette, he did not need to entrance her, he hadn't needed to entrance any of his lovers. He did not like influencing people to have sex with him, he felt it was cheating. He was more than confident that he could have anyone he wanted with just a little charm. He had not been mistaken.

"Annette, why don't I see you in my office at...oh, let's say one o'clock?" He asked as he stroked her hair. Annette struggled to remember something, there was something she had to do after work. Just when she was going to tell herself to 'forget about it' she remembered.

"Oh, I can't, I'm meeting my friend after work. We're supposed to be celebrating her new job. Otherwise..." she rose from her seat and ran her hands down Darian's chest. She had wanted to do that the moment she first laid her eyes on him. It was all that she thought it would be and more. He was firm and muscular under the soft thin fabric of his black shirt. She could feel his muscles tightened against her touch. It was then, she decided that Darian, was the epitome of a sexy male.

Darian was set back, but not too disappointed. "Very well, perhaps tomorrow night then?" He asked as he took her hand and led her to the door. "Oh and by the way, did you want the position?"

Annette remembered now, the reason she was called into his office in the first place. "Oh yeah- yes! Most definitely! Thank you, sir." She said excitedly.

Darian raised his hand in protest. "Please, when we are alone like this, call me Darian." Annette blushed, she hoped it did not show. She nodded her head. Darian saw this as a perfect opportunity to steal a kiss and seal the deal. He leaned forward slowly and brushed his lips against hers. He could feel her lean into him, into his kiss. Ah, it was a thrill he felt often, it was a thrill he sought. He pulled back and opened the door for her. Annette smiled and walk out of the office. Darian watched Annette swish down the hallway and he smiled. He knew she was putting an extra little sway to her hips for his benefit and he was pleased. Then his gaze shifted to Xavier and he widen the door and walked away, leaving the door open for Xavier to close when he entered the room.

"So you just wasn't going to share with me, were you" Xavier teased as he leaned against the door frame.

"I was trying to get a taste test. So why was I interrupted?" Darian asked, one eyebrow raised as he leaned against his desk, arms folded across his chest.

"Anthony's here, shall I bring him in?"

Darian's smiled returned. "Yes." Xavier beckoned John inside the office. John had Anthony in his grip. The front of Anthony's white t-shirt was spotted with blood and his blue jeans were so faded, they looked to have been several years old. Anthony's hands were tied behind him and a black silk bag covered his entire head. Anthony stumbled into the room, John pressed hard on his shoulders forcing him to his knees.

"Anthony, so nice of you to join us tonight." Darian said as he walked towards the kneeling man. He snatched off the black bag and peered into Anthony's eyes. Darian ran his fingers through the other man's hair, then grabbed a handful of the blond locks and yanked his head upwards, bringing Anthony's gaze to meet his. Anthony cried out at the pain that shot across his scalp as his hair was wrenched in Darian's powerful grip.

"Anthony, Anthony, Anthony, tonight just isn't your night, is it?" Darian asked as he ran a finger under Anthony's bloody nose. He raised his finger to his mouth and slowly sucked the blood away. His gaze drifted towards Xavier, who was already under the bloodlust. Xavier had not yet fed and had been waiting patiently for Anthony's arrival. The smell of Anthony's blood in the air was making the wait unbearable. Xavier could taste the blood on his tongue and desparetly wanted the real thing. He had control but his control was weaker when he was under the *Thirst*.

"You should never have betrayed me, Anthony," Darian was saying as he beckoned for Xavier to come closer. "Goodbye, Anthony." The horrifying truth finally dawned on Anthony. His death was inevitable. He mentally cursed himself for not booking town. He should have never tried to wait for her. He should have hightailed it out of the city on the fastest plane to

Timbuktu. He should have never opened the door, he should have known they'd come for him. Now he was going to die. A spark in his brain told him to try to escape.

"NOOO!!!!" Anthony screamed and tried to rise up from the floor, but John's strong hands held him in an iron grip. He could not move an inch, not even to struggle. He watched in horror as Xavier stood in front of him, then kneeled down. He cringed when Xavier caressed his face, softly with both hands. Tears rolled down his cheeks and Xavier leaned forward and caught a tear drop on his tongue, savoring his fear. A low groan rumbled through Xavier's chest that was a mingle of pure hunger and lust.

"Shhhh, quiet," Xavier cooed. "You die tonight, but you die as the chosen. Fear not, you are lucky to die tonight by a vampire's kiss." Xavier whispered into Anthony's ears. Xavier extended his silent command-coaxing Anthony to relax. Once Xavier felt the other man's muscles relax, he leaned closer to the pulsating artery underneath the smooth soft skin of Anthony's neck. Xavier's mouth opened, fangs extending for the feeding. Anthony gasped, his back arching as Xavier's fangs broke through the skin. As Xavier began to feed, audible sucking noises filled the room. Low moans were coming from the two men, both enwrapped in pleasure, both sharing this special union. Darian watched closely, he enjoyed watching the vampire's kiss in motion. He delighted in watching other people enjoying pleasure in all forms.

Anthony let out a long shivering moan, his body twitched once, twice and then, fell limp in Xavier's arms. Xavier continue to feed, draining the body completely. He savored the warm delicious, thick fluid as it filled his mouth and flowed down his throat. He could not, would not give this sensation up for anything in the world. He tilted his head slightly, to widen his mouth and capture more of the blood that warmed him. It excited him, he could feel it spread throughout all of his limbs. His body tingled as though little electric shocks where bursting over his form. He had grown hard during the feeding as all vampires do, and he felt his passions rise to the crest.

Xavier had to contain his disappointment when the blood stopped flowing. He forced himself away and let Anthony's corpse slip from his hands. His head rolled back, eyes half open, mouth parted slightly, blood stained his full shaped lips. He ran his hands down the length of this torso, past his stomach, to caress his groin. His body twitched as he massaged his organ. Darian smiled and waved John out of his office. John nodded and bent down to retrieved the lifeless body of Anthony, he threw the body over his shoulder and exited the room. Darian walked up behind Xavier and he peered into Xavier's grey eyes and smiled. He squatted beside Xavier, his arm encircling

41

the other man's chest. He held Xavier against his torso with his left arm, while his right hand slid up Xavier's chest to caress his throat. He grabbed Xavier's chin held his face up to his. Darian's tongue darted out to lick up the spilt blood from Xavier's lips. Their tongues met and the two embraced in a passionate kiss. A low groan escaped from Xavier as Darian began to caress Xavier's chest, he slid a hand inside his shirt, his fingers sought the firm nipples and gently rolled the delicate flesh between his fingertips, sending shivers through Xavier's form. Darian's other hand, slid further down to caress Xavier's crotch, massaging the hardness through the denim material. Ragged panting moans filled the room as Xavier begin to feel his climax. Then all the sensation stopped when Darian released Xavier and rose from the floor.

Confused and disappointed, Xavier looked up, a questioning look on his face.

"Why?"

Darian smiled and lean down and whispered in Xavier's ear. "An eye, for an eye, my beautiful *inomorato*. Tomorrow night, we'll share each other's passions, but not until then." Darian teased seductively then walked out of the room, leaving Xavier unsatisfied, forced to subside his lust. *Payback can sure be a bitch.* Xavier thought as he remembered interrupting Darian's seduction of Annette earlier.

Chapter 6

"Hello?" Xander inquired, his deep British accent was smooth as silk.

"Xander this is Warren. I just got this new case and I think you'll want to see these pictures from the crime scene. It's some sick shit let me tell you. Right now, I've never seen anything like it before." He paused "I know you'll want to see this; I'm in my car now. I'll be at your place in about…let's say, ten minutes."

Xander could hear the anxiety in Warren's voice, he knew well enough when Warren was upset. "Very well, I'll be waiting for you when you arrive. It will be good to see you after all of these months. The Family will be overjoyed to see you again, especially Adrian." Xander said with a smile. "I'll see you soon," he hung up the telephone and sat back in his recliner. He enjoyed the comforts of the mortal world, that was one thing he could not deny.

He smiled again at the thought of Warren and Adrian seeing each other after all this time. The last time Warren was home, Adrian was away on vacation. Adrian had been most upset when he learned that he missed the opportunity to see Warren again. Though the two are the best of friends and grew up together, they managed to become lovers, in spite of their differences. Xander did not opposed that at all. Adrian was his son and Warren had been raised by him. He did not mind them experimenting with their relationship. However, he did not believe that their romantic relationship would stand the test of time. It was apparent that both men were very dominate and Adrian had always been the more dominate of the two. They broke up for the second time ten months ago. Adrian never stopped trying to get Warren back. This night would prove to be an interesting one. Xander sipped his coffee and turn the page of his geographic magazine. He was becoming most fascinated with the various cultures of the different tribes in Africa. He thought it would be interesting as well as entertaining to take a return trip to Africa, perhaps for a second honeymoon. He had been once, a long time ago, but at that time, he was romancing his now current wife.

She had been a volunteer with the *PeaceAroundTheWorld* organization and they were there to feed the hungry. He had been on a safari hunt and had came upon their camp. Their scents attracted each other, she was in heat, her aroma was as strong and intoxicating as the scent of blood. It called to him, and his scent to her. They made love that night, they talked about past time… they fell in love. They were married after a year of dating, or as it is called inside the pack, mating.

His wife came into the room, she was tall five-feet-nine inches, slender frame, her smooth milk chocolate skin glowed in the moonlight. She wore her long dark brown hair braided in cornrolls that flowed down her back. Her full luscious lips parted in a smile as she looked lovingly at her husband. Her light brown eyes danced with excitement at the very sight of him. She loved looking at his broad muscular shoulders. Her heart skipped beats as he gazed at her with his silver eyes. She wanted to run her fingers through his waist length straight brown hair.

"Hi darling, Dinner is almost done, are you going to eat in here or in the dining room with the rest of us," she joked. Xander smiled, he closed his magazine and rose from the chair. He covered the distance between them in only a few quick strides, then he held his lovely wife in his warm embrace. He smiled at her and leaned forward and kissed her soft lips. He nuzzled his nose to hers and she smiled and giggled. His hands caressed her lower back as he squeezed her tighter, almost as if he did not want to let her go.

"I'll eat in the dining room with everyone else" He whispered in her ear. "And darling, we have a guest tonight, our headstrong young one returns. He has a case that he wants me to look into." His wife pulled away, and looked at him.

"Am I to understand that Warren is coming home tonight?" She asked, a look of humor played on her face. She was well aware that this night was going to be a long one.

Xander nodded. "Yes, he seemed pretty upset about a case. It must be a shape shifter involved. I will need to see for myself if it's something I think I may be able to handle. But for now, I'll let you go and finish dinner." He released her reluctantly. She smiled and headed towards the heavy oak-carved double doors, then stopped. She turned to face her husband.

"Xander?" .

"Yes, Tatiana?" He answered.

"Please don't let Adrian get out of hand tonight. We both know how our son can behave when he is around Warren."

Xander nodded, and smiled. "I'll try." He couldn't promised that Adrian would not act out. Adrian had been headstrong and cocksure since he was a young boy. And when Xander first accepted Warren into his home and introduced him to the others, Adrian did not like the new male near his own age, taking away some of his father's attention. He did not like the fact that Warren was scared and sad and always, always had someone comforting him. It was not until his father sat him down and told him that he should help, he could have a friend in Warren if only he were nicer to him. Adrian did not believe that he was lonely enough to want a friend, let alone, "Warren the whiner". He had been wrong. They had became the best of friends, and later as the years passed, they had become the worse of lovers.

The two fought constantly about who was the aggressor in their relationship. Neither man wanted to claim the more submissive role and they could not share the dominate one. Adrian always felt that since he pursued Warren first and he was one year older and stronger, then he should no doubt hold the title. However, Warren saw things differently and because the arguments about who should be on the top, never seemed to end, Warren could no longer endure Adrian's controlling personality. Warren decided to end the relationship. Adrian never agreed to the ending of the relationship and as far as he was concerned they were still dating, only on hiatus.

Xander made his way to the grand dinning room. The room itself had been remodeled to accommodate all the extra people that had moved in with Xander over the years. The extra long redwood table sat in the middle of the room. The wood was polished to perfection and reflected the rainbow specter from the four crystal chandeliers that hung overhead. The thick burgundy carpet covered the floor and remained stainless. Xander always enjoyed art, and it showed throughout his home. He had purchased priceless artworks from such artists as Monet, Botticelli, Michael-Angelo, and even one hit wonders. He enjoyed the self-expression the art projected. It was like delving into the artist soul, and seeing the passion that may have been hidden otherwise.

The sound of the door bell chiming alerted him that Warren had arrived. He walked from the dinning room to the front room that was decorated as tastefully as the rest of the house. The silk burgundy upholstery that covered the sofas and chairs was spotless and looked brand new. He did not allow anyone to abuse his furniture. Once in a rage, Adrian had threw one of his thousand dollar chairs across the room, splintering it and Xander had made him pay for it, dearly. He loved the feel of the thick burgundy carpet under his feet, on some rare nights when he was alone, he would trace the pattern of the carpet with his bare toes, smiling to himself at the simplicity of it all and marveling at the handstitched designs. He also purchased hand sewn rugs, "artwork for the floor" he once called it. Some rugs he considered too beautiful for the floor and hung them up on walls. He reached the front door, he could smell Warren's scent already from the other side of the door, he could hear him breathing. He opened the door and smiled.

"Warren, how good to see you again. Come in," He frowned as he watched Warren enter the house. "Where is your key?" He asked curiously.

"I lost it about three weeks ago. I'll need another one." He tilted his head up and his nostrils flared as he smelled the air. "Is dinner ready?" He asked almost excited. Xander chuckled.

He nodded "Yes, dinner's almost ready, I think. Come, let us go into the dinning room. Everyone will be so happy to see you." Xander placed his arm around Warren's shoulders and led him into the dinning room that was already filling up as hungry wolves smelled dinner. They all looked up recognizing Warren's scent as he entered the room, and were pleased to see him.

"Hey Warren!!! Welcome back man!" A tall slender man with pale skin, in a red t-shirt and black jeans said as he made his way around the table to greet Warren personally with a big bear hug. He was followed by ten other people all gathering around to hug their pack brother. They all wished he would stay home, at least to visit more than he did, but they all had their ideas of why he did not and some of those ideas included Xander's strict rules, and Adrian's lust.

"How's everyone!?" Warren asked, obviously happy to see everyone and to know that they were all doing fine.

"Everyone's well, Warren, real well. Why don't you visit more often you bum! You know how much everyone misses you, you jerk." Said a female in a hot pink halter top and white capri pants that were so tight, Warren doubted if she could even stick her finger in the back pocket.

"I'll try to visit more often, but you know this job keeps me pretty busy sometimes." Warren said, and shrugged.

"I can keep you even more busy." Said a rich, deep voice from across the room.

Warren looked up to see Adrian enter the dinning room, carrying a huge platter, his mother and matron of the house, Tatiana, following behind him with a bowl of vegetables. Warren had hoped that Adrian was still at school, teaching and working on his doctorates in English Literature. He would have preferred to avoid this reunion. Adrian was always difficult for him to resist, this was going to be a long night.

"All the more reason why I visit when I can afford to visit." Warren said smugly. Adrian smiled, he knew what Warren meant and was banking on it. He wanted Warren there, with them, as it was supposed to be. Not frolicking around with the government funded police, turning in his own kind to the mortal firing squad.

"We'll have to work on that then, won't we." It was more of a statement than a question. Adrian left the room to gather more food from the kitchen. Warren sat down in the seat to the left of Xander. He leaned closer to whisper something to Xander, he knew everyone in the room would hear anyway, but only Xander would know what he was talking about. He opened his mouth to speak but Xander raised his hand and shook his head slightly.

"Tell me later." He said. Warren nodded. Adrian returned, carrying another heavy platter filled with meat. He leaned in front of Warren to place the platter on the table, he made sure his crotch brushed against Warrens elbow, causing Warren to tense slightly.

"For the guest of honor" Adrian said as he leaned closer to Warren's ear. "I'll have your desert if you still have room for it…I'm sure you will." He stood up, smiling wide and walked back into the kitchen for the rest of the food. A few of the other pack members chuckled and batted their eyes at Warren teasingly. After about three more trips to and from the kitchen, the table was covered with platter upon platter of delicious smelling foods. Everyone was seated at the table, fifteen hungry wolves reached out for slices and chunks of the pork and beef roasts. Platters of slow roasted cornish hens, tender sliced roast turkey cutlets, smothered in gravy were passed around the table. Two people argued over the bowl of mashed potatoes with homemade gravy. They passed the bowls of fresh string beans, broccoli and cauliflower amongst them. Sounds of metal scraping glass echoed in the room as forks and knives scooped up portions of food and was followed by sounds of finger sucking, lips smacking, moaning, and thirsty swallows. Someone burped loudly and others laughed at the table. Xander frowned, he was well aware of the nature of wolves, but he did appreciate a *little* table manners. After a stern look from the pack master, the laughter subsided.

After dinner, Xander and Warren went to Xander's sound-proof study for privacy. Xander had settle comfortably into a high back leather chair with leather armrest. He leaned over and opened a box filled with Cuban cigars. He offered one to Warren who politely waved it away. Xander sat back in the chair and lit his cigar and gestured for Warren to go ahead and speak.

"Well, I know how you wanted me to inform you whenever we get a case that may involve a shape- shifter." Warren said as he settled into the seat opposite Xander's.

Xander nodded. "And you think there is a wolf involved," he asked.

Warren nodded his head, and opened a file and handed some photographs over to Xander to look at. "Those were taken today, this morning actually. The body was discovered around 9 am. There were no witnesses, just the poor schmuck who had the misfortune to have discovered the body" He watched Xander flip through the photos, one after another. He looked at the frown that formed on Xander's face. He knew that Xander was thinking the same thing he had when he first saw the condition of the corpse.

"Do you think a werewolf did that, one of us? Whoever did it, I think, enjoyed it." Warren said when he thought Xander had taken in enough of the photos to catch his meaning.

"Please do not refer to our kind with that ridiculous human terminology. And yes, I think you may be right. But where's the blood? To have his head ripped off there should be blood all over this area." Xander asked looking at the rest of the pictures again to see if he had missed anything.

"Yes, you're right. The body was missing most of its' blood. That is what makes me think a vampire might also be involved. But I'm not sure, see. I know that a vampire is strong enough to rip off a human head, but I caught a scent of a shape-shifter, a wolf, it was faint but it was enough, I don't think the body was killed there, I think it was deposited there. And I don't mean dragged either. The killer had to have driven to that spot and dumped the body to throw off the scent trail. Someone is doing their homework."

"If there is a shifter involved then why is the body not mangled? Surely a shifter would want to feast? Was the scent you smelled in the area on the body?" Xander asked. Trying to make heads or tails of all that he was taking in. Warren shook his head, he seemed confused. He sat back in the chair, his chin resting on his hand as he traced back in his mind the scene of the crime.

"No, as a matter of fact, the only scent I caught was the scent of the body itself. And that is the thing that bothers me. I could not smell any other scent on the body except for blood. There wasn't even another scent on the man's clothes! It was like whoever committed this murder, did this before and they are skilled enough to not leave easy clues. I have no idea of knowing if that scent I caught was from the murderer or just a wolf that was in the area." Warren seemed bewildered. He was getting a bad feeling about this case, call it intuition,. The last thing he wanted was a supernatural serial killer. It was bad enough when a human decided to become the next Ted Bundy. It's even worse when you have a supernatural psycho on the prowl.

"Take me to the scene of the crime, I want to get a whiff of this scent. I may pick up something you did not." Xander said as he rose from his chair. Warren followed and both men headed for the door. Warren open the door only to find Adrian on the other side, hand poised to knock. Adrian smiled and caught Warren in his embrace and planted his lips on Warren's. Xander smiled, rolled his eyes then walked past the two men. Warren pushed Adrian away and looked into his eyes both men were breathing heavily, both men remembering the sensation of each other bodies mingling together all too clearly.

"We're not together anymore Adrian, remember." Warren insisted, as he tried to leave the room. Adrian's arm blocked his exit, keeping him from leaving the room.

"No, what I remember is going off to college to teach and to get my degree and coming home to find out that you had joined that fucking government police squad. What the fuck for, I don't know but that's what I remember. As far as I'm concern, you're still my lover. Besides, who knows you better than I?" Adrian smiled his wolfish grin. Then he pushed Warren back into the room and closed the door behind him. He pounced on top of Warren, knocking him down. He held Warren's hands down against the carpeted floor. He pressed his hips into the other man's and slowly started grinding their crotches together.

Warren pressed up and moaned, he could feel himself growing harder under the other mans erect groin. Warren closed his eyes and savored the sensation of Adrian's body against his. Adrian's soft lips lock with his in another passionate kiss. He open his eyes and gazed into Adrian's silver eyes. It was one of the better features he shared with his father. Staring into those eyes always made Warren want to get kinky fast. And getting kinky fast was not what he wanted to do, not now, not with Adrian. He came back to his senses and bucked and pumped under Adrian, trying to throw the other man off.

"Adrian, get off of me now! Don't do this, I broke up with you months ago!" He said as he became angrier the longer the other man held him down. "Face it, we just can't make it work!"

"I like when you play hard to get, keep fighting me, I'm almost there." Adrian panted breathlessly through clinched teeth. Warren stopped fighting long enough to see the pleasure spread across Adrian's face. He realized the other man was enjoying his struggles a little too much. This angered him even more, he wanted Adrian off of him and fast. He continued to struggle, he could feel Adrian hardness grinding against his own. He saw Adrian's mouth open wide, his breath coming faster and faster until it stuck in his throat. He saw Adrian's eye close and a look of sheer ecstacy wash over his face as his body tense and jerked several times.

After what seemed like forever, Adrian collapsed on top of Warren, breathless, spent. His grip lessened on Warren's wrists. Warren sat up pushing Adrian off of him onto his side. A huge wet spot stained the front of Adrian's pants. Warren punched him hard in the left arm forcing Adrian to cry out and grab his arm. Adrian laughed as he rubbed the pained spot on his upper bicep.

"Ow, man, what was that for!?" Adrian asked as he rose to his knees in front of Warren.

"What was it for!? what was it for!? Do you even have to ask!?" Warren asked annoyed. "You know what Adrian, sometimes you can be a complete asshole. And you wonder why I broke it off with you." Warren said and he looked down to see the wet stain in front of his own jeans. "Look what you did, you asshole." He said as he smacked Adrian on the side of his temple. Adrian fell back on his side laughing. It tickled him to see Warren again and he knew Warren was happy to see him even if he did not want to show it.

"Oh, don't be this way Warren. You know you're happy to see me. We belong together. We were meant to be together since day one. Come on, let' s go back into my room and fuck for real." Adrian said as he managed to crawl onto all fours in front of Warren, who just shook his head and rose to leave the study.

"Where are you going?" Adrian asked.

"I'd love to beat the shit out of you right this moment but your father and I have something important to do. And I know you can't possibly figure out what could be more important than your immediate desires but I have business to take care of." Warren said as he closed the door to the study. He was relieved to be out of the same room with Adrian. If he had been in that room one minute longer, he may have done a thing or two he would regret in the morning. He was more than happy to drive Xander to the scene of the crime after that little evil trick Adrian just pulled. He met Xander by his car, he noticed it was a brand new automobile, one of those two hundred thousand dollar numbers. He hoped Xander did not want to drive that to the scene of the crime.

"Please tell me this isn't the car we're taking. We won't get passed the city limits!" He said chuckling to himself. He pictured Xander and himself getting car jacked and then he stopped chuckling when his vision played the reality that Xander would probably kill the would be car-jacker without the slightest hesitation. He shook his head to clear the thought and smiled at Xander.

"Well, it happens to be my favorite car at the moment. The drive is always smooth, even on some bumpy streets, but if you insist on us taking a less luxurious form of transportation then I guess I'll have to settle for the BWMX." Xander said as he walked towards a silver two door BWMX E52 Z8 Roadster.

Warren laughed outright. "You call this toning down!?" He had tears coming from his eyes. Xander looked at the car, then looked back at his Ashley Marin and smiled.

"Yes, I do. Now are you going to stand there laughing like an idiot or are we going to investigate this crime." Xander asked as he opened the car doors and climbed inside. Warren nodded his head and climbed into the passenger seat. He did have to admit, it was lovely to be rich. He knew Xander would provide him with just about anything. But he wanted to own his own living. He gave directions to Xander as he played with the state of the art sound system. He fished through Xander's CD collection of opera and classical music, he frowned.

"Don't you ever listen to anything where the composer's still alive and it's not in french or Italian?" He asked as he placed a cd in the six count cd changer.

Xander smiled. "I'm sorry, I left the Wu Lang cd at home." He said as he cut the curves in the road as if the car was on rails.

Warren laughed. "Who's Wu Lang?"

"Some rap group that Kevin listens to constantly. He loves this song called '*Big Baby Balls*'." He held up his right hand to stop Warren from speaking "Don't' ask me. It's by someone from the group called-and get this, Old Fat Bastard. Kids these days, no taste." Both men chuckled as they headed towards the city limits.

"Okay, just make a right at the light right here and pull into the alley, can't miss it, look for the police tape." Warren said as he directed Xander towards the crime scene. Xander pulled the car behind a parked black Cobra. A sleek black sports car that Warren had wanted. Both men got out of the car and walked toward the yellow and black police tape that was plastered between the wall of a bakery and the wall of the travel agency. They walked under the tape and immediately, Xander caught the scent that Warren had smelled earlier. He also smelled the scent of the body that was there earlier as well.

51

"I smell it also, but this scent...' he inhaled deeply through his nose to get a better whiff "this scent, I do not recognize." He walked down the alley to see if the scent left a trail, but it stopped at the end of the liquor store. Xander stopped walking and re-traced his steps back to Warren. "I don't smell any blood with the scent. It's likely that it might just be a stray wolf. You know, this might be the work of some deranged humanist group."

"How could a human do all this? You saw the pictures, how could a human do that?" Warren asked, he wasn't so sure of Xander's new take on things, but wasn't quite willing to cast it aside either.

"Simple, but first lets get out of his rancid alley, my senses are picking up scents I'd rather not smell." Xander said, Warren nodded in agreement, and they headed for the car. Both men climbed inside and Xander began explaining his theory.

"Think about it, people would love to prove just how dangerous the supernatural race is to them. This could be an elaborate set up. One of these radical groups that consist of morbid humans that have nothing better to do than kill our kind. Well, thanks to the new law they can't do that so easily anymore. The government is still in debate over how many bills to add or take away concerning our co-existing with the humans, a murder like this one, done in a such a brutal fashion would not look good for us." Xander merged the car with traffic on I-90 heading northbound.

Warren pondered the whole scenario. He had never thought that a radical humanist group would do such a ghastly thing just to make supernaturals look bad, but then the longer he though about it, the more sense it made.

"Understand, humans always believed that life has a price, for them, life is expendable. If they thought that doing this sick crime would push vote 287 in their favor, what's one more dead man sacrificed for the cause." Xander enlightened. Warren nodded, it made perfect sense.

"It makes perfect sense, unfortunately, it's going to be a bitch to prove and even harder to to convince the government to see that it is possible that a humanist group did this." Warren said as he settled into the car, wondering how he was going to present this new theory to his partner.

"People always want to think the worse of everything and everyone, Warren. That's what humans do. It makes all their evil seem less evil if there's someone out there they believed is worse than they are. So that they can say 'at least I don't do that.' I've seen it time and time again. All I'm saying is don't rule out humans and what they'll do for what they believe in." Xander said as he entered I-55 expressway heading towards the western suburbs, going back home. He glanced over at Warren and smiled, he decided to lighten the mood.

"I noticed earlier that you and my son got reacquainted, rather... personally. I take it you'll be staying the night...no, no I insist that you stay the night. Go back to work in the morning, but spend the night with us, your family, for a change." Xander said. Warren had blushed when he realized what the other man meant when he said 'reacquainted', he had forgotten about the wet spot on his jeans thanks to Adrian's spent passions. He frowned when he thought about it.

"I'll stay tonight, but not for Adrian" Warren said, and they sat in silence as they drove on.

Chapter 7

Natasha woke up, her eye lids heavy as the sleep slipped away from her body. She sat up in the bed holding the sheets close to her chest. She wiped her eyes and looked at the little digital clock on the night stand beside the bed. The little red numbers said 11:35pm.

"Shit!" She exclaimed as she climbed out of the bed, her foot was caught in the sheets causing her to fall, banging her knee on the floor. All the air left her body and her knee ached. She sat up on the floor to inspect the damage. A small red mark was already appearing on her knee.

"Shit! Great! just great! This will not interrupt my dancing, our celebration is on tonight!" She said pumping herself up for the celebration she wanted to share with her friend, she had to get ready right away or she'd be late. She hated being late. *Especially* since she loathed waiting on anyone else. She took a quick shower using her favorite body products from *Anisi Bath and Beauty*. Her body felt soft and smooth as she ran her hands over the finished product of her grooming. She smiled, getting more excited about the nights future events as the minutes passed.

She went to her closet and retrieved the outfit that she brought earlier. She removed the tags and slipped on the white denim halter top and tied the bow behind her neck. She then slipped on the matching denim mini that had the audacity to have two splits up the sides. The halter top had been the most daring article of clothing she had worn since her weight loss. She felt a little more confident in wearing the top with the peek-a-boo belly cut. She went to her shoe rack and found her knee length white gogo boots with the three inch heels. Normally two inches was more than enough height for her taste but tonight she was not going to pull any stops.

She removed the rollers from her hair and pinned her hair up leaving some spiral curls flowing down over her smooth shoulders. She took the little hand held razor and proceeded to trim her eye brows slightly. Her eye brows were naturally thick, arched and beautiful, she just wanted to add a little more definition to them. Then she applied her make up, she enjoyed the smokey-eyed look and since she was going to a dance club she thought it was appropriate. She gave herself the once over, smiled and headed to the kitchen to grab something to eat before walking out of the door to catch a cab.

"Taxi!!!" She yelled and a yellow and black cab pulled to a stop. She carefully walked to the cab and climbed inside. She took one glance at the driver then looked for his license. Once satisfied he was legitimate, she told him the name of the club she was seeking.

"The Slayer's Lair, please" She gave him the address and settle back against the leather seat of the cab. She loved the smell of the cab's interior. She knew this cab was kept clean. She had smelled some unsavory cabs in the past. She was happy she did not have to spend the long ride in the back of a smelly cab. She watched the city's scenery from the window as the cab sped through the nighttime streets. If she was not so worried about his meter, she would have asked him to slow down. She watched the night time crowds doing their weekly or nightly rituals, seeking a place to party. She looked at the skyscrapers that Chicago is known for. The architectural paradise that land-marked the city was sprinkled in golden lights from windows throughout the buildings.

She looked at her watch, the time was 1:13am. "Shit, I'm already late. There! There it is, right there! You can let me out right here." Natasha said as she fished through her little white denim purse for the twenty-five dollars to pay and tip the cabby. "Here you go and thank you." She handed him the bills and climbed out of the cab. She looked for her friend, she expected her to be waiting outside the club. She stared into the crowd for five minutes before her eyes spotted Annette. The building had polished metal walls that reflected objects like a mirror. Natasha wondered if the inside was similar. The main entrance was protected by an ultraviolet door frame that beamed light on all patrons who entered to keep out vampires. The bouncers stamped everyone hands who entered with a sterling silver stamp to ward off shape-shifters. If vampires were to attempt to enter the building, the ultraviolet lighting system would burn them, possibly killing very young vampires. In the instance of a shape-shifter having their hand stamped, their flesh would burn as a reaction from the silver.

"Annette!" She called as she made her way over to her. The other woman turned around and waved frantically for her friend to join her. The two woman faced each other and hugged. Natasha stepped back and opened her coat to show off her ensemble.

"Oh my god girl, you look great! I told you, you would look good with some meat on your bones. Ooh, look at you, with your little belly hanging out and shit!" Annette said as she poked Natasha's belly under the peek a boo shirt.

"Oh stop, if any more of my belly would have been exposed I would not be wearing this outfit. And lets get inside so that I can sit down, I have been standing in these damn boots for fifteen minutes and already I want to take them off. I hope I can survive the night." Natasha said as she danced from one foot to the other, trying to relieve the pain that threaten to settle into her feet.

"Okay, we're lucky my friend is working the door tonight, he'll let us in, we don't have to wait out here with the unfortunates." Annette said as she grabbed Natasha's hand and led her pass the line to her bouncer friend.

"Hey, Randy, this is my girl, Natasha, be nice to her if she comes here without me, I'd hate to have to kick your six foot four ass, got that!" Annette joked. The tall white bouncer just chuckled. He uncrossed his massive muscular arms to unhook the velvet rope. His hand rested on the hook as he looked at them

"What cha, wearing?" He asked. Annette smiled and opened her trench coat. Natasha reopened her coat. He glanced at Natasha and nodded. Then he focused on Annette, really enjoying her silver rhinestone piece of clothe that resembled a handkerchief tied around her waist and neck with the matching mini skirt that barely covered anything.

"Okay, ya passed the dress code…especially you." He pointed at Annette and she flashed him a smile as wicked as it was lustful. Natasha shook her head, she did not want to stand out there in the cold with her coat opened freezing her ass off, while her harlot of a girlfriend and the mountain of a bouncer made goo goo eyes at each other.

"Thanks, um…Randy." Natasha said as she slid past the huge man and made her way into the warmth of the club. She felt the soft heat from the protective door frame as she walked into the main area of the club. The interior matched the exterior, metal beams, steal columns and mirrored glass walls. Natasha thought it was kind of dark and sexy for a club.

"Natasha wait for me! Damn girl. Just forget about me!" Annette said breathlessly as she caught up with Natasha at the coat checker's counter.

"Well, I thought you were busy and I was starting to get cold and what is that you're wearing?" Natasha asked as she took the ticket for her coat.

Annette looked down at her attire. She did not see anything wrong with it.

"What? Girl shit, I look good. Besides it's more than I've worn all night. Oooohhh, oh my god, guess what!?" She asked excitedly, remembering her good fortune earlier that night.

"What?!" Natasha asked, excited because her friend was excited.

"Oh my god girl, I got promoted!!! As soon as I got to work tonight, I get called into the big boss' office, right. And I'm nervous as hell because I heard that if you get called into the boss' office, more than likely, your ass is getting fired. So I'm just on ten right, and I go inside and mind you, I've never seen the boss, so I'm really nervous. But I go inside his office and girl, let me tell you! This man is GORGEOUS!! Oh my god! You would not believe how gorgeous he is. I swear my mouth almost dropped when I saw him." Annette placed her hand over her heart and closed her eyes thinking about the moment when her eyes first met Darian's. And his voice as he spoke to her, the silky feeling of his hands on her skin.

"What happened next? what does he look like?!" Natasha asked, plainly interested in a good looking man.

"Well he has long black hair, it's really wavy, shinny and smooth. And it flows past his shoulders, almost to his ass. He has the most beautiful green eyes I've ever seen. They're like dark green or something, like emeralds or something like that. And his voice, his voice is so deep and smooth, like butter baby! It felt like his voice was caressing me as he spoke. Oh! And his body, girl this man has a body out of this world!!" Annette was getting excited again just thinking about her boss and the last thing he said to her.

At her last job she would have gladly kicked her boss's ass for propositioning her and for all the trouble he gave her and the other employees. But she loved working at this club and she welcomed Darian's advances even more. Tomorrow night was looking better and better. She could hardly wait.

"So, besides how fine he is, anything else happened tonight that's got you all excited?" Natasha asked, ready to stop beating around the bush. Annette thought about telling Natasha that she almost had sex with her boss then decided against it.

"Well like I said, I was promoted to daytime assistant manager! I'll be making double what I get paid now and it's salary. I might still be able to strip on some days, making all that extra money, I'll be able to get a new car." Annette said as she just realized her good fortune.

"Well, it looks like we both have something to celebrate. I'm so happy!"

"You're damn right, I'm going to get scummy tonight and so are you, I demand it, then you can go back to being pretty and pristine all over again after tonight." Annette said as she ushered her friend towards the bar .

"I'll have a drink or two, but I have no intentions of getting 'scummy' you got that heathen!" Natasha joked.

"Yeah, yeah, we'll see, when that music starts hitting you and the drink starts working, I want to see the wild woman unleashed." The two women sat at the bar and ordered Long Island Iced Teas. They began to sip the drinks as they looked around for potential dancing partners.

The club was packed, it was a Friday night and it seemed like the whole world was unwinding at the *Slayer's Lair* nightclub. The multicolored neon lights blinked on and off throughout the club adding excitement to the already charged atmosphere. The marble floor ended just where the huge dance area began. There were all sorts of vampire slayer memorabilia hanging from the walls, such as whips, cross bows, crosses, fake wooden stakes hung from the ceiling. Framed photographs of world famous hunters real and fake hung on the walls. Such as; Ivy Harthorn, the famed female vampire slayer who killed thirty- two vampires before she met her death eight months ago.

There were a lot of men dressed in brightly colored clothes standing against the walls or leaning on the marble columns throughout the club. As always, or so it seems to be this way at most dance clubs, the dance floor was mostly populated by seductively dressed women out to have a good time and a lot of them danced with each other. Natasha was not sure if the majority of the men standing by the walls simply like to watch women dance with each other or they just did not want to dance, if that's the case, *'then why come to a dance club to look like security?'*

The two women scoped out the club and sipped on their drinks and chatted. Annette was working on her second long island ice tea and Natasha was still nursing the first one. She was starting to feel the effects of the alcohol relatively fast, since the beverage she was drinking was a mixture of several different liquors. She thought it might have been wiser to have selected a more tame drink, maybe a breezer or something. She did not drink and she did not want to feel drunk either. However, Natasha was starting to feel relaxed, almost floating. Annette had jumped up from her chair and grabbed the first guy that walked by. She pressed her body against his and started grinding against him.

He led her to the dance floor where he and his buddy sandwiched her between their bodies as their hands groped her hips and back. They tried very carefully not to caress her butt and breast which is where their eyes were focusing as they danced with the spirited woman. Natasha wished she had Annette's confidence. She always thought that Annette could be the perfect poster girl for that company who's motto was: "just do it" and that is just what Annette did, if she wanted to. Natasha sat her drink down on the bar top. She settled against the bar seat feeling bubbly. Annette would make fun of her if she knew that half a glass of alcohol had gotten her intoxicated or at the least, a bit tipsy. She didn't care, like she said, she had no intentions of getting "scummy" and she was keeping that in mind. She did not want to feel what a hangover would feel like, getting drunk was never that important, nor alluring.

"Do you want to dance?" A tall gentleman asked Natasha. He was handsome, about six feet two inches, coffee colored complexion, dark brown eyes, strong bone structure. She would not mind dancing at this moment, especially with a handsome man like this.

"Sure, let's dance" She rose from her chair, a little too quickly and she had to catch herself by clinging to him.

"Whoa, are you ok? can you handle yourself or do I have to carry you?" He joked, but behind the joke, he was serious.

"No, I just stood up too fast, I think, I'll be okay." She smiled gaily, she was definitely drunk. There was no doubt about it now. She let him lead her to the dance floor. Where he wrapped his arms around her waist and the two begin to grind their bodies together to the beat of the music. The DJ had switched from disco beats to raggae. Natasha began to loosen up even more, she let the beat of the music guide her hips as she danced with the man. He smiled at her as she danced erotically to the island music, her hands coming up to caress her hair and trial down her waist. Her eyes closed as she turned around.

She looked up and over her shoulder as she felt his chest against her back. She had thoughts about going home with this man and having a one night's stand with him. It had been a long time since she'd gotten laid. Annette told her and even urged her to get laid. She had said, if she got some, 'it might help get her out of her depression.' *Some people think sex is the answer to everything,* Natasha thought. *'Oh you got cancer, better get some sex, that'll knock that shit clean out your system.' yeah right!*

She looked over to see Annette dancing with three men at one time. She knew that Annette was the kind of girl some people used to hate in highschool, but wanted to be like. Natasha was never one of those girls. She was always the one that people liked as a friend and was well known enough

Desires Unleashed

not to be a victim of bullies but never to be selected by the "in" crowd. Annette, on the other hand was the leader of the "in" crowd. She played the pipe and others followed. She wondered if she ever followed, maybe she was following now, that would explain the fact that she was drunk. The man she was dancing with looked towards Annette's group, he wanted to see the hot commodity and slowly started dancing over in that direction. Natasha became sober enough to become angry. *He asked me to dance!* The night had just took a turn for the worse.

Natasha went back to her seat and ordered another drink, she wanted to brood over all the men fawning over her friend. For some reason, when she received her drink her mind told her to chug it down and she did, immediately regretting it because the room tilted then straighten itself. She placed the glass gingerly on the bar top and sat very still. She ordered a glass of water. She decided her night of drinking should be put to an end. She looked at Annette walking towards her, sweaty and a trail of men behind her, all trying to buy her a drink each, hoping that she'll pick him for a rendezvous later that night or in the week.

"Bartender, I'll take another Long Island." Annette said as she looked to one guy to pay for her drink. He gladly reached in his pocket and pulled out a ten dollar bill and handed it to the bartender, who later gave him two dollars and fifty cent change. Annette smiled at the man as he cozied up to her, plainly claiming his spot as the dominate male who won the young ladies heart. Natasha thought it was like watching some strange mating ritual on national geographic. She watched Annette seduce the man by running her finger tips down the front of his shirt and circling one of his buttons. He smiled and sat down in the chair next to hers and chatted in her ear. Annette turned from him and looked at Natasha.

"So Natasha, I saw you dancing with that cute guy, are you having fun?" Annette asked, her southern accent, slightly slurred due to the giddiness the alcohol was causing.

"No I'm not, I think I had too much to drink, and I don't feel so good right now, the room's spinning. I think I want to go home Annette." Natasha said as she laid her head on the bar top. Annette leaned over her friend and brushed some of her curls out of her face.

"Yeah, you do look a little green. Please tell me you didn't take your medicine. Do you feel like you're going to puke?" She asked, concerned.

Natasha nodded her head slowly. "The room won't stop spinning and this damn music keeps pounding in my ears. But I did not take my medicine tonight."

"Damn girl, you are a lightweight, I'm sorry I asked your ass to drink with me tonight. I didn't think you'd get fucked up like this." She said as she noted her friends damp pale skin. She turn to the man next to her and told him they needed to leave, that her friend was not feeling well right now. She finished her drink and rose from the bar stool. The man she had been talking to offered to take them home.

"Naw, that's okay, we'll catch a cab, I would hate for her to puke in your car. Look let me get your number and we'll get together." Annette said as she headed towards the coat-room to get their coats. The man gave her his telephone number and offered once again to give them a ride home. Annette refused but thanked him for his kindness. She walked back to her friend, who looked even worse now than she did a few minutes before. Annette really started to worry about Natasha. She believed Natasha never finished her long island, and she assumed she had a full stomach or at least she hoped Natasha ate something before she came to the club. If she did not, that would account for Natasha's sudden sickness.

She walked back to the other woman and helped her put on her coat. After assisting Natasha with her coat, she put on her own, she then slid her arm around her friends waist and led her out of the club. A drunk man bumped the two women causing Natasha to stumble, but Annette caught her. The man dropped his car keys and Natasha picked them up. The world seem to spin but she kept her feet to the ground. She looked at the man, who seem to be barely standing himself.

"I can't let you drive, you're drunk." She said, her words slightly slurred as she held the man's car keys in her hand.

"Give me my keys bitch, I don't need no one looking after me." He said, his speech heavily slurred. He angered Natasha, drunk drivers always did. She felt that if a drunk driver caused an accident, they should be convicted under the charges of attempted murder. If they killed someone, they should get the murder wrap for certain, where they could be made to face the death penalty. She thought that might help with toning down people like the man in front of her.

"No, I'm not giving your drunk ass these keys. Annette, take these to the bartender, I'll wait right here." Natasha handed the keys to her friend. Who took them with a look of concern, she wasn't so sure she wanted to leave her friend in the same area with this man. But she knew Natasha was right.

"You wait here, I'll be right back." Annette said and then disappeared into the club. The angry drunk man followed, cursing Natasha as he disappeared into the darkness of the club. Annette returned shortly and went to the side of her friend.

"Geez, what a jerk. I hate assholes who drink and drive." Annette said as she flagged down a cab. Natasha could not agree more. They both climbed into the cab and Annette gave directions as the cab took off on the road, heading in the direction of their three story apartment building on the southeast side of the city. The traffic was heavy and Natasha drifted off to sleep. They were about four blocks from the club when Natasha had a vision of dropping her keys on the ground then fumbling for them. Then the next vision she saw, she was driving, the lanes seem to fade in and out, she had her lights on and the lights from the passing cars were so bright, so blinding. She saw a yellow car in front of her, the car wasn't moving. The lane seem to go on forever, then there was not enough lane, her foot slammed on the brakes but not in enough time, she felt herself being propelled forwards and then everything faded to blackness.

Natasha opened her eyes, unnerved by the dream, she looked up at the cab driver who seemed to be confused as he looked through his rear view mirror. She looked at the mirror and was blinded by bright lights and a second later, the cab was rear ended and knocked off the road. The cab continued to fishtail until it hit a tree, knocking it over, the tree fell onto the cab pinning both Natasha and Annette inside the car. Both women were knocked unconscious.

Chapter 8

Darian walked down the dimly lit hallway until he reached a huge tapestry on the wall. He brushed the tapestry to the side to reveal a small sensor in the wall. He pressed his hand to the sensor in the wall and the red light at the bottom of the sensor turned blue then a hidden door slid open. He walked onto the elevator and pulled a key out of his pocket. He inserted the key into the slot on the elevator panel to start the elevator downward. One level down, he exited and walked down another short L-shaped corridor to his private skybox overlooking an octagon shaped arena. He settled into one of the four comfortable leather chairs facing the see-through glass paneled wall. He looked around the arena to see that the soft cushioned seats were already full and everyone was anticipating the tournament. All the bets had been made. One could bet on a fighter per night, thus increasing their chances of winning. Or they could pick a Champion to win the whole tournament and receive one lump-some. There was a little under one hundred million to be won this night, which was very good for an opening night. Darian had already placed his bet on the fighter known only as Draco. Xavier had been most impressed by the fighter's skill and Darian decided to choose Draco as his champion.

It never ceased to amaze Darian that the human race would no doubt do just about anything for money. They put a price tag on their own lives. Darian had never met one vampire that could name the price of their own immortality. Darian figured mortals thought they were immortal, that life will always grant them another day, until of course, their last day came before they could blink their eyes. Darian no longer worried about having his life snuffed out so easily. It would take a lot more than a virus to kill him, of that he was pleased.

The announcer came out through the sliding double doors with two beautiful female vampires dressed in red sequence bikinis and top hats with white sequence bow ties and matching six inch heels, they stood by his side, hands on their hips. The Announcer wore a red sequence tux with tails and matching hat and a white silk shirt with matching gloves. He was a tall male with black hair and pale skin. Though he was not a vampire he could easily pass for one. Vampires are always pale before their first feeding. Then when their bodies are filled and warmed with blood, they can pass easily amongst the human race, unless a nifty human can detect the subtle differences in skin and hair textures and the shine of a vampire's eyes.

The announcer ordered some film footage of the fighters to be ran on the huge television that was suspended over the arena. The crowd 'oohhhed' and ' ahhhed' as they witnessed the talents of the new tournaments fighters. There was a mixture of female and male martial artist and grappling street fighters. Darian could hear a few murmurs of those who wished they could change their bets. And he smiled, *too late*, he thought. The footage ended and the crowd hushed, everyone waited for the theatrics the announcer provided. The lights dimmed to darkness, leaving only one spot light on the announcer. Who looked around the crowd as he raised the microphone to his mouth.

"Ladies and gentlemen, tonight you are in for a treat. Once again, we have gathered all of the world's best fighters to battle it out over the next three days, for a total grand prize of five million dollars!!!" He said this with raised hands. The crowd cheered and applauded. Darian laughed and clapped as well. He like the energy from the audience, it was like an appetizer to the hunt or in this case, since he had fed already, it was more like dessert.

"Tonight, we begin a new tournament with twelve vicious fighters, all willing to tear each other's heart out for that money. I hope you have placed your bets, ladies and gentlemen, and I hope you have placed them well, because there is no way of telling who will win the *'Champion of Gods Tournament*!!!'" Once again the crowd cheered and applauded. "Now, without further ado, let us begin." He turned to face the sliding double doors as they opened, and a female walked out into the arena. She was tall, about six feet two inches. She reminded Darian of the fabled "Amazon" women. Her dark olive skin was scarred. She had two large scars one on her left cheek and one on her right. A long ragged looking scar trailed her left shoulder down her arm to her wrist.

She carried a chain with her as her choice of weaponry. Her hair was cut short, almost like a buzz, but only an inch in length. Her brown eyes reflected only two things: greed and confidence. Darian could not wait to see her opponent. He never saw any of the people chosen for the tournament. He left the hand picking to Xavier. He seem to enjoy the auditions more so than Darian. The announcer began to give her stats.

"Coming to the arena, is a behemoth of a woman, standing at six-feet-two-inches, one-hundred and eighty-five pounds of lean mean muscle. Her weapon of choice is a chain whip, she vows to rip the skin of her opponent with her trusted weapon, put your hands together for Viper!!" He yelled her name to pump up the crowd. It worked, the crowd cheered and stamped their feet and applauded. Viper held her hands in the air and whipped her chain around one good time before the crowd hushed, all eyes on the door again and the announcer.

"Ladies and gentlemen, welcome to the arena, a man that stands at the staggering height of six feet six inches, two hundred and sixty-nine pounds of hard hitting muscle. He has no weapon, the only weapon he says he needs are his bare hands. Please put your hands together for Draco!!!" The arena burst with cheers and jeers. Darian settled comfortably in his chair, putting his feet up on the leather footstool. The lights illuminated and filled the arena with brightness. The Announcer and female vampire's (that had gestured to each entering fighter) left the arena floor. There was a buzzer and the two fighters circled each other like two lions preparing for battle.

Darian suspected that was how every living being prepared for battle, he had caught himself doing it before in the past when he had been challenged for territory or another vampire wanted to take him and make him their slave. They soon found out he was not an easy target. Darian leaned forward to get a better glimpse as the two fighters collided with each other, the taller man knocking the female to the ground. She regrouped quickly and rolled away from his huge foot that was trying to follow up the first blow with another. She swung her whip and caught Draco across the face, slicing open the skin, blood started to ooze out of the wound. Darian caught the first whiff of that succulent scent and was glad he had fed already.

The fighter touched his cheek wiping away some of the blood and bringing his fingers to his lips, his tongue darted out to lick the blood away. Both fighters smiled at each other, please with the effect of their approach. He charged her suddenly, she whirled her whip around striking him across the chest, she then whipped it around several times, each blow striking various parts of his body, leaving bloody trails seeping out of the wounds over his skin. Darian was beginning to wonder if he made a wise bet, it most certainly would not be the first time that he lost a few million on the wrong fighter. He tried to pick his fighters based on their lust for blood, their ruthlessness and above all…greed. He had seen lesser skilled fighters walk away with the prize. However, he was expecting more out of his pick for tonight's match.

Draco, caught her whip in his hand and attempted to yank it from her but Viper had double wrapped the whip around her knuckles so tight that the harder he pulled the whip, the more it began to cut into her skin. Darian could see the blood oozing out of the cuts that were getting deeper the harder Draco pulled on the chain. In one final tug, Draco pulled Viper close to him, causing her to lose her balance. He punched her hard in the stomach, causing her to gasps and cough, attempting to bring air back into her lungs. Darian heard her ribs crack when the blow had struck and wondered how much longer Viper would be in the match. The intestinal fortitude of human beings to survive never ceased to amaze him, it was only matched by their hunger for money and power. She wanted that money as much as Draco did. Viper rolled away from the follow up attack, Draco was stronger, but he was not faster. As she rose, Draco punched her in the face, knocking her against the thick plexiglass wall of the arena. Her blood splattered the wall as he punched her again, her body falling against the walls as she tired to roll away. She pulled a knife from her boot, Darian smiled at the deviousness of it all, there were no rules in the coliseum, it was kill or be killed, win or lose, live or die. Viper waited for her opponent to approach her, before she shoved the blade deeply into his groin and twisted it.

The tall muscular man screamed gutturally. His eyes closed tightly as his mind registered the damage. His hand swung out and caught Viper hard across the cheek, knocking out three of her teeth. The crowd erupted with hoots and jeers as the two battled on. Blood stained the arena floor and glass walls. Darian smiled, day one of the tournament was only beginning. There were five more matches for the night. Draco pulled the six inch blade out of his groin, grimacing all the while. He rose hunched over, blood dripped profusely from the wound, making a puddle between his legs.

Viper had risen to her feet and was spitting the blood from her mouth onto the floor. She grimace and revealed a dark area where her teeth used to be. Her face had begun to bruise and swell. Her nose had been broken and her skin was cut above her left eyebrow. The vicious wound was dripping blood into her eye, causing her to blink constantly to clear her vision. Draco had bloody wounds all over his upper chest and calves. A huge bloody stain in the front of his pants and his nose had also been broken.

He tried to walk towards her but his legs gave out from under him, he had lost too much blood and the pain in his groin was crippling. He grabbed his groin and fell over on his side, his skin began to pale as the blood continued to pour out of the open wounds. The announcer entered the arena again and the crowd cheered and applauded, some knew what was going to follow. The moment they had all been waiting for, the winner and the loser, the one who would leave the arena for tonight the victor and ten thousand dollars richer. Then there was the fighter that was left, the one who's life depended on their generosity. Many had lost tens or hundreds of thousands of dollars, some even millions on this fight. Darian had been most disappointed but it proved the old adage true, you simply can't judge a book by it's cover. It was one thing Darian always admired about the female species. They were damn resourceful. He had lost one million dollars on Draco and though he was tempted to participate in his fate, he decided to stick with his own tradition and sat back to watch as the crowd cheered and booed the fallen fighter.

"We have the winner of this match, ladies and gentlemen! Viper!!" The announcer said as he gestured towards the tall battered woman, who would no doubt need all the rest she could get, because she had two more fights over the next two days to come. Viper held her hands in the air, she had won the ten thousand dollar prize for the preliminaries, but her goal was the five million. The crowd began to hush as the announcer raised his hands for silence. The lights dimmed slightly to add ambiance to the arena. He stood over the prone body of Draco.

"Ladies and gentleman, here we have the fallen opponent, he fought, he failed. You decide!" He pointed around the arena. The faces he pointed at smiled and nodded and applauded. "You decide if he shall live or die." The crowd raised to their feet, cheering. Darian inhaled deeply as the scent of blood pumping in their bodies rushing to their heads, filled the arena.

"Shall he live?" The announcer held up his thumb as the crowd booed, only a few cheers and claps could be heard over the disappointed crowd, "or shall he die?" His thumb turned downward and the audience applauded and cheered. The announcer gave Viper a slow nod and walked away from the prone man. The sound of the excited audience thundered throughout the arena as Viper picked up her chain whip and wrapped it around the dying man's neck. She pressed both feet on his back and pulled with all her might as he struggled weakly, fingers clawing at the chain, trying to free himself from the pressure. His eyes bulged, pupils dilated, chest heaved one last time, then all the air in his lungs emptied as the crowed rose to their feet in thunderous applause, pleased that they played god. Draco's body was dragged from the arena floor as the Announcer came back out to introduce the next two fighters.

"I knew I'd find you here, Darian." A soft female voice said with a hint of a french accent. Darian knew who it was, he did not need to turn around. He could smell her even before she entered his private box seat. He smiled and held his hand out and gestured to the chair next to his.

"Elise...how are you doing tonight?" He asked as he turned to face the feline beauty at his side. His beautiful green eyes roaming over her sumptuous body.

"I'm feeling fine, even better now that I'm finally in your presence. It's unfortunate that you're a vampire, I always have to wait until sunset to see your beauty...to feel your touch." She took his hand and pressed his knuckles to her lips and kissed them gently. Darian smiled. He had helped her once and was taken by her beauty and aristocratic charm. Though he did not doubt his sexual power to seduce, he never expected Elise to become so entranced with him.

"You've just missed a very good match. I've manage to lose one million dollars on a fighter I was most certain would win or at least make it to the next round, but this just proves that even I can be wrong... once in a while." He smiled. Elise still holding Darian's hand, ran his finger tips down the front of her shirt and then she pressed his palm over her left breast so that he could feel her rapid heartbeat and her mounting passion.

"I see you've missed me very much, no?" He asked as his fingers began kneading the soft flesh of her breast.

"*Oui*, I have. Do we have to stay here and watch these matches, don't you want to sweep me off of my feet and whisk me away to your bedroom and make love to me until the sun rises?" She asked in her most enticing tone. Then she climbed slowly out of her seat and onto Darian's lap, her skirt rising above her hips to her waist

"I would love to sweep you off your feet and whisk you away but I think it would be more exciting for both you and I to have sex right here, right now. I'm sure you can smell the blood in the air, the fear and excitement of the arena. I can feel it, can you?" Darian asked as he ran his fingertips lightly over her jaw line. He ran his right hand down her back, bringing goosebumps over the surface of her skin.

"Yes, I can." She said breathlessly as she leaned forward and kissed Darian full on the mouth. Her tongue probing the inside of his mouth to caress his tongue. Their lips stayed locked together as they fondle each other, letting their hands explore each others' heated flesh. Darian removed her sheer black shirt, better to see the black leather bra that covered her pale bosom. Her own

68

hands sought the buttons of his shirt and undid each button, before sliding the black shirt slowly off of his broad shoulders.

Her hands ran over his warm flesh, feeling the muscles underneath his skin. Her mouth parted from his to kiss lightly along his jaw line. He closed his eyes, a low moan escaping his throat. Elise continued down his neck, she suckled the soft fragrant skin there, taking in his personal scent even as it mingled with his expensive cologne. His hands trailed up her back and found the little clasp to her bra and undid the hook. He ran his hands over her smooth shoulders and found the straps and pulled them down, exposing her breast. His hands sought the soft mounds of her bosom and he fingered the little pink erect nipples between his fingers, flicking his fingertip lightly over the tip of the nipple causing Elise to gasp and tremor.

"I want you inside me, now!" She growled into his ear and her nails dug into his flesh as she gripped his shoulders. He chuckled deep in his throat. She could hear the vibrations of his voice, she felt the wetness between her legs increase, soaking her black lace thong panties. Darian smiled, he could feel her wetness dampening the front of his pants while she sat astride him.

"How badly do you want me inside you." He growled. Her body jerked as his breath brushed over her ear. He looked positively gorgeous to her in his all black ensemble. There were no words to explain how badly she wanted to make love to him.

"If I don't feel you inside me in the next three seconds, I'm going to simply burst!' She hoped that was specific enough. She wanted to feel his hard naked body against hers, it was the only thing that mattered at that moment. Darian smiled. He was more than willing to oblige, especially since his earlier attempt at seducing Miss. Balfour had been ruined. He lifted her slightly off his lap and worked at his zipper and top button, Elise's right hand wrapped around his smooth erect penis pulling it free from his pants. She smiled as she looked at the un-circumcised organ. Darian yanked her black lacy panties, ripping the fabric. He brought the remains of her thong panties to his nose and inhaled deeply and moaned as her sexual scent assailed his nostrils. Elise began to grind slowly over his penis, she reached her hand between them to guide him inside her. Darian released the panties and groaned as he felt his organ slide into the soft, hot, wet flesh of her vagina.

He gripped her hips with one hand as he raised up to pump deeply into her. His other hand ran over her shoulders then around her waist to press her closer to him and help glide her over his groin. His mouth closed over her breast, running his tongue over the erect nipple, teasing it, nibbling the delicate flesh. He chuckled deeply as he heard Elise cry out. He could hear some members of the audience discuss what they were seeing in his private skybox, but he cared little. He heard the crowd cheer as the next two fighters went at it, beating each other to bloody pulps. He could smell more blood being spilled and it heighten his lust as he was sure it heighten Elise's as well.

She began to grind harder and pump faster on his groin, he could feel her flesh constrict around him, with each movement of her hips. He relished the heat that enveloped him as his penis stroked her fire. He became hungry for her orgasm, he wanted to feel the heat rise to the boiling point and spill over her in that one instant, that one magic moment, where nothing else mattered but the intense pleasure that followed. He pumped faster and harder, a wet smacking sound filled the room. He began to grunt and moan, as he felt his own climax building, he could sense Elise's own passion mounting. He licked her breast while his hand took hold of the other one, massaging the tender mound, stroking her nipple between his two fingers. He heard Elise cry out and he felt a rush of heat erupt from her body.

He felt his own body reach the point of no return as his penis harden all the more and pulsated as he released himself deep inside her. A low growl flowed from his throat through his clenched teeth as his orgasm whipped through his body. Elise's body remained tensed as spasm after spasm rippled through her. The room seemed engulfed in heat as they shared the moment. Elise finally collapsed on top of Darian's chest, panting, her body still shaking from the effects of their sex. His own body relaxed comfortably into the chair. He stroked her soft brown hair, brushing some loose strands away from her eyes.

She smiled as she looked into the forest green of his seductive gaze. She felt like she could get lost in those eyes, happily lost forever. She snuggled even more closely to Darian and exhaled deeply as she felt his strong arms encircle her body. Darian sat there with her for several minutes, basking in the afterglow. He listened to the announcer introduce the fourth match. Darian was slightly disappointed he missed two of the tournaments matches. He would have to settle for a playback video. The crowd went wild when a seven foot tall giant of a man entered the arena. He was black and had a thick muscular build. He carried with him a steal bat. The announcer introduced him as The Destroyer. Darian chuckled. He had to wonder where these people picked up their stage names.

He raised Elise up and kissed her lightly on the lips, just a soft brush of his to hers.

"Darling, I know you want to stay here forever, but we can not." Darian said. Elise looked at him sadly. He was right, she had to get back to Sergio, who would no doubt be combing the club for her. Reluctantly, she rose from Darian's lap. Both of them shivered slightly as Darian slid smoothly out of her. She pulled down her skirt as he put himself away and fastened and zipped his pants. He could still smell the sex in the air, and on their skin. The smell enticed him.

She reached down and retrieved her black sheer shirt and bra from the floor she snapped the bra back into place and pulled the shirt over her head. Darian reached over and picked up his black shirt and pulled it on, and began buttoning the shirt with quickness and ease. She plucked her leather coat from the chair besides Darian's and pulled it on, smiling at Darian as he watched her dressed. Darian's gaze darted towards the arena just as the seven foot tall giant was brought to his knees by a five foot seven Asian male who was brandishing a large sword called a kodachi.

"Hmm, so tonight's just full of surprises." Darian whispered to himself. He knew Elise could hear him, but that didn't matter.

"I hope I was one of those surprises?" She asked playfully, but serious at the same time. Darian looked up at her, smiled and nodded.

"Always, my dear. Shall I escort you upstairs?" He asked as he rose from his seat. She extended him her hand, and he took it and laid it gently on his forearm as the two headed for the elevator. He was hoping he might catch the last match of the night, but he was not counting on it. Like he said, the night was full of surprises. They reached the top level and walked off the elevator and entered the hallway. Darian turned to her with a puzzled expression. He had realized this before and wanted to mention it at first sight of Elise in his private box but never got around to asking, now was the time.

"Elise, how did you get to the arena?" He asked as they headed for the dance club.

Elise smiled. "Now if I tell you, then I won't have any secrets, and a girl's got to have her little secrets, or didn't you know that my darling bloodsucker." She pinched his chin lightly between her finger and thumb. Darian smiled, but was slightly annoyed. He had an idea of who let her in, that is IF she was let in. He hoped she did not break in by breaking through his security system. Nevertheless, he would have to have a long discussion with Xavier.

They entered the huge dance area and were accosted by Sergio, who looked positively livid at the sight of Darian. He walked over to Elise and held out his hand. Elise became stubborn and refused to take it, until Darian released her hand and directed it towards Sergio's. She seemed slightly disappointed. She did not answer to any man, so why was Darian putting her in Sergio's care? The two men stared at each other. Sergio's grey eyes bore deeply into

Darian's forest green eyes. The aura of both men was rising, filling the little space between them, almost stifling.

"I'll only say this once. Stay the fuck away from her Darian. She's mine. I've sat by long enough and watched you use her over the past six months and I'll stand for it no longer." Sergio said, his words squeezed through his gritted teeth. His anger thickening his Italian accent. Elise was taken aback, she was also upset that he would dare try to claim her. She was queen of the pride, she answered to no one.

"I beg your pardon!? Sergio, I think we've had this discussion before, I'll will not be treated like a piece of meat-" She said but Sergio cut her off.

"You treat yourself like a piece of meat." His teeth still gnashing together. He never took his gaze away from Darian. It angered him even more to know they had sex. It wasn't supposed to be this way. Never this way. "If you can't get control of yourself, then I'll do it for you. You need to take responsibility for the pride. You're not doing that, instead you fornicate with this dead son of a bitch and I can't stand it."

Darian smiled. He had to admit, he liked Sergio. He had guts among other things. Darian could respect anyone who took the initiative to set things in their favor. Those were the people who controlled the world, those who would see to it that the world would be created as they saw fit and would except nothing less. However, he would only stand to be threatened and insulted for so long before he would have to act. He respected Sergio and understood his situation but he was a master vampire, and this leopard standing in front of him needed to understand that.

"Sergio, I do not make the decisions for Elise, she has decided to share my bed. Perhaps you need to change your approach to make yourself more appealing to the lady. Whatever the case, do not come into my establishment and threaten or insult me. I do not take kindly to insults to say the very least. Now if you two are going to continue to argue, please do so elsewhere." He looked at Elise. "Elise I will see you later." After that, he turned and headed back down the long hallway.

Sergio reflected on Darian's warning. He did not like Darian, but there was something about him that he had to respect. The power emanating from him was almost suffocating. He knew he could never go toe to toe with Darian but he was still willing to fight for his queen. He looked at Elise, he couldn't read the expression on her face, for there were too many emotions being played out, but he guessed one of them was sadness and he knew why. Darian did not try to fight for her, he did not try to defend her honor. He hoped it was an eye opener for her. He hoped it showed her the truth. To Darian, she was just a piece of ass and nothing more.

"Elise, I apologize for my sudden action, I was rude. Come on, let's go home, we need to talk, we really do. Please, let us not argue tonight. Let's just talk, talk about us and our pride, the important things." Sergio took Elise's hand as he led her without resistence, out of the club. It was early in the morning and only two hours before sun rise. They climbed into Sergio's sports car and drove home.

Chapter 9

Adrian had crept softly and slowly as possible into Warren's bedroom. He hoped that he could climb into the bed before Warren woke up to stop him. Adrian took off his thick royal blue bathrobe and pulled back the black linen covers and climbed on top of the bed, then slid in beside Warren. Warren smelled his scent and woke up groggy but alert enough to know that he was no longer alone.

"What the hell are you doing!?" He asked as he looked over his shoulder at Adrian, who was smiling and scooting closer to him.

"What does it look like I'm doing? I'm getting closer to you so that we can make love." Adrian said as he ran his fingers down Warren's spine. Warren shivered slightly and moved away from Adrian, he sat up in the bed and looked at Adrian, who was resting his head on his arm, watching him. Adrian's beautiful silver eyes sparkled in the moonlight, a wonderful gift from his father at conception and Warren wanted to kiss his soft full lips. He wanted to feel Adrian's tongue enter his mouth. He wanted to run his hand along that smooth caramel colored skin.

"Look, Adrian, we aren't together anymore, remember?"

"Look, Warren, we never officially broke up, remember?" Adrian asked sarcastically.

"Adrian, yes we did and we can't do this, we should just remain friends and pack brothers because we both know neither of us want to be the bottom boy in this relationship. Besides, you are too fucking controlling!" Warren stated, as he reached to turn on the light. Adrian stopped him, grabbing his arm and bringing it back down to his side.

"We can both be versatile, I'm willing to let you conquer me, we can switch. Look, Warren I want you and I can smell that you want me, you've got this whole room filled with the scent of your desires. Let us satisfy each other." He pressed his body closely to Warren. He could feel Warren's hardness against his thigh. Adrian could smell his own lust in the air mingled with that of Warren's. It had been two months since the last time that Warren had sex, which was a record for him. It would be a record for any of them. It was not like he was trying to start his own record, it was just that his job had kept him so busy lately he didn't have time to date.

Warren looked into Adrian's handsome face, he felt himself leaning closer to those soft full lips, losing his resolve. He closed his eyes and felt the softness of Adrian's flesh as their lips met in a passionate kiss. Adrian hands slid around Warren and he pulled Warren on top of him. Their legs entangled as they kissed deeper. Adrian's hands caressed Warren's back, moving further down to massage the round firm mounds of his buttocks as his hips grinding into Warren's groin. Both men moaned softly as their tongues danced in each others' mouths.

Adrian rolled Warren over and licked his neck, trailing his soft wet tongue down his chest. He sucked gently at first, on one nipple then the other. He then increased the pressure of his lips as he pulled on the tender flesh, rubbing the nipple in his mouth, flicking the tip of Warren's nipple with his tongue. Warren's body jerked as he felt the sensations Adrian caused, making small gasps come from him at every delightful assault.

Adrian smiled as he watched Warren's facial expression change to that of rapture. He moved lower and lower, licking the fine curly dark hair that trailed down to the tip of Warren's boxer briefs then disappeared under the clothe. Adrian rose slightly to kiss the smooth skin of Warren's stomach, he continued to kiss his way further down as he pulled back the rim of Warrens' underwear.

Soft dark brown hair sprang up from the waistband of the boxer briefs. Adrian swirled his tongue through the hair as Warren jerked, his body tensing the further Adrian's tongue traveled. Adrian pulled the underwear off completely and smiled down at Warren's circumcised erection. He leaned forward and flicked his tongue delicately, smiling as Warren spasmed at his touch. He ran the tip of his tongue along the hardness sending tremors throughout Warren's body. Warren's fingers gripped the black linen sheets tightly as Adrian teased his manhood.

"Please…" Warren said breathlessly as he fought the urge to push Adrian further.

Adrian wrapped his fingers around the base and raised his head to look up at him. He loved the feel of the smooth hot flesh as he stroked it lightly in his hold, squeezing slightly at the same time as his wrist and fingers work the hardness of Warrens' manhood.

"Please what? What is it that you want me to do…exactly?" He asked teasingly. Warren looked down at

Adrian's smiling face. He licked his lips to moisten them.

"You know full well what I want you to do."

"Ahhh, no I don't. I think I need thorough instructions." Adrian chuckled as he continued to slowly stroke the hardness in his hand. Warren moaned loudly and arched his back, his toes curled and his grip tighten on the sheets.

"I want your wet mouth on me now!" Warren panted. Adrian smiled and lowered his head slowly until his mouth covered the entire length of Warren. His head bobbed up and down in a smooth slow rhythm as he worked Warren over. Warren cried out as Adrian increased his speed. His hips thrusting

forward to meet Adrian's mouth as it came downward on his shaft. Adrian could smell Warren's climax coming he could hear Warren's heartbeat increase, he pulled away leaving Warren looking surprised and disappointed.

"Roll over." Adrian instructed in his deep masculine voice. He watched Warren gather enough of his senses to slide one leg around him and roll over onto his stomach. His knees raised at his sides, his buttocks poised upward. Adrian reached into the pocket of his bathrobe and pulled out a small packet. Warren watched over his shoulder as Adrian ripped the little packet with his incisor and squeezed the contents into his right palm. He worked his right hand over his own hardness, muscles twitching causing his pecs to jump at the pleasurable sensation his hand was causing on his manhood. When he thought he was lathered up enough, he slid his hand over Warren's back and caressed his shoulders. He pressed his legs against Warren's drawn up knees.

"Relax,' he whispered into Warren's ear as he guided himself into Warren. He heard Warren cry out in a mingling of pleasure and pain as he enter passed the sensitive barrier. Adrian grunted in ecstacy the further he pushed into Warren.

Adrian continue to pump in and out of Warren in a smooth languid movement. Both men moaned, caught in the vortex of pleasure. Warren's fingers clenched the sheets so tight that his knuckles began turning white. Adrian hand slid down Warren's arm, reaching Warren's hand and interlocked his fingers with his. His other hand coming underneath, to grasp Warren's hardness, stroking the organ in time with his thrust. Adrian kissed his shoulder blade and spine. He planted soft kisses on the nape of Warren's neck. Warren pushed up to meet Adrian's thrust each time, their rhythm sped up and increased in pressure, Adrian did not hold back as he pummeled faster and harder into Warren with an animal abandon. The strong scent of male aroma filled their nostrils. Warren loved the feel of Adrian's hardness gliding inside of him. Adrian closed his eyes tightly as he felt an energy tingle throughout his body, it began to boil from between his legs, and it spread through his limbs, then erupted from his organ. Both men threw their heads back as they cried out when the pinnacle of their lovemaking rushed through their bodies. Adrian convulsed before collapsing on top of Warren, weak, barely able to catch his breath. They laid there trembling, panting, sweaty, their eyes closed, fingers still locked together.

"That…was…amazing, Oh my god!" Adrian said through breathless gasps. He was the first one able to speak. He reluctantly rolled away from Warren who was still lying on his stomach with his eyes closed, content. All he could do was nod his head. Adrian leaned closer and kissed Warren's mouth, a soft peck of the lips, he placed soft kisses on Warren's cheek and shoulder blade. He reach over and took hold of the other man's waist and rolled him on his side, so that he could move closer and spoon Warren as they drifted off to sleep. Both relieved and relaxed.

Warren was awakened shortly after sun rise when his little cell phone began ringing in that annoying little tone. He searched through his pile of clothes on the floor and found the little silver phone. He flipped the headset and lifted it to his ear.

"Hello?" He asked groggily.

"Warren this is Matthew, look we have ourselves another body. I need you here at 95th street, right off Jeffery. Did you get that?" Matthew seemed tired and stressed at the same time. Warren was worried about him.

"Yeah, I got that, hey. Are you okay?"

"Me? Yeah I'm fine, I just don't like the feeling I'm getting about this case."

"Yeah tell me about it." Warren thought about the other theory that Xander had given him about the murder and did not want to dismiss it without sharing it with his partner. "Look, I've been thinking about another scenario, just hear me out. What if one of the rebel humanists group committed this murder to make the supernatural race look bad so that congress would reverse the bounty hunter law?" (A law established at the beginning of the *Exposure*, before the S.U.I.T. organization was created, that permitted individuals the permission to obtain bounty hunter licenses to hunt down and kill suspected supernaturals.)

There was a silence over the phone, then Matthew spoke. "It's doubtful, how could a human rip off a head and slowly?"

"It could be done and easily, think about it, they could have drained the body and then tied the body to a machine and stretched the neck until the head snapped. I know it's far fetched but I don't want to rule it out. Right now we need all the leads and motives we can get." Warren said as he glanced at the clock. The time was 6:15 am. A most ungodly hour by any standards. He looked over his shoulder as he felt Adrian stir behind him. He knew the phone woke them both up and Adrian was probably awake and listening to every word he and Matthew said.

"Well it's a motive, that's for sure but you need to see the condition of this body before we further explore that option. Oh and Warren…?" Matthew started.

"Yeah?"

"You may want to eat some of that *steak tar tar* you like so much. Because this one isn't nearly as nice as the last. Okay, I'll be waiting on your ass to get here." The phone clicked off and then came the buzz that meant the connection was long gone.

"You're leaving?" Adrian asked in a groggy voice.

"Yeah, I've got a case I'm working on." Warren said as he climbed out of the bed to head towards the bathroom for a quick shower. Adrian sat up on his elbow and watched the naked form of his sometimes lover enter the illuminated room. He heard the water running and decided it would be nice to share a shower. He threw back the sheets and climbed out of the bed determined to follow Warren into the shower.

"Who told you I wanted to share." Warren stated as he watched as Adrian climb into the shower closing the frosted glass door behind him.

"I thought you could use some company. Besides someone has to wash your back." Adrian said as he reached for a wash clothe and began lathering it up. "Turn around," he said playfully. He worked the soapy rag over Warren's shoulders and back. He then massaged the soapy rag over Warren's butt cheeks, making Warren chuckled. Adrian loved the feel of Warren's muscular, trim figure. He enjoyed running his hands over the soft dark hair on his smooth tanned skin.

"I swear, you are so damn predictable it's not even funny. Look I can't shower with you like this now. So let me just rinse off and get out." Warren said as he moved away from Adrian as fast as he could, lest he would not be leaving anytime soon. He stood under the nozzle as the warm water rinsed off his soapy body. Adrian watched the suds cascade down his lovers body as he rinsed off. Adrian climbed out of the shower first and toweled himself off then he handed Warren a towel when he climbed out. Adrian walked back to the bed and laid down and began chatting with Warren as he quickly dressed.

"So this case must be about shape-shifters or vampires or some shit like that sense the S.U.I.T. division was called in." He said matter-of-factly.

"Yeah, but I'm still not sure which one. There is a new body I have to view today. I told Xander about the first one and he's not sure if it's a shape-shifter or not but I caught the scent of one of us in the vicinity but not on the body, so it's hard to tell what the fuck is going on." Warren said as he finished tying his boots. He enjoyed wearing blue jeans, t-shirt and boots.

"So what else did my father say, which supernatural does he think the murderer is? I know how he tries to find one of our kind before the humans do and set them on the right path. But from what you're telling me, I don't think he's going to interfere with this one" Adrian said as he settled more comfortably in the bed.

"Well, he thinks it could be one or the other as well as a rebel humanist group trying to set us up. Ok, I've got to go. I'll probably be back but for now I have to go to work." As Warren walked past the bed Adrian's hand darted out and caught his wrist. He pulled Warren on the bed, close to him and planted a huge sloppy kiss, thrusting his tongue into Warren's mouth, giving him a reminder of their earlier activities of that morning. He finally released him.

"Okay, now you can go to work." He smiled and pulled the sheets over his head.

Warren looked at him and couldn't help but smile. He did miss Adrian and his body tingled still with the sensations of what they had done, only three hours earlier. He picked up his truck keys and left the room. He hit I-55 and headed towards Chicago.

Chapter 10

Natasha woke up to see a young nurse checking her IV. She licked her dry lips to moisten them. Her head hurt, along with her arm, back and neck. She touched the bandaged on her forehead and found the source of the throbbing inside her head.

"May I have some water?" She asked the nurse, her voice sounding as dry as her throat felt.

"Sure," the nurse said in a most cheerful voice. She stood five-feet-two inches. Her dark brown hair was combed back into a bun. She wore a multicolored-floral printed shirt with white pants. She smiled at Natasha as she reached over to the night stand and poured Natasha a tall glass of water and then handed it to her. "Here, now drink this but drink it slowly. You have a mild concussion and some cuts and bruises but you'll be ok. You were lucky to have survived. God blessed you." The Nurse said as she kissed the little silver cross that dangled from the silver chain around her neck. Natasha forced herself to remember what happened.

"There was another woman with me, is she okay?" Natasha asked somewhat frighted but still groggy from the drugs she had been given.

"Your friend is ok, she suffered a broken arm and some minor cuts and bruises. She'll be ok." The nurse continued to check her chart and fiddle with the bedding. "There, are you comfy?" She asked, smiling. Natasha nodded.

"Which hospital am I in? How long have I been here? What happen to the drivers?" Natasha asked consecutively.

"You're at County General Hospital, you came in several hours ago. I'm not sure about the other two drivers, I think it's going to be on the news. Right now you need to get some rest, doctors orders. Oh," the nurse replied, looking at her chart "I wanted to know if you're on any type of medication?"

"Yes. I take some medications for my headaches. I've been taking the medication since I was a child. But I did not take my medicine last night because I knew I'd be drinking. The last thing I remember was feeling really sick, my head was hurting and spinning at the same time. And I fell asleep in the cab..." Natasha said as she struggled to remember the events of last night.

"Do you remember the name of the medication you're taking?" The nurse asked as she scribbled words down on Natasha's chart.

"Yeah, Triadonex, is there a problem?" She asked. The nurse looked up from her writing and smiled. She shook her head.

"Oh heavens no, it's just better for both of us to know if our patient's have any medications they're taking or allergies. Speaking of allergies, do you have any?"

Natasha thought about it for a minute. "No. I don't believe I do."

"Excellent. Now you lay back and get some rest. The bathroom is over here if you need to used the restroom. And here's my call button, right here" the nurse pointed to a red button beside the bed. "And the remote control for the TV, here." She informed as she gestured to a black controller on the table. They will be serving breakfast in about fifteen minutes. Is there anything else you need?" The nurse stood there to see if Natasha had any other questions. Natasha shook her head.

"Okay, call me if you need me." The nurse said as she covered Natasha up to her neck in sheets. She placed the chart on the edge of the bed and left the room. Natasha did not know what happened. She was concerned about the drivers but it was the vision she received seconds before the accident that worried her. Did she have a premonition? Or was it just a freak coincidence? She thought about the man she took the keys from. *That bastard bartender must have given the damn keys back!* She hoped he would be fined for that. *You just don't let people drive drunk, and now two people might be dead since the nurse did not mention that they were brought to the hospital with her and Annette, the two injured.* She was angry and sad, it all could have been avoided.

She looked around the little room. She could hear the beep and clicks of the machines and the soft snores from the patient next to her. She looked over at the bed to her left and saw an elderly lady asleep. Her wrinkly pink skin took on a pale luster. There was a thin layer of sweat on the woman's skin. Natasha watched her chest rise and fall at a normal pace. She continued to survey the room. There was a little thirteen inch color tv suspended from the wall in the far upper left corner of the room. Two clothe upholstered chairs sat in the room, one by the elderly patients' bed and one beside her own. The room had white plastered walls and a white cement-tiled floor. There was a huge window on the far left wall, the curtains were closed to prevent the morning sun from shining in. The sun was exactly what Natasha wanted to see just to make sure she survived for real. The bathroom was conveniently only a few feet away from her bed. For which she was grateful for, because the pressure in her bladder was almost unbearable. She pulled the thick white sheets away from her neck and slowly slid both legs to the side of the bed and scooted her aching body off the edge.

She had never felt such pain. Her whole body felt like it had been hit by a mack truck. Once when she was a child, she had fallen from a tree while climbing up to her best friends treehouse and dislocated her shoulder, until this moment that had been the worse pain she had ever felt. Every muscle in her body ached. To stand up straight was proving to be more difficult than she thought. She felt a painful spasm through her body as she erected, she cried out and had to grab hold of the steel bar on the side of her bed to keep from falling.

She could feel the effects of the painkiller wearing off and thought hastily about reaching for the nurses button and pushing it repeatedly and asking for a dose of the *good shit*. Once again, she was reminded of the need in her bladder and had to cross her legs tightly to keep from having an accident. The last thing she wanted was to have to push the nurses button to report that she wet herself. No that was not an option. She took hold of her IV stand then put one foot in front of the other and forced her body to work those aching muscles.

Once inside the bathroom, she closed the door and turned the little lock to secure her privacy. She looked at the toilet with the steel bars on either side. She remembered being a kid in the hospital when she dislocated her shoulder and wanting to play with all of the gadgets inside the hospital room, now all she wanted to do was to leave and never come back. She did not like hospitals, she hated them, she always felt that the germs were just festering in the air, and with every breath you take, you were bound to catch something. Whenever she had to visit a person in the hospital, she tried very hard to hold her breath as she walked down the halls. Holding her breath now was not an option, at least her roommate was not coughing up a lung over there, or she might have panicked. She was never very good around sick people.

She squatted over the little white toilet and balanced herself over the opening, gripping the steel bars for support and released the pressure in her bladder. She felt tiny pleasurable tingles work its way through her limbs causing her to shiver just a bit. It was funny to think about all the little things that can bring pleasure at any given time, at least *she* thought it was funny. After she finished and washed her hands with the little brown square soap. Natasha considered taking the cosmetics when she leaves. She slowly walked back to her bed, she felt tired. She looked at the clock on the wall and noticed that the time was 6:50am, she may have only had about four or five hours of sleep. Natasha tried to remember what time it was when she left the club with Annette.

"Annette!" She thought about her friends condition and felt sorry for her, she wanted to go and visit Annette but first she would give her a chance to rest. She would visit her later, she hoped by that time she would be feeling better herself and would make for better company. She climbed back into the bed slowly and pulled the thick white covers back over her head. She lay still in the bed thinking about the freaky dream she had before the crash. It unnerved her that she could see something like that coming and knew who was the cause of it.

She wondered how she did that. Natasha thought about what could have caused the connection. In the vision she had of the man, who was probably dead, she saw him drop his keys on the ground. She remembered picking up his keys, she could not explain it. As she laid there in the narrow little bed she thought about all the events that led up to the crash. She had not taken her medicine that night and had gotten drunk for the first time in her life, (though she vowed never to drink again,) she thought that might have had something to do with the "premonition" maybe it was just a freak thing that happened. Maybe she just dreamed about the man since he was the last thing on her mind before she had drifted off to sleep.

Maybe she felt the blinding lights on her closed eyelids which made her open her eyes in the first place to see the headlights reflecting in the rearview mirror. It made sense to her, *that must be it and nothing more.* She decided that was the most logical answer for what happened. And she snuggled deeper under the sheets and drifted off to sleep. She only dreamt about her friend sleeping in a little narrow bed with white linen sheets like hers .

Chapter 11

Warren took the less crowded exit off the I-90 expressway. He hated the city's rush hour traffic, people always drove at their worse. They would race to get to work on time before they were fired or written up. And after the grind of the work day, everyone is rushing to pick up the kids, groceries and get home in time to cook and enjoy a little prime time before they had to start the rat race all over again the next day. An erratic driver cut him off causing him to swerve his car. He thought about letting him go, so that he could get to the crime scene but then traded against getting breakfast and decided to give the guy a ticket for driving recklessly, he could have caused an accident!

Warren took the exit to Lake Shore Drive to escape the stop and go traffic of the Dan Ryan expressway. Exiting the Drive, he turned onto Stony Island, he was almost there now. He knew right away when he reached the scene of the crime due to all of the police squad cars that held off oncoming cars and the uniformed officers that redirected the traffic. He pulled his black Diamond Back S5-20 four door truck over to the side opposite of the crime scene. He reached into his glove compartment and pulled out a pair of latex gloves.

He took a few deep breaths then climbed out of his truck. He could smell the blood in the air, it made his stomach growl. He immediately regretted not taking his partner's advice and grabbing a whole lot of something to eat along the way. The scent of the blood was so enticing he felt his mouth water. He swallowed hard and reached into his pocket to pull out his badge and ID to show to the uniformed officer who was protecting the crime scene from intruders and media. He surveyed the crime scene, the body had been discarded on the shoulder of 95th street. There was a small patch of wild grass that had grown four feet high and behind that, just huge patches of gravel.

He stepped under the yellow and black tape that always decorated crime scenes everywhere. He could see the M.E. forensics expert taking pictures of the body from all types of angles. As he walked closer he realized right away why forensics were walking around the area taking pictures. The crime scene was a horrific sight. The body had been dismembered; mutilated chunks of bloody flesh had been strewn around the area. A uniformed officer rushed past him and began puking on the curb next to a squad car. He used the car's hood for balance as his stomach heaved its contents onto the pavement.

Warren looked closely at the mutilated, disembodied chucks of flesh, his senses did picked up a slight scent from the body but it was highly over shadowed by the scent of blood. He wished that whomever the pieces of flesh belong to, was murdered here at this location and not somewhere else like the last victim. It would help him with the scent of the wolf. Now he knew for certain that a wolf was involved. He just wished he had a more defined scent to work with. Well at least one thing could be ruled out. Xander's theory of foul play from the human race was out of the question from this stand point. This was the work of a supernatural and it was the last thing the supernatural race needed....*more drama. More ammunition for the humans to throw at them about how they should all be rounded up and destroyed.*

He watched as blood dried to a dark red tint on the exposed chunks of torn ligaments and muscles. Ragged pieces of skin clung to the chunks of flesh. He counted five pieces of the body ranging from small to medium. The largest chunk of flesh he saw, was what remained of the torso. He stepped closer to examine the bite marks in the flesh where the wolf tore threw the skin and muscle. He looked inside the cavity and saw that the ribs had been splintered, little particles of white bone sprinkled the remaining intestines of the shredded abdomen. There was no blood splattered around the area, just small puddles of blood poured from the pieces of the corpse. He fought the urge to kneel on all fours and plunge his face deep into the feast at hand. He licked his lips and swallowed the saliva that had gathered in his mouth. His stomach growled loudly this time. He heard footsteps coming closer and looked up to see his partner approaching.

"I can hear your hungry ass from over there. Didn't I tell you to eat something before you brought your ass out here." Matthew said as he approached Warren, he then kneeled down beside him and examined a bloody chunk of the corpse. Warren gave him a sad smile. He looked at Matthew's attire, a black sweatshirt with the faded letters of Rosenthall-Krest University on the front and a pair of faded and obviously worn blue jeans. His boots were the newest thing he had on, they still had that new store brought shine to them.

"You did, but I didn't think I'd have enough time to stop." Warren lied.

"You had time, at least enough time to pull into a *Burger Town* or something and grab a dozen breakfast sandwiches. Anything would have been better than having you drooling over the body." He took another look around the area. "Or what's left of a body. We can't even tell if this was a man or woman, young or old. I guess it matters little. As it stands now, this is a John or Jane doe. Shit, Im not even sure if it's human!"

"It's a human, Matt. Has the coroner found anything extra about the body from yesterday? Has it been identified?" Warren asked.

Matthew nodded. "Yeah, the victim was a man named Wallace Gram. He owned a cleaners down there on 69th street. His wallet was missing from the body but his wife had reported him missing two days before his body was found. She of course doesn't know why anyone would do this to her husband, she said he was a good and caring person who always gave back to the community. I guess she did not realize that supernaturals don't take that into consideration." After Matthew said what he said, he wished he could have taken it back, because the look on Warren's face made him regret it.

"You sound like the rest of them!" Warren said as he gestured to the other officers surrounding the area.

"You know I did not mean it like that. It's just, ah shit man, you know how I feel about all this. I know that humans are just as capable of this as the next being it's just-"

"Most supernaturals were human, so I supposed that's were they get it from." Warren said matter-of- factly, then walked over to another piece of the body. He did not want to get into this kind of debate with Matthew, not right now, not in public. He was grateful that no one was standing close to them as they exchanged words. He would hate to have to explain his sympathy for the supernaturals to humans who would not understand.

"I guess, nevermind, we'll talk about it later I suppose." Matthew said and he rose and stood over the largest piece of flesh and bone. Warren was grateful Matthew knew how to take a hint. It helped since he was trying to hide his own nature from the world.

"This looks like part of a femur right here." Warren gestured in a circular motion around a fragment of white bone jutting out from a football size chunk of bloody flesh. Matthew walked over and bent forward to get a closer inspection.

"Yeah, it looks like it. It's still to hard to tell if it's female or male, it's just not enough left to make that determination. Perhaps the bone marrow will aid the coroner in determining the sex, it's his job."

"Well, it looks like the wolf took what he wanted and then mutilated the body afterwards so that we wouldn't be able to pick any details from the remains, thus making it difficult to determine concrete evidence from these remains. We know that the murderer is planting these bodies on the southeast side of the city. We have also determined that these are not just natural feedings Matthew, the murderer is toying with us by leaving us little to connect. But there's something more…" Warren gestured for Matthew to follow him towards his truck. He needed to get a breather away from the immediate scent of the body. He needed to eat something as soon as possible or end up eating one of the people at the scene of the crime.

"I have to get something to eat and *now*." He whispered breathlessly as he wiped the sweat from his forehead with the back of his gloved hand. He snatched the gloves off and climbed inside his car. Matthew climbed in on the passenger side and looked at Warren who was gripping the stirring wheel so tight his knuckles began to sweat and turn white.

"Hey man, are you going to be okay? Shit, should I be sitting next to you right now?" He asked seriously.

Warren nodded. "I'll be fine, I just need to get away from here. I really should have eaten but I don't know how much good it would have done. I wasn't prepared to walk into a crime scene like that." He pressed his forehead to his knuckles and took several deep breaths before sitting up and starting the engine. He threw a glance at his partner and smiled.

"I wouldn't eat you. You would probably taste like shit anyway." He joked.

"Oh please, I'll probably be the best thing you ever had in your mouth." Matthew said winking at his partner. Warren gave him a wolfish grin. That one line meant more to Warren than he would let Matthew know. He had thoughts about how good Matthew would taste in his mouth and he wasn't thinking as an entree either. He had always thought that Matthew was extremely handsome. He also enjoyed Matthew's personality, he liked how Matthew always remained calm, even when he was pissed. He reminded him of Xander. He didn't have any sexual lust for Xander but a calm cool temperament was always a turn on for him.

He wished Adrian was more like his father, it would have kept their relationship from getting so rocky. He sat in the driver's seat and drove his truck to the nearest Pancake Palace. He wanted a real breakfast, something that was going to coat his stomach. He thought about Adrian and the feel of his body stroking his, inside and out. It made him blush. If it was one thing that made a shifter think about sex, it was the sight and scent of blood. He could feel himself growing hard and fought against it. He did not want to have to explain to Matthew why he was sporting an eight inch boner.

"What was it you were going to say back there at the crime scene? You looked like you were going to say something, then just trailed off. What was it you were going to say?" Matthew reminded, bringing Warren out of his sex filled trance.

"Well, this shifter, it's a wolf."

"You mean werewolf?"

"Yeah, but inside the shifting community, we don't refer to ourselves as 'were' anything. If you change into a wolf, then you're just a wolf or cheetah, etc. you get it?"

Matthew nodded. "So it's a we-wolf, what else."

"I'm pretty sure it's toying with us. Baiting us, or something. Whatever it's doing, it's laughing it's fucking ass off. But this is the thought that was on my mind. I think it may know that I'm a shifter and may be trying to expose me."

"Why do you say that?" Matthew asked, obviously concerned.

"Well, it's a hunch that I have. for one thing, if it's just feeding and tossing the remains then this wolf is hiding its' scent pretty fucking well. I went back to the first crime scene last night with the oldest and strongest of our pack. He picked up the same scent I did. But nothing else. And I'm sad to say that the scent from that crime scene did not match the scent I smelled at this crime scene. So either it's two wolves working together. Or that first scent was just a wolf passing through."

"How would this wolf know about you, why would they be trying to expose you?" Matthew asked as they pulled into the parking lot at the breakfast restaurant on 87th street. The restaurant had been one of Warren's favorites. He loved getting quantity with quality for his buck. He liked the wooden interior design of the restaurant, it reminded him of a bed and breakfast he stayed at while camping and hunting with Xander and the pack. The booths had blue and red plaid upholstery coverings, the big bay windows allowed for plenty of sunlight. He adored the shining hard wood floors and the atmosphere, which was very friendly and laid back.

"I don't know, I've never smelled the scent of this wolf before, so how this shifter knows me is a mystery. Unless…this wolf returned to the prior crime scene after we had investigated, that would be one way, but it still doesn't explain the motive. It has been my experience that most serial killers try to hide their bodies for fear that the tiniest linking evidence would lead to their capture. But this murderer wants to play cat and mouse and this shifter is leaving only the clues he/she want us to have. Matt, this murderer does not fear us." Warren speculated as he climbed out of the truck, followed by Matthew.

"When we get back to the precinct, we have to look at the most recent missing persons reports. We have to try and make a link from the missing persons to the murder victim. We have to find out where this killer is finding it's victims." Matthew said as he held the door open for his partner. Both men were seated right away. Warren's stomach growled louder, he felt the rumble deep inside his gut.

"Damn man! Let's get you something to eat, A.S.A.P.!" Matthew joked. Warren just smiled, but he did want to eat A.S.A.P. A plump black waitress in a black dress with a white apron came over to the table and set two glasses of water on the table in front of them.

"What can I get you two handsome gentleman?" She asked in a friendly voice. She held her ink pen poised, ready to jot down their order.

"Well I would like a coffee and two scrambled eggs with a side of french toast. My friend here will just take everything on your menu." Matthew chuckled. Warren gave him a crossed look then opened the menu to see what he wanted to order.

"Do you need some more time?" The waitress asked. Warren nodded.

"Just give me about one minute and then you can come back, I should be ready to eat a horse by then." he smiled. Matthew gave him a knowing look. The waitress smiled and walked away. Warren looked at Matthew.

"What?" He asked, shrugging.

"Yeah, I bet you *could* eat a horse, probably have at some point."

"Do you really want to know?"

Matthew shook his head. "No, not really." Warren laughed and went back to looking at the menu. Their waitress returned to the table ready to take his order. He was ready now, with an appetite to boot.

"Okay, I'm ready now, I'll have the number four with an extra steak-rare. A side of southern style hash browns, Canadian bacon and…a side of strawberry buttermilk pancakes and a large coffee." He closed the menu and smiled at the waitress, who was still writing what he had listed as his "breakfast".

"Will this complete you order sir." She asked, smiling at him, she just knew he was going to say, 'oh and I forgot this.'

"No, that's what I want," he said smiling. She nodded her head and walked away. Matthew looked at Warren and chuckled.

"Tell me how is it you're not fat as hell? If I ate the way you ate, I'd be dead by now from high cholesterol and clogged arteries." Matthew stated as he leaned closer across the table. Warren looked into his friends soft brown eyes and smiled.

"Well, we've got pretty high metabolism. So we burn fat and protein relatively fast. If you ever see a fat ass shape shifter, it's because that shifter never stopped eating. He/she probably fought the urge to run as well. So in reality, I can eat whatever I want and just about never gain a pound." He was glad they had a booth set away from the other booths in the restaurant, so that their conversation was not overheard by all.

"What do you mean, 'urge' to run?"

"Well, since we pretty much turn into wild animals, we have a natural instinct to go running and hunting. In addition, feline shape-shifters have the urge to climb, and most take plenty of naps. I'm sure you can imagine the canine shape-shifters love to run, which is why I can enjoy chasing down a suspect on foot. It's the hunt, the chase." He shrugged one shoulder. "We also have the urge to mark territory, the males, I mean." Warren added with a wicked smile. Matthew chuckled, then continued.

"I hope you don't mind me asking all these questions and shit. When I first found out about you, I had to absorb the reality of it. Then I just did not want to know anything... well anything outside of what might get me killed. But now that I'm pretty comfortable with the whole idea, I'm just curious." Matthew said as he leaned closer. Their waitress returned with Matthews order. She gave them both a look. She thought they were lovers. The way that Matthew peered into Warren's eyes had given her that idea.

"Your order will be ready in a few minutes, sir." She told Warren. He nodded and thanked her. He watched Matthew dig into his eggs and his mouth started to water all over again. His stomach rumbled a bit more.

"Keep your eyes off my food." Matthew joked. Warren chuckled and clasped his hands in front of him on the table.

"Back to what you were saying, I don't mind if you ask questions. As a matter of fact, I'm glad that you are asking. I wanted to tell you myself, but I did not want to freak you out or anything. But I'll answer any question I can." He looked around the restaurant. He did not catch a scent of another shifter in the vicinity. But he was starting to get a little unnerved about discussing his "condition" in public.

"Better yet Matthew, when we get back into the car, I'll tell you everything you want to know, but for right now, let's just stick to the case." Warren said as a second thought.

Matthew nodded, then stared forward like he was in deep thought, then shook his head. "I'd rather not talk about the case while I'm eating," he said. Warren actually agreed. Though discussing the case would not have bothered them, if it was not for the condition of the remains. It both sickened Matthew and enticed Warren.

Warren's eyes widened as the waitress came closer to their table carrying a large brown tray that held the several plates that completed his breakfast.

"Here you go sir." She said as she placed a large platter with two sixteen ounce skirt steaks accompanied by a three-egg omelette stuffed with cheddar cheese, green and red peppers, onions topped with fresh made salsa. She then placed down a bowl of hash browns with mixed green and red peppers, onions and diced spicy apple-glazed chicken sausage. Then came a medium size plate stacked with four thick fluffy buttermilk pancakes topped with strawberries, powdered sugar and whipped cream. She placed a serving of strawberry syrup next to the plate of pancakes and a bottle of katsup and steak sauce next to his platter of steaks and eggs. The last was his large cup of coffee.

"Is there anything else that you'll need gentlemen?" She asked, looking from one to the other. Both men gave each other a look and shook their heads. Warren was already cutting into the steak when she smiled and walked away. Matthew looked at the spread before him and just couldn't see where Warren put it all.

"I still can not believe you're going to finish all that." Matthew said. Warren simply nodded his head as he stuffed fork-full after fork-full of steak into this mouth. Other people surrounding their table threw quick glances at their booth. Trying hard not to watch Warren eat, because it is considered rude. Matthew just finished his french toast and sipped his coffee as he watched his partner put away two sixteen ounce steaks, four pancakes with fruit, three eggs and about a half a pound of hash browns all with vegetables and shook his head.

He wondered if they would win a free dinner if he ever took Warren back to his home town in Texas to his favorite restaurant and had him order the "Cowboy". He pondered that for a minute. Not only would the dinner be free for you and whom ever was in your party but you get fifty dollars and your face on a plaque that would hang on the "Wall of Champions". You would become a legend. It's not everyday that one person can put away a sixty-five ounce steak in an hour, at least not without dying half way through. He would present the offer to Warren later.

After twenty minutes, Warren had finished his breakfast and was sitting back looking over the empty plates in front of him. He looked at Matthew and smiled.

"And you thought I couldn't finish this." He said as he shook his head as if to say '*for shame*'.

"Shit, you weren't supposed to. By all rights you should be passed out somewhere on a gurney." Both men erupted into laughter. Warren could just picture what Matthew was envisioning. Him laid out, arms and legs dangling off the edge of the gurney, face still greasy from the breakfast as the paramedics performed emergency CPR, the thought made him chuckle. They settled in their seats for a few more minutes, Warren savoring the breakfast. Then he reached inside his pocket and pulled his wallet free. He held up his hand in protest as Matthew started for his own wallet.

"Hey, don't worry about it, it's on me." He said as he pulled out two twenty dollar bills and one ten.

"You sure?"

"Yeah. What's your seven dollars to this." He gestured to all his empty plates. He raised his hand to call the waitress over, who walked towards them. "Here and keep the change. Thanks for everything."

"Oh, you're welcome." She said smiling at her ten dollar tip. She hoped he came back, she like the big tippers. She did not get tipped that much where she worked at. The two men left the restaurant and headed for Warren's truck. They climbed in and Warren started the engine. He glanced at Matthew.

"Okay, now ask me whatever it is you want to ask." Warren said.

Matthew looked at him and nodded. "I know some things about shape shifters since the job but not the behind the scenes shit, you know. Do *you* belong to a pack or something like it?"

Warren thought about the question. If Xander knew he was revealing so much private information to his friend, he would no doubt want to kill Matthew. He would make sure he never told Xander he was telling Matthew anything.

"Well, yes I do. I could live with them if I wanted to but because of the job, I don't. There are about fifteen adult wolves in my pack and three children. We have a leader who controls all the goings on within the pack. For example, he decides who's to be made a wolf. He also tries to makes sure none of us gets into trouble. If we do get into trouble, he has to decide the best way to deal with it."

"So he's the top dog and shit, right?" Matthew asked, not realizing his play on words.

"Yeah, he's our Alpha, we do like that term to best describe the leader of the pack. He has a lifemate, the matron, our alpha married her. I was raised by them when my parents were killed by hunters. They took me in right away and have been like parents to me."

"What do you mean by 'matron?'" Matthew asked.

"Well, she's the mother of the pack, the queen so to speak. She is the provider, our Alpha is the protector. She can heal us if we're sick or wounded. She also helps raise any children born within the pack." Warren said, then he glanced at Matthew. "Do you need to go back to the crime scene to pick up your car?"

Matthew shook his head. "No, I hitched a ride with a black and white."

"Okay." Warren said as he entered the I-90 expressway heading towards downtown. The street was not nearly as congested as it was only a few hours ago. The morning rush hour traffic was thinning and it made for easy traveling. Warren lane surfed between eighteen wheelers easily.

"What do you mean by heal?" Matthew asked, all of this was intriguing him. He was amazed at how organized Warren's world really was. He was glad to be getting a peek over the other side of the fence.

"Well, she has a certain power within herself to heal. She can also lick the wound to heal." He gave Matthew a sideways glance out the corner of his eye. He wondered what was on his mind.

"Do you lick your wounds clean and heal them?" He asked

"Lick them clean? I can and I do if I'm alone but they heal on their own as you've seen. But if it's a more serious life threatening wound, then we all go to her and drink of her healing blood as she licks the wound with her healing saliva. Not every female can be the matron as I'm sure you realize." Warren said with raised eyebrows.

"Yes, I suppose. Okay, what else? What taste better? Cooked food or raw?" He asked.

Warren thought about his answer for a moment. "Raw. But that's if I'm in wolf form of course. If I'm in human form, then I'd have to say I like the meat seasoned and cooked rare. At least I don't *really* get food poison, if I do, I pretty much puke it up within minutes of digestion and then I can go about my business, no long hours of night sweats and agonizing pain."

"Lucky you, I don't even want to remember the last time I was sick like that. Okay tell me more about the pack."

"Like I said, we have a king and queen who combined, protects and provides for the pack. On full moons we hunt together. Where my pack lives we have a private forest which is our hunting grounds. However, only natural born wolves can shape shift at will and hunt when we choose. Bitten wolves are at the mercy of a full moon night before they can join the hunt, but they're exceptions to the rules here as well," he paused.

"Go on." Matthew urged. Warren threw him a sly smile, flashing a row full of pearly whites.

"If a bitten shifter comes into the hunt and gets a strong scent of the blood from the kill, they might change, the hunger forces the body to change so they could feed. Our human form doesn't digest raw deer carcass that well, you know with the bones and all." Warren smiled, Matthew chuckled then Warren continued. "Our digestive track changes specifically for a different type of feeding. Also, another thing that can induce the change is extreme fear or anger. If we are terribly afraid or upset then the change could be triggered." Warren exited the expressway at the Ohio Street, East exit. He drove towards the precinct that was eight blocks away.

"I forgot to ask before, I know how thorough you are, did you get everything we needed to make our report from the crime scene today?" Warren asked as he stopped at a red light.

"Yeah, you know I did. Man, I'm still trying to digest all this. So exactly how strong *are you*?" He asked.

Warren thought about it for a minute or two. "I could probably take one of these steel stop sign poles and bend it into a bow easily. If I exert my strength I could really do some damage. I have to monitor myself. I have to make sure I don't handle things under extreme emotions." Matthew nodded his head, remembering the two times Warren broke his car door handle. He seemed to be thinking about times since their partnership were he had noticed Warren seeming more tense of body than usual as if he was struggling to contain something.

"One more question?" He asked as Warren pulled the car into the parking lot of the precinct.

"What's up?"

"How in the hell do you keep passing inspections and shit, all these test we've had to take?" He asked genuinely curious.

"Well, it's not easy, I can tell you that. My pack leader helps me out in that department. We have someone who's brother is in our pack, she looks out for my records. She also does all the analysis and blood work for the precinct. And when I went to the military base, she hacked the files before anything went public. She's a life savor, let me tell you." Warren said with a nervous chuckle.

"You wouldn't be talking about Sara would you? Sara Washburn?!" Matthew asked, surprised. Warren nodded.

"Her brother was bitten ten years ago. She hides his identity, being as he's a lawyer and his career would be in the toilet, if all of his rich high-priced clients knew what he was. Even though the supernatural race has been exposed, we still have to hide. It sucks but it's a fact . My pack took him in and help him through it. So to show her gratitude, she helps us out from time to time. My pack leader doesn't really want me to be a cop but he won't force me to switch career choices, unless he thought it would threaten the pack."

"What does he have against you working on the force?"

"That's a long story, a lot of my kind feel like it's a betrayal. My leader has mixed feelings about it. He'd rather not turn a shifter over to the humans, but if it can't be avoided then he turns the other cheek, if you will. Now we got to go or people might start to think we're having a deep passionate conversation." He said with a chuckle. Both men stepped out of the truck, and headed inside.

They walked side by side into the brightly lit station. Uniformed unit officers were walking around talking with each other and looking over files. One thing Warren knew for certain was that he really liked the S.U.I.T. division's I.T. (Infiltration Team) uniforms. It's reminded him of S.W.A.T uniforms, only better, more stylish. The black vest was equipped with hooks for ultraviolet grenades. The outfit had numerous pockets on the vest and pants legs for knives, ammo and other things. A protective thin steel collar and cuffs were sewn into the turtle neck shirt that you wore under the padded vest. Steel toed combat boots that snapped closed, securing your feet inside the boots. Yeah, Warren really liked wearing the outfit when they were zeroing in on a suspect. But as a detective, he was not required to wear the infiltration team uniform.

They signed back in at the front desk and walked to their desks to look up some of the most recent files on missing persons. Warren's desk was a cluttered mess, files spread askew over the surface. While Matthew's desk had all of his papers and files stacked neatly on top of the desk in one pile or placed in alphabetical order inside his file cabinet. Both had computers on their desk, both had telephones equipped with speaker and caller ID. They sat at their desks and turned on their computers. Warren tried to straighten up the mess on his desk but was unsuccessful, so he stopped trying.

"Okay, I'm going to look up the records of people being reported missing in the past forty-eight hours. What are you going to do?" Matthew asked Warren. He looked at Warren differently now. He felt like he understood him better, more intimately. He was glad he put away his barrier of not wanting to pry and decided to ask questions in spite of himself, thinking it to be rude. He found a certain appeal to his partner now. He wasn't sure if it was because he always thought Warren was one of the sexiest men he'd ever seen or if it was because he was accepting Warren's animal side? Was this just the effects of him being under the spell of his animalistic attraction or both of the above? He wasn't sure if he should say anything about the way he felt.

He wasn't sure if *he* could be the *lover* of a *shape-shifter*. He thought about that possibility many times after discovering Warren's true nature. Knowing a little bit more about the life behind the hype was truly an eye opener for him. He cleared his mind of the rampant thoughts and tried to concentrate on the troublesome situation at hand. They had to track down and catch a killer, and they had very little to go on. He scanned through the files on his computer, reading the newest missing person reports on the list. It was sad to see so many people reported missing. This list had seventy-five people on it. There were forty-five throughout Illinois and the other thirty in Chicago alone.

"Shit, I've got about seventy-five people here in Illinois alone that have been reported missing, thirty just from Chicago. Think it's safe for us to rule out the other states, or no?" Matthew asked, hoping that Warren was on the same page as he, in thinking that the people reported missing in the state of Florida were still in Florida. He wanted to narrow their search as much as possible. They did not have a motive, except that Warren suspected that whoever the killer was may also know what he was and possibly wanted to expose him. That could be true and may very well hold water but he wasn't willing to bet his whole paycheck on it, not yet at least.

"I think we should focus on Illinois, mainly Chicago's south side and the areas closest to where we're finding the bodies. I want you to know…this shit really sucks." Warren said as he read Matthew's report of the most recent murder scene. "Even though the body was not in the same condition as the first one, it was still missing a lot of blood and it's head. And I think it's the same killer. We need to go down to the coroner's office to see what he could find." Matthew nodded in agreement as he printed out the long list of names and all their information from the missing persons' report.

They rose from their seats and headed towards the chilly basement to the coroner's morgue. They had their own autopsy specialist who worked in the same facility. He was to deal with the victims of supernatural crimes only. They walked through the double doors of the morgue. The walls were painted grey, the light grey cement floor shone with a soft glow, reflecting the bright florescent lighting equipped with ultraviolet lights for emergency back up. There was a long wall that was layered from top to bottom with drawers for the numerous corpses that frequented the morgue. A small stainless steel sink was in the middle, right beside two draining holes. They saw Marshall Galen six-foot -three, thin frame hunched over the remains of the body they viewed earlier. He was working with silver tongs and scalpel. His salt and pepper hair needed a trimming, his lose curls dropped low covering his eyes. his thick black rimmed glasses were smudged. He was wearing worn brown loafers, grey wrinkled slacks and a long white lab coat over his green button up shirt. Warren thought about Xander and Adrian and how they would want to drag him away to make-over heaven.

"Yo, doc find anything interesting? Anything we can use?" Asked Warren as they approached the carcass on the steal slab. Marshall erected himself looking at the two officers and exhaled a deep breath, that meant that he did not have good news. He took his glasses off his face, pulled a handkerchief from his back pocket and proceeded to wipe his glasses clean. After holding them up to the light, he placed them back on. He looked at the two men again.

"Well gentleman, there wasn't a whole lot left to this person." He said as he gestured to the five chunks of flesh decomposing on the stainless steel examining table.

"So can you tell if it's was a man or woman? That might give us a pattern we can trace." Matthew inquired.

"Man." Warren said. Matthew gave him a questioning look. Warren shook his head as if to say, *'don't ask yet'*. He looked at the coroner. The coroner was looking at him curiously.

He shrugged. "Lucky guess, I suppose. Do you think I'm right, doc?" Warren asked to cover up his blunder. Marshall Galen gave him a small nod, apparently satisfied with Warren's explanation.

"From the size of the fragment of bone in this piece here," he poked a chunk of red flesh so that Warren and Matthew could get a better look. The blood inside the flesh oozed out more when he moved it. The torn muscles and nerves dangling from the boulder of flesh like tentacles. Matthew paled a bit and shifted from one foot to the other. Warren was happy he had a full breakfast, his stomach did not betray him now.

"See gentlemen, the fragment here is pretty thick in circumference, which suggest a male." Both men nodded.

"And furthermore, you see this?" The coroner said as he pointed to a dark dryness inside the bone fragment. "And this tells me that this body belong to a mortal man about average height..hmmm, what's this?" He said as he leaned closer to the rotting flesh. Even though the room temperature was very cold, the smell of the numerous corpses, past and present filled the room with a thick stench, like rotting meat. Warren did not particularly care for the scent of rotting flesh. The smell in the room made it easier for him to control his hunger, that and the fact that he had a full belly.

"Is this what I think it is?" Marshall asked as he looked closely at several strands of silky black fur between his tweezers. Warren and Matthew moved closer to get a better look. Warren gestured for the tweezers and Marshall handed them to him. He took the tweezers from Marshall and held them up to the light. He turned his back to the coroner so that he would not see him smell the fur, taking in the scent. He then turn towards Marshall and returned the fur with the tweezers.

"Well that just confirms what we thought already. From the way the flesh was torn, it looked like a shifter murder." Matthew said as he walked towards the grey double doors, followed by Warren. "Just fill us in if you find out anything else Marshall, thanks." When they stepped outside the morgue, Matthew turned to Warren, he wanted to know the answer to the question he could not asked until now.

"How did you know it was a man's body?" He asked.

Warren smiled slightly. "I could smell the iron in the blood. It was stronger than the amount of iron that's in a female's blood stream." He said, his smile widen.

"How come you couldn't tell that earlier when we were at the crime scene? The blood was a little more fresher then?"

Warren sucked air through his teeth, making a 'smacking' sound. He stopped walking and caught the other man's arm to stop him from going any further. He leaned closer to his partner to whisper in his ear. "Well, at the crime scene, I was focusing too much on controlling and maintaining my hunger and composure to focus on my senses. Now, I'm not hungry, the flesh doesn't smell all that appealing and I'm able to concentrate. That's why I wanted to smell the fur he found. I got a more defined scent. I don't know how much that's going to help us, but at least it's a fucking start." He whispered. He did not want anyone to hear that little bit of information. He knew there were cameras throughout the building and didn't want to get caught revealing this aspect of his nature.

"You two look like love birds." Observed an officer walking down the hallway who had caught Warren invading Matthew's personal space by leaning against his ear like a lover whispering sweet nothings to his mate.

"Well, we're not, asshole! So you can keep walking!" Warren said as he flipped officer Ronen the finger. Officer Ronen held up his hands as if he was preparing to defend himself from an attack. His blue eyes widen as he shook his blonde crew cut head from side to side.

"Hey, alls I'm saying is, it looked questionable. What you two do in the privacy of your bedrooms is certainly none of my damn business. I'm just saying keep that shit in the bedroom where it needs to be." He said jokingly but with a hint of sarcasm. Those two always seemed a bit sexless to him. Never flirting with the female officers in the division or a female period. He could not remember a time when he ever heard either of them ever talking about fucking a female. He just assumed they were both gay since they weren't married or involved.

Both Warren and Matthew rolled their eyes and walked away from Officer Ronen. He watched them walk away side by side down the hallway. One word formed in his mind and he whispered it through his lips

"*Fags.*"

Warren's ears picked up the insult, his shoulder's tensed. He fought the urge to turn around and march right back to that *prejudice son of a bitch and put him in a hurtlock, before planting his body into the plaster covered cement wall.* Instead, he continued to walk away. It would be hard to explain how he heard him when he was more than fifty feet away in the first place. Very hard indeed, especially since superhuman hearing is a standard characteristic of the very being they were trained to police.

"What an asshole!" Warren said as they stepped into the elevator. Matthew pushed the number two button and the mirrored doors closed. Leaving them with their reflections staring back at them.

"Yeah he is, which is why he can't keep and fucking partner longer than six months. No one wants to work with the motherfucker. The partner he's got now has lasted the longest, they might be birds of a feather, ya know. Both assholes." Matthew said. Both men chucked as they walked out of the elevator and headed towards their desk to look over the list that printed out on the most recent missing people.

Chapter 12

Sergio lifted his head up lazily and looked at the sun shining brightly through the floor length french windows of his bedroom. He lifted his hand to shield his eyes from the light, then let his head fall back, face first into the pillows. He was trying to will the sleep out of his body. He knew it was late in the afternoon and he had slept most of the day away. He rolled over on his back and stretched the long length of his well formed body on the bed. His back arching up high, to ease his muscles. Once he relaxed, he stared at the ceiling, letting his mind wonder. His hands resting lightly on his stomach, two fingers playing with the black curling hair trailing down his abdomen to his groin. He sat there, thinking about the night before and what he and Elise were going to talk about. He had to figure out a way to make her see him, she needed to be with her own kind. He did not like Darian, but he respected him for being honest. He knew right away from Darian's behavior that he never promised Elise the life she fantasized. He never claimed that he loved her. Sergio allowed himself to wonder just how good Darian was in bed to have a woman like Elise so enthralled with him. He thought it was safe to think that Elise was…*what do you say when a woman is "pussy whipped"? "Cock slapped", perhaps?*

He looked over at the clock, the time was 1:45pm. He composed himself then crawled out of the bed. He felt the urgency of his needs pressing him and made his way to the bathroom. Afterwards, he stood over the pedestal porcelain sink with the round porcelain ball handles and began to brush his teeth. He turned on the porcelain and gold handles in the shower to adjust the water temperature and forcefulness. He liked the water to hit him hard, it relaxed his muscles and felt like a massage. He prepared his towel for afterwards, and stepped inside the steamy shower and closed the door behind him. He let the hot water pour over his body as he lathered up his smooth olive colored skin. Once his hair and body were clean, he rinsed off all residue then stepping out of the shower, toweled off. He wrapped the towel around his narrow waist and walked towards his closet. He pushed clothes backwards and forwards on the rod, looking for something comfortable to wear. He would really have to go shopping soon, this was getting ridiculous

He found a pair of black denim jeans and a red v-neck t-shirt. He pulled it on and looked at himself in the mirror, he looked down and adjusted his crotch. He never wore underwear so he preferred to have himself tucked comfortably in the left pants leg. Many of the female leopards had chosen him when it became their time for mating to satisfy them when they were in heat. Not only was he well equipped, he knew how to brandish his sword. He wanted to show Elise more than anyone, that he could contend with the best of them, even Darian.

Once he approved himself, he walked across the black carpeted floor past his king size bed, through the double doors and into the active hallway. Two members of their pride were walking pass and talking about what movies they saw at the theater, what movie they were going to see at the theater or what movies that should not have ever made it to the theater. The hallway was brightly lit, crystal chandeliers hung from the ceiling, the floors had beige carpeting all the way down the stairs until you reach the main floor. The main floor was beige and white marble. The room was decorated with cream and tan wood trimmed french furniture.

Elise loved the craftsmanship of the French, seeing as she was french herself. She would go out of her way to find the most exquisite and rare pieces of furniture she could fine, the best money could buy. She would pay craftsmen to design chairs, sofas, lounges, armoires, ottomans, etc, just for her home. She was a fan of art and adored the french painter, *Monet*. Many of the walls were decorated with his paintings. She had marble statues decorating the hallways and main parlor. The pride enjoyed her famed sense of taste in both fashion and furnishings but sometimes, the more masculine of the pride, like Sergio, thought the house was just too feminine and needed to be toned down.

Elise would resent having to remove even the smallest bit of furniture to appease her other pride members but it was her duty. She was to keep the pride together and take care of them. So as it was, she had to make their living quarters bearable for all. Pity. Sergio once made her get rid of a pink fountain that she had installed in the main parlor. The fountain had several naked cherubs floating on clouds, they were surrounding and looking adoringly at a true-to-life replica of Elise herself carved out of alabaster. Sergio declared that it was over the top and in the way. She protested but then was finally out voted against by everyone in the pride. Thus, the fountain now adorned the garden patio.

He made his way to the kitchen, he was starving. Sleeping the day away did nothing for his appetite, it was raging. He peeked his head inside the den and said hello to pride members in the room. Some lay stretched out on the soft thick brown carpeted floor and divans as they watched tv, others wrestled with each other playfully or laid napping. He reached the kitchen and headed straight for the refrigerator. The kitchen was a state of the art masterpiece. Built in everything, from microwaves to the electric stove top, separate broiler, oven, and roaster. The Refrigerator itself was built into the walls and wooden cabinets surrounded the other three walls of the kitchen. Sergio opened the refrigerator and searched for something quick and good to eat. His eyes spotted the lunch meat, cheese, milk and fruit. He pulled it all out and began making himself two triple decker sandwiches stacked with several thick slices of chicken, turkey and beef lunchmeat. Three slices of cheese per sandwich. Lettice, tomatoes, onions, green peppers mustard and mayonnaise. He filled a twenty ounce glass with whole milk and grabbed a pear and apple from the package, and headed into the den to eat his meal.

As he entered the den, four pair of eyes looked up at him, two of them were silently begging for just a small taste. Sergio threw them a glance and sat down in the comfortable tan recliner and began eating his sandwiches. He began watching what was playing on the television. It was a rerun of the *Dave Lappelle Show* that someone had recorded. It was a new episode to him. He enjoyed the sketch comedy show, he liked the daring comedian who was the star of the show. Laughter erupted from everyone in the room as a sketch played out. Right away, he knew either Devin or Arianna, recorded this show. They loved watching the sketch comedies on the *Dave Lappelle show.*

"Can I have some?" Asked a greedy fifteen year old teenager of the pack. It was Sebastian, Sergio's son. He wasn't a full fledged leopard yet, he hadn't come of age, when he hit maturity he would experience his first change and then it would be complete. As it stood now, his senses were more acute than any human his age, his speed was faster but not abnormal, so was his strength. He stood at five feet four inches, fair of skin and freckles that sprinkled over his cheeks, arms and legs. He was wearing a pair of cut off shorts and a wrestling t-shirt featuring several of his favorite wrestlers. He brushed his dark red bangs away from his grey eyes as he focused on the sandwich as it went into Sergio's mouth.

"I was waiting for one of you cats to start begging for my food." Sergio chuckled. "No, no and no! No one can have a piece or just a little bite or a taste, none of that! If you are hungry, there's plenty left, make yourselves a sandwich just like this one." He said to the entire room in his thick Itallian accent, hoping he got the message across that he was far too hungry to share. There were a few disappointed looks from the potential beggars.

"Dang dad!" Sebastian exclaimed as he rose to make himself a sandwich. He knew his father was the dominate male in the pride but sometimes he thought he was too possessive, he could have given him a bite, *dang it*! Two more rose and walked out of the room, and they all returned ten minutes later with two huge sandwiches apiece. Sergio chuckled to himself. *It wasn't until someone else made something look good, then everyone would want a piece of it.*

He stood up from his chair and stretched again. It felt great to him to tense and relax his muscles. He felt like going for a run, he was thinking after his talk with Elise, he may do just that. He was dreading the talk he had to have with Elise. She had a way of toning out things she did not want to hear and making excuses for things she wanted to do or did to try to get people to see things her way. Well, he was not going to see things her way. Not about what he needed to discuss. He left the room and headed for her bedroom, He hoped she was still there.

He knocked on her bedroom door, he wondered if she was still asleep or just ignoring him. He knew she could smell his scent outside her door, because he could smell her. He wondered if she was still sulking about Darian's dismissal of her from the night before. He would be if it were him. He wanted her to understand that dismissal is something she would never get from him. He knocked harder and waited… no response.

"Elise let me in," he waited. Nothing. "Elise, I'm coming in." He said as he open the door and saw her laying on the bed, not even pretending to be asleep. He sat on the edge of the satin and lace covered bed. He looked down at her. He brushed the brown curls from her beautiful aqua-green eyes. It was as he hoped and feared, she was thinking about the dismissal, Darian had hurt her feelings and for that, he wanted to kill him, even if he was already dead.

"Elise please tell me you're not sitting up here in this room, sulking over him. Fuck him! Baby, that's why I'm here for you, always, always." He stroked her cheek softly with the back of his fingers. Her eyes settled on his but she did not move. He fought the urge to grab her and shake her. He wanted to slap her face to bring her out of this stupor, even if it meant getting the shit beat out of him afterwards. Elise was stronger than him physically, now he wanted her to be stronger than him in spirit. She was the Queen of the pride, her torch was a heavy load to carry.

"Elise, come run with me, right now. It would make you feel better, get your mind off of things you don't need to be worried about. Come on, I'm not opposed to pulling you out of this bed." He said as he stood up, holding her hand lightly in his. He looked down at her and smiled. "Come on," he urged. He tugged a little on her hand pulling it towards him, lifting her slightly from the bed. She groaned and tried to pull her hand free but his grip tightened and she did not fight when he reached down and scooped her into his arms effortlessly and plucked her out of the bed.

He looked into her eyes and smiled. His gaze lingered on the aqua green of her eyes then to her full shaped lips. He leaned forward and kissed the tip of her slender nose. His gaze then took in her complete form, he tried hard not to smile at her nakedness but failed. He couldn't help it, normally it did not bother him to look at the others naked but it was her he desired. *The things I would do to that flesh if she would only let me, would blow her mind,* he contemplated. He led her out of her soft satin, lacy bedroom, with the lace curtains, satin and lace bedspread and pink satin sheets, into the hall.

"I was going to go running alone to get some exercise but it'll be way more fun if we go together." He said as he led her to the back of the house. He opened the door to the huge piece of land that they owned. Elise had brought the mansion because of the many bedrooms but mainly because of the large private forest the mansion had. It made for great hunting never having to leave the grounds. They stepped outside, the cold freezing winds of the winter did not effect them, their bodies could acclimate to *almost* any climate. Sergio ran off first, giving Elise the temptation to chase him. It worked. The more she ran, the more she began to enjoy herself and grow into a more playful mood.

She caught up with him in a patch of bushes. She pounced on his back and they both tumbled to the grass. They rolled several times with Sergio ending up on top, just as he planned. His legs were tangled with hers, his elbows resting on the ground beside her head. He peered into her aqua-green eyes, he wanted to swim in the deep ocean of her eyes. The moment froze between them and their heads gravitated to one another and their lips met in a passionate kiss. Sergio's tongue entered her mouth and delicately brushed her tongue. This kiss lingered for a few moments and they ended it with two soft pecks.

Sergio rolled away from her and stood up. He grabbed the bottom of his shirt and slowly slid it over his head, making sure she could see the muscles of his torso flex with each movement. He pulled it off his head, tossing it aside. He looked down at her. She laid on her side, legs folded together bent slightly, ankles crossed, hands resting on the grass. She gazed at his body. She always loved his light olive complexion. She wanted to run her hands over the smoothness of his flesh, to feel the heat rise from it. She wondered what his body would feel like if they made love.

His fingers undid the buttons of his jeans. He rolled the zipper down slowly and parted the flaps to show a tuff of his dark curling pubic hair. He watched her expression as every piece of him was slowly revealed. He grabbed the waistband of his jeans and slowly slid them down to his feet. He pulled off his shoes and threw them aside. He stepped out of the jeans, picking them up, tossed them with his shirt and shoes. He stood before her completely naked, erect. His body temperature had risen and his skin had darkened with his lust. Her own body was reacting to him. Her nipples had harden, she felt a wetness between her legs that she knew he could smell. Her heart beat had become rapid. She crawled to all fours and began her change. She mentally prepared for the amount of pain the change always brings, the excruciating pain that was almost crippling.

Sergio dropped down beside her, and willed his change to take place. He growled low in his throat, feeling his body temperature rise to a fever pitch. Sweat poured from all his pores, the skin began to vibrate. He grimaced and looked at Elise who was almost through with her change. Her body was fully covered with black fur. Her nose had turned into a snout, her whiskers continued to grow to their full length of four inches. Her mouth filled with razor sharp teeth her canines two inches in length, and as sharp as daggers. She could change in an instant, it took him a few moments to complete his transformation. Black Fur began to sprout from pores all over his body, he could feel his inside churn and constrict, his intestines reformed themselves to mold with his new form. He could feel nothing but pain as his mouth and nose compressed together as fur covered his face, his teeth grew from his gums and became sharper and longer. He felt the bones break and muscles reform in an instant to accommodate his animal form. A long fur covered tail sprouted from his tail bone. His hands grew wider, fingers receding, turning into paws, his nails turned black then turned into thick strong three inch claws, that retracted into their sheaths. He could feel his whiskers grow five inches from his cheeks and eyebrows

When his change was complete, he shook himself all over, from head to tail. They both stood side by side, their sleek black bodies, touching, she was three and a half feet from the ground up, he was four feet in height, a full sixty pounds heavier than she was. Fully changed, they could weigh anywhere from two hundred pounds to three hundred pounds. In rare cases, they could weigh about four hundred pounds, Elise walked up to him and licked the side of his muzzle. He returned her love by brushing his body alongside hers and rubbing his head down her neck. She growled low into his ear and licked the inner shell. His head tilted towards her and he groaned softly. He pulled away from her and ran off after a white rabbit. The change had taken a lot of energy and he was hungry again. The rabbit ran as fast as it could but Sergio closed in on the hare and caught it by the back of it's neck. He shook it twice in his powerful grip, breaking the bones of it's neck. The feet jerked three times, before going limp in his mouth.

He walked back to Elise he knew she was hungry as well, he dropped the dead rabbit at her feet, and licked her muzzle, one side then the other. She leaned towards the dead rabbit and sniffed it. She pawed it and held it to the ground. She began to bite into the rabbits furry back, ripping at the flesh, tearing it from the bone. Blood spurted from the wound as she ripped the flesh, swallowing it in one gulp. Sergio walked off to find a meal for himself as Elise ate the rabbit. He caught another rabbit and brought it over to Elise and began eating it as she finished her meal. When she finished with the rabbit, she snatched the remains of his from his grip and ran off to eat the rest. He chased her, he saw her ripping at the flesh. He walked behind her and stuck his nose into her crotch. She batted him with her paw, hooking her hands in his head and dragging him to the ground. They wrestled and rolled around on the ground. He stood up first, grabbed his rabbit and ran off to eat the rest. Elise let him eat in peace.

He finished the rabbit off and walked back to Elise. He stuck his nose back to her crotch. He could tell she was coming into heat. In the past, she would not give herself to him for mating. She would allow him to grind against her as his fingers played with her but it never went past making out. He wanted so much more. He licked her crotch and sniffed again. She pawed his head away and laid on her side on the grass. He walked around her one time then laid next to her, resting his head on her ribcage. They drifted off to sleep under the late afternoon sun. three hours past before they woke up.

Sergio awoke first and raised his head and licked Elise's muzzle several times, cleaning the blood away from her face. He stood up and stretched his huge feline body, arching his back completely. He would love to go hunting now that the sun was down but he wasn't hungry. He really wanted to talk to Elise, he had postponed the talk earlier because she was upset but he did not forget that he wanted to have it. He willed himself back into human form.

The processed reversed was much faster but not less painful. Elise saw that he changed back and she followed suit. They sat on the grass, both panting and sweating. He spoke first when he was more composed.

"Elise, this pride, it needs a protector. It needs it's king, and you, you need a mate." He leaned closer to her, their cheeks brushing. He rubbed his cheek against hers. His hands encircled her waist, pulling her closer to him. A low growl vibrated from his throat. "Can't you see…look at me." He pulled away and took her chin into his hand guiding her face to his. His eyes stared deeply into hers. "Look at me." He whispered sensually. She looked into his beautiful grey eyes. She raised her hand and ran her fingers lightly through his black silky curls. Her fingertip trailed over his muscular jaw line. She was looking at him in a different way, in a way she never allowed herself before.

"I am your mate Elise. Don't push me away, don't deny us. Together we could care for this pride. I have fought to maintain my presence, I am the most dominate male, is it my duty to protect the pride. It is my honor! Elise, the pride should not be only yours to deal with. I love you, Elise…look at me." He forced her eyes to focus on him once more. She had looked away, trying to hide from his words. "I am all the man, the only man, that you will *ever* need." He let her go and looked at her. He wondered what she was thinking. She sat there quietly for a long time. He watched her, never moving.

"It is true, the pride needs it's protector, more than what I can provide. When Adam died, I became the sole care taker of the pride. I did not want to share that power. In a way, I still don't but I know my limitations, they are few but I know them. I will name you my King and pride protector. You will be honored as such." She said as she rose to her feet brushing the grass off of her legs. He looked up at her, she was forgetting something.

"And what about us Elise?" He asked.

"There is no us. You are our protector, our king and nothing more." She said harshly. She wanted to embrace the anger, she did not want to share her power with anyone. She controlled the pride but she thought of the benefits. If she gave some of the power of the pride to Sergio, it would allow her more time to be with Darian. There was always two sides to every coin. She looked at Sergio, she knew she did not say what he wanted to hear. She felt that he could not compete with Darian. She could not remember any man in her past who could.

"Have you listen to anything I've just said?" Sergio asked, obviously holding in his anger and frustration. He slowly lifted his head to look at her.

"I heard what you said. I felt your seduction but you can not compete with him, we are lovers and you have to accept that." She said matter of factly.

Sergio looked at her, his face twisted with rage. He laughed in a harsh sound. He shook his head.

"Unbelievable, un-fucking-believable. How can you be so beautiful, yet so…" his voice trailed off, he did not want to say anything he would regret. He stood up and looked at her. He could show her better than he could tell her, if need be. He wanted to pump the poison from her veins. The poison being her lust for Darian. He grabbed her by the back of her head with a speed no mortal could have seen and planted a kiss on her lips, forcefully, passionately. He radiated desire and heat. His other hand wrapped around her waist pulling her closer to him, pressing her body against his, their hearts beating fanatically in their chests. His tongue exploring the heat of her mouth, his lips working expertly over hers. He could fill her knees go weak, and he held her still.

He pulled away, her eye's opened slowly, lips still slightly parted. His gaze never left her face. He peered into her eyes, unafraid, unashamed. He would show her what she was missing if he had to. He leaned down to her ear, his tongue darting out to lick along the inner shell of her ear sending tingles down her spine. Her knees buckled and he held her still. His lips sought her lobe and sucked gently as his tongue licked along the rim of her lobe. A small whimper escaped her lips.

"I can make you tremble anytime I want. All I have to do is kiss you…" He leaned towards her lips and brushed his lips against hers in a soft kiss. "Lick you…" The tip of his tongue darted out and licked her bottom lip lightly. "Touch you." He whispered seductively, his thick Italian accent sent the words rolling over the surface of her skin bringing up goosebumps. His hands slid further down past her buttock, between her legs. His fingers explored the soft wetness there, causing her to gasp in pleasure. After he achieved his goal, he let her go, she stumbled but did not fall. She looked at him lustfully, yet confused. He brought his fingers to his nose and inhaled her scent, his eyes closed savoring her scent, his tongue snaked from between his lips to lick away the sticky wetness. He opened his eyes and looked at her.

"Delicious." He whispered sensuously as he turned and walked back towards the house. He turned before reaching the back door. "I suppose we should tell them about my becoming king so that we can plan the celebration." He was watching her from across the courtyard. She gathered herself, she had to take in what just happened. Her mind raced with random thoughts about Darian, her and Sergio. She walked back towards the house.

Both entered and she told Marianne to gather everyone for a big announcement. Marianne did as she was told and in moments, everyone, all twelve leopards sat in the parlor. She had fetched her bathrobe and put it on. Sergio stood before the others still naked. His nakedness distracted her. She wanted to tell him to put some clothes on but nakedness was not a taboo among shifters. They saw each other naked all the time. To ask someone to put on some clothes would have seem rude and demeaning.

"I've gathered you all here to tell you great news." She paused for dramatics. Everyone watched her and waited for the news. "I have picked our King, our protector, Sergio." Everyone applauded. The pride was made up of four males and eight adult females.

"It's about time," said Devin and he walked up to Sergio to congratulate him. "Does this mean you have picked Sergio as you mate Elise?!" Devin asked excitedly. Everyone was hoping for a positive answer. No one approved of her sleeping with a vampire, and on his terms, they wanted her to keep a mate within the pride, being as she was the queen of the pride.

"No, he is not my mate but he is our King. You will treat him as such. Prepare for tonight's celebration." She said as she turned to leave, not wanting to see the truth of their eyes. Sergio watched her walk away, he had lost the battle, but not the war. He turned to face those who were still congratulating him. He winked at Devin. He thought about turning up the heat on Elise. *Round one goes to Elise, let's see where round two ends up.*

Chapter 13

Xavier's eyes open suddenly in the pitch black darkness of the room. He blinked once, then twice as he gathered his senses. He focused on the crystal chandelier hanging over the king size bed. He turned his head to the right to see that Darian was still being lazy and lingering in the bed with his eyes closed. He rolled onto his side facing Darian and poked him in his arm.

"Get up, I know you're not sleep. It's way past sunset." He said teasingly. Darian smiled, then chuckled. He looked at Xavier and his hand came up to lightly stroke the side of his cheek, caressing the soft skin with his fingertips.

"Aren't I allowed to daydream?" He asked, eyebrows slightly raised.

"What were you daydreaming about if I may be so bold as to ask?" Xavier said as he propped himself on his right elbow. Darian turned his eyes towards the ceiling.

"I was thinking of repainting this room. It's been this design for ten years, I need a change. You know how I am about redecorating. I was thinking of adding a forty-eight inch screen tv, there." He pointed to a wall in front of the bed that held a painting of the Chicago Fire. "I want to have it constructed so that the TV will be built into the wall and the wall would slide back to reveal the tv when we wanted to watch it." He glanced at Xavier for a response. Xavier sat, dumbfounded. For a moment, he thought when he asked the question, Darian would tell him some profound statement of enlightenment or something along those lines. But there he was, talking about redecorating their bedroom.

"I think that would be nice, after we make love, I could turn on the sports channel for the climax." He teased jokingly as he crawled out of the bed. Darian gave him a sly look.

"Very funny, after we make love, you won't be able to do anything but close your eyes and drift off to sleep, having sweet dreams about me, my little audacious *inamorato*." He turned to stare at the wall again. "So I take it that you like my ideas. I think I'll call a contractor, and have him come over right away." Darian said. He folded his arms behind his head, showing off his strong biceps and triceps. He rested his head on his arms and turn to watched Xavier walking towards the bathroom. One minute later, he heard the shower running.

"Are you going to the club tonight?" Asked Darian.

"Yes, but first, I'm going to the hospital." Replied Xavier as he climbed into the shower.

"Why?" Darian asked, as he sat up in the bed.

"Well, Annette, our new day manager was injured last night. Some of our human people saw her get into a cab with a friend of hers and they saw a car rear end their cab. They said that ambulances took Annette and her friend away. The drivers of the cab and car did not survive. Seeing as the cab collided into a tree after being rear ended, I'm surprised they're not dead as well." He said as he lathered his body all over, massaging the foaming suds into his skin for fragrance.

"Mortals are so fragile." Darian said lazily as he laid back on the bed and looked at his hands as he held them in front of him. "I could crush one in my hands as easily as one would squeeze a marshmallow." He climbed out of the bed and walked into the bathroom, gazing lustfully at Xavier's soapy body. He had intentions of caressing that body later on that night. He would have done it then but he did not want him to miss the hospital visiting hours.

"Well, if you're gong to visit our dear Annette, give her my love and regards. It is quite a shame that we could not make our rendevous tonight. Give her my well wishes for a speedy recovery. Inform her that we will have a temporary replacement for her until she can return of corse. Also, give her a bouquet of flowers to express my heartfelt sincerity at the thought of missing our date." Darian said as he leaned against the doorframe. His powerful pale arms crossed over his broad pale chest.

"I take it she was going to be apart of this threesome you wanted tonight, am I right?" Xavier asked as he rinsed off his body.

Darian nodded. "Of course. I wanted to taste her last night before I was so untimely interrupted." He said sarcastically. Then turned and made his way back to the bedroom. "I need to feed. I think I'll go hunting tonight. To bad you'll be too busy cheering up hospital folks to join me. Maybe next time." He chuckled suavely. Xavier emerged from the bathroom, a pale blue

111

towel wrapped around his pale waist. He felt the pangs of his hunger gnawing at his stomach. His entire body thirsted. He could not deny himself blood, not even for one night. He was still too young to play the starvation game. Old ones, like Darian, could go at least five nights in a row, until the need forced them to feed the hunger. He went to his closet and searched his bounty of clothes for a nice sleek ensemble.

He settled for a hunter green ribbed turtle neck sweater, black boot cut denim jeans, which where his favorite style of jeans. He loved the way the boot cut denim elongated his already impressive leg height and he favored the way the cut embraced his buttocks. He put on the outfit and pulled on a pair of black steal toe boots, he laced them up as he sat in a straight back black soft leather chair beside the bed. Darian watched him dress. He admired the way Xavier looked in those style of jeans. He delighted in watching him walk away, looking at his buttocks moved from right to left with each step.

Darian thought that Xavier had the body of an adonis. Smooth, strong, slim and muscular, his manhood was impressive enough but it was the total package that caught Darian's eye. Xavier was beautiful and beauty should last forever. Darian wasted little time bringing Xavier over to him, the night he found him laying on the ground, dying. He had been shot and left for dead by one of Al Cantone's goons. Xavier had been trying to get into the closed-nit gang for years. But all he had become was an errand boy, then target practice over some numbers that had gotten misplaced.

Darian remembered vividly as he walked up to the prone bleeding body of Xavier's and kneeled over him. He looked into that beautiful face, grey eyes stared back at him, pleading for help. Full sensuous lips parted to beg for him to save his life. Darian had been without a companion for two hundred years and he felt it would be nice to have one as beautiful as Xavier by his side, under his wing. He had lifted Xavier's head off of the cold wet ground. He pulled back the high collar on Xavier's brown jacket to reveal the slow pulsing vein. Without hesitation, he bent closer and buried his face into the crook of Xavier's neck and pierced his skin, fangs entering the vein causing the other man to gasp, hands out to grip Darian's forearms. He began to drink the blood slowly from Xavier, he drank enough to bring him to the point of death so that he could be reborn. He withdrew his fangs and looked into the face of the young man. Xaviers' eyes were half closed, only a hint of whiteness showed underneath the pale lids. Darian had sank his fanged teeth into the blue artery in his own wrist and lowering his wrist to Xavier's open mouth, he whispered this one phrase: "Drink from me and you shall live forever and ever, my beautiful one."

Xavier had no idea what he meant but he was willing to try anything at that point in time. He opened his mouth and Darian lifted his head, Xavier pressed his cold bluish lips to the hot bleeding wound and he began to suck gently. At first, the shock was settling in his mind that he was drinking blood from a man's wrist. Then all that seemed to fade away as the delicious flavor and sensation filled his body, reinventing all that was dying away. His body tingled with wondrous, orgasmic feelings he received with each swallow he took. His limbs regain strength and his hands reached for Darian's wrist. He held the bleeding wound to his mouth with all the strength he had and all that he was gaining. He sucked harder, his breath coming faster and faster as the blood traveled from Darian's veins to his stomach. His eyes were closed and he saw tiny colored spots dancing in the darkness. Low moans escaped them as both men seemed to swoon. Darian was grunting and panting as he fed Xavier, he could feel his own life draining through his veins, leaving him feeling cold, weak, lightheaded and sick.

He had pulled away, snatching his wrist from Xavier's hungry bloody mouth. He had fallen back against the cobblestone street holding his wrist. He looked at his wrist and bit his tongue he could taste his own delicious blood in his mouth. He ran the tip of his tongue over the open wound, sealing it instantly. The skin healing until no mark were visible. Xavier had sat up, eyes glazed over, glossy. His tongue ran along his lips smoothly, licking away all the spilt blood. A tremor ran through his body, he closed his eyes savoring the last drop. Then he opened them, he looked at Darian. His sight had changed, it had become sharper, he could see his master's features clearer. Instantly, he felt a connection to Darian, a mental and physical one. He knew then that he would never lust after the power of Al Cantone. He had found a higher power. A more promising one.

Darian had held his hand out to Xavier, who took it and secretly vowed, to never let Darian go. That had been over seventy years ago. This was not the longest relationship that Darian ever had but it was his most precious one. Xavier did not try to control him or change him. He understood him, better than any of his other offspring. He understood and accepted Darian's jaded personality. He knew that he had been alive a long time and probably seen dynasties rise and fall and that very little surprised him. He also knew that Darian would never be monogamous. Xavier understood that, he would never ask that of him. Darian was a free spirit, a lover of both men and women. He could not be contained. Xavier enjoyed the nights they spent together but he also learned to enjoy the nights they spent sharing their bed with others.

"I'll see you later. I haven't' forgot what we 'discussed' yesterday, when you left me…compromised." Xavier said as he pulled on his soft, dark-brown leather bomber jacket. His voice brought Darian out of his reverie, and he smiled, nodding.

"I'll be at the club, tonight is the second night of the tournament. Speaking of the tournament, thanks to you, I lost one million dollars!?" Darian said playfully, but slightly disappointed.

"Me!? Well you're the man who can see them coming! Wow, you lost a bet. Oh my!" Xavier said as he placed his hand over his heart and pretended to stumble towards the door. Darian laughed as he clapped his hands.

"Yes-me, I did not see last nights match coming. Last night was full of surprises. But you better leave now if you want to make it to the hospital in time. I'll see you tonight," he said then he sprawled on the bed and gave Xavier a most seductive look. Forest green eye's glazing over, hand pressed to the satin sheets in front of him. "Try not to keep me waiting too long." He whispered seductively. That voice made Xavier want to forget about the hospital and just climb back into the bed, shedding his clothes along the way. He knew he had better leave now or he never would. He nodded his head and quickly turned and left the room.

He ran into a fledgling that lived with them. Darian had about seven vampires living with him. He did not mind a coven, he swore protection to all vampires in his territory that asked for it, so if it meant some felt safer under his roof, he allowed them shelter. As long as they obeyed his rules of course. His rules varied slightly from those he had for his city territory in general. No killing on his territory of any mortal without his permission, was rule number one. If this rule was broken, on one of Darian's good nights, he would cast you out of the city. On a bad night, he would cast you out of existence.

Rule number two was to respect what was his. Darian had plenty of expensive artwork, sculptures and furniture all around the house and at no point did he ever want to see any of his belongings damaged or ruined. Braking rule number two would most definitely get you kicked out the house. But at least you get to stay in the city. Rule number three, was no stealing. If found breaking this rule, it would mean death to the perpetrator. Other than that, the house was laid back and entertaining. Darian hated only one thing, being bored. So he found plenty forms of entertainment in the mortal world. He enjoyed their entertainment and technology. He'd decked his house in both forms and every time something was created or updated, he would go out of his way to obtain it. Money was never an object when it came to Darian getting what he wanted.

Xavier looked at the fledgling who was obviously running late for work. He was new to the city, Tony's lover and fledgling of three months. He stripped at the club. If you were going to beg upon Darian's good nature, he required absolute gratitude for his service bestowed. For all vampires that had come to him for protection, even those that did not live with him, he put them to work at his hot night time club *Desires Unleashed*. They tended bar, mesmerized foolish mortals that wanted to come get a closer look at the *sharks*. Stripped or provided sexual pleasure in his bordello. There was only one section of the club that vampires hated and that was the "Colosseum". They did not hate it because of the violence and blood. They were leery because for those vampires who broke Darian's rules, he would pit them against each other in the tournament. Who ever won, would be allowed to leave his city with their life. It would prove his point to other would-be rule-breakers as well as bringing him double the money than normal tournaments. For Darian, it was a win/win situation.

"You're running late I see. Since you're already late, come here." Xavier gestured for the young vampire to walk towards him. Gary walked towards him. His long shoulder length blonde hair bounced with each step. His blue eyes brightened the closer he came. He knew that Xavier was Darian's lover and right hand man. He hoped that Xavier wanted to have sex, he had had a thing for Xavier the moment he saw him in Darian's office when he came to ask for protection. Well to tell the truth he had a thing for both Darian and Xavier. His tight leather pants did not allow enough room for a full stride. Xavier smiled as he came closer, he looked through the see-through shirt displaying his erect nipples. He knew Gary's attraction for him. Tonight he would kill two birds with one stone. He would feed that attraction and his hunger simultaneously.

When the young blonde reached him, he braced his hands on the vampire's shoulders holding him firmly in his grip. He leaned closer and brushed his lips softly over Gary's. He let Gary lean into him, setting his weight on his chest. Xavier's right hand came to Gary's chin and turned his head to the side to reveal the pulsating vein in his neck. Xavier leaned forward, tilting his head, feeling his fangs extending, he placed his mouth over the vein and sank his teeth through the warm tender flesh. He heard Gary gasp and felt his grip tighten around his waist. He closed his mouth over the hot blood flowing out of the wounds. He began to suck the delicious blood from Gary's veins.

Gary began to moan loudly, his grip becoming weaker, his body trembling with ecstacy. His orgasm began to build deep within him. He felt it gather itself up from the base of his feet as Xavier continued to feed. He felt it grow, becoming more powerful. Xavier's mouth open wider against the flesh, a hoarse moan escaped Gary's lips as his whole body exploded with pleasure, the indescribable kind. Xavier's moan was muffled against the skin of Gary's neck as they shared the dry orgasm. Both of their bodies shook with the climax that always followed the sharing of blood between supernaturals. It was highly pleasurable to share blood with a mortal, but never climatic, a mortal could never survive long enough to bring a vampire to climax on blood alone. Which is why most mortals were bitten during the height of sexual gratifications so that the climax would be more intense for both mortal and vampire. Xavier released Gary's vein, retracting his teeth. He licked his lips catching the blood that spilt while he feasted. He gazed into Gary's eyes. They were glazed over, the look of an addict who just got the hit of a life time.

He steadied Gary. "Are you ok, can you stand?" He asked. Gary mouth moved but no sound came out. So he just nodded his head weakly. Xavier chuckled and let him go. "Good, take the night off, get some thing to eat and rest, I'll find your replacement." He said as he walked to the door. He walked to the garage and opened the door. The garage was packed wall to wall with sport cars, luxury sedans, huge towering trucks and SUVs. Xavier set his sights on a silver, sleek two-door 2004 Boa 300s Series. He went to the key locker and pulled out the correct key and climbed into the comfortable black leather interior of the car. He put the keys into the ignition and smiled as he heard the soft purr of the engine. The dashboard navigation panel lit up the multicolored buttons and knobs.

"Almost as good as any woman." He commented as he put the car into gear and drove out of the garage down the curving driveway. He hit the side street, and took quick peeks at the various mansions on the block, only a few acres of land separating each mansion. He was glad to be living the high life with Darian. He never wanted it to end. He drove to the highway, entering the I-55 then the I-90 to the hospital where Annette was staying. He saw the tall white five story building, as wide as two city blocks. He pulled into the parking lot for visitors only. Unfolding his tall frame, he expelled himself from the tiny sports car and adjusted his clothing, he walked towards the main desk. The woman behind the main desk looked up as she heard the little bell chimed as Xavier walked through the automatic sliding doors carrying a bouquet of pink lilies . Her smiled brighten when she saw the devastatingly handsome man walking closer to her. She fiddled with the collar of her dress but did not want her primping to be too obvious.

"Can I help you sir?" She asked, letting her eyes do her flirting for her as she batted them in his direction.

"Ah yes, I'm here to visit a friend who is a patient of yours, one Miss Annette Balfour. Can you tell me which room she's in." He flashed her his most charming smile and her face reddened. She instantly wished the gorgeous flowers in the crystal glass vase were for *her* and he was her knight in shining armor coming to swept her off her sore feet and carry her out of her grueling rat race. She cast aside the thought, chiding herself for her foolish fantasy and pulled the room number by looking up the last name in the directory. She turned to look at him again and smiled.

"She is in room 314 sir. Is there anything else...I can do?" She asked imploringly. He lowered his head and looked up at her bashfully.

"I think that's all I'll need...for now." He said and gave her a devilish grin as he walked towards the elevators. He stepped in, and watched as the metal doors close in front of him. He pressed the number three button and waited patiently for the ride to end. At the sound of a tiny bell the doors opened, indicating that he was on the third level. He walked off, using the room number signs to navigate. He found room 314 and knocked politely on the door. He waited till he heard a soft female voice bid him entrance. He opened the door and entered the room, with the flowers out before him. He saw Annette's face brighten as her eyes peered into his face. She recognized him as one of her bosses. She thought it was sweet that he would visit her in the hospital and bring her flowers. She had already been visited by her mother and father, they fawned over her until she told them to go home. And two of her co workers had come baring outside food, which she was grateful for. She was worried about Natasha though, she had not seen her friend *all day* and wondered how serious her injuries had been.

But now as she smiled at Xavier she would talk to him. She immediately remembered the date she had made with Darian. She regretted laying up in a hospital bed. She knew by the way that man kissed that he could no doubt take her to paradise and back for a return visit. He made her feel like a school girl with her first crush. She looked at Xavier and wondered if Darian knew she was in the hospital. She hoped he knew she did not stand him up, would never stand *him* up. Xavier sat the glass vase full of flowers on the table right next to her bed. Annette leaned over to take a deep whiff of the fragrant flowers. She smiled.

"These are from Darian, he regrets that he can not be here with you right now to help ease your suffering. He wanted to wish you a speedy recovery." Xavier said in his deep smooth voice. Annette thought his voice was extremely sexy, it flowed over her body like cascading water. She wondered if it was just how older vampires talked or was it a skill, some kind of trickery that they learned to seduce mortals. Either way, she wasn't one to ruin the moment.

"I have to remember to thank him when I see him next time. They're lovely. Lilies are my favorite, how did he know?" She asked, she sat up in the bed, not wanting to slouch in front of such a beautiful man. She hated that her arm was in a cast. Two of her ribs had been bruised and she had numerous cuts and bruises all over her torso and face. She wished she did not look so beat up at this moment. She always wanted to look her best in front a pretty piece of man-flesh. But now, in her opinion, she looked like the missing link. *Life just wasn't fucking fair.* First she damn near gets killed in a car accident along with her friend. Then she misses out on fucking the hottest man walking the earth and now here she had the second hottest man in her hospital room. *Here I am, wearing an ugly hospital gown, with the ass out, to allow for easy entry. But no, I have to be in too much pain to get frisky, life really sucks right now.* She thought to herself.

Xavier had been watching her facial expressions, he wanted to laugh, it did not take a mind reader to know what was on her mind. *She wanted to fuck him, probably fuck both himself and Darian and probably at the same time. She would have gotten her wish. Funny how things work out,* Xavier thought, as he settled in a chair next to her bed. He crossed one leg over the other, arms raised behind him, his fingers locked together, to support the weight of his head.

"Do you know how happy I am to be alive right now!" She exclaimed, trying to spark up conversation. Trying to keep her mind off of sex.

"I do, I know what is it like to have a second chance." He said calmly, he knew from experience. Annette looked at him, she wondered just how old he really was. He looked composed, not like some of the vampires she worked with but not quite like Darian either. She wondered how old he was too. The fact that they lived forever really amazed her. Sometimes she would look at one of the young vampires she worked with and become envious. They would still be here, beautiful, young, when she would not. She would be dust in the ground, forever forgotten.

"You sound like you're talking from experience," Annette said. He smiled and nodded.

"I was dying when my master made me a vampire." He said, not offering anymore information.

"I hope I'm not prying but who's your maker…master…er…whatever.." she trailed off. Xavier chuckled. He thought she must be very nervous. He had hired her but they did not keep personal acquaintances. This was the most personal they had been since the day of her interview. He pulled his hands from behind his head and leaned forward, staring into her brown eyes. She began to become even more nervous. The look on his face suggested things. Things like sex but more so lust or hunger. She wasn't sure she liked being looked at like that. If he was a mortal man, the meaning would be different...or would it? Xavier knew he was unnerving her and decided to call off the dogs. He sat back in his chair and stretched his long legs out before him. He looked at her again and smiled.

"Darian's quite the number, isn't he. You know he fucks both men and women?" He said, watching her expressions closely. He enjoyed shock value most of all. He liked surprising and unnerving mortals. Especially the ones that would come into the club looking for a little excitement, entertainment that only a vampire can give them.

"I had heard a few rumors. Nothing concrete or anything like that." She said carefully. Ok now she was nervous. He had successfully made her nervous. She thought about pushing the panic button for the nurse. And have him ushered out of there. She might have if she thought it would help. She knew vampires could hypnotize mortals.

"I'm not trying to scare you," he lied.

"You're not scaring me," she lied

"I just wanted to know if you knew this. He probably wanted to add you in a threesome" He made an offhand gesture. "That's in the past. He really wanted me to tell you that he was going to have a temporary replacement for you for daytime assistant manager. That is, until you feel strong enough to come back to work." He said as he sat up straight in the chair as if he was preparing to leave. Annette was slightly confused, she had mixed feelings about Xavier. She did not know if she wanted to have sex with him or run. If it weren't for the fact that he could snuff out her life in a blink of an eye, her decision would be easier. She looked at his gorgeous face again. She thought about it. She came to the conclusion, she wanted to get into his pants.

"Thank you, both of you, I was really excited about the promotion and now this. I appreciate you holding the job for me, I really do." She said honestly. She just knew she would have to go back to stripping after the accident. Not that there was anything terribly wrong about stripping, that section of the club made some nice money and had nice tippers. But the A.M. position paid double what she could make on salary and was less work. They both looked at each other for a moment. Xavier saw the beauty in her that

Darian did, he knew why Darian wanted to have sex with her. Looking at her now, he wondered if Darian would have shared her.

~****~

Natasha woke up in her hospital room and noticed the tv was on, her room mate seemed to be enjoying a sitcom she did not recognize. She wiped her eyes and tried to take in her surroundings. She noticed two chairs in the room, she knew where the bathroom was. She sat up and looked at the clock. The time was 7:30pm. She had only gotten about five hours sleep sense the last time she was awake. Her parents had come barging into the room, so happy to hear their baby girl was alive and well. They had stayed and talked to her and listen patiently while their daughter talked about her new job and the night club she went to the night before. Even though she was happy her parents had visited her, she was glad when they left. She wanted to be able to get some sleep. Whatever drug they had given her to dull the pain was knocking her out. When she woke up for the second time, she was surprised how fast time went by. She was happy she did not feel wiped out like she did earlier. She climbed out of her bed and could feel the stiffness in her muscles but it was not as bad as it was before. She grabbed a hold of her IV stand with bag and made her way to the little bathroom.

After she finished her daily needs, she washed her hands and found the tooth brush, proceeding to brush her teeth. She could not stand having a mucky mouth. She looked at her hair in the mirror, it was a mess. Her curling locks were tangled and matted sitting on the top of her head. Her face was bruised on her left cheek and she had two bandages covering up two stinging wounds on the right and left side of her forehead. Her eyes had dark circles under them. For better choice of words, she looked positively dreadful, like death warmed over.

"Damn girl! Look at you! The 'undead' ain't got nothing on you." She said jokingly to her reflection. She turned off the bathroom light as she walked out of the little room. She was picking up the telephone to call the front desk to ask for her friends room number when she heard the news reporter talking about the deadly crash that took place last night on the corner of Roosevelt and Clark that ended with the deaths of both drivers and the hospitalization of two passengers. The reporter was saying that the doctors said that both passengers were in healthy and stable condition, with only minor injuries. The doctor stated that the one passenger did withstand a broken arm. The camera flipped back to the pretty blonde anchorwoman who mentioned the fact that the driver of the car that caused the accident, was driving on a suspended license and DUI, with an alcohol level high above legally drunk. Well, Natasha thought, that answered her question about what happened to the two drivers. It also made her sad. But she was even more relieved that her friend was truly ok. She picked up the handset and dialed '0' for the operator. She heard the phone ring twice and a female voice answered on the other end.

"Operator, how may I help you?" The soft friendly voice asked.

"Hello, I'm a patient here in the hospital and I would like the room number of my friend Annette Balfour. We came in together last night." She said and then waited for the nurse to look up the name.

"She is in room 314." The nurse said

"Thank you." Natasha said as she hung up the telephone. She grabbed her IV bag with traveling pole and walked out of her room. Her left hand held the back of her gown closed. She hated these hospital gowns. She was going to ask for a second gown to use as a robe, when she got back to her room. She walked down the hallway, grateful that she did not have to do that much traveling. She stood in front of the door, and knocked.

"Who is it?" Annette asked.

"Girl its me, Natasha!" She said through the other side of the thick door. "Damn, can I come in?" She asked slightly annoyed. She heard Annette bid her to enter. She turn the nob and walked into the room. She first noticed a gorgeously handsome man rise to his full height of six-feet-two inches as she entered the room. He stepped aside to offer her the chair. But she waved her hand nonchalantly . If this was one of Annette boyfriends, she did not want to intrude. She just wanted to check in on her, but it was quite obvious that Annette was alive and well. She looked at the man again and was taken aback by his beauty. She had seen beautiful men before, but normally in a magazine or on a TV screen. He looked like a model, his clothes fit him like a model's, better than a model! He still continued to stand in the room, not wanting to sit, if Natasha did not. He was so charming to her as he smiled at her politely. His smile could brighten a room. It most certainly did brighten this one. She stared into his soft grey eyes, they were watching her with a keen interest.

"I don't want to intrude." Natasha said. "I just wanted to make sure that you were ok. Are you? I mean, I see you're as much of a mess as I am, but I just wanted to check in on you." Natasha walked closer to the bed, she gripped the back opening of her gown tightly, not wanting to give Xavier a peek. She gave her friend a soft embrace. Her body was still sore, but not nearly as much as before. The two women hugged each other lightly.

"Oh my god, we are so blessed to be alive. Annette I saw on the news that the driver of the car and the cab driver died in the crash, instantly!" Natasha said obviously still in shock. Annette nodded her head, she had heard the unfortunate news. Her mother had brought a newspaper in when she came to visit as proof of how God had blessed her and her friend.

"Yes I know, I read about it earlier. The newspaper article said that we were both unconscious when medical help arrived. Considering what happened, we're lucky. I thought we'd be in worse shape since we were in the back seat." She said, analyzing the situation. Natasha nodded her head,

"There's no doubt about it." She said softly, distractedly, her gaze slowly moved towards Xavier. He stood there quietly, letting the two women reunite after their ordeal. He watched them praise God for their lives. He never thanked God for anything, he thought perhaps he could thank him for bringing him Darian but considering the nature of their existence, he thought it might be sacrilegious in some manner of speaking. Annette caught the wondering eyes of Natasha then remembered she had long forgotten her manners and introduced Xavier.

"Natasha, this is Xavier Richards, Xavier this is my best friend Natasha Hemingway." She said, she struggled to sit up in the little narrow bed, Xavier reached over, and helped prop her up comfortably without any effort at all. He smiled at Annette then turned his head towards Natasha. He walked over to her taking two manly strides and held his hand out. She smiled and put her hand in his thinking they were going the shake hands. Instead, Xavier bent forward and pressed the warm softness of his full lips onto the back of the tender flesh of her hand. His grey eyes never leaving hers as he poured on the charm.

"Charmed." He said as he erected himself. Natasha heart raced a few beats when he kissed her hand. She had never even been this up close and personal with a man this beautiful. She did not want to blush, but she still felt the blood rushing to her face, reddening her cheeks. She wanted to place her hand daintily on her chest and batt her eyes at him. She wanted to flirt insanely. She looked at Annette questioningly, she wondered if he was a boyfriend of hers that she never new about, if so, Annette had some explaining to do, girl talk. What was he like in bed, how big is it, the usual. She searched her mind for the right words to ask such a delicate question. She did not want to come on too strong if this beautiful man *was* Annette's boyfriend.

"So," she started, looking from Xavier to Annette. "Are you two together?" She asked, hoping it was subtle enough, not too embarrassing.

Annette laughed softly. "No, no we're not, Xavier here is my boss. Well, he's like the second in command at *Desires Unleashed*." Annette said. Xavier glanced at Annette and smiled. Then his eyes returned to Natasha. He felt sorry for the fact that they were both injured so badly . He could still see their beauty underneath all of the bandages and bruises. As he looked at Natasha, he peered into her mind. He wanted to find out about her, he wanted to use that information to seduce her. He was immediately intrigued the moment he laid eyes on her. He wanted to take her into his embrace, gaze into her eyes and make her moan in pleasure, absolute pleasure.

When Annette said that Xavier was her boss at the club where she worked, that instantly set off warning sirens in Natasha's mind. The fact that he was her boss let Natasha know that he was a vampire, or at least not human. She had never been eye to eye with a vampire before, at least not one that she *knew* was a vampire. All of a sudden she began to panic. Her heart raced, but in a different sort of pattern. She had the urge to run back to her room and lock the door. She set nervous eyes on Annette who did not seemed to be scared at all. This beautiful man standing here, was more deadlier than anything Natasha had ever known or seen. *He was a killing machine, like any predator in the wild. He hunted his prey then ate them alive.* She felt herself backing away. Now was the best time to leave. She felt that if *Annette wasn't worried about the boogy man, then she was on her own.*

"Well Annette, I'm going back to my room now, I'll see you later." She said in a rush, as she turned to leave.

"Wait." Said a rich, mellow, sexy voice. It stopped Natasha dead in her tracks. Xavier walked up beside her. He took her hand into his, he had spied her rampant thoughts about what he was, he fought the urge to laugh out loud. He thought her analogy was correct, Darian would be impressed. He wanted to reassure her that she was not in harms way. He looked into her frightened eyes and using a trick that Darian taught him, he projected his calmness onto her without using hypnotism. He slowly led her away from the door. He sat her into the chair and kneeled down in front of her, he looked into her battered, but beautiful face. And smiled his million dollar smile again, exposing his pearly whites, no fangs.

"I realize that you may be frighten of me but you have no need. I would never hurt you or Annette." He said as he gestured to her friend sitting up on the bed. Annette seemed to be caught in a trance, she looked at the two of them, eyes darting from one to the other.

"Natasha, you never need to be afraid of me. But if you simply must go back to your room, please allow me to escort you." He said then he erected himself and held his hand out, palm upwards, towards Natasha. She placed her slender hand into his and he held it as he guided her out of the chair.

"Well, I am still tired. I was trying to get some sleep earlier but my parents had visited me and kept me awake for about four hours." Natasha said as they walked towards the door. Xavier was glad she wanted to go to her room, it would allow him a little private time with her. She looked back over her shoulder to say goodbye to her friend, who waved. Xavier smiled at Annette as he closed the door behind them.

"So, where's your room?" He asked as they walked down the white corridor with the polished and sanitized cement floors.

"It's just down the hall here." She said as she pointed down the hallway. Xavier nodded his head and walked her to her room. She opened the door and he followed her and closed the door behind himself. Natasha was a little nervous to have him in her room, but he did say that he would never hurt her. She looked at the clock on the wall, the time was 8:32pm. She knew full well that the visiting hours for the hospital had well since passed. Why was he still here.

"So, you must have someplace to go, I want to thank you for walking me to my room." She said politely trying to give herself a clean easy way to be rid of him. He still made her nervous, even as his pearly white smile brighten the room and his grey eyes kept her blushing. She wanted to run her fingers through his soft lovely dark brown hair, but dare not try.

"Actually, I must admit, I wanted to get you alone. I wanted to talk with you on a more intimate level. Natasha, I think you are an extremely beautiful woman. I would love to get to know you better." He stood in front of her and held both hands up, palms exposed. "No tricks, no games, just you and I talking the way two people do when they're interested in each other."

Natasha looked at him, was he going to ask her on a date? She could not believe her ears. He was a vampire, most certainly, he could have any person he wanted and he was interested in her. Why not Annette, who was obviously interested in him, everyone looked at Annette. But now, in her little hospital room she gets hit on by the most beautiful man she'd ever seen. She couldn't help but blush. She lowered her head. Still unnerved by him, she supposed if he wanted to kill her, she doubt that she could ever stop him. He did seem genuinely interested, she considered his statement.

"Why me?" She asked. "I mean Annette likes you, I think we can both tell that." She stated. He looked at her, his head slightly cocked sideways. An expression of amazement on his face. His lips parted in a smile. Natasha felt her face grow hotter, more blood had rushed to her cheeks, she was sure by now even her forehead was turning red.

"Yes, I'm aware of Annette's attraction to me." Xavier said "She is a wonderful woman and very friendly, she is also my employee. I only wanted to give her my well wishes for a speedy recovery." He stated. He noticed Natasha shaking her head. and continued. "My interest in you is sincere, the interest of a man for an intriguing woman. I hope I'm not being too presumptuous. But are you dating anyone currently?"

Natasha shook her head "So, here you are in my hospital room while I have nothing on but this thin gown and you're telling me you're attracted to me? I bet you say that to all the girls you find in hospitals." She laughed nervously, it was his turn to laugh now. And he did, throwing his head back and belting out a deep throaty laugh. He made Natasha squirm on the inside. He was so manly, so sexy, two of her weaknesses . When it came down to characteristics she looked for in a man. She loved a man who looked like a man, who acted like a man, who could take care of things like a man. If she went on a date and the man ordered a salad and nothing else or some kind of vegetarian meal, he lost points as a man in her eyes. *Real men don't eat tofu as a meat substitute.*

"Well, unfortunately, a hospital…"he made a wide wave of his arm around the room for emphases "is where I first saw you, so I must work within the limits." He smiled at her again, throwing on the charm full force. He took her hand and led her to the bed, he picked her up with ease causing her to yelp in surprise. She had never been swept off of her feet, literally and carried anywhere. He held her in his arms effortlessly, as if she had the weight of a feather. Her arms locked around his strong neck, and she gazed into his lovely soft grey eyes. She liked how the light danced around his pupils, never getting caught in them. He placed her on the bed softly. She smiled at him, she felt her heart pitterpat inside her chest. She was being swept away, she thought he was a fairytale, *men like this just did not exist.* She almost forgot he was a vampire.

She never imagined her first official meeting with a vamprie would be like this. She felt an attraction towards him even though he was a vampire, he looked to be a human man. She was beginning to wonder what kind of relationship they could have. She wondered if his body functioned like that of a mortal man's. She decided she'd let curiosity kill the cat and came on out with it. If she was going to consider allowing this vampire in her life she wanted to know if they could be compatible.

"Can you, you know, do you…um…Does your…okay, there's no nice way to ask this of you." She took a moment to form the best sentence.

"Yes, I can. I can 'do it' just like a human man, even better," he smiled. "Years of experience. I can last hours longer…if need be." He said, taking the pressure off of her. He did not need to read her mind to know what she was thinking. It was the same thing he would have thought if he was in her place. He smiled at the expression of shock she couldn't hide. He could tell by now that her mind was probably playing out an erotic scene this instant. He turned and sat down in the small uncomfortable clothe-cover chair beside her bed. He stretched out his long legs, hands resting on the armrest. He looked at her.

"What are you thinking. I can see the gears turning in your head. Knowing you women it's something lewd." He joked. She looked at him, her eyes widening.

"Knowing us women! Thinking something lewd! Naw baby, that's how you men think. Your minds are always in the gutter. Women are sensible. I don't know what the hell is wrong with you men. Right now, I bet you're looking at me and I no longer have on this hospital gown, you have already mentally undressed me." She said matter-of-factly. Xavier was caught off guard and it showed and he laughed outright again. He would have to tell Darian about this beautiful, exciting woman. He definitely wanted to get more acquainted with her.

"Well, you do have a pretty good understanding of men, I did mentally undress you, about twenty minutes ago. But, that doesn't mean you were not having lewd thoughts, just now." He said, looking at her knowingly. she laughed.

"Yes, so what of it!" they both laughed. He settled himself again, and studied her.

"So what do you like to do?" He asked.

"Well, I like to go to the movies. I like to eat out in restaurants, I love seafood, and no, I don't mean I love whatever food I see, either." She joked, Xavier flashed her a smile, then shrugged innocently. She smirked, then continued. "I'm the kind of girl that will go on a date and order food to fill me up, not to impress. So I will order a 10 ounce steak, eat half and take the rest home for later. I'll order appetizer and dessert. A lot of men I've gone out with in the past think that entitles them access to my after hours lounge, but that's not happening." Xavier laughed at her choice of words for intercourse. The more she revealed, the more he found himself enthralled by her. It was easy for a vampire to become enthralled with a mortal. It was how mortals became vampires in the first place. He gestured for her to continue.

"Well, I just got a job with the *Chicago Word* and that was what I was trying to celebrate last night, before I started to feel sick."

"Sick, why? What happened?" He asked, concerned.

"Well, Annette wanted to celebrate with me and she said that I needed to get drunk, or at least have a real drink for the first time in my life."

"Not much of a drinker are you?" It was more of a statement, than a question.

She shook her head. "No, I'm not. I supposed I should not have ordered the long island iced tea." She was thinking in retrospect. Xavier whistled.

"Nope, wasn't the best drink to start off with if you're a lightweight. So you got sick?" He asked encouraging her to continue.

"Well, I didn't throw up or anything like that, I just felt like I wanted to, that's why we left the club. But enough about last night. How old are you...your real age?"

He smiled. "How old do you think I am?" He asked.

She shrugged, "I don't know. It's hard to tell, it still freaks me out that you guys exist-let alone live forever. So I guess one hundred years old?"

He raised both eyebrows. He knew she was guessing but it was a damn good guess. "Well, you're pretty damn close. I'm one hundred and four years old." He said, then watched the shock spread across her face.

"Oh my god I can't believe you're that old, you look so young!!!" She exclaimed surprised. Her room- mate who had long since went to sleep, let out a long loud snore that startled her. Xavier had looked up as well, he almost forgotten what a snore sounded like. He no longer snored when he slept or even breathed. His body rested lifelessly during the sunlit hours, as all vampires did during the day.

"Well, I was very young when I was made a vampire." He looked at his watch. Then drew up his legs and rose from his seat. Natasha could tell he was getting ready to leave and she felt a sadness come over her, the most unexpected sadness. She felt they got along very well, she felt calm around him. He wasn't what she expected a vampire to be. She supposed, *you really can't judge a book by it's cover.*

"Are you leaving?" She asked, disappointedly.

He nodded his head. "Yes, I have to go to the club, you know our assistant manager is out of commission so I have to pick up the slack. And besides, you need your rest." He noted her disappointment "Is it ok, if I visit you tomorrow night? We can talk some more." He walked over to her and leaned forward, she could smell his sexy cologne, he kissed the soft caramel colored skin of her forehead. He looked down at her and smiled. It was a bold move, he knew, but he could not resist.

"So, I'll see you then?" He asked. She nodded her head. "Good, until tomorrow, goodnight." He said as he left her room closing the door silently behind him. She stared at the closed door, still wondering what had just transpired between them. She laid in her bed and thought about everything that had passed in the last twenty-four hours. She began to feel tired. She allowed the exhaustion to relax her body and deliver her to a blissfully, deep sleep.

Chapter 14

Elise sat in her room, her mind raced with thoughts of both Darian and Sergio. She cared for Sergio, he was also part of her pride but Darian was the one for her. She just had to figure out a way to bring Darian closer to her. She did not mind the fact that she would have to share Darian with Xavier. She did hope that after being with her, he would see no need to have Xavier she could satisfy his every desire. She wondered what she could do to seduce Darian into taking their relationship more seriously.

As she prepared her bath, she turned on the water adjusting the temperature making sure the water had just enough heat to make steam, but not so hot that it caused discomfort. It would take some pretty extreme temperatures to effect a shape shifter but she did not want to take any chances. Once the tub was filled to the desired amount, she slid her pink satin bathrobe with the cashmere cuffs off of her smooth creamy shoulders. She tied her long thick brown curling locks into a bun so that her hair would not get wet. She reached into her cabinet and removed the little Egyptians bottle of bath oil that she had imported from Egypt. It was designed to moisturize the skin making it baby soft. From what she could tell, as she ran her fingers over her silky skin, the oil did the job effectively.

Elise poured a few drops into her heated bath water and put the bottle back. She put one foot then the other into the deep porcelain tub. She adored deep tubs, the kind with the four legs for support. As she settled into the tub the water covering her passed her breast touching her chin, she laid her head on the bath pillow on the back of the tub and closed her eyes, she began to think about Sergio-naked, changing in front of her. In the past that had never bothered her. But since his relentless approach to her, she had been forced to take notice of his qualities. He was without a doubt the most handsome male in the pride, truly worthy of kingship. She had heard the other females praise his bedroom skills when they mated with him. But she never had. She wondered if that aspect alone may be the cause for why she had his affections. She was not sure, if it was because he wanted her for companionship or because they have not mated yet. She knew she would be in heat soon and would need to mate, in the past she would only allow him to touch her but never enter her. It had annoyed her as much as him, but she was not ready to claim a mate. That was before Darian, now she could fulfill her need without the threat of pregnancy or having to share control of the pride, she was not ready to bare a princess. To bear a daughter, would be to secure the new queen's role in the pride. The sole provider was a hierarchy . She liked being the Queen and was not ready to prepare someone else to take her role.

She knew she would have to soon. She was over two hundred years old and the oldest shape shifter that ever lived, was a natural born that lived to be five hundred and fifty years old, before dying of old age. She had aged over the past two centuries. She picked up the hand held mirror from the side of the vanity beside her bath tub. She looked at her skin and complexion in the little round polished tortoise shell mirror. She looked at the little fine lines that were beginning to appear on her face. She hated the taletell signs of age. She focus on the small lines at the corner of her mouth and eyes. She was born an aristocrat, she then married a Duke and became a French Duchess. Men would fall at her feet. She once had the great self proclaimed emperor in her bed. He had been most taken by her beauty, and had promised her diamonds, pearls, all the riches of the world. He had promised her what all men promise her. And she expected no less. Now as she looked at her reflection she wondered what the future had in store. She wished for just an instant, that time could be frozen for her like it remained for vampires.

Shape-shifters had prolonged life, but not life everlasting. There was always a grey shade to every rainbow. She placed her mirror on the vanity and picked up her loofa sponge. She soaked it in the fragrant water and ran the sponge over the surface of her soft skin. She liked fragrances, though strong scents affected her senses. She could tolerate and even enjoy some scents only if they were soft, like a musk. Anything stronger would cause her to have a headache, the same affected all shape shifters. After bathing her body, she rinsed off the soapy oil and climbed out of the bathtub, water dripped off her body onto the fluffy pink floor rug. She loved the way the rug felt on the soles of her feet. If it was one thing she had to have, it was comfort. She grabbed one of the double thick fluffy pink towels from the towel rack and patted her body dry.

She walked out of the bathroom with the towel wrapped around her torso, she walked to her closet and opened the white double doors. She looked for a cool sheer outfit for the nights festivities. This night would be the inauguration of a new King of the Pride. The pride had not had a king in over fifty years. The last king had been her mate. He ruled the pride with an iron fist, making her only the Matron of the Pride. She wanted more. When he died of old age she took over completely and did not want to have to relinquish her hold over the pride. But Sergio had been right, a Pride without a protector, a male protector was considered weak and would be a target for other Prides that would want their territory. Chicago was prime real estate for any supernatural. She did not know any of the other Supernaturals in the city besides Darian and those few of his coven. Knowing Darian did help when one of their pride members was arrested for hunting on unsanctioned grounds. The government had a zero tolerance for such things and one of her leopards would have been sentence to death had she not sought Darian's help. Sergio had hated the outside help. He wanted to rescue their pride member by any means necessary. Elise did not want to cause a scene. She was comfortable in the city and did not want government harassment. Sergio was a strong male presence, a Natural Born, he understood the role of protector, she did not have any doubts that he would help keep the Pride under control. She could not afford another incident.

She found the attire she wanted to wear. A sheer pink two piece pants suit. A button up top that would reveal her creamy breast and matching pink sheer pants. The entire outfit hid nothing, it's sole purpose was to add a pink shimmer to her skin. She took the pins out of her hair letting her brown curls cascade down her back. The curly ends of her locks nearly brushing her buttocks. She applied a small amount of lipstick and blush. She stood back from the mirror and smiled. She may be aging and that was unfortunate, but she was still gorgeous, and of that she was certain.

Elise walked out of her bedroom to the back entrance of the house. She stepped outside the house and looked at the decorations that had been set up in preperation for the inauguration. Stone pillars had been mounted and set aflame, lighting the aisle leading to an alter. On the alter was a gold chalice for the ceremony. And a dagger with a jeweled ruby and diamond handle. She looked at the pride that had gathered for the ceremony. Everyone was naked kneeling in a semi-circle, they were all waiting for her, looking at her. Sergio stood tall and naked at the front of the alter. Elise walked slowly towards Sergio, the other members moved a few paces back to give them room to perform the ceremony.

Elise took Sergio's face into her hands and kissed him lightly on the lips, then on both cheeks. Sergio lowered his head so that she could kiss his forehead. Then she released his face and turned towards the alter. It was up to her to claim a new mate and in doing so, a new king. However, she was braking tradition by not taking Sergio as her mate, who would protest? Who would dare? She removed her clothing, letting the sheer pink shirt fall off of her shoulders to the grass covered ground at her feet. Sergio grey eyes watched her every move, eyes trailing over her body as she undressed. She let the pants fall into a puddle at her feet before stepping out of them. She was undressing herself for the hunt to complete the ceremony but she would be omitting one part of that ceremony. She would not be consummating their partnership, her duty was to mate with Sergio on the alter. She picked up the jeweled dagger from the alter and held her wrist over the gold chalice. She held the blade firmly in her hand and she ran the sharp end over her skin, slicing a deep cut an inch in length. Blood oozed out of the open wound and began to pour into the chalice. Everyone's eyes were focusing on the ruby red liquid that filled the bowl. The scent of her blood, the blood of the Matron filled the air. Some of the members licked their lips and moved a little closer to the alter. The only member that was not completely affected by the scent of the blood was Sebastian. Sergio's son he fathered when he mated with Madeline sixteen years ago. He had mated with her since then, when she had gone into heat, but Sebastian was his only child and it was the responsibility of the Pride to raise all natural born leopards. Sergio let out a low growl as the scent of Elise's blood assailed his nostrils. The growl curled from deep within his throat. It made the hairs on the back of Elise's neck rise.

She pulled her bleeding wrist from the chalice and began to lick the wound closed. The healing properties in her saliva could heal all wounds, even deep life threatening wounds with the aide of her blood. Only a natural born female had the ability to heal, as the ability of a natural born male was to form a link to any member of the pride that he shared blood with. Thus allowing him to scan their minds as well as control their change. Except on full moons. She continued to lick the wound until it was completely healed. She placed her hands around the gold chalice and slowly lifted it off of the alter. Sergio, his hands at his side, kneeled in front of her, awaiting her next move.

Elise then lowered the chalice to his face, he raised his hands, accepting the chalice from her. Tilting the golden cup to his lips, he drank deeply of the blood that would transfer some of her power to him, sharing the leadership of the pride. His throat worked as he swallowed deeply. Elise could tell he savored her essence that was in the blood. She knew that with sharing her blood with him they were creating a link that would stay with them until death. Sergio, drank all of the blood, and taking the dagger up, cut an identical wound and now held his bleeding wrist over the golden chalice. Everyone watched as his blood filled the chalice. Placing his wrist to his mouth, healed his own wound. Elise took the chalice and drank the blood deeply, emptying the chalice. Sergio threw his head back and roared, triumphantly, in a mixture of animalistic and human sounds gurgling from his vocal cords. The rest of the pride roared as well, all except Sebastian who yelled to support the inauguration.

Sergio stood up, tall and strong, penis erect, this would be the moment when he would claim his queen, his mate. Elise turned her head towards the alter, then away from both the alter and Sergio. His frustrations were evident, but he had known that it would come down to this. Until she could free her mind of Darian, he would have to walk the tight rope. This did not mean that he could not try to convince her otherwise. He held her hand in his and licked her palm, she locked her green eyes with his grey and she shook her head. Disappointed, Sergio released her hand. He turned towards the members of the Pride and held his hands upwards. They roared again. Happy to have a king.

"Tonight we hunt to commemorate the ceremony!" He yelled, the pride cheered and clapped. He lowered himself on the ground and began his change. The other four natural born members lowered themselves on all fours, also willing their change. The members of the pride that were bitten and not natural born stayed in the human form. They would cheer on the hunt, but were unable to celebrate the hunt unless their king willed their change. To do that, he would have to share blood with them. The groans of pain from those transforming soon disappeared, to reveal five beautiful silky-furred leopards. Two: Sergio and Elise, were black spotted on black, also known as black leopards. Devin was snow white, and Madeline and Daniel were spotted orange and black. Their sleek bodies rubbed against one another. Then they walked over to the other members of the pride and rubbed against them.

The remaining members rubbed their faces against the animal forms of their family, bathing in each other's scents. Low growls echoed through the air as they all shared the moment of bonding. The leopards licked the faces of the human form pride members to build loyalty. Then Sergio roared and the other four echoed, before they ran off into the woods, to hunt down a buck. They hunted in a pack, using their super senses to smell live stock. Their eyes saw clearly in the night sky. They spotted a deer drinking at the pond one hundred yards away. Slowly, together they crept low to the ground, moving stealthily towards their prey. The deer was unaware that he was targeted, he only stood drinking the cool water from the man made pond.

The muscles in their body allowing them to move as one smooth quiet unit, until they converged on the deer. The deer looked up in time to see Devin, lunging, a harsh growl coming from his throat. The deer took off in a sprint, running further into the woods trying for cover. The five leopards took off after it, Elise leading the chase. Their sleek bodies moved through the thick bushes easily. Elise gained on the pray, her paws reaching out, claws extending as she gave one final lunge for the deer, catching the hind legs under her claws. She could feel the flesh and muscle rip under the pressure of her nails. Blood spurted out of the wounds, and the animal cried out, but did not stop trying to run for it's life. The wounds slowed it down, but it was Elise's claws, now embedded in it's hind legs that sealed it's fate.

Elise clawed her way up the length of the deer and buried her two inch incisors into the flesh under the deer's neck, cutting the vocal cords and crushing the windpipe of the deer. The other leopards snaked up alongside the prey and began to rip off chunks of flesh from the deer as it lay twitching, dying. Paws held the deer down and teeth ripped at skin and meat, pulling it away from bone. They ate their fill of the carcass. Elise bit into the neck of the remains of the deer and lifted it in her mouth carrying it back towards the others. The rest following behind her, but Sergio walked alongside of her and licked her nose and whiskered cheeks.

They reached the other members of the pride, and Elise tossed the carcass on the ground before them. They all surrounded the bloody carcass, some licking the blood from the carcass, others taking small bites out of the carcass. Sebastian sat back and watched. It would be a few years before his body would undergo his first change, and then he would be able to enjoy the hunt. He felt a little left out of the celebration due to that fact. Even though the other's never made him feel as though he could not participate, he knew he could not, and therefore, he felt the way he did. The other members that were still in animal form began to eat more of the deer carcass. Until there were only fragments of bone with small bits of flesh left in a pile on the blood soaked ground.

Sergio, Devin and Madeline stayed in animal form, Madeline was in heat and both Sergio and Devin could scent it. Both waited to see whom she would choose to mate with. Madeline rubbed against both males, but licked Devin's face. She lay in front of him and exposed her opening. Sergio gave a low growl but left the area to change forms. When he was fully in human form again, he looked at Devin and Madeline, Devin had mounted her and had her neck in his teeth as he pounded deeply into her. Sergio knew that she wanted another child. Everyone knew that Madeline was the motherly kind. So she had picked a different male to father the second child. It really did not matter who the father was because any child born into the pride would be parented by the pride. So when a child misbehaved, he or she could end up getting several reprimands in one day for the same thing, by several different members.

Sergio walked inside. He was tired, normally, like all of their kind, he could stay up all night but that was only if he slept the majority of the day away. Right now after the hunt and activities he had for the whole day, his body was tired. And he retired to his room for a good nights sleep. But before he could sleep the night away into the day, he wanted to get the blood off of his body or the scent of the blood would never let him sleep. He climbed into the shower and soaped his body, working the unscented suds over his skin, rinsing off when he was satisfied with the results. When he could no longer smell the blood of the kill in his pours. He toweled off and climbed into his bed. He closed his eyes and dreamt about Elise. It was a good dream, she had finally excepted him as her mate and they were making love in the dream Sergio could feel himself smiling, even in his sleep.

Chapter 15

Xavier sat at the bar, his eyes scanned the dancing mortals. The blood pumping in their veins, mixed with their young energy filled the area with a succulent aroma. Xavier inhaled deeply and smiled. He thought about the beautiful woman he met earlier that night. He wanted to have her, to make love to her, to taste her. He wanted to tell Darian about her, Darian would be amused that he would be so entranced over a human. He turned around and looked at their vampire bartender, Tony and gestured for him to come closer. Tony finished up his trick he always did to entertain the crowds. He would toss bottles of alcohol into the air, spin around a few times, performed a few tricks, then catch them, before pouring numerous drinks for flirtatious women and men. He was a huge crowd pleaser and attraction to the club. Darian, always made wise decisions, like hiring the sexy looking bartender. Tony began walking towards Xavier his skin tight leather pants squeaking as his thighs rubbed against each other. He was wearing a fishnet shirt and you could see his twin nipple piercing. Looking at the little barbels made Xavier want to twist them lightly between his fingertips. Tony's ocean blue eyes locked on Xavier as his hands came up to brush his long blonde bangs away from his face.

"What can I get for you boss?" He asked as he stood in front of Xavier.

"The usual, but with a little more kick."

The bartender smiled and reached behind the bar and opened up a brand new bottle of synthetic blood, he then reached again behind the bar and pulled out a bottle with a plain black label of the special mixture he personally concocted, he did not want anyone to steal his special ingredients. This was the only bar in all of Chicago, maybe even the country, where a vampire could get a real drink and become intoxicated. He refused to tell anyone what he put in the drink and for good reason, he would charge an arm and a leg for his signature mixtures. It had tickled Xavier the first time he saw Darian drunk off of one of Tony's…"Contenders." Darian never lost his charm. Still, It was nice to see him grinning for no reason and babbling on about anything that popped into his head at that time. Darian ordered the drink regularly and was the only one who never had to pay for them, Xavier would just run up a tab, then pay it at the end of the week, he never really mind paying, he was rich through Darian and so it was always Darian's money that paid his tabs.

Tony, poured the drink with the same flare in which he did everything else. He tossed the bottled blood in the air, spun around and caught the bottle behind his back, then juggled both bottles and pausing only to pour the right amount into the glass, then serve the drinks with a flourish to the waiting customers. Even though Xavier enjoyed the show, sometimes he just wanted his drink, but he let Tony put on the performance. It always brought more people to the bar and the more people that came to the bar, the more money the bar would make. He looked at the gathering crowd and thought to himself that Al Cantone had nothing on Darian.

"Here ya go, boss." Tony said, as he slid the glass down the length of the bar to Xavier, who caught it without looking. He brought the drink to his lips and took a deep swallow. Halfway through the glass, he began to feel the effects of the secret ingredients, his body felt warmer inside, and whatever tension he held in his shoulders, now gone. He could feel himself becoming relaxed, giddy. Tony had indeed made himself a hot commodity. Tony had come to Darian two years ago, his master had used him for sexual pleasure and would beat him and threaten to destroy him if he would not comply. Tony managed to escape, practically killing himself in the act. He hid himself during the day underground, making his way to Chicago. It's forbidden to enter a vampire master's territory without permission. To do so, would mean death at the Master's discretion. Tony pleaded with Darian to let him stay and to protect him. Darian had agreed, but for a price, Tony was more than happy to pay, and that is how he got the job bartending. Darian did have to eradicate Tony's old master, a foolish young vampire who did not respect the older one, untill it was too late.

Over the past seventy years or so, Xavier had seen Darian challenged for the city many times, and he's seen Darian viciously and skillfully dispatch his opponents. He's even seen him let some of the weaker challengers battle it out in the arena of the Coliseum, the grand prize… their existence, it was during these types of tournaments that Darian would raise the normal admission fee of one hundred thousand dollars to five hundred thousand. Beside how many times would mortals see two vampires fight to the death, and be able to choose the losers fate? Always thinking about personal gain, that was Darian. He was one of the most ambitious bastards Xavier ever met.

Xavier wondered if Darian would still be busy watching the semi-finals of the tournament. He looked at his platinum Rolex watch, with the diamond dots to mark the quarter positions. He shook his head. The time was 2:42 am. The tournament was long over. At three, he was planning to leave. John could handle the rest. He had appointed John Fallon to take up Gary's place in the Strip Club section of the establishment. He could tell John did not want to get on the stage and strip for the hysterical mortals who wanted to see a vampire in the buff, but Xavier had been most insistent. He watched the crowd react wildly to John as he relaxed more and more for his audience. It became apparent that he enjoyed dancing for cash. Xavier shook his head and laughed as he saw John seduce the human crowd, tease them with the last bit of clothing he had on that covered his genitalia. When the crowd began to chant "take it off" John had teased them a bit more, before submitting. But now the strip section of the club was also closed, and John had reassume his regular duties as manager once again. He also did not mind the extra few hundred dollars he had stuffed in his pocket.

Speaking of the devil, John walked up to Xavier who was by now feeling *very* mellow. He sat down on the bar stool next to him. And surveyed the energetic mortals.

"It seems that they never get tired, doesn't it?" He asked.

Xavier nodded. "Yeah, it does. They love the night life after the grueling work day, I suppose it's the only thing that makes them feel alive." He said softly. "That is the one thing we have in common with the humans, we both love the night life." He finished his drink and placed the empty glass on the bar top. He rose slowly, taking his leather jacket off the back of the seat. "I'm going home now. I'll leave all of this in your hands, remember to remind Jennifer that she has to cover for Annette until she returns, Okay."

"Yeah, boss, I won't forget."

Xavier looked at him and smiled. "You enjoyed stripping, didn't you?"

John, blushed slightly, then nodded his head. "Yeah, I did. At first I did not think I would, but it's pretty exciting to be up there, everyone loving everything about you. Shit, I even did a personal dance for these two chicks in the back who wanted to know what it was like to touch a vampire." He said smiling, eyes staring forward suddenly as he remembered the moment with the ladies.

"Well, I hope you did not let anything get out of hand, did they want you to feed from them?" Xavier asked, looking at John suspiciously.

"Well, yeah, you know how these mortals are these days. We're like a new aphrodisiac to them, they can't get enough of us. I think we have successfully replace heroine, crack and cocain!" John said with a chuckle, Xavier couldn't help but laugh. "But, I behaved myself, I only took a little, just enough to give them a thrill." Xavier nodded, pleased. He put his coat on, and walk towards the parking lot. He climbed inside his sports car and headed home.

Xavier looked at the night sky, the stars shining bright against the darken clouds. He could see the sky so clearly, better than any mortal would ever be able to see it. To him, the night was beautiful, he felt it was the best time of the day. He arrived at the mansion and entering the huge garage, proceeded to the second level. The four walls of the double decker garage were all glass. Darian had wanted to be able to see the cars even before entering. Xavier had thought it a bad idea to tempt a crook but Darian paid no heed to the warning. They were burglarized shortly after that discussion, by a foolish band of mortals who thought it would be easy to get in and get-out with as many of the high priced cars stored in the two-story garage as they could. What they did not know was that the huge two story mansion with sixteen acres of scenic landscaping was owned by a powerful master vampire that had no qualms about killing humans.

That night all six vampires that lived with Darian, which at that time, consisted of Xavier, John, Tony, Annabelle, Miko, April and the man himself, feasted greedily on the five mortals that dared to enter their territory. Xavier navigated the car to the second level of the glass garage and parked it. He walked inside the house, the house itself was full of luxuries. Crystal chandeliers hung from the ceilings, hand made carpeting covered the floors. The mansion was built in the 1930's and had a classic look to it. The arched doorways were decorated with engraved rose vines. The rooms without carpeting had dark hard wood floors that were hand polished. Darian's mortal servants lived on the premises and protected the coven during the day as well as completed daily house chores. That was how they earned their room and board, and a handsome salary to boot.

Whenever Darian had human servants, it was primarily for day time protection and very little else. He might have sex with them but it was rare, he picked mortals that were menacing and strong, with little or no family ties, who would scare off would be groupies who wanted to look at a vampire sleeping, or slayers. For slayers, Darian had zero tolerance. He had caught four slayers since the "Exposure" who attempted to destroy him. To these idiot mortals, he did one of two things; either killed them instantly, or placed them in a tournament. But never, ever did he turn them over to the police. Xavier passed two human servants in the hallway and nodded at them and they returned the nod. He walked into the extravagant bedroom that he shared with Darian. The huge king size canopy bed was draped with sheer black curtains and covered with black satin sheets. The room smelled of orchid incense. The floor had white carpeting, a daring move, with the constant amount of traffic in and out of the bedroom. The armoire and dresser were made of solid black marble. As was the frame and pillars of the four-poster canopy bed. The high arched roman style windows, reaching from ceiling to floor, were covered with thick black velvet drapes to keep out the sun. Darian did not sleep in a coffin, he enjoyed the comfort of waking up in a bed every evening and Xavier had to agree.

Xavier could hear sounds of water splashing from the bathroom. He headed in that direction and opened the door, allowing steam to escape from the room. He leaned against the door frame and crossed his arms over his chest. He looked down at Darian sitting in the huge round marble tub that was built into the floor, it was big enough to swim in. He was pouring handfuls of scented water over his muscular chest. Darian looked up at him and smiled.

"Home already?"

"Yeah, well, the fun sections of the club were closed. All that was left was the dance section, and well, the mortals were filling the place up with the most delicious scent." Xavier said as he twirled into the bathroom, arms outstretched. Darian lowered his head and chuckled.

"You're drunk." He smiled, the cute dimples in his cheeks made Xavier blush.

"Yeah, I had one of Tony's concoctions, the patented 'contender.'" He smiled gaily.

"I could have had a 'contender'." Darian joked mischievously. He poured more handfuls of the hot water over his muscular arms. Xavier watched as the water flowed over the soft skin. He sat down on the edge of the tub and looked down at his lover.

"Mind if I join?" He asked as his hands came up to unbutton his shirt, working slowly on the buttons.

"Not at all." Darian submerged himself under the fragrant, soapy water, and came back up. Water trailed down his body, his long, wavy, jet-black hair plastered to his face and chest. He looked at Xavier, who was removing his shirt and leather jacket at the same time. He stood up and unbuttoned his pants and pulled them down. His semi-erect penis sprang forward. Darian laughed outright, then he moved away from the edge of the tub to allow Xavier access into the heated water. Xavier climbed into the water and moved closer to his lover. Darian opened his arms wide and took Xavier into his embrace, pressing him back against his chest. He tilted his head and kissed Xavier's temple lightly, Darian truly loved Xavier and would do all that was in his power to take care of him. He did not feel that way about many people, even some of his own offspring, but he felt that way wholeheartedly about the one laying comfortably and safely in his arms. Darian lifted a handful of water and poured it over his lover's chest. He watched the water run in rivulets over his nipples to settle into the ridges of his muscular stomach. He tilted the other mans head back, pressing it to his chest and planted delicate kisses alongside Xavier's cheek and mouth. Their tongues met in a gentle kiss.

"I met someone today." Xavier said, when they broke the kiss. Darian looked at him, his long, thick straight black lashes brushing his cheeks as he looked down into Xavier's eyes.

"Who?" His hand continued to pour warm water over Xavier's head and body.

"A beautiful, enchanting woman. She was with Annette the night of the accident. Oh, Annette wished she was here right now, but unfortunately, she's laying in a hospital bed. Her arm's broken, and she has a few cuts, stitches and bruises here and there."

Darian frowned slightly, "did she like the flowers?"

"Oh yes, she did, and she also had her eyes set on me, I think she would have been willing for that threesome." He chuckled.

"What of this other woman you met tonight?"

"Oh, that's right," He smiled and looked up at Darian, head tilted against his chest. "She's gorgeous, light green eyes, full luscious lips, smooth brown skin, incredible figure, she was delicious to look at. She has a smile out of this world, and she's funny. Let me tell you what I read of her mind." He proceeded to tell Darian of her thoughts about them being predators. Darian smiled and chuckled. He listened as Xavier told him more about his conversation with Natasha.

"You were pouring the charm on kind of thick, don't you think?" He accused questioningly.

"Well yeah, but you would have too, if you had seen her. But I guess, you're just too smooth, women throw themselves at you, all you need to do is pretend that you're going to look their way and you've got panties thrown at your feet, you lucky bastard!" Xavier said playfully, as he splashed water into Darian's face as he laughed.

"I would not go that far, I do have to put a little effort into seducing the *ladies.*"

'Picking out the right designer suit doesn't count...well...doesn't count for much. Face it, you've been blessed with a face for billboards, and a body to boot." Xavier said, Darian smiled, he thought the same of his young lover.

They bathed each other in the tub then Xavier reached over and pushed a silver button, that released the raining waters from the shower heads mounted in the ceiling. Warm sprinkles of water rained from the ceiling rinsing off the soap and residue from their bodies as the water drained from the tub. Darian held Xavier in his arms and began to kiss his shoulders, his hands caressing Xavier's stomach, and pecs. His fingers teased Xavier's erect nipples as he pressed his back closer to Darian's chest. Darian's hands trailed down Xavier's stomach to his fully erect penis, he encircled his hand around the base and began to lightly stoke the smooth hardness, causing Xavier to moan. A small tremor ran through Xavier's body as his eyes closed, letting his body relax and enjoy the pleasure.

Releasing Xavier and turning the shower off, Darian rose to his full height of six-feet-three inches, he lifted his lover in his arms and carried him to the bed. Using telekinesis, he pulled the curtains away from the bed, making way for him to lay Xavier down on the satin sheets. Darian laid Xavier down on the mattress, he looked down at Xavier's body, catching his breath at the sight of his beautiful lover's naked form. He climbed in behind him and kissed the soft lips, that parted in a smile as their tongues met. Darian pulled away slowly and reached into a drawer to retrieve a small glass vial filled with fragrant oil. He poured the fragrant contents of the bottle into the palm of his right hand and cupping both hands together- rubbed. He then placed both hands onto Xavier's body, rubbing the warm fragrant oil into Xavier's chest, giving him a soft soothing massage. Darian's hands kneaded the hard muscles underneath the soft flesh of Xavier's arms, legs, and shoulders, as Xavier moaned and squirmed in delightful pleasure on the bed. Xavier raised his hand to caress Darian long silky locks. Darian caught Xavier's hand, he began to kiss his palm, trailing soft, moist kisses along the sensitive skin of his inner arm. Xavier moan in anticipation as Darian reached for Xavier's erect hardness again and began to stroke it slowly in one smooth rhythm. Xavier arched up and cried out, as he felt himself coming to the height of passion.

Darian withdrew, smiling wickedly at his lover. He pressed his hand on the other man's shoulder, urging him to roll onto his stomach. Darian covered Xavier's body with his own and he began to plant soft tender kisses on Xavier's shoulder blades, moving lower to the rise of Xavier buttocks. His tongue found Xavier's inner passions and Xavier cried out arching his back as his hands gripped the sheets. His eyes closed tightly as his mouth opened, panting. After a several minutes, Darian rolled him over onto his back, he gently tortured Xavier with grazing nips of his teeth, before satisfying their mutual longing by pressing his lips to Xavier's in a passionate kiss. Darian's tongue teased, tasted before he withdrew, he lowered his head to plant a single kiss on Xavier's neck.

Xavier moaned deeper, he pressed himself closer to Darian as his lover's hands slid under his legs, placing his calves around his waist. Darian reached for the bottle of oil he used earlier and poured more into his right palm. He rubbed it on himself, groaning softly in the pleasure of the act. Then he poured the remaining oil over Xavier's opening, while inserting his fingers to assure for an easy entry. Darian moved forward and Xavier felt him penetrate him, his arms encircled Darian's shoulders, his legs tighten around his lover's waist. He began to feel the delirious pleasure spread throughout his body as Darian began thrusting into him. He moaned loudly with each thrust, nails dug deep into his lover's back, drawing blood. The scent of the blood mingled in the air with their lust, heightening their passion.

Darian began to pump faster as he felt himself coming to the point of no return. The pleasurable sensation started at a low boiling heat deep within his groin, then like a rocket, it shot throughout all of his limbs, and he pushed hard one final time, biting his bottom lip, unable to contain his ecstacy, he cried out. Xavier's entire body tense along with Darian's final thrust, he echoed Darian's cry, his grip tightened around his lover as he felt the searing release erupt from their bodies. Darian collapsed on top of Xavier, they lay entangled as they kissed softly. Small tremors still rippled through their limbs as they relaxed in the afterglow. Darian looked into Xavier's eyes and smiled.

"You know that I love you, don't you?" He asked

Xavier cocked his head, and smiled brightly. "Yes, and I love you." He kissed Darian deeply for several moments, before the older man rolled reluctantly to the side. He put his hands behind his head, and stared at the opening in the four-poster canopy bed, looking at the chandelier. He smiled. He looked over at the window and saw the first sign of the morning coming through. He looked at Xavier, who was already fast asleep. He chuckled, and climbed out of the bed to close the heavy, thick, black-velvet drapes. He knew that the other vampires were tucked safely in their own bedding. Once the room was surrounded in darkness, he climbed back into the bed and pulled

Xavier's body to his, resting his head on the other mans' chest as his arm held him close. He closed his eyes and let the sleep take him.

Chapter 16

Natasha woke up in the little white hospital bed, the light from the bright sun, burning her eyes. She raised her hand to shade her sensitive eyes from the heated rays. She looked around the room and she saw her room mate sitting up eating breakfast. The little grey haired old lady was grinding the mushy food in her mouth. She looked at Natasha and smiled, her dentures had been removed and all Natasha saw were a mouth full of pink gums. She shivered mentally then she thought about that being her fate in the next fifty or so years. The young never wanted to age. She smiled at the lady.

"You look better today, how are you feeling?" She asked the woman.

"Oh, darling, I'm feeling a lot better, but how about you, you laid there in that little bed and whimpered all throughout the night. Kept saying something like, 'don't drive'. Were you one of those young gals hurt in that terrible car accident that was all over the television news?" She asked.

"Yeah, I am, wait a minute, you say that I was talking in my sleep? That's funny, I don't recall ever talking in my sleep. I also keep having these weird dreams. One right after another. They were really strange, I don't normally dream unless I forget to take my medicine or something and that only happened once. But this is really weird, I know I sustained a concussion in the accident and that may have something to do with it." She looked at the old woman sitting there, watching her babble. "I'm sure you don't have the faintest idea of what I'm talking about do you? Don't worry about me, I'll probably get better once I get out of here."

"Why do you say that?" Asked the petite elderly lady. Her thinning grey hair resembled a tangled mop. She looked to be about sixty-five years old or so to Natasha.

"Well, I hate hospitals, hate them, I get all anxious when I have to come to them, I keep thinking someone else's illness is going to jump out of their body into mine. I know it's ridiculous, but come on, it's a hospital, all sort of germs and unidentified viruses are floating around. To me, it's a war zone in here!"

The elderly woman laughed until tears ran from her eyes, she slapped the side of her thigh. Natasha sat there stunned for a moment, she hadn't meant to be comical, that was just how she felt. Then she thought about how she must sound to the elderly woman who had seen so many years pass. And the thought of such a young woman having a fear of hospitals was just as endearing to her as it was absurd. The elderly woman took a napkin from the table and dabbed her eyes with it.

"Ohh, that was precious. Sweet heart, I've never heard of anyone becoming ill in a hospital. All the dangers are out there, honey child, all the crazies and creepy crawlies are out there. I mean, can you believe that all these dead people walking around drinking our blood, and these monsters that turn into animals, it's like the normal world has been warped into some kind of horrible horror movie!" She said, obviously upset about having to live with the supernaturals. Natasha couldn't blame her. Until last night, she felt the same way. But there was something about Xavier that was more humane than most men she'd ever met and she was willing to take a peek over the other side of the fence.

"Well, I know what you mean, ma'am. It's like, you have to worry about all sorts of things now, when you walk down the street, not just at night either, but during the day as well. I've never met one of those shape shifters, and I don't think I ever want to. It still creeps me out that my body smells like food to them."

"Tell me about it. I saw one of them damn animal people one day on the news. They were doing some kind of report to try and ease our anxieties, or so they said. But the damn report only made me more nervous! It was like actually looking at proof that they really do exist!" She shook her head.

"Yeah, I know what you mean," Natasha said as she sat up in her bed. "When I first heard about them, I thought it was a hoax, you know? I mean, really, vampires and werewolves. But it's as real as it gets. I heard that they all have superhuman strength and power-"

"And.." the elderly lady cut her off. "It ain't nothing like the movies, ya know! Garlic, crosses, none of that works! But at least the silver bullets work for them damn animal people. That's good news." The woman said as she nodded. Natasha wasn't so sure if she could determine who were the most

146

dangerous. Mortal men, who have plagued her and every other woman who dared walked the streets at night, or a supernatural creature. She put them both even, if you could call it even.

"So, if you don't mind me asking, why are you in here." Natasha asked.

"Are you afraid I might give you something." The lady joked. Natasha had not thought about it until just then.

"Well, now that you've mentioned it.." She said laughing.

"Well, I was attacked by one of those damn bloodsucking monsters. I was coming home from my job, when one of them grabbed me and carried me in an alley." She paused, remembering the horrifying experience. Natasha's mouth had dropped open, here she was, sitting in the same room with a survivor of a vampire attack. It was even more amazing than a survivor of a shark attack. The elderly woman continued. Her thinning grey hair, a messy mop on her head. Natasha wondered if she had any family, would anyone come to comb her hair, or talk to her. Natasha hadn't seen any friends or relatives come to the elderly lady since she'd been there. She was starting to wonder if the woman had any loved ones…that returned the love.

"The thing bit me! And I screamed darling! Let me tell you, I screamed like I've never screamed in my life! Those long sharp painful teeth went into my neck. Then there was something else. It made me feel funny inside. These bloodsuckers are some dangerous things." She was nodding her head, agreeing with herself.

"So how did you survive?"

"Well, I thought I was going to die, my body felt light and there was this good feeling I was feeling in my arms and legs and…" she blushed and trailed off, Natasha, choose not to press the intensity of a vampire's bite. She had heard rumors and had her own speculations and was not very interested in hearing about this sweet old lady getting off on vampire sex. No, no, not at all. The thought made Natasha shiver with repulsion.

"Well, this tall dark haired man came out of no where and saved me, he threw the vampire off me. And the funny thing is, he told the mean vampire to take care of me. At first I was scared that meant that he was going to put me in a dumpster or something but he brought me here, then ran away, strange isn't it?" The lady asked obviously perplexed. Natasha nodded her head she wondered who the ladies savior was. The elderly lady did not know it, but Natasha guessed that the other man was also a vampire, a stronger vampire, she wondered if Xavier would know anything about it. Then she wondered if the woman's savior was Xavier, he was tall, and handsome, and had dark brown hair, she thought about how romantic that would be, Xavier, a knight in shining armor. Keeping the streets safe for damsels in distress. Then she came back to herself. Xavier was probably at the club when this elderly lady was attacked. But he was still a handsome gentleman, who's to say he could not be a knight in shining armor?

Natasha began to feel the pressure in her bladder the longer she sat on the bed. It was obviously time to climb out of the bed even though she did not want to. Her body was still slightly sore, like she had a good two hour workout after not working out in years. Even her buttocks hurt a little. She pulled the sheets back and headed for the bathroom. After she finished doing her business she began her morning ritual of washing her body, and brushing her teeth, these things simply had to be done. After about twenty minutes she emerged from the bathroom, turning her attention to the TV. The elderly woman had turned on one of the reality court tv shows, where two people battled over who pays who, because they found so and so sleeping in their bed with their best friends dog, or some crazy shit like that.

"You like your court shows too, eh, just like my grandmother used to. She loved that one court show, every afternoon, she had to watch Judge Walter." Natasha said as she climbed back into the bed. The old woman laughed and nodded her head, then began to explain to Natasha what was going on in the court drama. Natasha pretended to care, she was not sure if it was a good idea to pretend to care. That may spark up more details which she did *not* want to know.

"Oh, really, well, I hope she gets paid" Natasha said to appease the woman, who had just explained that a lady was suing her landlord for not installing a fire detector in her apartment. thus she lost her fur coat and other belongings in a fire that she started in her bedroom, because she had fallen asleep smoking a cigarette. The landlord was countersuing for damages done to the apartment to do the fire. *What was the world coming to.* Natasha thought as she buzzed the nurse, she wanted to have something to eat, even if it was hospital food. The same nurse from the day before came into the room, smiling.

"How are you feeling today Miss. Hemingway?" The nurse asked as she removed the IV bag and the needle from Natasha's arm. Natasha was relieved, she had wanted to pull the vicious little needle out and toss it across the room from the very first day.

"Oh, I'm fine, just starving, what's for breakfast?" She asked knowing that it was nothing she really wanted to eat. No wonder people always lost weight when they go into the hospital, one thing was for certain, forget about *Slim and Trimmer* and all the other lose weight fast diet plans, all one needed to do was admit oneself into the hospital for two weeks and come out looking like a brand new person. Natasha smiled to herself as she thought about the weight loss alternative.

"Well, we have the lunch menu ready, that will be a side salad, strawberry geletin, and turkey sandwich." The nurse said as if she was at a restaurant, where the food was actually desirable. Natasha fought the urge to gag. She just smiled at the nurse.

"Well, I'm pretty hungry, so I guess I have no choice but to eat what they provide me."

"That's right" Joked the nurse. Natasha made a face, and chuckled. The nurse finish checking all the machinery and her chart, she walked over to her room mate to check on her.

"Hello, Mrs. Harnett. How are we feeling today? You'll be pleased to know that you will be going home today. As a matter of fact, both of you are going home today. Mrs. Harnett, we're still trying to contact your son, we have not been able to get hold of him, do you have another number so that we may be able to call him, and tell him that you're ready to go home?" Asked the nurse as she removed the IV bag that dangled on the stainless steel hook connected to the pole. Mrs. Harnett seemed sad. She had not had one visitor while she rested in the hospital. Natasha felt sorry for the old woman, here she had a son who did not even want to know what happened to his mother. Natasha had seen Mrs. Harnett attempt to contact someone in her family so they could visit her, no one ever picked up. Natasha imagined how lonely the elderly woman must be. She would hate to be that lonely. What was the point of having kids if they did not return the love and compassion.

"That's the only number he gave me, he said I should call it if I need to talk to him. I've tried to call my daughter, but I haven't gotten an answer." She smiled sadly, she knew when she wasn't wanted, no one wanted to have to take care of the old hag who took care of them. It made Natasha angry. She would love to set her eyes on these two good for nothing children of this kindly old woman and tell them a thing or two about themselves!

"Well, if I'm going home today, my mother will most likely take me home. I can give you a ride, Mrs. Harnett." Natasha said from across the room. The elderly lady looked up, her eyes brighten. She seemed to relax all of a sudden. Natasha figured the woman was stressed out trying to figure out how she was going to get home on the bus or train, or both. She was still weak from her ordeal, it would be nice to get a ride home, well now she had one if she wanted it. Her mother always taught her to treat people the way she wanted to be treated. And there was no way she was going to let this kindly old woman feel alone in her time of need.

"Thank you dear, I really appreciate that. I'll have to get on those two children of mind. So busy, too busy for their own mother." She said, she tried to hide her sorrow by making light of the situation.

"Cut them out of the will, that'll teach their ungrateful asses!" Natasha said, nodding matter of factly. Mrs. Harnett looked at Natasha blankly. She did not know quite what to think of the young lady, but she liked her. She nodded her head.

"That is an option." She smiled. The nurse smiled and nodded, she left the room to get Natasha something to eat. Natasha called down to her friends room. She waited for her friend picked up the phone.

"Hello?" Asked Annette.

"Hey, how are you feeling?"

"Shit girl, my back still hurts, and my arms are sore, man, this sucks. I see partying with your ass is bad news." She joked.

"I could say the same about you." Natasha responded. "They said I could go home today. So I have to call my mom, hopefully, I'll be outta here before they serve me this nasty ass hospital food. If I have to eat one more bland bowl of jello, I'm going into cardiac arrest." Natasha said. Mrs. Harnett laughed across the room, she had heard the young lady complaining about the hospital cuisine and had to agree. She too was glad to be leaving.

"So, miss, 'I'm going to walk off into the sunset with my best friends hot boss', what were *you two* doing last night?" She asked slyly.

"What do you mean, what could we have been doing?"

"Oh, lots of things, like getting your freak on, I saw the way you were looking at him. Fear not, I hold no grudges, the man is gorgeous. I'm not mad at you, trust me, if I wasn't aching all over, I would have made the moves on him myself, you would have came into my room and found yourself in a predicament let me tell ya!" Annette laughed as she imagined her friend walking in on her and her hot boss with her bent over the hospital bed while he gave it to her from behind. Natasha knew why her friend was laughing, and she shook her head.

"You are nasty. I know what your dirty mind is thinking of."

"Good, don't act like you weren't thinking of switching places in my fantasy. So, getting back to the question at hand. I thought you were too scary to be around the….unnnnndeaaad." She said, dragging the last word out, making it sound eerie. Natasha did have to admit that the thought of being in the same room with a vampire did unnerve her. She did not expect to meet a vampire like Xavier, he was so romantic and such a gentleman, she had a hard time imagining Xavier feeding from a live mortal victim. She could in fact imagine him wrapping his soft full lips around a bottle of Synblood. She wondered what Synblood tasted like to a vampire. She imagined it was like tofu to her.

"Well, we just talked, that's all. He seems so nice." She began reminiscing about their time together and smiled to herself. She wanted to see him again, she remembered she did not have his phone number, did he even have a telephone? At least she knew where he worked. She was leaving the hospital later that day and she wanted to be able to give him her telephone number so that he could call her. She had no idea why she felt so comfortable around him, she barely new him, but for some reason he did not seem dangerous to her. She wondered just how dangerous he really was, when he wanted to be.

"Uh hmm 'just talked,' you say. So why do I hear something else in your voice. You like him don't you!?" Annette asked, trying to get all of the juicy gossip.

"Well if you must know-"

"Yeah, I must know! I got to know!"

"Yes! okay! yeah, I like him, happy!?"

"Are you happy? I know how scared you were, do you think you can trust him not to eat you?"

"I don't know, I mean, I can't stop him if he chooses to, but it seemed like that was the farthest thing from his mind. I think he wanted me in another way and let me tell you girl, the feeling was very mutual. It has been a long time for me. But I'm still kind of like, "egh" on having sex with a vampire. I wanted to ask him if he could but did not know how to form the words right." She whispered, trying to make sure that Mrs. Harnett did not hear her discussing a sexual fantasy she had about a vampire, she did not think that would be good for her to hear, seeing as Mrs. Harnett survived a horrible vampire attack.

"Yeah, I think they can fuck better than a mortal man!" Annette speculated, her southern accent adding a certain twang to the words. She remembered how Darian made her feel, and a small tingle ran through her body.

"Yeah? I started to ask him and he just answered for me. He said that they could have sex and they could do it for hours if need be. I don't think I could even last for hours, If it is really good, I don't think I could last an hour!" Natasha joked.

"Okay! Girl, guess what? Xavier's is so fucking beautiful but you should really see his boss, the man that promoted me. Darian Alexander. This man is…you know what? If you looked *'Unbelievably Gorgeous'* up in the dictionary, you'd see a picture of him smiling holding a rose. That's just how fine he is."

"Really? Well, that's a dangerous type of 'fine', Xavier's bad enough, already I'm thinking of him as a potential lover."

"So, why not, he can't do no worse than any mortal man. Less I bring up the last contender." Annette said gravely.

Natasha frowned "No, miss *rain on people's parades,* you don't have to bring up that asshole. I know, I know that 's the only reason I'm even considering giving Xavier my telephone number. Think I should? What would you do, well wait a minute, I know what you would do. Do you think I should?" Natasha asked, she was doubting the relationship would grow. She had spent a good part of two years avoiding supernatural hangouts and now here she is faced with the decision to date one, even have sex with one.

"Well, I say go for it. What's to lose, either you do or you don't, hard to say, you' ve got to ask yourself if you want to put up with his night time hours, his appetite for blood and whatever else he brings to the table. "Annette said. Natasha was silent, the other woman made perfect sense, she had to think about this whole situation on a totally different level. She wondered if the relationship could work out, she really wanted to give him her telephone number so that he could call her and they could set up a date, just to talk.

"Okay, since I'm going home today, I need for you to give him my telephone number, and that's if he stops by, what's the number to your job?" She asked

"I can't believe you are really considering this." Annette said, obviously shocked at her friends new found courage to delved into the unknown. Natasha seemed so straightlaced to her, never wanting to party hard, never wanting to have a drink, always content to stay at home and read, or watch tv, never wanting to do anything at the spur of the moment. Now here she is, trying like hell to make a connection with a vampire. A beautiful, smart sexy vampire, but a bloodsucker nonetheless.

"Okay, I'll give him your phone number if he comes by, what makes you think he'll come by?" She asked

"He said he would, test number one, can he keep his word?"

"Shit, you can say that again, men seem to have a hard ass time keeping their words. Which transcends into keeping their vows, which is why I'm totally against marriage. You can lie to me, but don't lie to god, if you have no intentions of staying with me till death do us part, let's not waste the lords time. That's how I feel about it. Bastard ass men, I hates them and loves them!' Annette said.

Natasha laughed. "It's the men that believe wholeheartedly in that 'till death do us part' that you have to worry about, that vow didn't say anything about dying of old age, only as long as you both shall live. Besides, you just hate spending any amount of time with them that would equal a real relationship, you like sleeping with them and what comes in their wallets."

"Well yeah, shit, they got to be good for something, damn. Don't you think? I mean, I love men but they require entirely too much attention. And some can be down right annoying. Like taking care of a big ass baby." Annette said chuckling. Natasha knew her friend had a personality on her. She just loved Annette, she always made her laugh.

"So don't forget to give him my number, ok, I have to call my mom to let her know she can pick me up, today. I'll go grocery shopping, we need some food in the fridge."

"Okay, good, I hate shopping for anything but clothes. I can shop for clothes all day."

"You have more clothes than you need."

"Ha! Says who!"

"Okay, got to go, I'll stop by your room before I leave, talk to you later."

"Bye." Annette hung up the telephone and laid back down on the bed. She was smiling thinking about Natasha and Xavier, *who would have thought?*

Natasha picked up the handset and dialed her mother's seven digit cell phone number. She waited as the phone rang, she hoped her mother had her phone with her, she had told her mother time and time again to turn on the cell phone whenever she left the house, what was the point of having a cell phone if you're never going to leave it on. By the forth ring, her mom had answered.

"Hello?" she asked cautiously, not recognizing the telephone number on her caller ID.

"Hey mom, it's me, they said I could go home today. I'm still really sore, but I'll be okay. Can you come and get me?" Natasha asked. She looked up as the nurse and doctor came into the room, both remained quiet while she was on the telephone. The doctor removed her chart from her bed and proceeded to look it over. He was medium height, about five feet nine inches. Kind of short for the modern day man...or was he? He had salt and pepper hair cut short and combed back. His hazel eyes scanned over her chart, dark eyebrows knitting slightly.

"Sure, what time shall I pick you up?"

"As soon as possible. Oh, and mom, my roommate here doesn't have a ride home, she's an elderly woman. Hold on, let me get her address." Natasha pressed the receiver to her chest and looked at Mrs. Harnett.

"Mrs. Harnett, where do you live?" She asked. The elderly woman looked at her and smiled.

Mrs. Harnett gave Natasha her address. "Is that going to be out of your way, because if it is, don't worry about me dear, I don't want to be an inconvenience."

"No, no, not an inconvenience at all" She lied. She put the receiver back to her ear, "Mom, -"

"I have already heard." Her mother sighed, she did not mind helping out her fellow man, it was out of her way but she'd do it. She did teach her daughter to help those in need. "I'll be there in a little while, okay. Probably about fifteen minutes after twelve, is that going to be alright?"

"Yeah, perfect, bye mom."

"See you later," her mom corrected her. "You know how I dislike the word 'bye'"

"Yes mom, see you in a few."

"That's better." her mother said, before hanging up the telephone. Natasha looked at the doctor.

"So what's up doc? I hear I can go home today, I was just calling my mother to tell her she could pick me up." She smiled, happy to be getting out of the germ infested hospital and nothing anyone could say to her would make her think otherwise. The Doctor nodded as he looked at the file then up at Natasha.

"What would be the reason why you're taking. Triadonex?" The doctor asked.

"Well, I've been taking Triadonex since as long as I can remember, I started getting these head aches when I was a small child. So my family doctor put me on the medication, why?" She asked, she had sat up in the bed more alert.

"Well you put down that you take it for migraines, but Triadonex is a dream suppressant. Do you dream much, Miss. Hemingway?" Natasha thought about it and shook her head. She had no idea the medicine she had been taking all her life was not what it seemed. Why the hell was she taking dream suppressants?

The doctor looked at her and smiled. His calm hazel eyes eased her mounting anxiety somewhat. She was going to have to talk with her doctor to see why she was kept on the medication. She seemed at loss all of a sudden.

Had she been lied to for over twenty years, or was there some other reason why she had been taking the medication? She was starting to feel uneasy.

"Thanks doctor for everything. I don't think I'll be taking any more of this medication until I know the truth. And no, I didn't normally dream, but since we're on the subject, I've been having a lot of random dreams, one after another." She said, obviously frustrated.

"Like what? Can you remember anything? Any portion of these dreams? Would you like us to run a few tests?" He asked, hoping to gain more money. He took out his little medical light and was holding Natasha's head upwards as he looked at her pupils.

"No, that won't be necessary doctor." She did not want to owe the hospital any more than she already had to, she especially did not want to add on any unnecessary costs. She just landed a brand new job and her insurance plan had not even been established yet. She had mentally calculated the current cost of the ambulance ride over, the medication, the emergency room assistance and the hospital stay, in retrospect, she kind of wished they had left her in the back seat of the cab, *I would have gotten home ok, no worries.*

"Ok, well, you're free to go at anytime. I see you called your mother, so I'll just sign your release papers and you can be on your way." He smiled. Mrs. Harnett thanked them both for taking such good care of her. The doctor assured her it was nothing. Natasha wanted to laugh. *Sure, it was nothing, but you'll still get the bill,* she thought to herself. Then both the nurse and the doctor left the room to allow the two ladies to get prepared to go home. Natasha combed out the tangles in her hair, she couldn't believe Xavier had been interested in her when she looked the way she did. Maybe there was hope yet for the relationship. She came out of the bathroom and Mrs. Harnet went in. While Mrs. Harnett was in the bathroom bathing. Natasha put on her club outfit, there were some dried blood stains on the clothes. She hoped her mom would bring her a fresh change of clothes. Her mom normally thought about things like that. Mrs. Harnett came out of the bathroom just as her mother came through the door.

"Hi mom!" Natasha said excitedly, as she gave her mom a big hug. "Did you remember to bring me a change of clothes?" she asked, keeping her fingers crossed.

"Yeah, I brought you a change of clothes. I've notice you lost a lot of weight, honey. I'm so proud of you. Never let anything get you so down that you'll neglect yourself. Besides, there is a man out there who will know the treasure that you are, understand me, young lady?" Her mother said sternly.

Natasha nodded. "Yes, mom." no point in arguing, her mom was right. She took the bag of clothes her mom had brought for her. She looked into the bag and thankfully saw a pair of blue jeans and a red ribbed turtle neck sweater. Her mom always had excellent taste. She turned around and introduced her mother to her roommate who would be getting the ride.

"Mom, this is Mrs. Harnett. She couldn't reach either of her two children to come and pick her up, so I offered her a ride home." Natasha said as she walked into the bathroom to change.

"I hope I'm not causing a problem?" Mrs. Harnett asked sincerely.

"Oh, no, no, not at all, I wouldn't feel right about leaving you here to fend for yourself. Not in this day and age" Mrs. Marian Hemingway said to the grateful elderly lady. Natasha emerged from the bathroom fully dressed, the pants were a bit large but the clothes would do. She walked over to her bed and gathered all of her belongings, which weren't much along with all the free stuff she was going to take from the hospital. She left the bed pan. The three women exited the little white room and headed for the elevator. Natasha remembered she was going to stop by Annette's room before she left.

"Mom, one minute, Annette's here too, I promised I'd say goodbye to her. I'll meet you downstairs." She walked towards Annette's room without waiting for a response. She knocked on the door and heard a faint 'come in' and she opened the door. Annette smiled as she entered the room, she was looking a little better on this day than the day before. The dark circles under her eyes were lightening up, and her skin complexion had improved. Her arm was still in a cast and the cuts and bruises were still there, just like her own. She walked over to the bed and hugged her friend lightly.

"I'm leaving now, but I'll visit you tomorrow and bring you some real food, okay." Natasha said.

"Your ass better, cause if you don't." She held up her good fist and shook it to prove her point.

"You're not going do to anything." Natasha joked.

"I'll beat you in your sleep, that's what I'll do, you don't have to be awake for me to extract my revenge." Annette said trying to not laugh.

"Un hmm, well, I'm off. Talk to you later." Natasha gave the other woman one last hug and a kiss on the cheek. She felt bad having to leave her friend in the hospital alone. Maybe she would surprise her and come back later on that night. She thought about how sore her body was still and decided against the two bus rides and one train ride it would take to come back to the hospital on public transportation. She would stick to the plan. Tomorrow she'll visit. She left Annette's room and got on the elevator. She met her mom and Mrs.

Harnett in the lobby. They walked to her mom's red 2003 *Diamondback Sahara S4*, she liked her mom's car, it was perfect for her. They all climbed in, Mrs. Harnett sitting in the back, was thankful for the comfortable seat. Natasha's mom put the car into gear and headed towards the outer drive going northbound.

Mrs. Harnett gave directions the closer they got to her neighborhood until they pulled in front of her little yellow frame house with the red brick foundation. Natasha helped her out of the car before she climbed back into the passengers side. They sat in the car and waited as Mrs. Harnett to fished through her purse for her keys to open her door. She waved goodbye, then walked inside. The conversation on the way to Mrs. Harnett's house had been between her mother and Mrs. Harnett. The two women discussed the current situations with the supernatural race vs. the human race, the crime rate in this country and above all, the good old days. Natasha wished she could have tuned them out but she could not. Her stomach growled, she had escaped the hospital in time to avoid eating the food but now she was starving. She wondered how Xavier felt when he first woke up, was he ravenous? Would he recognize her before taking a bite?

She let her thoughts run wild in her head, she looked at the busy city streets as they drove on. They passed *China Town*. She always liked going to *China Town*. The buildings in China Town had the Chinese architecture added to them, the shingled tiered roof tops, the dragon statues and mini towers. She wondered if it really looked like a piece of China, she wasn't sure, but she loved the food. There was a particular restaurant she loved to frequent when she had the money that made the best smoothies, bar none. Her mother continued to drive until she told her to pull into a super market so that she could get some groceries. Her mother parked the car in the lot and both women climbed out. Natasha could move a little more easier than before, the pain killers were really kicking in and making everything more bearable. They walked through the automatic doors and her mom grabbed a cart.

She aided her daughter in reaching for items off of the shelf. Natasha had made a list and she gave her mom half. Her mom took her half of the list and walked off to retrieve the items. Natasha walked down the aisle looking at the directory signs overhead. She was searching for the can goods section, she rounded the corner and collided into a boulder of a man. She lost her balance and would have fallen and probably ended up back in the hospital had he not caught her. Her hands brushed the watch on his wrist and she felt a little shock through her fingertips. She looked up into his face as he steadied her.

He was huge, standing at least six-feet-nine inches tall. He was the biggest man she'd ever seen.

He looked at her with cold blue eyes, his brown hair was cut short in a military buzz cut. His shoulders were almost as wide as the aisle itself and she could tell he was all muscle. He was a real man, no doubt about it. He held several packs of beef clutched in his right arm. His leather vest smelled new. His jeans were worn and had holes in the knees. When she was finally out of harms way of falling, she gave him a bashful smile.

"I'm so sorry, I did not see you, I know that's probably something you've never heard anyone say." She joked, trying to make light of the situation. It was something in the way he looked at her that made her nervous. He smiled a wolfish grin, revealing rather sharp incisors. They looked like little fangs to Natasha. She wanted to get away from him as soon as possible.

"No need to apologize," he said as he walked away towards the check-out line. Natasha looked at him, the feeling was still close to her. He really freaked her out. She walked away, with a slight shiver and finished her shopping. She reunited with her mother who had completed her half of the list and they walked to the check-out line. She paid for the groceries, put them into the car and climbed back in. Less than fifteen minutes later, she was in front of her apartment building. Her mother helped her carry the groceries into the apartment. She stayed around to see if her daughter needed any help.

"Mom, I'll be alright, you don't have to stick around. Thanks for everything." Her mom said, and she walked over to her mother and gave her a big hug, as strong as her body would allow.

"Okay, you just call me if you need anything, alright?" She asked as she headed for the front door. Natasha nodded and waved. She loved her mother, but she did not want to hear anymore motherly advice, She had heard enough on the way home. How she needed to get her own car, not to let people talk her into doing things she would not normally do, such as getting drunk and so on. She was glad to be at home. She remembered that she wanted to catch Xavier to let him know that she was no longer in the hospital. She reached in her pocket and pulled out the piece of paper with *"Desires Unleashed's"* phone number on it, and dialed the number. The telephone ranged several times before a female voice answered.

"Desires Unleashed, where all of your fantasies can come true. How may I cater to your desires?" The voice asked seductively. Natasha wondered if she received a lot of calls from men who just wanted to hear a sexy voice.

"Hello, my name is Natasha Hemingway and I'm trying to get in contact with Xavier Richards." She paused

"Mr. Richards, will not be in until tonight, you can try back after five or six pm."

"Well, can you leave him my number for him to call me? I'd really appreciate it."

"Will do, what's the number?" She had taken on a more normal tone of speaking. Natasha wanted to chuckle, must be cool to work under a facade. She gave the woman her ten digit phone number, area code included. "Ok, as soon as Mr. Richards gets in tonight, I'll give this to him. Is there anything else?" The woman asked.

"No, that was it. Thank you. Goodbye." Both women ended the connection. Natasha sat on the sofa for a few minutes thinking about Xavier, she smiled, feeling giddy. Then her stomach rumbled and she decided it was time to make something to eat. She walked into the little yellow and white daisy covered wallpapered kitchen. She hated the wallpaper, wanted to tear it down but Annette said it reminded her of the kitchen she grew up in back home in Charleston, South Carolina. Natasha did not argue, but she still thought it was ugly. She looked into the refrigerator and shuffled a few items around till she found the sliced roast beef she brought and some lettuce, cheese, tomatoes and onions. She placed all the food on the counter top and began making herself a double stacked sandwich, adding two layers of everything. She wondered if her eyes may be too big for her stomach but there was no law about saving some for later. She made her sandwich and poured herself a tall glass of juice and she sat down comfortably on the sofa in the small living room. The living room was only big enough for the brown sofa and two matching chairs, a wooden coffee table and the thirty-two inch screen TV she and Annette had saved and paid for together for Christmas a year ago. She reached for the remote and turned on her cable, she surfed through the channels and complained that there was never anything worthwhile on cable.

"Hundreds of channels of garbage." She whispered out loud as she passed channel after channel of reruns, music videos and sports. She finally settled on an old movie she had once seen as a child and loved. She settle back and watched a marathon of classic movies, featuring unforgettable actors and actresses. The sky grew darker, she had drifted off to sleep when the telephone rang and jarred her out of her sleep. She sat up quickly upsetting her equilibrium and almost falling off of the sofa. She paused for a second and grabbed the telephone receiver.

"Hello?" She said groggily.

"I'm sorry, did I wake you?" Asked a deep sexy voice. Natasha did not recognize this strange man calling her house.

"I'm sorry, but who's calling?"

"It's me, Xavier, you left your telephone number, you wanted me to get in contact with you. Is this a bad time?" His voice was smooth as silk. It purred through the receiver, goosebumps surfaced on Natasha's skin. She remembered how beautiful he was and wanted to talk with him about other things.

"No, no, I did want you to call me. I wanted to talk."

"Do you want me to come over?" He asked

She gave him her address. "It's a three story apartment building with a red awning in the front. There's an intercom, I'll have to buzz you in, the name on the intercom is…"she sighed. "Two hotties." She could hear Xavier chuckle softly, she couldn't blame him, it was ridiculous but it had been Annette's idea.

"Ok, I can be there in about thirty minutes. Are you hungry?' He asked smoothly.

"Um, a little, but you just make sure you're not. I don't want to look appetizing to anyone." She said sternly. Xavier chuckled. He admired her blatant honesty, and her unique form of expression was charming.

"I've already fed. I just want to take care of you. I'm on my way. See you then." He hung up. Natasha felt her heart jump in her throat, here she had invited a vampire into her house. She felt the excitement throughout her body, she could hardly keep still. She walked through the apartment making sure no unmentionables were visible. Once she had feminine-proofed the apartment, she waited. She looked at her clock, the time was 7:42 pm It had only been twenty minutes since she talked with Xavier, she hoped he would be there within the thirty minutes. Before she had time to think any further on Xavier's promptness, her intercom buzzed. She jumped off the couch, then paused as the pain in her muscles forced her to calm down. She slowly walked to the intercom and hit the button.

"Hello?" She asked, leaning into the intercom speaker.

"It's me, Xavier" Even over the loud disruptive reception of the intercom his voice was clear and sexy. She buzzed the door. And before she could take her hands off of the release button, she heard a knock at her door. She walked to the door.

"Who is it." It couldn't have been Xavier, she just buzzed him in, this must be a neighbor.

"Xavier." It was him! She couldn't believe how fast he got up to the third floor! She peeked through her peep hole and sure enough, there he stood looking down the hallway. She unlocked the door and opened it. He turned to face her and smiled. He was breathtaking. He was wearing a smoke grey blazer over a black silk shirt and smoke grey front pleated pants. The cut of the pants really showed off his flat stomach, and impressive imprint in the groin area. She smiled and stepped to the side as he walked past her carrying a pizza box. Natasha's stomach growled as the aroma of the pepperoni and cheese pizza whiffed up her nostrils.

"Where should I put this?" He asked, holding the box of pizza.

"Oh, you can put it right there." She pointed to the coffee table in front of the sofa. He sat it down, then took a seat on the sofa, he crossed one long leg over the other, his right hand resting in his lap, the left, resting on the armrest, he looked at her.

"Are you going to come a sit down, or no? I promise I won't bite." He joked. She smirked at him then walked over to the sofa and sat down... cautiously. She looked at him, she definitely felt an attraction to him, acknowledging her desire for his body, but she was also afraid of him. She decided to play it cool, he still did not seem to pose a threat. She opened the pizza box and looked at the delicious smelling pizza topped with onion, black olives, mushrooms, green and red peppers, sausage, pepperoni and double layers of cheese. She looked at him, and smiled.

"What are you trying to do, get me fat?" She joked as she reached into the box, pulling away a slice and taking a bite out of it, working the long strings of melted cheese into her mouth with her lips. Xavier smiled as he watched her eat.

"I picked their deluxe, everyone there said it was the best thing on the menu," he said.

"Well, it's delicious, thank you." She looked at him "I'd like to just talk, if you don't mind. There are some things I like to ask you. I've never really seen a vampire in real life...at least not one I was aware of. And well, I wanted to know more about you." She said with all honesty. He looked at her, he seemed thoughtful.

"Okay, whatever you want to ask me, feel free, I'll answer all of your questions to the best of my ability."

"Are any of the myths true?"

"Like crosses and holy water? No. Neither can harm us, or irritate us in any way. The only thing that can kill us or do us harm is the sun, fire, or decapitation. That's why I have to take my hat off to the mortal world for

161

equipping themselves with all of the weapons necessary to protect themselves. Really! Ultraviolet bullets are simply amazing." He seemed truly astounded.

"What about, when you go to sleep, do you sleep in coffins, or in dirt?"

He laughed outright. His hand slapping his thigh. "No, I don't sleep in a coffin," He stated still chuckling. "I choose to sleep in a bed, but there are some of our kind that choose to sleep in coffins, or even underground."

"Can you make, well, do you...you know, when you have sex?" The blood had rushed to her face, and her cheeks were reddening. He looked at her, his head slightly cocked sideways. He smiled.

"Well, let me explain it this way. When we have sex, there is a release with the orgasm. But we are sterile, we can never reproduce. Our bodies are reanimated, so to speak, nightly, outwardly functioning much like a normal human body, after we've fed. Which is why it's hard to tell one of us from one of you. Our skin is warm to the touch, but if you notice, we sweat, we can cry, and we can ejaculate." Natasha's eyes were as huge as saucers as she listened to Xavier. Her mind raced with every detail he revealed.

Xavier continued. "Unfortunately, we can not digest human food, wait, I'll take that back, the oldest of our kind are practically invincible. They can carry on lives just like you. But for me, I'm too young to be able to have such luxuries. I have to feed nightly, I can not digest human food, or go out into the sunlight, I'm well asleep before day break. I haven't seen a sunrise, or sunset in over seventy years." he smiled sadly as he watched her reaction. She appeared sadden by his information. "I know that once we get a certain age, we become resilient to the sun. Older vampires can walk around in the sunlight, just like any mortal, and even enjoy food. Mind you, they do not receive any nutrients from human food, just the thrill of eating, and the taste of the different cuisines. However, they must rid themselves of the food in the very same method that humans do, you can imagine how an ancient vampire views this options. Many of them choose not to eat human food. I have a long time, before I can see those days come." Xavier said.

"Do you regret any of it, not being able to have kids, or anything else?"

He thought about her question for a moment. "Sometimes. But there's always a price to pay, and we pay for our immortality." It was now Natasha' s turn to think about his response.

"Why do you want to go out with me, you're a vampire, wouldn't you prefer your own kind?" She asked

"Why? why not? I find you intriguing, beautiful, humorous and kindhearted, besides the alternative of not being with you is unthinkable.

The only thing standing in the way of our having a relationship, is you. Can *you* date a vampire?" He asked, turning the tables.

"Well, yeah, I guess I can try, I mean I like you, I can give it a shot, it's still really weird to me, I'll need time to get to know you better, but I can still give it a shot." She said as she finished her third slice of pizza.

"Good." He smiled, then a thought came to his mind, *should he tell her about Darian now or later?* He decided to wait for later. After they got better acquainted. He sat back and asked her questions about herself, what where her hobbies and her least favorite things.

"See, I enjoy going to the movies as well. We both like the same actors and actresses, well, except for that one guy, I don't particularly care for him." Xavier said as he lounged on the sofa. Natasha had settled in the chair next to the sofa. She chuckled at his jokes, he was surprisingly funny. And she began to feel very relaxed in his company..

"So," she asked getting more serious. "You're a vampire and now that we are here together, you seem like a regular guy but just how dangerous are you, have you ever killed anyone?" He lifted his head and looked over at her. He pulled himself up into a sitting position.

"Well, I was waiting for that question." He chuckled softly. "I live a different life than you do, *vampires* live a different life than *mortals*, yet it's a similar type of life. We have wars, and betrayal, we handle it in our own way which can be violent. As far as how dangerous I am, I can be very dangerous and yes I have killed people. Does that upset you?" He asked, his expression had grown serious.

Natasha looked into his grey eyes. She knew that he was telling the truth and that earned him some major points in her book. She doubted a mortal man would be so totally honest. *Were vampires more honest, or did it just seem that way?*

"No… well… in a way, it *does*, as of right now, I don't know what I think about that. I have my thoughts, but then I realize you're not like me and that has to be taken into consideration." She sighed. "I need to think about all this but now I have to get some rest, I'm exhausted." She said rising from the chair. Xavier took the hint and rose as well, he picked up his coat from the arm of the sofa and put it on. They walked towards the exit, he opened the door and stepped out into the hallway, then turned to say good bye.

"Why don't I give you my number so that you may contact me." He took out a pen from the inside pocket of his blazer and a piece of paper and he wrote down his number and handed it to Natasha. "Call me anytime, um, after sunset" He chuckled. She took the paper and looked at it. She smiled knowing he had given her his phone number. She looked up at him.

"May I ask you something,? Can you enter a house without being invited?"

He grinned mischievously. "Yes." He said, then turned and walked down the hall. When he had reached the top stair, he looked back at her. "Call me. I'll be thinking about you." He blew her a kiss and vanished as if he teleported instantly, Natasha wondered if he had. She would have to ask him about that later. She closed the door still experiencing mild fatigue. She decided she needed to get some rest and fast. She wanted to be alert for her first day on the job. She walked into the bathroom and took a shower, using her favorite *Anisi 's* bath products. She rinsed and toweled off then put on her pajamas. She climbed into her bed and drifted off to sleep the instant her head hit the pillow.

She stood over a prone figure of a woman crying as she lay tied to a metal blood stained table. The woman was begging her for her life. She could hear herself laughing, a deep husky laughter. She ran huge manly hands over the woman's body, suddenly claws started to extend. The woman screamed and began thrashing against her restraints. The clawed hand stabbed the woman in her stomach, thick dark red blood bubbled then flowed from the wounds made by the clawed fingers. She could feel the fur-covered-clawed hand as it ripped the woman's flesh, disemboweling her while she cried, screamed and begged for her life. Natasha had never heard anyone scream in agony, true agony, it made her skin crawl. Blood and tissue poured freely from the wound as several yards of intestine came spilling out of her abdomen. She could feel the hunger rise inside of her, she could smell the scent of the blood. She could hear the laughter of another, feminine laughter. Her eyes looked up to see a beautiful woman with pale skin and long black hair that reached to her thighs, enter the room. She wore a black leather catsuit with black four inch heeled boots. Her fangs had extended and her eyes glowed bright red. Natasha felt herself panic, she forced herself to wake up. The first thing her eyes could see were two bright red eyes staring at her from across the darkness in the room, she screamed and quickly turned on the lamp on top of the night stand. She looked frantically around the room, her sheets were soaked with sweat. Her hair was plastered to her face. Her heart pounded in her chest. She felt thirsty. She climbed out of the bed and went to get a glass of water from the bathroom. She drank the water down quickly and just as quickly refilled the glass for a second round. Afterwards, she set the glass down on the edge of the sink and looked at herself in the mirror. She looked frightened as she stared at her reflection in the mirror.

"It was just a dream! Just a dream, you're being ridiculous. Go back to bed, it was only a bad dream. Everything is okay." She told herself, she felt herself calming down. Taking several deep breaths she walked quickly back into her bedroom. She slowly looked around the room giving everything a thorough inspection. After she made sure she was the only one in the room, she climbed back into bed but was restless and unable to fall asleep. She laid in bed, sheets pulled up to her neck staring at the ceiling. She looked at the clock, the time was 3:42 she had to get some sleep, she closed her eye and willed herself to fall asleep.

She was awakened by the TV alarm coming on and the channel seven news was blasting in her ears. She opened her eyes and the sun was shining brightly into her window. She shielded her eyes and looked at her clock, the time was 7:05am.

"Shit!" She said as she jumped out of the bed and stumbled into the bathroom. She rushed into the shower and brushed her teeth at the same time. Then she hopped out of the shower and toweled herself off as she walked to her closet. She had picked out something really special to wear on her first day at work and she was excited about that. She sat on the bed and pulled on her stockings, she looked up at the TV to see the news anchorwoman announcing another gruesome murder.

"…And the body of what police think, may have been a woman, was found today in an alley located on 55th and Garfield. It was reported that the head was missing and the body was devoid of some of its internal organs, S.U.I.T. detectives are on the scene. Let's go live to Brain, who is at the scene right now and have one of the detectives with him. Brian." The anchor lady announced as the camera cut to Brian, an African American male with a bald head wearing a long brown trench coat, he was pressing his ear piece closer so that he could listen for his cue.

"That's right, Amanda, I have with me right now, Detective Warren Davis from the governments Special Unit Investigation Team. He and his partner, Detective Matthew Eric have been on these gruesome and disturbing cases since Friday, Amanda." He put the microphone into the face of the handsome detective."Detective, do you have any information for us?" Natasha looked at detective Warren and wondered where all of these beautiful men were coming from. She loved looking at hot cops, what woman did not like a man in uniform. Especially one as physically fit as this one. She stopped her dirty thoughts long enough to listed to what he had to say.

"Well, it is pretty early in this investigation, we have a few leads, but nothing concrete. We'll keep you posted. That is all for now, thank you." He said as he walked away. Natasha felt her throat tighten. The dream she had last night was really weird. She would never have dreamed that, would she? Maybe it was because she ate pizza before going to bed. Maybe it was her lack of medication. She shook her head, she would not dwell on that she had a big day, she had to go to work then go visit her friend in the hospital. She put on the rest of her clothes, a black wool-blend skirt with matching double breasted jacket, a white pullover satin shell underneath. She checked herself out in the mirror, aside from the bandages and a few dark purplish bruises here and there on her face, she was satisfied with the finished result. She grabbed her keys, purse and left for work.

Chapter 17

"This fucking son-of-a-bitch is pulling our damn chains!" Warren cursed through his teeth as he climbed into his car and slam the door shut. He sat in the car trying to regain control over his anger. Matthew had slid in the seat beside him and stayed silent not wanting to irritate Warren with questions. When Warren had finally calmed down, Matthew spoke.

"This wolf, do you think he might be watching us now? Think he's in the area?"

Warren shook his head. "Not likely, I would have caught his scent, but I'm sure the bastard's watching the fucking news. We look like fools, we have nothing to go on, I've scanned the crime scene practically putting my fucking nose to the ground and can't find shit! They picked their spots wisely, like the shoulder on the side of a busy street. They do it for fun and..well, it's like this." He adjusted himself in the seat so that he was facing his partner. "You got exhibitionist who fuck in public for fun, it's the excitement that they might get caught even though they don't want to, but the thought of getting caught adds more excitement, only with a murderer like this, he's killing these people in one place and then putting the bodies in public places leaving little or no traces. They know what they're doing, that fur left on the body the other day wasn't an accident, they wanted us to find it!"

"Why do you think it's taking the heads?" Matthew asked, he did not like this case one bit, Warren was right, they were working with professionals. The kind of killer that sometimes takes years to capture. The kind that liked the chase, that like eluding the cops for the thrill of it.

"Trophies. I'm willing to bet that somewhere there's about three heads, shit, maybe more mounted on a wall with blood dripping from the torn necks. When they put the body on the side of the road like that, they did it in the middle of the night, probably around two or three in the morning, not many people driving along the road at that time, most won't stop nor do they care why a car is pulled over on the road. So that allows them the excitement of getting rid of a body in the open public and no one seeing anything. I can't fucking understand how this wolf is shredding these bodies to pieces and I can't find a scent to trace." He shook his head, perplexed. He turned back in his seat and started his car.

"Let's go back to headquarters to see what they may have found on the body from this morning." Matthew suggested. This case was really frustrating him, he now knew for certain that he had another serial killer case, like that child murdering freak from a few years back. And *he* had been *human*, Matthew did not know what to expect from a serial killing werewolf. *Would now be a good time to retire?* Matthew speculated.

"I looked over the body, thoroughly I don't know how much more Marshall's going to find." Warren said as he drove down the crowded streets, he beeped his horn at people who did not seem to care that he had the right-of-way. The rudeness of some people annoyed him. He drove back to headquarters only stopping once along the way to pick up some of his favorite donuts. He and Matthew ate a few on the way and left the box in the car. They entered the elevator and pressed the button to the lower level. Once they reached their destination, they exited the elevator and turned down the gloomy hallway towards the morgue walking through the double doors. They saw Marshall Galen, bent over the remains of the female corpse that was discovered earlier that morning. He was wearing a light blue t-shirt and a pair of brown worn-out jeans that slightly sagged off of his waist. *This man really needed a make over*, Warren thought as he walked over to the corpse, Matthew stayed a few paces back while his partner glanced at the mutilated body. Matthew had avoided getting a good look at the body at crime scene. The sight of the insides hanging out all torn and shredded made his stomach turn.

He walked away, gagging, both Warren and Marshall glance up watching him. Warren wondered if Matthew was going to puke. Matthew struggled with his nausea and turned around facing Warren, taking deep breaths. Warren could see Matthew's flesh turn a pale green.

"Are you okay, buddy?" He asked.

Matthew nodded. "Yeah, I'll be alright, let's just do this." He said, it intrigued Warren about what could turn a person's stomach. Like himself for instance, if he saw anyone eating anything molded, spoiled, or rotten, he would become instantly nauseous. He once saw a movie where the actor supposedly ate a chicken wing that was spoiled to the point where the meat was green and a greenish gelatin liked substance had formed on it, Warren barely made it to the bathroom in time. Still to this day, just thinking about that particular movie made him sick to his stomach. Needless to say, he never finished watching it. Warren looked at his partner one last time, then turned to face the corpse.

Marshall Galen had discovered very little. "Who ever is doing the killings, they're covering their tracks, better than anyone I've ever seen. This killer damages the bodies far to much for anything to be recognizable. Look at these entrails," He held up a handful of long intestine, bits and pieces of torn flesh and globs of dried blood slid off of the intestines and plopped back into the exposed abdomen. Warren felt his mouth gather saliva. He did not want to take any deep breaths that would only make it worse. From behind him he heard an ugly sound, followed by the sound of retching. He turned around to see Matthew leaning over the sink puking up his breakfast. Marshall looked up and frowned and shook his head. He thought these specially trained cops would be used to this type of stuff. And here is one of the best cops on the unit, barfing in his stainless steel sink. *He* knew one thing, *he wasn't going to clean it up!*

Matthew had finished retching and turned on the faucet rinsing his mouth as he rinsed away all of the vomit. His face was pale, but he could feel the blood rushing to his cheeks, he was embarrassed to have lost his breakfast. He was known to have a cast iron stomach but the conditions of this last victim sickened him.

"Feeling any better? Do you want to wait outside?" Warren asked in a slightly teasing voice. "Do you need to lay down, put your feet up, want a pillow?" He chuckled. Matthew grimaced at him and flipped him the finger as he headed for the double doors. Warren chuckled. "So what do you think, doc?" He asked.

"Well, I think this shifter is playing around with you guys. The intestines are ripped to shreds and the spleen and kidneys are missing. It ripped into the stomach and you can say "fished around" for the goodies, so to speak. You two got a real sick puppy on your hands, literally. Get out there and do your job, try to keep my morgue empty, alright boys?" He pleaded, as he placed the intestines back into the abdomen. He packed them in, pressing down on the entrails to get them to stay in place. Warren felt his hunger rise and decided now was a good time to leave.

"Will do, doc. Will do." He said as he followed his partner. As he stepped outside, he took a deep breath. Matthew was leaning against the wall head

169

down, his skin color had returned. He raised his head and looked up a Warren.

" Can't believe I lost it in there."

"You lost it! I *almost* lost it, face it, we make a pretty fucked up pair."

"Yeah, but I've never seen you get sick."

"Nope, but I'm more likely to eat the evidence, and that's worse, come on." He gestured to his partner and they walked down the hallway back to the elevator. They were still at square one and couldn't do a damn thing, except sit there and twiddle their damn thumbs.

Chapter 18

Natasha had a rough day at work, she worked for hours on her feet taking photos of various crime scenes, the corpses were long gone, but they wanted to photo-document the crime scenes for tomorrow's news scoop. They were calling this killer the "HEADHUNTER" it was grim to Natasha, she hated how the media had to add sensationalism to every maniac. She wondered why they always gave criminals jazzy names like the "CHICAGO HELL RAISER", or "THE MIDNIGHT STRANGLER" so now, the perpetrators could clip out news paper articles about themselves featuring their new cool nickname. Why not call them "THE CRAZY ASSHOLE," or "THE SICK COWARDLY FUCK" because that's what they were, call it like it really is, that's all she wanted.

She almost did not want to stand up when the train came to her stop but she promised Annette she would visit her. Several of the other passengers were nice enough to offer up their seats after they saw how bruised and battered she was, that helped. But she really just wanted to go home. She had not gotten much rest the night before and she was feeling the effects now. She stepped off the train and walked down the platform with the rest of the evening rush hour crowd. She walked down the steps slowly, as people rushed past her throwing her nasty glances until they saw her face and thought they better keep their mouths shut. To them, Natasha either liked to fight or just gotten beat up pretty bad and did not look like she needed any more drama.

She reached the bottom and walked to a restaurant that was close to the hospital and ordered her friend an Italian combination with cheese and mixed peppers. She got an order of seasoned fries on the side, she ordered the same for herself. Even though she knew it wasn't helping her diet, that combined with the pizza from last night was definitely breaking the rules. After she paid for her order she left and walked the eight blocks to the hospital. She decided after the walk to the hospital she'd gotten her exercise for the week and Annette was not going to be home to harass her about it either. She walked to the front desk, the nurse behind the desk looked tired, stray wisps of hair framed her face, her eyes were dulled from fatigue, when she spoke, her voice was low and weary. It made Natasha feel bad for bothering her for a visitors pass. The lady did not bother saying another word once Natasha told her who she was coming to see. She wrote her name down on a white label and tossed it on the top of the counter. Natasha did not appreciate having things tossed at her but she did not want to get into a confrontation, so she swallowed her pride and walked to the elevator. She pressed the number three button and got off on the third floor. She arrived at Annette's room and the young woman turned to look at her, smiling as she entered the room.

"About time, you brought your sorry ass in here, don't you know 'people hungry'?" She asked jokingly, as she held her one good hand out, fingers outstretched and wiggling to indicate her desperation for the food. Natasha laughed and walked over to the bed, but out of arms reach and dangled the bag of food in front of Annette, who began to whine. "Awe, come on, gimmie, gimmie, gimmie!"

"Man, I don't get a 'happy to see you,' or a 'thanks for visiting my stankin' ass!', nothing, geezs, what an ingrate! Here!" She chuckled and tossed the bag that had the room smelling with its aroma, into Annette's lap. The woman quickly opened the bag, snatched the sandwich out of it, unwrapped the aluminum foil hastily before shoving the juicy sausage and beef sandwich into her mouth with only the use of one hand. She took a bite and pulled the sandwich away from her mouth, long strands of melted cheese connected the sandwich to her lips. Natasha gave her friend a look of disgust and shook her head.

"You look nasty eating that sandwich, makes me not even want mine!" She laughed . Annette shrugged, when she was able to free her mouth she had to explain.

"You obviously forgot in your twenty-four hours, just how disgusting hospital food is. I feel like a starving woman being tossed a cracker, this sandwich is the best damn sandwich I've ever eaten!" She said, greedily swallowing the last of the sandwich.

"Yeah, I guess I blocked the horrible experience from my memory, we are never to talk about it again." She joked. "What are you watching?"

Annette looked towards the TV. "The news, nothing special, only have fifteen channels, you think they would have more channels for you to watch when you're in a hospital, you know what I mean? I mean it 's bad enough you're depressed cause you had to go to the hospital, even worse when you wake up in one and your only form of entertainment is fifteen lousy channels, it ain't right!" She shook her head, looking grim. Natasha chuckled. Annette always made her laugh, they made each other laugh, even when they were sad, which was the best time to laugh. Natasha looked at the small square thirteen inch color TV and watched as the news anchor reiterated the gruesome details of the crime from earlier that morning. Listening to the details again made the memory of her horrific dream flash in her mind. She turned to Annette.

"I have to tell you something that happened to me last night." She said apprehensively.

"You got laid? Did you fuck Xavier?! Awe shit, I bet it was the bomb!" Annette said excitedly. Natasha frowned and shook her head.

"No, you gutter mind! We talked last night and that was it, I'm still trying to make up my mind if I want to go that route, it's still weird to me, you know, it's different...but I am still interested. But that's not what I wanted to tell you." She reached behind her and grabbed the uncomfortable leather chair from the corner of the room and moved it closer to Annette's bed. She sat down in the chair and a low hiss escaped through the leather bindings. She looked up at her friend, perplexed.

"Last night, I had this weird ass dream, every since the accident I've been having all these weird dreams. I had decided not to take my medication and it is as though I've opened Pandora's box. I've been seeing what I think may be premonitions! God! I hope not, cause this fucking sucks if it is!"

Annette looked at her friend with concern. "What was your medication for?"

"Well, every since I was a kid, I was told I was taking it for my headaches... "She trailed off. "I don't remember having a lot of headaches in my youth, but I do remember having weird dreams." She said thoughtfully. She stared off across the room as if she was recollecting some long lost memory. She caught herself staring off and bringing herself back to the present-looked reflectively at Annette who waited patiently for her friend to continue.

"I used to have weird dreams, I think my parents lied to me about my medication. A doctor at this hospital, told me the medication I have been taking every night for all these years was a dream suppressant. But now that I'm not taking them anymore, it's like my mind is being flooded with all of these fragments of..I don't know quite what to call it." She said clearly frustrated, her hands hovering beside her temples. Annette felt sorry for her friend. She did not know what to say.

"Are they like visions?" She asked.

"Yes!, that's exactly what they're like. It's like I saw you in the hospital last night eating grape geletin, but I saw all this through, *your* eyes, first person's view." She held her fingers above her eyes, as she looked at her friend. "You think I'm losing it don't' you?"

Annette shook her head. "I *was* eating grape gelatin last night. You got a gift, Tasha. You can see things as they're happening. You don't have to think you're a freak or something like that. God granted you with this gift, for a reason, you should embrace it. See god knew who to give it to, cause if it were *my* gift, I'd be trying to see people's bank account information, cause I'm a heathen like that, and broke, people need money!" She laughed outright. Natasha chuckled, she knew her friend had the craziest sense of humor, and she also knew that she wouldn't make her feel abnormal if she told her. She felt compelled to tell her the rest of her discovery.

"I think I saw the murder that happened last night!" She said in a rush of words. Annette looked at her, her smile fading as what Natasha blurted to her registered in her mind.

"What do you mean? The dead woman they're talking about?" She asked, her good hand pointing towards the TV. The news had just went off, and an evening sitcom had just come on.

Natasha nodded. "It was as if I was looking through the eyes of the killer, I think it was the same one, I don't' know but I could see the hand, it was a huge hand then it grew fur and thick sharp nails formed from normal human looking nails. There was a woman in front of me. In the dream..um...vision, she was crying and begging for her life. Then the hand started ripping into her flesh, just tearing away her insides!" She closed her eyes tight, hands covering her face. "The worse part of it is, I could feel what the killer felt!" She shook her head, she did not want to believe she saw the murder, could not believe it, to do so is to claim insanity.

"No, no...there's got to be a logical explanation for all of this." Natasha moaned. "This doesn't make sense. None of it." She exclaimed in anguish, as she rose from the chair and began pacing in front of Annette's little bed. The other woman watched her, trying to think of the possibility that her friend could see things. And if she really did see this murder, what was she going to do about it?

"Natasha, listen to me. If you get another one of these visions of this murderer, you've got to tell the police." She said, Natasha stopped pacing, she looked at her friend, shaking her head.

"They'd laugh at me, and probably lock me up. They would not take me seriously. What am I supposed to say? I had a dream about the killer, I saw how he did it. Yeah right, that's how you get committed." She shook her head. Annette wanted to reassure her friend that not everyone would laugh, especially not in this day and age.

"Natasha, the next victim could be you or me or your mother, my mother, father, a child, innocent people are dying! You have this gift that may help the police catch this murderer. If you sit on it and not do anything and day after day you hear about a new body found in a back alley and you knew that you could have prevented it, you would never forgive yourself. You might as well be an accomplice!" She said, she hated to be so blunt but she wanted to give Natasha the cold hard truth. It worked. Natasha found herself slumped in the leather chair, tears suspended in her eyes.

"I don't want this gift, curse, whatever, I don't want it Annette, you did not see what I saw!" She said trying to hold onto her composure.

"No I didn't, but you're the only one who did. And you're the only one who can do something about it. If you embrace your ability to help people, then it can be a gift. If you choose to ignore it and all that it brings to you, then it *will* be a curse. Can you live with that? How do you know the visions will stop? Just because you don't want to see them, doesn't mean they won't come. I read about something like this in a magazine article." She adjusted herself in the bed, to get more comfortable. "This woman could predict the future, you may be seeing the future and not actually the present, did you think of that?" She asked.

Natasha nodded her head dejectedly. "So how can you sit there and try to escape this!?" Annette asked. "Yeah, it's a bum wrap for you, real shitty, but Jesus had a bum wrap too. This is your cross to bear, so use it for good." She looked at Natasha who was looking down at her trembling hands clasped together in her lap. Annette's tone grew softer. "Tasha, you must go to the police and tell them what you saw, what you know, even if they laugh at you, you have to do something, as it is now everyone is in danger. I know you're scared and unhappy, but you can't run from these visions."

"If I take my medication again, I'll be okay." Natasha said, stubbornly. Annette's face flashed with anger.

"You got to be kidding me, did I just waste my breath here!? Sure, you can run and hide behind your meds and pretend that you did not see what you saw and delude yourself. But you'll always know the truth. Look, it's your choice Tasha, but I hope you make the right choice even if it's the hardest one." Annette said, she was angry with her friend, but she could empathize with her. In less than forty-eight hours, Natasha had discovered she's a psychic and had witness a horrible murder take place, through the eyes of the sadistic son of a bitch that committed it. She figured Natasha's world just flipped upside down. But she couldn't except Natasha letting people die when she could prevent it, or at least try to prevent it just because she was afraid.

Natasha sat in the leather chair, and reflected on everything her friend said to her. She thought about everything that had happened to her in the past two days. She wanted to go home, to think. She needed to be alone. She rose from the chair and walked to her friend's bed and gave her a hug. They embrace for a long time, she thanked Annette for her advice.

"Think about all of it, Tasha, okay? I love you, be careful, really careful." Annette said as Natasha closed the door behind her and headed for the elevator. She pressed the lobby button, and walked off the elevator when she reached the ground floor. On the train ride home she thought about it, she weighed her options, she could take the medicine again now that she knew what it was. Had her parents been thinking about her well being when they gave her the medicine to suppress her dreams or was it because they did not want to be troubled with a 'special' daughter. She wondered about that as the bus rocked slowly. She walked into her apartment and decided she needed to talk to her mother. She sat down on the sofa, picked up the telephone and punched in the seven digit number. She glanced at her watch as she waited for an answer, the time was 10:05pm. She waited for several rings, then came the sound of her mother's voice .

"Hello?" Asked her mother

"Hey, mom, it's me, Tasha. I need to talk with you." She said, there was a short silence over the phone, then her mom responded.

"Okay, you know you can talk to me about anything, baby girl, what is it?"

"Mom, why did you and dad put me on this medication and further more, why did you not tell me about it in all these years. I've been thinking I'm taking this for migraines and I'm not. I can see things, can't I?" She asked, her voice was laced with anger. Anger at her assumed betrayal by her parents.

"How did you find out? At the hospital?"

"Yeah, I did, I must have looked like a fool to them." She said.

"We did it for you, we did not want to see you suffering. when you were only four years old you started seeing these visions. You would be so confused and terrified. You thought they were nightmares and at first, so did we." Her mother paused.

"So what happened?"

"You would come up to us in the mornings sometimes, but most of the time it was during the night, you would wake up screaming after you had a dream. And you would tell us what you saw. Like I said, we thought they were only nightmares. But then one day, you came to us and you told us a disturbing dream you had about your best friend Michelle, from next door. You were very upset and you said that she was playing with her father's gun and it went off, then everything went black." Her mom's voice trailed off to silence.

"Mom, go on, what happened!?" Natasha said, earnestly.

"She died the next night. She was playing with her father's gun, just like you had said and the safety wasn't on and it went off and the bullet entered her head, she died instantly." Her mother's voice quaked with tears. Natasha's tears fell freely from her eyes. They trailed down her cheeks. She remembered her friends funeral. How sad she felt that her best friend had died. Her parents never told her how she died. Now it sickened and angered her to know her friend's death could have been avoided.

"Did you even try to tell her parents what I saw, even if they laughed at you? Did you!!!" She yelled into the phone overcome with anger, sadness and frustration. Her friend Annette was right. She would not sit on this ability and let people die, not like Michelle had died twenty years ago. She could hear her mother crying, she felt the sadness set in. The situation hit her like a ton of bricks. She might have been able to prevent someone from dying, but there was no telling how many deaths had happened that she might have foreseen, and changed the fate, if she had just accepted the truth last night. That woman might still be alive. No one to blame but herself. She would not live with that fact, ever again.

"We did not tell her parents. Natasha, believe me, I have had to live with that all these years! I was too sick at heart to believe you could see the truth, I did not want your little mind to suffer. I could not sit there and watch my only child, go through mental and emotional anguish, night after night. There was no telling what you would see, how it would have haunted you. You were a baby, how were you to understand what you had. We did what we thought was best for you, to give you a normal life!" Her mother said passionately.

"I haven't been taking the medicine for a few days, mom. I've seen things. Things I can't let go of. I've seen through the eyes of a murderer, mother. I don't know how I have the connection, or why, but I do. I've seen him kill someone. And I think it was the murdered woman that was on the news

177

today. I don't know much detail right now but If I get another vision I will not disregard it or any more in the future. Can you support me?" She asked.

There was a silence over the phone. Then her mother spoke, softly. "If this is what you truly want to do. I will support you. But think about it. You may never be able to stop these visions or control them."

"I know. First I need to figure out how or why I only see visions of certain people." She said thoughtfully.

"We took you to all sorts of specialists, they could not tell us much about your ability. Then we took you to one who said you make connections through personal items that you've touched. For your friend, you had played with her toys, you were the best of friends, your connection was strong. It's a mental bond, or so I was told. The doctor said that the brain waves have to be really active, strong, for you to form the connection, he hinted that you may have a touch of clairvoyance which accounts for part of the connection."

It was Natasha turn to be silent, she remained quiet for a few minutes, then she spoke softly. "I can't believe you knew all this for all of these years, and never told me."

"What parent want's their child to suffer."

"Certainly not the parents of the people I could have saved, mom." Natasha felt the anger boil again. She knew her mother meant well, but she would have wanted the choice. She understood she was being unduly harsh, but the past seventy-two hours was hard on her, and she was having difficulty controlling her emotions.

"I fear that you would go insane from what you would see. I didn't want that. Are you sure you want to stop taking the medication?" She asked concerned.

"Yes, mom. You know, Annette said this was a blessing and now I see why. I can't throw it away, nor can I hide. Mom, I realize why you and dad did what you did, and I forgive you. I love you, both. But I have to go."

"I love you, too, honey. I will talk with you later." They finished their goodbyes and Natasha hung up the phone. She sat in the living room and looked around. She laid down on the sofa slowly. She knew now that going to sleep would mean something entirely different from the norm. sleep would never be sleep for her ever again. She stared at the ceiling, she pounder the 'cross' she was preparing to carry. She slowly closed her eyes and prayed for the vision again. Soon she drifted away from the busy sounds of the street. The constant car honking, people screaming, sirens, all of it faded into silence. Then there was nothing.

She sat down on a black dust covered chair. Her long thick muscular legs stretched before her. Her thick strong fingers, laced and resting on her stomach. She looked at a man laying naked, stretched out on a metal table . He was scared, this man, he begged for his life, eyes brimming with tears, his body was covered in sweat. His wrist and ankles were bound to the four corners of the table, a stream of urine trickled to the floor from the table forming a small puddle. She laughed at the man her tongue running over her lips, a large thick bulge grew between her legs. Her left hand trailed down her denim jeans to caress the bulge making her moan slightly. Her eyes closed for a moment to savor the sensations.

"Stop playing with yourself." A sensuous feminine voice said. A tall woman had entered the room, she wore a red leather body blouse revealing the cleavage of her tightly pressed breast causing her bosom to rise high on her chest. She wore a pair of skin tight red leather shorts. The shorts barely covered the paleness of her buttocks. Her red high heel boots click-clacked on the concrete floor as she walked closer to the male form on the table. Her blue eyes peered into the man's pleading face, her right hand in her hair, fingers twirling the black locks between them.

"Why don't *you* come over here, and play with me." The male voice said, it was thick, deep and husky. It came from Natasha's own throat, this man's voice. He continued to massage his groin then fingers reached for the zipper and fingers dug into the opening of the jeans, and freed the bulge. Thick fingers massaged the hardness. She could feel the sensation the fingers were creating. It sent tremors down her spine. Her back arched in the chair and a low animal sound came from her throat, a growl would best describe it.

"Should we save him for tomorrow night, or feast on him now?" Asked the beautiful lady. As she looked in Natasha's direction.

"Let's save him for tomorrow night. He's strong and he definitely looks tasty. But right now, I have other things on my mind. I want you on my mind." Her male voice said as fingers pointed at the hardness. The female threw her head back and laughed. She looked at the form sitting in the dusty chair and began to walk over to it. Through the eyes of the killer, Natasha watched as the female climbed into his lap. Her hips began to grind on the hardness, causing a deep masculine moan to escape his mouth. Thick hands gripped the slender hips of the beautiful woman. His face leaned forward, Natasha felt as if his own tongue licked along the neckline of the woman, sending shivers through his body, his back arching. The male form on the metal table, began to scream for help. The woman turned around and looked at him, both of them laughed at him. Before continuing their love making.

179

Natasha could see the emptiness of the room. The windows were blocked with thick wooded boards. The floor was covered with several layers of dust and grime. There was no electricity in the room, only a few candles burned around the prone man.

The man screamed until his voice became hoarse, despair started to sink in. He began to cry again and pray. The beautiful woman began to undress, revealing two perfectly creamy breast, her pink nipples erect. Natasha could feel her mouth closing around the nipples, her tongue licking them hard. She could feel the softness of the other breast in her left hand, her fingers groping the tender flesh. She could feel the woman's hotness between her legs over her erect groin.

Natasha opened her eyes, she stared at the ceiling as she lay still gathering her thoughts. She remembered where she was, who she was. She knew that she saw things through the eyes of a man, she knew they planned to kill the male victim on the next night. She knew she had a time limit. She sat up on the sofa and looked around the room, wiping her eyes to help clear her vison. She looked at her watch, the time was 5am. She rose from the sofa and grabbed her coat. She ran down the block and caught a bus before it pulled away from the curb. She paid her fare and sat down in the back of the bus, until she reached her stop. She switched from the bus to the train and rode the train until she arrived at Grand street, she got off. The police station was just a few blocks away.

She saw the white and tan building, a full square block including the parking lot. She was a little nervous about what she was going to do. She hoped that they would not laugh at her or call her names. She hoped that they would take her seriously. She walked into the huge station and looked around. The main lobby had several grey benches where a few dozen people sat quietly, waiting to be seen. The floor was light grey cement-tiles. Florescent lights illuminated the huge room, adding a certain glow. Uniformed officers walked by, decked out in black pants and black zippered jackets with enough pockets to store all kinds of things.

She walked up to the front desk and placed a trembling hand on the counter, the desk officer looked up at her. His cold grey eyes looked tired. His bald head glowed under the lights.

"Can I help you, ma'am?" He asked, his nostrils flared as he spoke.

"Um, yes, I need to speak with the officer that's dealing with all of these murders in the city, um." She paused, she knew she would probably need to be more specific. "The dead body found earlier this morning, I need to talk to the officer who's working on that case." She looked at the officer behind the desk. His eyes trailed her up and down, then he reached over to the telephone and dialed. A deep male voice came over the speaker.

"Yeah?" The voice asked.

"Yeah, I got a woman out here, that says she needs to speak with you about the murders you're working on. Come round." Said the desk officer.

"Will do," said the voice. Natasha felt a little embarrassed as she fantasized about the man who owned the voice she heard over the speaker. She wondered if it was the same man she saw on the news that morning. . His voice was clear, rich and sexy. She was anxious to find out. She look towards the active hallway were uniformed and plain clothes officers walked to and fro until her eyes located the extremely handsome man from the news report approaching. He was wearing a pair of black jeans and a form fitting white t-shirt that hugged his chest tight enough to show off his perfect abs and biceps. He walked gracefully towards her. She was surprised he knew she was the woman the officer had mentioned. Then her gaze flicked to the desk cop, and she saw him pointing in her direction. She was a little disappointed. He stood in front of her, even more handsome than he was on TV. She could feel herself blushing then forced it back, now was not the time to be bashful. She had something to say and she had to be as serious about it as she possibly could.

"I have information about the murders you're investigating." She said softly. The detectives eyes widen, he told her to follow him and he grabbed her by her arm lightly and led her into the main work area. The open space was lined with desks and filled with noises of people arguing, telephones ringing, and keyboards being typed on as officers worked diligently at their desks. He directed her back to his desk next to where his partner was sitting. He sat her in a chair adjacent to their desks. Warren sat down at his desk and looked at Natasha. She looked at his partner who was wearing a snug dark blue t-shirt and faded form fitting blue jeans. She liked his light brown eyes, they made him look warm and friendly.

"Can I get you anything, are you thirsty?" The Detective asked.

Natasha shook her head. "No, no thank you."

Warren gave one quick nod and introduced himself. "Ok, I"m detective Warren Davis and this is my partner, detective Matthew Eric" He said, as he gestured to the equally handsome man sitting across from him. Matthew waved in acknowledgment. "And you are…"

Natasha introduced herself. "Oh, I'm Natasha Hemingway. I work for the *Chicago Word*. I've um, I've come to you tonight because I know some details about the killings and when the next one will happen and possibly where." Both officer's leaned closer, Matthew actually pulling his chair around to the

181

front of her. Warren sat at his desk, poised with pen in hand. They looked at her, waiting for her to continue. They prayed that it was something solid, for four days now, they had zero to go on and now this person said she knows something. This may be the breaking point in their case.

"I…I don't' know how to explain this completely, but I'll try my best. I've always been able to 'see' things, like premonitions." She paused to witness their reaction. Their eyes were still locked on her, there was no mockery in their faces. "A few days ago, I was in a car accident. I had not taken my medication, because my friend and I went out to celebrate that night. I just got a new job. And she wanted me to share a drink with her. So I thought it best not to mix my medication with the drink. But after one drink, I started to feel sick, so we left the club." Matthew interrupted her.

"Wait a minute, was this the accident a few blocks from that club, *Slayer's Lair*?" He asked.

Natasha nodded her head. "Yeah, this guy who was drunk, dropped his keys and I told my friend to take the keys to the bartender who obviously gave them back to him. I knew who it was, because, while we were driving away in the cab, I had a vision about the accident. I saw the accident happen through the eyes of the guy who rear ended us. I saw it right before I woke up and then I woke up and saw the lights getting closer. Then it happened. At first, I disregarded it. Sometimes people have those little unexplainable things that happen to them." She took a few seconds to breathe and relax.

"So you've seen this murderer?" Warren asked, getting her back on track.

"Yes, I've seen through the eyes of the killer. It's a man, a pretty big man, he's caucasian, at least six-feet- seven, or eight inches tall. He's very muscular and I think he's a …wait, I know he's a shape-shifter, his hands were…"She trailed off she had remembered the man she met at the supermarket. She did not have those dreams until she had bumped into him at the store. She struggled to remember what he looked like. Warren sat back in his chair. All this was really weird to him but he was willing to take any kind of lead he could get. He threw a glance at Matthew who shrugged, not sure if he was going to take Natasha's word for it.

"I think I may have seen this man!" She said excitedly. "I went to a supermarket when I left the hospital. I bumped into him, it was like hitting a brick wall. He caught me before I fell. I don't know what I could have touched that was his to make our connection. He had a handful of meat, ground beef and chuck roast, things like that." She said thinking back, trying to recapture any details that she could. Warren sat at his cluttered desk and thought about the descriptions Natasha had given.

"I saw them kill the woman that you found this morning." She looked at her watch, "well, yesterday morning. I could see him killing her through his eyes. That's how I see things, it's like I experience everything with the person. It's really weird and I don't like it. But I watched in my vision as his hand turn from a normal human hand to a furry claw. Then I saw him rip at her stomach, just ripping, as if she were paper…" her voice faded, tears welled up in her eyes. Matthew reached over and removed some tissues from the box on his desk and handed a handful of them to Natasha who took them gratefully, and began to blow her nose, and wipe her tears away.

"And you saw all of this. Just like you were actually doing it yourself?" Matthew asked genuinely curious.

She nodded her head and dabbed her eyes. "Yeah, I don't know how long she would have lived had I came to you guys then, but I did not want to believe it…I'm sorry." She said, her head down in shame.

"Don't beat yourself up about it, the important thing is you're here now, helping." Warren said, patting her hand to reassure she was not to blame.

"You said, 'them' as in more than one?" Asked Matthew. Warren looked at him then back to Natasha, who was nodding her head.

"Yeah, a female, I'm not sure what she is. Her eyes glowed red when I first saw her. The night they killed the woman. She had pale skin, jet black wavy hair, it was long to her thighs. She had blue eyes, when they weren't glowing red. She likes to wear a lot of leather-tight leather. Tonight, I had a vision of them. I could see through the male again. He was sitting in a chair, there was a man on this metal table. He was crying and begging for his life just like the woman before. And the man watched him, he was happy to hear the other man pleading for his life, it was like I could taste his fear." She explained to the two officers using her hands to emphasize the feeling she was receiving through her vision.

"As he sat in the chair, he began to masturbate." She said, her face flushing with blood. She could feel her body temperature rise. She squirmed in her seat trying to get more comfortable. Her arm knocked Warren's mug off of the desk and she caught hold of it but fumbled it and Warren caught the mug before it hit the floor.

"I'm so sorry, I'm just so nervous, I didn't mean to make a mess." She said apologetically.

"Don't worry about it, doesn't matter, lady you could break everything in the place for all I care, I'm thrilled with this information." Warren said as he placed the mug on the other side of his desk.

Natasha smiled because they did not laugh at her or think she was crazy. They took her seriously from the very beginning. She continued. "The other killer came into the room, she teased the male victim then she said, and I remember. 'Should we save him for tomorrow night, or feast on him now?' the male killer said that he wanted to save him for tonight because he looked tasty and he wanted to savor his meal. Then they began to have sex as the man laid on the metal table screaming for his life, they laughed at him. His fear seem to make them horn...hornier." She blushed more. And looked away. Then she looked at Matthew, who was quiet.

"If we could get a sketch artist in here, can you give us their descriptions?" Warren asked. Natasha nodded.

"I'll do my best." She looked at her watch, it was seven in the morning. She was tired. She would have to call off of work, it was only her second day, she might as well kiss that job goodbye. She felt sad, she enjoyed her first day at work, in spite of all that was going on. Warren dialed a number on the telephone, he sat there tapping his pen on his desk as he waited for the person to pick up the phone. Matthew leaned closer and continue to ask questions.

"Did you see what the place looked like where they were holding the man? Do you know where it's at?" He asked.

"Well, it was pretty dark in the room. The place looked abandoned. There were wood boards over the windows and the floor was really dusty and disgusting. The room was pretty big from what I could see. They had some candles burning around the small area they were at, but that's it. I wish I knew more. I might have to have more visions to be of further help." She said sadly. The thought of having to have more visions upset her. For it's obvious she would have to see more death and torture and the sight of blood sickened her.

"Trust me, you have done so much, even now. You've been the biggest lead we've had. We were going out of our minds trying to establish a suspect profile, nothing came up. But you have the best clues yet!. You have done more than enough." Matthew said pleased, excited about the new information they now had. Natasha smiled. She was very pleased that what she told them was so vital.

"Tell me, do you have to be asleep to see these visions?" Warren asked when he got off of the telephone.

"At this point, yes. I have to be completely asleep. Then the visions come. Some are just random, people playing, or having sex, or eating. Nothing terrible. But my doctor says it's the brain waves that help me form a connection with a certain person to the point where I can see *how* they see, *feel* what they feel." She said wearily, she yawned and covered her mouth. She looked up to see a middle aged man approaching her. He had a sketch pad in one hand and a set of pencils in another. His salt and pepper hair was combed back exposing a receding hair line...and he was wearing a wrinkled blue sweatshirt and jeans. He sat down in front of her and held out his hand.

"I'm David Foster. I'm the sketch artist. Why don't you sit back, relax and try to remember any detail about the face that you can." He said as he poised his pencil over the canvas. Natasha settled into the chair. She closed her eyes and tried to envision both of their features. She began to give details as the sketch artist's hand worked furiously on the canvas. His eye's darted to Natasha several times as he etched out the features of the male murder suspect she described.

"Do this look like the man you saw?" He asked as he held out the white sketch book. Natasha opened her eyes and looked at the drawing. Her mouth dropped open, amazed at the incredible likeness. It was her killer, no doubt about it. She pointed at the picture and nodded her head looking at both Warren and Matthew. The two detectives took the sketch from the artist and focused on the features. Warren could judge by the size of his head, that he was a huge man and an even more enormous wolf, even bigger than himself.

"Okay, I'm ready to do the other sketch." Said the artist, he retrieved his sketchbook, then turned the page. Natasha closed her eyes again and began to describe the female she saw in her visions. The sketch artist's pencil worked over the paper, she could hear the soft sounds of the lead pencil scratching paper as he copied her descriptions.

"Is this accurate?" He asked, once again holding up the canvas for approval. Natasha looked at the picture and nodded her head. She looked grim. Warren looked at the picture, Matthew stood behind Warren's chair and looked down at the sketching.

"Well, is that it? Do you need me for anything else?" Asked the sketch artist. Both Warren and Matthew shook their heads and thanked him. He gathered his belongings and left the room.

"So, what's next?" Natasha asked. Matthew had returned to his desk, he looked at Warren.

"Well, from your descriptions of this place, we should probably check all abandoned buildings in the south side area. That's were the bodies are being

Desires Unleashed

deposited. Even though the victims could be getting murdered in an entirely different area then brought there, we have to narrow our search parameter and start somewhere." Matthew said as he looked through some files on his desk, noting the locations of where the bodies had been found.

"Where did you say you lived?" Warren asked.

She told them her address, "it's an apartment building. I live on the third floor, though we're trying to get an apartment on the second. Why?" She asked. She looked at Warren, she thought he and his partner were two of the hottest cops walking the earth. *They were two cops you wouldn't mind pulling you over. Shit, you might just drive fifty miles over the limit, just to snag one.*

"Well, you did say that you saw him in the grocery store in your neighborhood. That might help us narrow down a prospective area to search." Warren said. He nodded to his partner and both men rose from their seats and began to put on their coats. Natasha looked at both men. She felt that they wanted her to go also, she wasn't sure and did not really want to ask, but she felt she should.

"Do you need me to go with you?" She asked apprehensively.

"Yeah, we do. You might remember something, a landmark, something that might help us identify the building they may be in." He held out his hand to her, palm upwards and she slid her slender delicate hand into his and he pulled her out of the chair with ease. Natasha appreciated the strength of a strong man. She felt herself attracted to Warren, she was not quite sure why but she felt some other sort of connection as well. She followed the two men to the garage as they led her to the sturdy black and silver squad car. The car had the new sleek design of the new 2004 automobiles, but was solid steel and had titanium gates with silver overlay separating the back seats from the front seats. In the back seat, there was an over head lighting system. Natasha wondered why the car was like that. They all climbed into the automobile, Natasha in the back, Warren at the wheel.

"May I ask a question?" Natasha inquired.

"Yeah, shoot." Matthew said.

"Why is the car, well, what's with this car?"

"We're a policing team specially funded by the American government to control supernatural crime. This kind of case would never see a normal police officer's desk file drawer. All weird cases like this, that's suspected of supernatural foul play, comes directly to us. Since we have to deal with it, we are equipped with the means to deal with it. This car has a powerful ultraviolet lighting system. In the case of a vampire getting out of hand, under the US law, we have the right to flip the switch and fry their asses." He turned in his

186

seat to look at Natasha, he wanted to see her expression. He suspected she would be wide eyed and opened mouth, he had guessed right.

"What about the shape-shifters, I mean, I've seen this guy, he's huge!"she looked at the titanium cage, "he could probably rip this cage and crush it into a small ball and go bowling with it!" She said chuckling nervously. She was wondering how the hell they were going to get his humongous body into this car, and keep him there until they could get him to the jail.

Warren chuckled he could imagine what she was thinking, he was thinking the same thing. "Well," Matthew continue, "the cages, are built inside the car, it's a part of the car, welded and cover in silver-the same for the insides of the rear doors, you know what I mean? Besides, if he starts to resist, then under US law, we reserve the right to put a bullet into his head." Matthew said. Natasha began to think about the judicial system for the supernatural and how it differed from theirs.

"How do you even hold a vampire or shape-shifter for questioning let alone prosecution?" She asked, she thought it was a valid question. Matthew and Warren glanced at each other, they seem to be sharing a secret and Natasha could not help but feel out of her league. She did not like feeling that way.

"Well, the law works in a strange way. Say we catch our killer today in the act, we don't need to bring him in for questioning or prosecution under the new US law that was passed, we have the right to shoot and kill on the spot while in the act. No 'freeze, don't move' just shoot to kill, for both shape-shifters and vampires. We have liquid silver nitrate bullets that explode on contact with the skin. So basically, it goes into a shape-shifter's blood stream, he can not survive and dies instantly. For a vampire, we have liquid ultraviolet bullets and they do the same thing as the silver nitrate ones." Matthew said. It amazed him just how little people in the world new about their current situation. He thought that every mortal in the world should want to know what's out there. Mortals should want to know what resources they had to better protect themselves.

"Okay, so how do you bring them in and restrain them?" She asked. She could not believe she hadn't found out all of this information before. She had been so deep into denial she did not want to know more about the 'others' than she needed to. As it turns out, she needed to know a lot more than she did. She was happy to be learning new things now.

"Well, we also work with flame throwers and these special guns" Matthew stated as he held one up to her. It was metal with a black handle, it looked like a miniature sawed off shot gun to Natasha. "This little beauty here can hold sixteen hollow tip silver bullets that carry a little extra "umph". They explode a millisecond after contact and can take off a head, a limb, or blow out a chest. When we bring them in, they have a chance to prove their innocence. But that's only if we don't have any real evidence against them. There are no other exceptions. The law is very biased in that aspect." Matthew said, as he gazed at his partner who had been quiet the whole time.

They drove the rest of the way in silence to Natasha's neighborhood. They drove around the grocery store, Warren parked the car and got out. He turned and leaned into the driver's side window.

"I'm going to go in and check some things out, you two stay here." He walked off without waiting for a response from his partner. Natasha looked at Matthew who seemed to be a little nervous about his partner going in alone, but he said nothing.

"So how long have you two been partners?" She asked, trying to kill time and the boredom of sitting in a quiet car.

"Hmm, for about five years. I was on the force before he joined. Then, and this is going to throw you through a loop, we were selected for this government special unit because the normal police squads weren't prepared let alone equipped to handle the supernaturals. So the government drafted ex soldiers and cops from across the country for specific training, there were over one hundred thousand of us chosen, but only about fifteen hundred passed the training. Warren and I being two of them. What really pisses me off is that we're stretched so thin. It's only one S.U.I.T. division per state. That's fifty-two units and about thirty cops per unit. Granted, states like Illinois have about forty officers in our division, it's still not nearly enough because we cover the entire state and then some if help is needed. You can imagine how stressful things can get." He looked out the window. "Here he comes." He said relieved as Warren opened the car door and climbed inside.

"Find anything?" Matthew asked.

"Warren shook his head. "Not really." he started the car, pulled out of the parking lot and began to drive down the street looking for abandoned homes and stores. He pulled the car over in front of a tall two story building with boarded up windows.

"Does this look familiar in any way?" He asked. Natasha looked at the building. And shook her head.

"No, it doesn't, but in the vision I was inside the building and it was really dark. I couldn't see anything distinct except the man on the table and the female. I wish I could tell you more but that's the best I can do for now."

"Miss. Hemingway believe me when I say this, you have been our knight in shining armor. We had nothing to go on, and it was eating at us, so don't be upset. If you remember or see anything else, just let us know, here's my card." Warren said as he handed her his card with his home and cell phone number on it. "You can always reach me with either of those numbers. I'll drop you off at home now." He said. Natasha looked at him, confused.

"I thought you needed me to come along with you?" She asked, somewhat disappointed, she felt like she was letting them down.

Warren shook his head. "No, we can handle this, if we do find the killers I don't want you in the middle of it. Like I said, you've done more than enough already. So let me drop you off." He pulled off in the direction of Natasha's apartment. The car stopped in front of her three story apartment building with white trim painted window and red awning. There was a small landscaped garden in the front of the building with a white fountain that was turned off due to the winter season. She climbed out of her car and walked to the drivers side window and peered in.

"If I see anything else I'll call you right away." She said.

"Call the cell phone, I'll probably be out late today. We might need you to come into the station at some point to complete some reports, I'll let you know. Thanks for everything take care of yourself" Warren said, Matthew smiled and nodded. Natasha smiled sadly at the two officers, she hoped they would be ok. She was worried for them, she would hate to be the one who had to deal with the supernatural criminals. It was truly a horrendous job, 'but she reasoned *someone had to do it.'* She walked away from the car and went into her apartment building. She dragged herself up three flights of stairs and by the time she reached her apartment, she had only enough energy to plop down onto the sofa. She closed her eyes as she regained her normal breathing pace. She began to feel extremely sleepy, she realized that she only had about five or six hours sleep at the most. And her body felt the lack of rest. She looked at her watch, the time was 10:46am. She walked into her bedroom and called her job and requested the day off. She hoped she would still have the job the next day. She laid down comfortably in the bed and decided to let the sleep take her.

She walked into the darkness of the room. She could smell the distinctive scent of another wolf breed in the room. She raised her gun, the hand that held the gun was a man's hand. It was strong, not a normal man's strength. She looked at her partner Matthew. Matthew looked at her and nodded slowly moving behind her, back to back. Her eyes could see very well in the darkness and she knew she was in an abandoned warehouse. She could see old boxes stacked on top of each other or strewn about. There was dust and grime on the floor and the strong scent of blood whiffed up to her nostrils, the scent made her mouth water. She could hear the soft whimpers of a mortal man near by. The scent of him mingled with the scent of old blood made her hungry. She knew instantly that she was seeing through the eyes of detective Warren Davis, and he was a shape-shifter. She could hear another voice in the room, she looked in the direction of the voice.

"I can feel the vampire here, they're close. Keep an eye out, do you see your wolf?" Asked a tall man, he was wearing a dark green ribbed sweater and black front-pleated pants, his long black trench coat flowed outward behind him as he walked around the room, scanning. His long black hair framed his gorgeous face, his dark green eyes pierced the darkness. "I can smell human blood, do you see your wolf? there is a human alive here, I can hear his heart beating." The man stated as he looked around.

"I can smell the wolf and the vampire." She catches a glimpse of movement behind the dark haired stranger. "Darian, behind you!" She yelled, through her male voice. She watched the other man defend himself with seeming ease as he fought with the female vampire. Who bared her fangs and swung her clawed hand towards the man named Darian. That vision began to fade into darkness and another started to form. She saw the three men looking around the warehouse, searching for something, someone. She knew who she was in the vision. She was the male shape shifter and he was setting his sights on Warren, she could see herself moving closer. A loud ringing sound filled her head. The sound began to pull her out of the vision. She woke up and stared into the darkness of her bedroom, she heard the phone ringing again. She sat up and lifted to receiver to her ear.

"Hello?" She asked, her voice groggy, drugged.

"Well don't you sound sexy first thing in the evening." A sexy smooth male voice said through the telephone. Natasha knew his voice, it sent tingles down her spine.

"Hi Xavier. Look, this is a bad time. I need to call you back, is that ok?" She asked. She was anxious to call Warren, she needed to tell him what she saw.

"Well, this is unexpected. Okay, call me later." He said as he hung up the telephone. Natasha noted that she did not get a chance to say goodbye, she hoped he wasn't upset with her. She thought about the last few days and was astounded by how fast her life had changed. Would it ever be normal for her again? She did not know. She dialed the cell phone number that warren had given her and listen to the telephone ring three times, before Warren picked up.

"Hello?" He asked

"Detective Davis, this is Natasha Hemingway, I need to talk with you, I had another vision!" She said excitedly.

"Are you still at home?"

"Yes."

"I'm on my way," and he hung up the telephone. She hung up the telephone and dressed quickly then waited for the detective to arrive. She looked at her watch, the time was 7:42pm, she soon heard a knock on her door, the knock was loud enough to make her jump. She wondered if it was Warren, if so, he made it to her house in seven minutes. She wondered where he had been when she called. She walked to the door, and looked through the peep hole, she saw it was both him and his partner Matthew. She opened the door and let them in. They walked past her and looked around her little apartment.

"What did you see?" Asked Warren, not wasting any time.

"I saw you, I mean, I saw through your eyes. I felt what you felt, and" she paused and looked at Warren, she walked over to him and gestured for him to lean closer. He did and she whispered into his ear. She whispered low, she knew he had excellent hearing. "I smelled what you smelled. I know what you are." She stepped back quickly, hoping she had not just made a mistake. She did not want to be dinner. Warren looked at her, he could not figure out how she could do what she did. He looked at his partner, then back at Natasha.

"He knows, you don't have to whisper." He said to her attempting to clear the air.

"Oh, okay. That's a relief, I'm not the only one who knows." She said happily, if his partner knew, then she might not be his dinner.

"What else did you see?" He asked. It seemed as though he did not care that Natasha knew his secret only that he could solve the case. Natasha was happy that he was on her side.

"The building is an abandoned warehouse. I'm not sure where, there were cardboard boxes everywhere and the place was all dusty and grimy, I have no idea what kind of warehouse it is, if I knew that, it would help narrow the search, wouldn't it?" She asked. Both men nodded. She paled. "I thought as much. Oh, there was another man there, he was helping you." She said. Both Warren and Matthew gave each other a surprised look, they couldn't possibly figure out who could be helping them.

"Who?" Asked Matthew.

"I think he was a vampire, he fought with the female I told you about, she was a vampire too. You called him Darian in my vision." Natasha said.

She looked at Warren to see if the name registered. It looked as though the name did. "Do you know him?" She asked.

Warren and Matthew nodded their heads. "He's the owner of that huge entertainment club called *Desires Unleashed*. He's also the master vampire in this city. Only reason why I know this, is because of my leader. Both of them have been in the city for a long time. The S.U.I.T.'s don't have a real record on him, such as real age, nationality, nothing of the sort. All we know is that he registered his business as a vampire owned establishment. Why would he help us? Why would he want to?" Warren asked, he seemed to be really pondering the notion.

"The female vampire looked to be strong and he was fighting her, I think you need him for a reason. I wouldn't go against the vision, oh, and the male victim is still alive, you could hear him somewhere in the warehouse."

"Well, I suppose we have to make a trip to *Desires Unleashed*. Let's go, we don't have time to waste. You did say they wanted to kill him tonight, right?" he asked Natasha as they headed down the stairs to the car. She nodded her head. "Then we need to haul ass." He said as he climbed into the drivers side. He turned on the siren and lights as he raced through the crowded streets, switching from lane to lane at break neck speed. Natasha began to wonder if they would survive the ride over. She watched Warren drive, his eyes locked on the road, his reflexes were perfect, inhuman, he didn't even flinch as he dodged two potential accidents. Ten minutes later, they arrived in front of the club her best friend worked at. Would Xavier be here tonight? Natasha wondered.

Chapter 19

There was a long line of people waiting to get in. Some of the people were dressed in black garments. Their eyes, nails and lips decorated with dark colored cosmetics. They looked excited about going in, they wanted to see a real-life creature-of-the-night. She climbed out of the car with the two detectives. A valet parking attendant walked over. His black hair was shaved low, he was wearing a black shirt and pants uniform, with a white satin vest.

"Excuse me, sir, but you can't park there." He said trying to get Warren's attention. He did.

"Look" Warren flashed his badge, and the man's brown eyes widen. No one of the supernatural race wanted to see that badge. He stepped back and watched as Warren flashed the badge to the door bouncer who made Warren wait as he called his boss on walkie talkie.

"Yeah, un hun, okay, okay…yes sir." He put down the walkie talkie and called over another bouncer who stalked over towards them. He was tall, he had a mustache and his head was shaved bald. He stepped up to Warren, looked him up and down and a snarl appeared on his face.

"Against your own kind, ain't that grand." He said disgustedly. Warren stepped up to him, the bouncer was two inches taller than Warren but it did not seem to matter.

"Do I have to go through you to get to your master." Warren said, the bouncer's snarl grew more tense, his body became ridged.

"That depends, why are you here, traitor!?" He hissed through his clench teeth. Warren took a deep breath and let it out. He became annoyed at the run around he was getting. Matthew stayed quiet, he did not want to tread in uncharted waters. Natasha took his cue and remained silent herself.

"I need to speak with your master, I need information from him, he's not a suspect so can we calm down the tough-son-of-a-bitch attitude. I don't have time for it." Warren said. His nostrils flaring slightly as he kept his temper in check. The two bouncers, who Natasha suspected might be vampires, looked at each other then nodded.

"Follow me," said the bald headed bouncer that was causing the stall. He led them through the crowded dance floor. They had to push past some of the rowdy dancers that did not seem to have any regard for the four of them passing through. Natasha looked upwards and was astounded that there were gogo dancers in skimpy black leather outfits dancing in cages suspended from the ceiling. She reckoned that was a real thrill for the party goers. She liked the vitality of the disco music the DJ was playing, she enjoyed the vibrations of the bass as the sounds thumped through her body. The only thing that annoyed her were the multicolored neon lights that danced around the club. She looked at the Bartender who was as sexy as all the other men she had been seeing lately. She marveled at his skills as he twirled bottles of alcohol for the crowd that cheered him on and praised his efforts with money. The bouncer directed them towards the employees only entrance and lifted the walkie talkie to his lips.

"Mr. Richards, I got two detectives here from the S.U.I.T.'s, they want to talk to the Boss. I'm bringing them to your office." He released the talk button and listened for further instructions.

"Two detectives? Did they say…nevermind. Go ahead and bring them to the Boss's office." Said a smooth deep voice, it took Natasha a few seconds to realize that it was Xavier's voice.

"Yes, sir." He said as the opened the door to the employees only entrance. The hallway was decorated with photographs of naked people, the photographs were done tastefully, no smut. The artist had truly captured the beauty of the human body in each photograph. Natasha found herself wanting to stop and look at the photos as if she was in a gallery but decided against it. Maybe she could ask Xavier to show them to her later. Then she thought about Xavier. *Was she really contemplating starting a relationship with him.* It seem to be a possibility to her. They were led to a set of double dark red wood doors. The bouncer knocked twice and a young blonde man opened the door. Natasha thought he was beautiful also but very young, his blue eyes gave them all a once over and he stepped aside and let them walk in.

They entered the room and looked around. Natasha marveled at the grandeur of the room. It was simply amazing, she wondered how much money it must have cost to decorate a room like this. Then her eyes spotted

Xavier, he seemed surprised to find her with the two cops, his eyes held a hint of bewilderment. She smiled at him and waved, she hoped that would ease some of his suspicions. This night was not going well for the two of them, so much going on, she hoped he would understand, if not, then that would be just one more thing to contemplate later. She looked at the huge three section black marble desk in the middle of the room and saw the most gorgeous man she had ever laid eyes on. Natasha fought hard not to stare dumbfounded. She wanted to photograph him, she wanted to kiss him, she wanted to touch him anything to prove that he was real, that his beauty was real, tangible. He sat comfortably in a black soft leather chair behind the desk. Natasha was willing to bet the chair vibrated from the looks of the rest of his office she would not be surprised.

He looked at the three of them, his eyes lingered on Natasha then darted over to Xavier. Natasha watched him observe Xavier watching her. She could not take her eyes off of this man, he held her captive in his gaze. He smiled and rose from the chair. He walked around the desk, practically gliding, Natasha wondered if his feet even touched the ground, his moves were so graceful. He leaned against the front of his desk and rested his palms on the top of his desk beside him. He was dressed as he had been dressed in her vison, hunter green sweater with black front pleated pants, the only thing missing was his trench coat. Warren had been watching him too, so had Matthew. Natasha looked at the two officers, she could see that they were looking at him pretty much in the same way she had looked at him. She began to wonder about their sexuality. She concluded that both Warren and Matthew might be gay.

"What can I do for you tonight, officers?" He spoke, this gorgeous man across the room spoke in a voice that matched his exotic beauty. Natasha could not tell what country he came from, his voice was low, but there was a certain hint of an accent when he spoke. It made his voice all the more sexier, more intoxicating. Warren seem to come out of a trance when he heard Darian speak, they all did.

"I'm detective Davis and this is detective Eric and Miss Hemingway." Warren said as he gestured to both Matthew and Natasha. "I don't know if you know about this, but there's been some murders around town." Warren said, his eyes darted around the room as if he was trying not to get caught in a spell. Natasha pondered if this beautiful man had put a spell on them then she looked at him from head to toe. She swallowed the saliva that had gathered in her mouth. And decided right away that this handsome hunk of man, had no need to cast such a spell, he was just blessed. He nodded his head, when Warren mentioned the murders, but did not seem too interested.

"Well," Warren paused and looked around the room, "can we talk alone?" He asked. Darian smiled and gestured for John to leave the room. John bowed and walked to the door opened it and left. Xavier stood in his place, not moving. Warren looked at Xavier but said nothing. He just continued speaking to Darian. "Well, we have a witness who has seen the murderers, one is a vampire. To make a long story short, we need your help. We know that they are going to kill someone tonight and we have to get to them before it happens, but we don't know where to find them, I think you can. Will you help us?" Warren asked.

Natasha looked at the man leaning against the desk. His expression was blank, as if he did not hear a word Warren said. Then his eyes darted to Natasha and Matthew, then back to her.

"Are you the witness?" He asked her. She nodded, it was all she could do, her voice was caught in her throat.

"And you want me to track down this rogue vampire and then do what?" He asked nonchalantly. Natasha was getting the feeling that he wasn't going to help them. She did not understand it, in the vision, he was there, he was fighting on their side.

"Well, I have weapons to deal with vampires, but let's face it, if this vampire is old, which I have an inkling that she is, I don't think I have the strength to fight her off and the wolf that's with her. Can you help us deal with them. She's killing people in your territory, this looks bad on you, don't you think?" Warren asked, trying to bring reason into the matter.

Natasha looked at the other man, this was the Darian from her vision. She was still at a lost for words. She watched as he shrugged his shoulders lazily. "You're the police squad, the government trained protectors of the human race, you take care of it. I do not pay taxes to do your jobs for you." He said sarcastically. He crossed his muscular arms over his broad chest. Natasha could not believe what she was hearing. Was he being obstinate?

"If we don't stop it tonight there will be more deaths, we need to find them, you're the only one who can help us!" Warren said desparately. Matthew had his hand on the hilt of his gun just in case things went sour. He did not know quite what to think of Darian. He watched Warren plead with the master vampire for help and wasn't sure if Natasha's vison was accurate.

"Humans die all of the time, either by their own hands, or old age, what do I care about a handful of mortals whom must meet their fate? You'll have to fight crime without me my young wolf, I see nothing in it for me." Darian said, offhandedly. Natasha saw red flash before her eyes, she could not believe someone could be that heartless. She looked at Xavier who stood silent. She stepped up to Darian, his forest green gaze lowered to meet the soft green of her eyes. One eyebrow raised slightly, he was curious about her.

"How can you stand there and say that, you would let people die horrible deaths and for what? You're being petty!" She yelled at him. He fought the urge to smile, he could always appreciate a feisty woman.

"I can resist easily, because I do not care." He chuckled.

"You know what, maybe you don't care but I do! I've seen what happens to these people, I see their deaths in my dreams! I can't just brush it off like some castoff thing the way you can. I see their suffering and I don't think you'd be all high and mighty if the shoe was on the other foot!" She could feel her temper rising. She looked at Darian who did not seem the least bit ruffled and it annoyed her even more. "People are dying, you can help, why won't you?" She asked, the tears welling up in her eyes, she imagine the male victim being gutted while they argued and it angered her even more. The more she looked at Darian, the less beautiful he was.

"You misunderstand me. This has nothing to do with me. I will not come to the aide of the human world as if I were some superhero in tights like your friend over there." He gestured languidly towards Warren.

"It is a shame that your condition will not allow you a moments peace, but even that holds very little concern to me." He said nonchalantly and Natasha felt an alarm go off in her head, she felt her hand rise before she could stop it and her open palm slapped Darian on the left cheek, before she even realized it was her hand that did the smacking. Their was a collective gasp in the room and she knew she made a mistake, she gave herself a silent prayer. Darian stood against his desk, his arms still crossed over his chest. A look of pure shock was plastered on his face. His eyes wide, lips slightly parted in amazement. He looked at Natasha, he watched her slowly back away from him, still he did not move.

Xavier came to stand beside Natasha, Darian's eyes still locked on her. A thousand thoughts filled his mind, yet he only settled on one. He had never been slapped by a anyone in all of his long life. It was a whole new experience. No one had ever thought to lay their hands on him in anger, Natasha intrigued him. He had never seen a mortal with such fire, such courage to challenge him. He was fascinated, he became instantly entranced with her. He could not take his eyes off of her. Natasha thought her life was over, she did not know if Xavier could protect her or not, but she prayed that he could. All she wanted to do now was to crawl inside a box, anything just to get away from Darian's deep gaze.

197

"Darian?" Xavier queried. Darian who had been staring at Natasha, seem to come out of a spell at the sound of Xavier's voice, his eyes slowly focused on Xavier. "Are you through speaking with the officers."Xavier said, trying to redirect Darian to another point of interest. Darian lowered his hands and walked across the room to where Natasha was standing. Warren stepped in front of her, blocking Darian's way as Xavier came to Darian's side, hand clasped on the master vampire's arm.

"Please don't hurt her, Darian, she did not mean it?" Xavier pleaded. Darian looked at him and laughed, a cool smooth sound vibrating throughout the room.

"Oh, she meant it. I don't think she does anything without meaning to." He looked at Natasha and walked forward. Warren held his gun out aiming it at Darian who stopped and looked at the gun, and in a movement too fast for anyone in the room to see, the gun was suddenly in his hands and Warren was left stumped, in shock.

"You forget what team you're really playing for wolf. Don't you ever point your weapon at me again. I have no intentions of hurting this beautiful young lady." He said as he handed Warren his gun. Warren took the gun, but he was still confused. Darian continued to speak. "As a matter of fact, I think I will help you in your investigation. Allow me to get my coat." He smiled and walked to the closet in his office and pulled out a long black trench coat.

"Wait a minute! Why do you want to help all of a sudden?" Natasha asked nervously.

Darian looked at her and smiled. "To get closer to you, of course. I'll have you know, you're the first person to have ever slapped me." He cocked his head to the side. "Not that I'm in total agreement but perhaps you're right, I was being petty." He pulled his long jet black wavy locks from underneath the collar of his coat and let the waves fall past his shoulders. He smiled at her again, his dimples brightening the smile even more, making him look innocent. Natasha hadn't even noticed his dimples before, to see them made her feel butterflies inside. She adored dimples on a man, she thought it was rather comical to so see this master vampire smiling like a school boy.

"Well whatever gets you to help us is fine with me, we have to go now, I hope we're not too late!" Natasha commented as she counted her lucky stars that she was still alive. She made a special mental note to herself. *Never hit a vampire.* She hoped he did not have intentions of killing her later, she hoped to God that he did not. She would make certain to stay close to Warren and Matthew. She looked at Xavier, who seem to still be perplexed.

"Are you coming?" She asked him.

"No, I have to watch the club, if it's a pestering bloodsucker on the prowl Darian can handle it, he doesn't need my help." Xavier smiled. He winked at Natasha, he wanted her to feel safe. He did not think Darian would kill her, he had been intrigued by her-just as he himself had. He watched his master smile at her and then Darian turned to Xavier and walking over to him, he leaned into Xavier's ear and whispered. Natasha could not hear what he said but she was sure Warren did, she have to let curiosity kill the cat and ask Xavier or Warren later about what it was that Darian had whispered.

Darian walked away from Xavier, he stepped up to Warren. "Okay, I've decided to help so lead the way." He made a sweeping motion with his hand towards the door. He bowed as Natasha walked past. She still did not know if she could stop shaking or not, but she knew she wasn't going to let her guard down. She knew running away wouldn't help her, but that did not mean she would not try. Darian walked gracefully behind them as they headed towards the main entrance. Natasha looked at the long line of party people still waiting to get in and shook her head. She thought it was too cold outside to be standing in such a long line just to party, but that was their decision. She followed Warren and Matt to the police squad car. Warren opened her door and she climbed in. Darian walked towards the police car and lowered himself to take a peek at the built in contraption of the car. He smiled and shook his head, chuckling. He erected himself and looked at the two detectives.

"Sorry, gentlemen, but I don't think I'll be riding in your death trap tonight. You lead the way and I'll follow." He glanced at the valet attendant who seem to know what his boss wanted and disappeared around the corner of the building. Darian stood waiting, his hands hidden in the pockets of his form fitting black pants. His long black coat flapping behind him in the wind. He looked in the direction of oncoming traffic on the street, the wind whipping through his long luxurious wavy locks. Natasha almost drooled as she looked at his perfect manly body. She imagined what he would look like naked, how his muscles would feel under his skin, as she trailed her fingertips over his body. She had to pull herself out of her fantasy, she did just slap him only about fifteen minutes before, she felt she was not out of the danger zone. Being around all of these gorgeous men wasn't doing her any good.....but then again.

The two detectives had settled into their seats and waited for Darian to get his car so that they could get a move on. Warren squirmed impatiently in his seat, eager to get to the scene before anything happened. All of the roadblocks were getting to him. The valet brought Darian's car around to the front, he climbed out and walked to his boss and handed him the keys.

Darian took the keys and glided to the drivers side of the car. The wind played with his hair and coat making him look like an ad for *Anisi Cologne For Him*. He climbed into his black Pavilion luxury sport car. Natasha loved that car, but she could only afford the half a million dollar set of wheels in her dreams. The car had automatic doors that closed after you get in, state of the art sound system with a three CD changer and three disc DVD player. The leather interior was climate controlled and there could be multiple moon roofs depending on the type of Pavilion you could afford. That was the car on the most wanted list for the insanely wealthy, nothing else could compare. What could she say? The man had style.

Warren pulled the squad car off and headed in the direction of the abandoned warehouses in Natasha's area. There were only three warehouses in the vicinity, the search would be short. Darian drove behind them, Natasha could not help herself and decided to look behind them. She saw him steer his car effortlessly. He winked at her and she blushed and turned back around and slouched in her seat. Warren turned to glance at her, he frowned.

"What's wrong?" He asked

Natasha looked up and realized he was talking to her. "Oh nothing," she responded, then she began to describe the warehouse. "The warehouse was dark grey on the outside. It was not tall and it did not resemble a factory, more like a loft. Like that one right there!" She pointed to a grey building with boarded up windows and doors. There was one window that did not have wooden boards on it, one side of the steel gate that surrounded the building had been pried apart. Warren pulled the car over and the three of them climbed out. Darian parked behind them and joined them as they stood looking at the building. Warren nostrils flared and an expression came over his face that indicated something Natasha could only guess as a recognition of a scent.

"I smell him here, he's marked territory as well. They're inside there now." He said as he walked towards the damaged gate and jumped over it easily. The rest of them walked towards the gate, Darian looked at the gate, but did not walk through it. Natasha looked up and noticed that he was already on the other side of the gate. She looked at Matthew, who shrugged as if to say *'your guess is as good as mine'* they both climbed through the battered gate to stand beside Warren and Darian.

"I can sense another vampire." Darian said he closed his eyes, exhaling a deep breath, his shoulders slouching slightly. "This one has a formidable aura. No, I don't think the three of you would have been able to handle this one alone. Very fortunate for you that I'm willing to help." Darian said condescendingly. Natasha threw him a disdainful look. *Arrogant bastard*, she thought. He looked down at her, and smiled flashing his dimples again. It made the disdain Natasha felt disappear. She did not know if she liked not being able to hold a grudge against an *'obvious asshole'*, but for some reason it did not seem to matter.

"Let's go." Warren said and sprinted off ahead of them to the broken window. He climbed in and Matthew followed. Darian looked at Natasha and held out his hand.

"Unlike those other two, I'm a gentleman, ladies first." He said smoothly, his voice cutting through her animosity like a hot knife through butter. She handed him her hand, and he closed his fingers lightly around hers and lifted her gently into the opening of the window. Matthew aided her as she climb through the window. Once she gained her footing she turned around to help Darian, he was standing in front of her. His super human speed unnerved Natasha. She remembered he could moved faster than she could blink her eye. She wondered if this other vampire could move as fast and if so, would bullets help? The four of them walked slowly through the pitch black room. Natasha trailed behind Matthew as the two of them used light from a flashlight to navigate around the warehouse. Darian had grown impatient and decided to walk faster, he stopped a few paces in front of them. His eyes scanning the darkness, his nostrils flared and he turn to face Warren.

"I can feel the vampire here, they're close. Keep an eye out, do you see your wolf?" Darian asked as he removed his hands from his pockets. "I can smell human blood, do you see your wolf? there is a human alive here I can hear his heart beating."

"I can smell the wolf and the vampire" Warren said as he turned around in a circle to scan the room, he turn to face Darian. "Darian-behind you!" He yelled. Warren watched as the slender figure of the female vampire appeared behind Darian, her clawed hand raised to strike. The hand came down in a slashing motion but Darian was no longer there. He materialized beside the vampire his own claws extended, he slashed ripping through the skin of the female vampire's back. Blood spurted from the wounds as she cried out and rolled away from his attack. Warren and Matthew ran towards the female vampire, guns out, but the other murderer, the male wolf pounced on their backs-knocking both of them to the ground. Matthew bellowed an agonizing wail as he fell to the ground, dropping both his gun and flashlight. Blood from the fresh scratches on his shoulder blade began to soak the back of his shirt. He grimaced in pain as he searched for his gun in the darkness.

Natasha panicked, her pulse quickened, she could hear her heart beating furiously in her ears. She knelt on her knees, her fingers patting the dusty, grimy, floor searching in the darkness for Matthew's gun. Her weak vision could not find it. She looked around the room frantically, she saw the flash light Matthew had dropped when he was attacked. Desperately, she crawled towards the light. She picked up the flashlight and guided by the sounds of scuffles, aimed it at the others in the room. She saw Darian tossing the female vampire against the wall. The female vampire fell to the ground along with little pieces of plaster and brick from the impact of her body hitting the wall. She began to rise weakly. The female hissed at Darian and continued to bare her fangs as he pursued her.

Natasha pointed the light along the walls looking for a door. She remembered Warren and Darian mentioning the scent of the mortal victim. She suspected he was still confined in a room somewhere in the warehouse. She heard gun shots ringing from behind her, and prayed that she would not get hit by a stray bullet. She spotted the door and ran to it. Her hand gripped the knob and turned it, but the door would not budge. She turned around to yell to Matthew to help her. As she pointed the light in front of her she saw first hand the huge black half-man, half-wolf standing before her. Her eyes froze on the huge bulging muscles under the furry skin, the long sharp teeth that lined the open muzzle. Her limbs froze, her mouth opened but no sound came out. She wanted to scream, but it remain caught in her throat. His massive chest heaved slowly, a low menacing growl trickled from his throat. His rancid breath, a sickening mixture of rotting flesh and decay pelted her face, assailing her nostrils. Her stomach lurched and she regained control over her limbs once again. She could see the silver eyes reflecting the moonlight shining through the open window. She screamed as a huge, clawed hand, slashed down. She felt white hot pain as his claws ripped through the flesh of her chest. Blood spurted from the open wound staining the front of her shirt and covering the wolf's fur. Warren regained his senses when he heard Natasha's scream. He focused his eyesight in the blackness of the room and saw the wolf standing over her. He smelled the spilt blood in the room. He looked around the floor and spotted a broken rusty pipe, it was spiked and jagged at one end. He raced over to the pipe and snatched it off the floor. Sneaking up behind the distracted wolf, he aimed the jagged end of the pipe, and ran the wolf through the back. The wolf howled in pain and turned to face Warren. His huge furry arm smacked Warren across his chest knocking him against the far wall, Warren slumped to the floor, dazed. The spiked edge punctured the wolf's heart and he fell to the floor. His hands flailing behind him, trying desperately to reach the steel pipe protruding from his back. Blood poured in a puddle beneath him as he fought to remove the pipe.

The female vampire screamed as she saw her lover suffering. Darian continued to stalk her, moving forward. Warren called out to him for help. "Darian, Natasha needs help she was attacked!" Darian turned around, the female vampire took the advantage and scurried away. Darian walked quickly to Natasha, and knelt beside her, taking her gently into his arms. Matthew had located his gun and tossed it to Warren who caught the gun with one hand. He walked over to the wolf and standing over the wolf he aimed the barrel of the gun at the wolf's heart, and fired off two silver bullets. The wolf howled in pain, his back arching, body twitching. His body slumped back to the floor and he slowly began to revert to his human form. His black fur began to recede under the skin and was replaced by human hair. They could hear his bones break and reform themselves into a human skeleton. His size was impressive in both his physical states. As a wolf he had been close to nine feet tall on his hind legs, now laying there dying in human form, he had been close to seven feet. The wolf lay still, lifeless the silver in his veins had turned his flesh a pale grey. The protruding veins underneath his skin had turned black like little connecting roads over his flesh. He was hideous.

Darian watched closely witnessing the wolf dying. He then fixed his gaze on Natasha, her shirt was ripped open and blood poured from the open wound, soaking the front of her shirt and jeans. Her skin had turned a pale ashen color and she shivered. The two detectives stood over Darian. Warren's eyes narrowed. He did not want this wonderful woman to get hurt. He was angry at himself for allowing her to enter the warehouse knowing the danger that awaited them.

"You're dying. You've lost too much blood. "Darian whispered in her ear. Natasha felt the tears well up in her eyes, she felt them slide down her cheeks. She began to whimper, she did not want to die.

"What are you going to do to her?" Warren asked. He supported his injured partner with one hand. Matthew's back had been clawed but the wounds weren't too deep. Warren had checked him over as he monitored Darian and Natasha.

"The only thing I can do."Darian said and he looked down into Natasha eyes. He caressed her hair, rubbing it back from her face. "I can give you my blood it will heal you, that is all. You will not be like me, do not worry, but you need my blood if you want to live." He did not have to tell Natasha twice, she was desperate to live. She nodded her head weakly moaning in pain. Darian shifted her body to his right arm and supported her easily as he raised his left wrist to his mouth. He plunged his fangs deep into the soft skin of his wrist and ripped it gently. The blood began to flow freely and he pressed his bleeding wrist to Natasha's mouth. She felt the first drop of the blood on her tongue and fighting the searing pain in her chest, immediately reached for his wrist, holding it to her mouth weakly as she fed.

Darian watched with a close eye as Natasha suckled on his wrist. A low moan escaped his lips, his eyes rolled upwards as his lids slowly closed over them. A spasm rippled through his body causing him to moan loudly in pleasure. He pulled his wrist free from her grasps. His right arm still supporting her but his left wrist he placed behind his back away from Natasha outstretched fingers. She wanted desperately to press his wrist to her mouth again. She desired the sensational pleasure of his blood coursing through her limbs. His blood ran its course through her body, ceasing the pain and healing all of her injuries. The bruises, cuts from old wounds and the claw marks had disappeared and all that was left was the drying blood that stuck to her clothes. The blood began to congeal on her skin. Darian's eyes focused on the blood, his nostrils flared, taking in the enticing scent but he held himself in check.

"How do you feel now?" He asked, his voice was breathless, he was panting, his chest heaving slowly. Natasha blinked twice clearing her vision. She looked into Darian's forest green eyes, she wanted to swim in his gaze.

"I feel better, thank you. What did you do?" She asked.

Darian smiled. "I gave you my healing blood. I'll explain further later, right now we need to get out of here." he rose to his feet with her in his arms. Natasha was beginning to get used to being carried by strong handsome men. Warren looked at her and smiled. He was so worried for Natasha he had forgotten about the trapped victim.

"Oh shit! The victim, he's here. I can smell him, this is the room! It smells like it!" He sat Matthew down on the ground against the wall and pulled hard on the knob. The door frame splintered and gave and he was able to open the door. He walked quickly into the dark room, his eyes pierced the darkness and he saw the man laying spread eagle on the metal table. His wrists and ankles bound to the four corners. He cried and begged for his life. The room filled with the scent of human waste, a smell Warren would rather not have to be introduced to. He ignored the putrid scent and rushed to the man's aid. He snapped metal chains that bound the victim without effort. The man's wrist and ankles were raw, bloody and swollen. Warren lifted the man in his embrace and carried him out of the room. He met up with the others. Natasha was still in the arms of Darian, and Matthew had regained his footing-gritting his teeth against the excruciating pain in his back.

The male in Warrens arms began to cry and pray, his limbs hung limply his body was starved and weak and soiled. "Let's get out of here. He needs to be taken to the hospital-you too Matt." Warren said as he walked towards the door. The other three followed. Warren kicked the door down and they walked to their automobiles. Darian placed Natasha gently in the passenger seat. And he climbed into the drivers seat. He looked at her and smiled.

"I'll take you home. Where do you live?" He asked his smooth accented voice sent tingles over her body. It seem to make her more giddier than before. She was not sure, maybe it was her imagination. She nodded and told him her address. He started the car and drove off. She watched though the window as Warren pulled the squad car out of the lot. He was heading in the opposite direction. She remember at that moment that they were leaving her alone with a powerful master vampire that she had slapped earlier that night. She felt a panic deep inside her stomach. She looked at Darian who's eyes were locked on the road. He felt her looking at him, and he turned to face her.

"You're worried that I'm going to kill you?" He asked. He chuckled. Natasha decided to be honest.

"Yes I am, I don't know why you saved me back there, I'm very grateful, yet I'm still a bit leery, I don't know much about vampire's or how you think, but if this were the movies I'd be dead wouldn't I?" She asked

Darian threw her a comical glance, his lips parted in a smile, his dimples giving his expression a more friendlier look. "The movies?" He asked, he chuckled again, a deep rich sound that filled the car. "It's hard to tell what a vampire would do in the movies and I'm far to old to try to emulate some mortals opinion of my kind. I'm not going to lie to you, when you slapped me earlier this evening, the thought of your immediate death did cross my mind." He threw her another glance, he wanted to catch her expression. He figured it would be horrifying and fearful. He had been right. Natasha inched a little closer to the door and Darian laughed outright.

"Don't worry, I told you, you intrigue me. It's very rare when a mortal can hold my interest, but you do. I have no intention of ever harming you Natasha. In fact, I'd like to get to know you better, perhaps on a more personal level?" He leaned over and placed his arm around her shoulders. His other hand navigated the automobile as he gazed into her eyes. "I find you beautiful, courageous and extremely sexy." His fingertips brushed the lose strands of her hair from her eyes. "I am powerfully attracted to you. I want you and I'm pretty sure that you want me as well. We can both have each other." His hands navigated the car from lane to lane as he eyes remained locked on Natasha's. it amazed her that he could drive without watching the road. She couldn't help it, she thought that was pretty damn slick!

"I can't I'm dating someone already." She said softly, she wanted to kiss those full luscious lips of his. She wanted to feel his tongue inside her and not just her mouth. Darian settle back into his seat and continued to drive, finally pulling the car in front of her apartment. He turned off the engine and shifted in his seat to face her.

"I know about Xavier and you already. I don't mind it at all that you two are together."

"Well, then you know why I can't be with you. Look, I don't want to talk about that, I feel funny inside, and I want to know why." She demanded. Darian allowed her to change the subject. He did have a few things he needed to take care of before daybreak.

"I have given you my blood. In doing that, I have shared with you some of my power. I want you to know that I do not share my blood indiscriminately. Like I said, I do want you but I wanted you to live. I could have easily made you my servant. However, I did not want to form that kind of connection through the blood. We do have a bond that was unavoidable." He paused.

Natasha looked at him, her eyes widening as she began to realize the price she must pay for survival. "What do you mean, by '*bond*?'" She asked

"I mean that we now have a mental connection." He paused, and frowned, a slight creasing of his brows, his lips pursed. "I hope you don't crave my blood in the future. It isn't a disappointing prospect, but that can happen-"

Natasha interjected. "What the hell do you mean, *crave*!? Like a crackhead!?" She asked nervously.

A perplexed expression flashed across Darian's face at the mention of the phrase, "crackhead." Then he nodded and chuckled. "But it's far more better drug than crack. It doesn't always happen, but it might. In the event that you do begin to feel a desire for my blood let me know. I can help you through it. The good news is; the mental bond we have now, will allow me to help you control your visions. What you see and what you don't want to see. As far as you being able to see or read the thoughts inside my head, you will not be able to see them. Of course..." His eyes linger seductively over her body. He leaned closer to her, she could smell the musk scent of his cologne. He raised his fingertips to her face and delicately caressed her left cheek. "Not if I don't want you to." He whispered as he smiled wickedly. Natasha blushed, she couldn't believe just being close to him, to hear his voice brought butterflies to her stomach like a high school teeny bopper.

"So let me get this straight-apart from me possibly becoming a blood addict, I'll have you dancing around in my head playing with my thoughts?" She asked sarcastically.

"Well, in a manner of speaking, yes. There is always a price for the blood. But it doesn't have to be viewed as a bad thing. As I've said, I will help you every step of the way."

"Yeah, I'm sure you will. Look it's been a long night and I need to get some rest. Between you and the murderers and all this horror, I just need some peace of mind." Natasha said and she opened the car door and climbed out. Darian watched her walk to her door. He made sure she was safely inside her apartment building, before he pulled off to return to his night club.

Chapter 20

Warren waited patiently in the hospital emergency waiting room. He had called his precinct and reported the incident informing them of where they could find the body of the shape-shifter he killed. His captain seemed pleased that they were making such great progress on the case, but was unnerve to discover that there were two supernaturals committing these murders. She had informed Warren that he could have any assistance he required to continue his investigation. He stretched his long legs out in front of him, hands resting on his stomach as he watched the morning re-runs on the nineteen inch color TV suspended in the upper far right corner of the room. He looked at his watch, he had been at the hospital for over four hours. He'd have to wait for the male victim to regain consciousness from the medication given to him in order to make a report. Matthew was still being sewn up and there was still one killer left out there for them to hunt down. Warren sat in the chair and reflected on his mistakes of the hours before. He should have never let Natasha come into the building. He should have kept a better eye out for Matthew. He wondered if it would have been wiser to change forms. His half breed form would have been better suited for battling the wolf, than his human form. He thought on the event of the past several hours then decided *what was done-was done* and should not be repeated again.

He rose and walked to the vending machine, he pulled a dollar out of his pocket and slid it into the automatic slot and pressed the desired button for an apple danish. He was extremely hungry and tired of eating the vending machine junk food. He had already consumed two danishes, three bags of potato chips, three chocolate candy bars and three sodas, and was still hungry. He thought if Matthew did not come out of the ER soon, he was going to have to desert him for a few hamburgers. He turned around to walk back to his seat and saw Matthew walking through the white double doors. Matthew looked a bit worse-for-ware but he smiled lazily at his partner.

"You look like shit, how do you feel?" Asked Warren.

"Shit, just like I look. I've have about sixty stitches in my back and it's sore as hell!" Matthew said as he shuffled closer to his partner. He put his coat on slowly, wincing in pain when he had to lift his arm to slide it into the sleeve.

"I can take you home.."Warren said, Matthew looked at him and shook his head.

"I know that look Warren. What are you planning?"

"Look, you're in no condition to go with me"

"Fuck that, I'm you're partner, you might need my help. Whatever it is I'm not letting you do it alone, so you might as well tell me what's your plan." Matthew said looking at Warren seriously.

"The female vampire is still out there. Last night Darian did not get a chance to kill her, he saved Natasha instead. It's day time, I want to see if I can track down her daytime resting place and put an end to her."

Matthew frowned. "That's going to be hard as hell, she's not stupid, I'm sure she's not at the same warehouse. It's going to be impossible to track her down. Nighttime comes faster now, we only have about eight hours to do this. Did you get a chance to talk to our witness in there?"

"Not yet, the nurse said he was still sleep from the pain killers. They had to bandage his wrist and ankles and give him a tetanus shot. But he'll pull through just fine. I figure we'll come back here in a few hours, but right now, I want to search for that blood sucking bitch." Warren said. Matthew nodded his head in agreement. And both detectives walked out of the hospital. They walked to their squad car and climbed into their seats; Matthew moving a lot slower than his partner.

"So, what's going to happen to Natasha?" Asked Matthew.

"I'm not sure. She was completely healed last night. Then Darian took her home. I trusted him with her, because he saved her life and if he would have done anything to her, I would have *killed* him, even if it cost me my life." Warren said sincerely. They drove back to the warehouse to look for clues. The warehouse was surrounded by yellow and black police tape, both men knew that the body of the shape-shifter was no longer present. They walked through the door and looked around. It was still dark inside and Warren went back to the car to retrieve the flashlight for Matthew. Matthew pointed the light around the warehouse looking for any hint of evidence that would help them locate the female vampire or any clue at all to why they did what they did. Warren walked into the dark room where the male victim had been held and looked around. The room still smelled rancid, but he ignored the scent once again. He found nothing in the room. He came back out and looked at Matthew.

"Find anything?" Warren asked.

"Just a piece of my shirt from last night." Matthew said, pointing the light on a torn piece of bloody fabric from his dark blue t-shirt.

Warren chuckled. "Well, at least it's not you!"

"Oh, you sick bastard." Matthew chuckled. "Look there's not a damn thing here. Lets get something to eat and head back to the damn hospital."

"I thought you'd never ask. I'm starving, shit I spent about twenty dollars in the vending machine alone." Warren said as they headed back to the squad car. He drove to the Pancake Kitchen, in the Hyde Park area. He enjoyed their food, to him they had the best breakfast in the whole city. They had to wait for five minutes before their number was called. The pretty hostess that led them to their table was wearing a black turtle neck and dark grey knit pants that fit her slender figure perfectly. Warren and Matthew watched her hips sway as she walked in front of them. She turned around and pointed to their table, both men smiled at her. Then they watched her walk away as they sat down in the wooden chairs. The restaurant was crowded and the tables were practically side by side. The hard wood floors were polished and the wooden ceiling fans circulated the air in the room.

The hostess left two menus on the table and both men reached for their menus to see what they wanted to eat. A waitress came by the table a few minutes later, she placed two glasses of water in front of the two detectives and removed her pen and pad from her apron and poised herself in her order taking position.

"What can I get for you two gentlemen?" She cooed. She wanted to flirt and was planning on flirting with them as long as they were there. She had seen them there once before, she knew they were cops but more importantly they were gorgeous and big tippers, she wanted to hook herself one or the other.

"Well," Matthew started. "I'll have the peach crepes and a large orange juice. Oh, and a side of these chicken hash browns." He said and he closed the menu and handed it to the waitress, who smiled broadly and took the menu. Matthew looked at Warren. Warren lifted his head up and smiled at the waitress. Causing her to blush.

"I'll take the strawberry crepes, the western omelette, the side of Canadian bacon, and the chicken hash browns, I also want a side of this apple glazed chicken sausage, and with the western omelette can I have strawberry pancakes instead of regular?" He looked at the waitress, who's hand was still busy jotting down his order. She nodded her head. "Good, that's what I want. Oh, and a large coffee and orange juice for me as well."

She finished writing down the order. "Will that be all sir? There are still some items left on the menu you didn't mention," she joked. Matthew laughed outright, hand slapping the table top. Warren pouted playfully.

"Well, now that you mention it…" he began, the waitress eyes grew wide and Warren laughed. "No, I'm kidding, nothing else, that's all I want." She chuckled and walk away to get the order ready.

"Having a good time over there, ya bastard?" Warren glared at his friend playfully.

"Ohh…I'm sorry…it's just…she said what I was thinking." Matthew said, between chuckles. Warren rolled his eyes and snorted.

"Shut up." Warren said as Matthew laughed harder. Tears welling up in his eyes.

"OW!" Matthew cried out as he was reminded of the fresh stitches in his back. He decided then it was a good time to settle down. He did not want any of the stitches reopening, because of excessive laughter. He looked at his partner. Who seemed to be in deep thought. "What are you thinking about? When you get quiet I know you're thinking about something, and it's bothering you."

"Natasha. You. This female vampire knows about us now, she knows that Natasha is human, she knows that you are human. She may try to attack either one of you for revenge. I don't want to find her when it's too late. I can't get it off my mind, I have a bad feeling and I just can't shake it."

"Well, I'm with you and I'm staying with you, it's daylight right now. So we can relax for a minute. Lets call Natasha after breakfast to see if she had anymore visions."

Warren nodded. After ten minutes past, the waitress brought Matthew his meal. Warren caught himself staring at the creamy peaches that topped and filled the crepes his partner had ordered. His stomach growled as he fought the urge to beg. The act of begging was synonymous with shape-shifters.

Warren commented, "why is it that I'm always stuck watching you eat first?" Matthew opened his mouth to speak "Don't answer that." Warren added. His partner chuckled and finished pouring peach syrup over his crepes. After five more minutes had passed, Warren's meal arrived. The waitress sat several plates in front of him. The delicious aroma of the dishes drifted to his nose and made his mouth water. He began to dig into meal immediately.

The waitress had just set the last plate of strawberry pancakes and syrup on the table. She asked him if he needed anything else and he shook his head. She smiled and walked away. She could not wait to finish the gossip she had started in the back with the other waitresses about the two of them.

The two men talked about sports and the movies, not wanting to discuss the case over breakfast. In spite of Matthew getting his food five minutes earlier, Warren finished his huge meal two minutes faster. Each plate that was in front of him was empty. Matthew still wondered where it all went. He knew his friend had a high metabolism, but it was amazing to watch him eat. The waitress brought the bill, both cops looked at the bill and reached in their pockets to leave a generous tip. They took the bill to the front of the restaurant to pay.

"Don't worry, this one's on me." Matthew said.

"Naw, I got it. You'll have lunch, deal?" Warren asked. Matthew smiled and nodded. Warren paid the bill and they left the restaurant and headed for the hospital. They hoped their witness was wide awake and able to answer some questions. They made it back to the hospital, going directly to the room their witness was in. There was a uniformed S.U.I.T. officer outside of the door. Warren had called the station and requested one, when they brought him in. They flashed their badges and the officer nodded, stepping aside allowing both detectives to walked in. Warren looked at the patient in the little narrow bed. The white sheets were pulled up to his chest. His eyes were opened but he looked confused, he did not recognize the two officers.

Warren walked to one side of his bed and Matthew leaned on the foot of the bed. Warren introduced themselves. "We're the two detectives that rescued you last night and brought you here. Tell us, do you remember anything about what happened to you? I know this may be difficult, but we need any information that you are able to give us." Warren said compassionately. The male survivor looked at both cops, he took a deep breath and nodded.

"My name is William Banner. I work at the *Discount Alley* on seventy-ninth street. I had to close up three nights ago and that's when they got me. They put a blind fold on me and threw me in the trunk of a car. The trunk smelled terrible, like something had died in there. I remembered thinking that I was going to die. I could hear them laughing from inside the trunk. They were two sick assholes and I hope they burn in hell!" He said venomously.

Warren couldn't blame him for feeling that way. "Do you remember hearing them say anything, that might lead us to the whereabouts of the female?" Matthew asked. Warren nodded in agreement. The survivor stared forward, trying to recollect the traumatic experience.

212

"Yeah, after they were through with me, they said they were going to own this city. They wanted to prove a point to the mortals, they said. They were sick, sick fucks!" He said in a shaken voice.

"Is that everything you can remember?" Asked Warren

"Yeah man, that's everything. Look I've been through enough already, thanks for saving me and all, but I don't know much information, it's not like they included me in their plans. I was a piece of meat to them and I really just want to get away from it all. Understand!?" He snapped at the two officers. Both Warren and Matthew nodded and left the room. They closed the door behind them.

"So much for fucking gratitude." Matthew said. "So, there's a chance that this chick might try to do one more kill, if she hasn't fled the city already. Even after that battle with Darian, she might just try to do it, to prove to us that we can't stop her."

Warren nodded. "What we need to do is go back to the station, and look through our database to check over our files. We need to find any murder cases matching ours. I looked some up before but they weren't exactly like ours. The problem with ours is that the bodies were never found entirely in the same condition. I don't know whether to call them serial killers, or just plain crazy fucking murderers!"

"Well, lets get back there and check it out, we might find something." Both men headed for the car and climbed in. Warren 's cell phone began to ring, the designated emergency ringer letting him know it was a phone call he needed to answer. He pulled the little cell phone from his pocket and flipped it open putting the handset to his ear.

"Hello?"

" Detective Warren, it's Natasha. I had another vision." She continued. She had another possible murder vision. This time, she knew a little more information.

"I'm listening?" Warren said, as he drove onto Lake Shore Dr, towards downtown.

"She's going to be at a club but I don't know which one, I did not see the name of the club in my vision. But I could hear the music from the club, she was with a victim-she was going to kill him and leave his body in an alley. I saw through your eyes and Darian was with you again but Matthew wasn't' with you. That's all I saw, my alarm went off. It seems every time I have a vision, it's interrupted. I wish I could tell you more."

"No, no, you're doing more than enough, remember what I said before. We wouldn't have gotten this far if it weren't for you. Natasha, stay home, stay safe, you got me?" It was more of an order than a request. Natasha did not argue, after last night she was not in any hurry to go dancing with death again.

"You don't have to tell me twice." She joked, but she was serious. Then a thought came to her. "Warren, how come I'm not like you?"

There was a short period of silence. Then he spoke, "because, you were scratched. The gene can only be transferred through the saliva of a shape shifter. If you were bitten, it would be a different story." He chuckled.

"What about the other bodily fluids?" She asked inquisitively.

"Semen, blood, breast milk and vaginal secretions can not carry the gene-strange, I know. The shape-shifter gene is only spread if the saliva of a shape-shifter directly enters the blood stream of an unaffected human being, mainly though bite wounds."

"What about kissing?"

"If the unaffected partner doesn't have any open wounds in their mouths, then he or she will be safe." Warren informed. "You really need to brush up on your supernatural studies." He joked.

"Yeah, tell me about it!" She chuckled nervously, but relieved.

" Look, get some rest, if you see anything else call me but don't leave the house, not tonight." Warren said as he pulled the car off the expressway.

"No problem, I did not want to go out tonight anyway. I'm on my lunch break now. When I get off of work I'll go straight home. I was going to visit my friend Annette but I'll just call her. You be careful too, okay?" She entreated. She really liked Warren and Matthew, she had felt a part of a team last night, but there was a price she had to pay for that. She now had a clear understanding just how dangerous their job was and she wanted them to be safe.

"Don't worry about me. You just be safe. Take care." He said, he waited for her to say her goodbyes and he hung up. He told his partner what she said.

"So, now we just need to narrow down clubs in the city. Probably some well known clubs. If she wants to make a name for herself." Matthew said, as he pondered the possible motive.

"Yeah, we finally found a motive. Not only that, but we have to get Darian to back us up again tonight. It was in her dream. If I don't' have him there, there's no telling how the situation can end. I'm strong and fast, but I'm young. She was fast...too fast! When the government created our team and our weapons I don't' think they were completely prepared for the skill of the old ones." Then he wondered just how old she was. He also wondered just how old Darian was.

"Yeah, I agree. Look lets get some different weapons and head out to Darian's club." They walked into the precinct, Matthew tried very hard not to look wounded as they headed towards the weapons locker. Warren selected a flamethrower just in case of extreme emergency then he pulled out an automatic machine gun and a 9mm, all fully loaded with ultra violet ammunition. He signed all the weapons out, the desk clerked looked them over and threw both of the detectives a sarcastic glance.

"What?" Warren asked.

"Oh, nothing, I was just wondering if you two were taking over a small country, that's all." Officer David Marks said. pushing his black rimmed glasses back on his nose.

"What country do you know of that is going to let us take over with these little ass weapons?" Warren asked sarcastically. David was always a smartass, but then Warren could be one himself at times. The desk clerk smirked at him and dismissed them with the wave of his hand. Warren took the weapons and walked out of the locker, Matthew trailing behind him.

"Do you think we need the flame thrower?" Matthew asked as they loaded the guns into the trunk of the car.

"I don't know, but it's mainly for you. If she gets close to you let her have it. I'd prefer if you stayed here at the station."

"No, I'm coming with you we're partners."Matthew stated with finality. Warren nodded his head. He decided not to argue, it wouldn't matter.

"Okay, good, let's go." Matthew said as he climbed slowly into the passenger side wincing with every movement. He hated that his back had to touch the seat. His partner climbed in beside him. And they headed for *Desires Unleashed.* When they arrived at the club the day manager walked up to them.

"What can I do for you two officers?" She asked. Her long brown hair in a thick braid down her back. She was wearing a black satin skirt and white satin blouse. Her black leather boots clacked on the tiled floor. Warren could smell that she was a shape-shifter, a cheetah.

"We're looking for Darian. Know where we could find him?" Warren asked. The female shifter threw glances at both men.

"The boss isn't here. And no I don't know where you can find him. You're welcome to stay here, and wait for him to arrive, though he might not come, he's normally here on weekends. Is there anything else?" She asked politely. Both men looked at each other and shook their heads. "Okay, well, if you will excuse me, I have some loose ends to tie up. You can show yourselves to the door." she said then turned and walked away. Matthew and Warren headed for the entrance when a female janitor mopping stale vomit off of the floor stopped them.

"I can tell you the address…for a price." She whispered. Warren looked at his partner then back at the woman. She was wearing a grey workman's jumpsuit. And a grey base ball cap.

"What's the price?" He asked.

"Fifty bucks, I tell you the address."

Warren reached in his pocket and pulled out a fifty dollar bill. He held it in front of the woman. Her hand snaked out and took the money.

"It's a three-story mansion on the outskirts of Chicago. His place is in Evanston." The female gestured for the two cops to come closer, they did and she whispered the address in their ears. Warren thanked her for her help and they left the club. They hit the I 90-94 expressway towards Evanston. It was an hour and a half drive, the traffic slowed them down considerably. They finally located the huge three-story mansion.

Matthew whistled. "Would you look at that. This place is huge, vampires live pretty damn good."

"Not all of them just old bastards like him. My leader lives in a similar shack. That reminds me!" He looked at his watch. He wanted to call Xander and tell him all that had happened. He noted the time was 2:32pm. Time was flying by. He pulled out his cell phone and called his pack leader.

"Hello?" Xander's voice flowed through the telephone. Warren remembered how that voice used to always make him feel safe when he was a frightened little child. There was still some element of security in Xander's voice even now and It made Warren smile.

"Xander, it's me. Last night, I closed in on the wolf. He was huge, I've never seen him before, he's dead. I killed him last night. He was insane, a pleasure killer. I just thought I should tell you."

"Are you alright? Was anyone bitten?"

"No, two people were scratched but that's it."

"Okay, good. What are you doing now, I can hear stress in your voice."

"I'm vampire hunting, the wolf shared his kills with a female vampire, she got away last night so now I have to prepare for her. Look Xander I have to go, I just wanted to bring you up to speed. I'll have to fill you in later on all the details."

"Very well, we will talk later. Be careful, Warren" Xander replied calmly. Warren assured Xander he would and hung up the phone, then looked at Matthew.

"Don't ask, I'll explain to you later. Now we have to convince Darian to help us again, I don't know if he will. Last night he helped because of Natasha. Now, I don't know, but let's give it a try." Warren said, as he exited the automobile, Matthew followed. Both men walked up to the front door and rung the bell. A few seconds later a beefy standing six-feet-four, two-hundred-plus pound black male answered the door. He looked at the two officers.

"May I help you?" He asked.

"I'm officer Warren Davis, and this is my partner Matthew Eric, we need to speak with Mr. Darian Alexander when he wakes up. We need to ask him some questions. We'll wait on the sofa if necessary. But we're not leaving. We can get a warrant but I rather not let it get that far." Warren said, hoping the bluff would be good enough to grant them entry. The body guard regarded both of them and opened the door wider to allow them entrance. They walked in and he pointed to a room off the main entrance. Warren walked into the living room. He noted that Darian's style was a lot more modern than his own pack leader's. he settled down on the black leather sofa, the soft cushions were incredibly comfortable, he could feel himself becoming relaxed. He felt he could fall asleep on the sofa, especially considering he hadn't slept in over twenty-four hours. He looked at the black marble coffee table and matching floor. The huge warm grey marble fire place was lit and the roaring fire filled the wide open space with heat. It was becoming more relaxing than Warren was comfortable with.

"Wait in here, I'll inform Mr. Alexander when he wakes up and tell him you're here. You leave this room and you're going to need more than a warrant." The body guard warned.

Warren looked at him. "Are you threatening us?" He asked challenging the body guard.

"No, just a warning. I don't necessarily have to be the one doing the punishing, though I wouldn't mind." He left the room leaving the two cops to ponder that statement..

"Nice help," Matthew joked.

"Tell me about it. Look, we've got about an hour before nightfall. Wake me up, I know this is completely unorthodox but I can't seem to keep my eyes open." Warren said as he struggled to fight the sleep.

"Yeah, take a load off." Matthew smiled. He watched his partner slump on the comfortable leather sofa. Matthew sat back and closed his eyes thinking about the night before. Then all faded to blackness and he ceased to think at all.

Chapter 21

Darian walked into the room. His human servant had told him about the two officers who came looking for him. He figured it was the two cops from the night before. He had been right. He leaned against the door frame watching the two slumbering officers lounging lazily on his expensive leather set. He walked towards Warren and tapped him on his shoulder. Warren's grey eyes focused on Darian's. He sat up and shook off his sleep. He looked at his partner who was sound asleep in the black chair. He looked at his watch, the time was 5:32pm. Almost two hours had passed.

"Shit!, Matthew! Wake up!" The other man stirred and opened his eyes, he looked at Warren, who had rose from the sofa, anxiously. "You were suppose to wake me up, not fall out, yourself." Warren complained. Matthew shrugged.

"I think we both got the same amount of sleep. What made you think I was more resistant than you? Hell, you know they got me all doped up." Matthew stated groggily.

Warren looked at him, annoyed and shook his head. "Look, none of that matters now." He turned to face Darian. He had to admit the man was dangerously good looking. He looked into Darian's dark green eyes and had to fight his own rising desire. He decided to get right to the point. "The female vampire that escaped last night, Natasha saw that she's going to be at a night club tonight, you and I are supposed to be there. Will you help us once more?" He asked the vampire.

Darian exhaled a long breath. "She is strong but she is not that old, she's only three centuries and her maker was strong." He cocked his head and glanced quizzically at both Warren and Matthew. "Let me ask you this, why is it you can not kill her yourselves? Do you not have the technology?" He asked.

"Yeah we have the technology to deal with really young ones that fuck up, not the more skilled of your kind, that have control over their powers. I can't do it alone, I know this. We weren't trained for this, not on this level, will you help us?" He asked once more, suppressing his agitation.

Darian was slightly annoyed with the manner of how he was sucked into this situation. But he wanted Natasha. She was a beautiful woman, she intrigued him. He would help if it would get him closer to her heart. "I will help you but I have not fed. I'm stronger when I feed." He moved closer to Warren and smiled wickedly. "You're a shape-shifter, you could take my feeding, and still be strong for tonight's battle." He said with a smirk. Then he turned away from Warren, shrugging his shoulders and continued "Or..." He paused, "I could waste time hunting for a mortal who won't mind me feeding from them. But I do not and I repeat, do not drink synthetic blood. So, what's your decision?" Darian asked, a devilish grin spread across his face. He always enjoyed the blood of a shifter, it was a delicious delicacy.

"You have to be fucking kidding?" Warren looked at Darian aghast. When Darian's expression did not change, he began to realize that Darian was serious. "Fine, whatever. We don't need to waste anymore time, enough has been wasted as it is." He shrugged his leather coat off of his wide shoulders and tossed it on the sofa.

"What now?" He asked.

Darian's smiled broaden. "Are you offering?"

"What does it look like? Yes I am. So what do you want me to do?" He growled.

Darian frowned. "Well you make me feel like some sort of leech when you say it that way." His arm extended, pointing a long finger at Warren. "Remember, you came to me, do not forget that I am doing you a favor." He commented. He lowered his arm. Warren's face grew sullen, he nodded his head in acknowledgment.

"You are quite right. It's just that I know someone out there is going to need our help and I want to get there before it's too late. So what do you want me to do?" Warren asked, a bit more cooperatively. Then he pointed to the sofa, "do you want me to lay down on the sofa or continue standing?" He looked at Darian.

"Oh I'd prefer if you lay down on the sofa." His wolfish grin returned. "It will be more comfortable for the both of us." Darian made a languid gesture towards the leather sofa. He watched with a predatory gaze, as Warren walked towards the sofa and laid on his back. Warren's eye focused on his. Matthew had been watching silently from the chair across the room. He dared not to say a thing, he felt this was a matter to be handled between the two supernaturals.

Darian walked towards the sofa and gazed down at Warren who watched him from his prone position. Darian placed one leg on the other side of Warren against the cushions to the back of the sofa. Then he lowed himself, straddling Warren. Darian leaned forward, his hands on both sides of Warren's head. He peered into Warren's grey eyes. Warren fought his desires, he wanted to wrap his arms around Darian and press his lips to his but he remained still.

"Turn your head, give me a look at that delicious vein." Darian joked, smiling sensuously at Warren. Warren smirked but cock his head to the side, revealing his carotid artery. Darian's vison grew more focused as he eyed the pulsating vein. He leaned towards the vein, his eyes closing slowly.

Warren gasped as Darian's long fangs broke through the flesh of his neck. His hands gripped the side of the sofa cushions, his breathing began to quicken. He began to relax as an extraordinary pleasure gathered in his limbs flowing through his body towards the two puncture wounds in this throat. He felt Darian grow hard against his own growing erection. A low moan came from Darian as he continued to feed.

Matthew watched both of the men as they lay on the sofa like lovers. Darian straddling Warren, his face buried in Warren neck. Matthew could hear the audible suckling noises coming from Darian as well as the breathless pants emanating from Warren. Matthew began to feel an uncomfortable arousal as he witnessed this intimate union. He wanted to leave the room but he did not want to leave his partner, or so, that's what he told himself. He watched, transfixed as he realize that both men were coming to a climatic state. Warren's expression was euphoric as his body twitched and jerked underneath Darian's own trembling form. Matthew face redden as he looked at Darian rise from the sofa, his expression relaxed, sated. His skin tone was flushed, pinkish, human. If Matthew had not known any better, he would have thought Darian *was* human.

Matthew looked at Warren, who lay on the sofa, motionless. After a few seconds, Warren seemed to gather his senses and mobility. Matthew couldn't help but wonder what it felt like to be fed on by a vampire, especially one as seemingly powerful as Darian. He had heard that the more powerful, thus skillful a vampire was, the more pleasurable their "kiss". He would ask Warren later if the opportunity presented itself.

Darian licked his lips, his eyes lost their cloudiness and began to focus. It had been a most precious treat to feed from Warren, not only was he a shape-shifter but a natural born wolf at that, very precious indeed. He watched as Warren's body regenerated the blood he lost during the feeding. His gaze move to linger on Matthew. He thought the other man was very handsome and brave. Not only to surround himself with supernatruals but to hunt them down as well. Darian thought that both men had a lot of fortitude.

"Well I feel like a million dollars." Darian smiled, "are you ready to go?"

"Yeah." Warren said as he slowly sat up on the sofa. Matthew walked over to him and held his hand out to him. He looked at Matthew and smiled. Then took hold Matthew's hand and pushed himself off of the sofa rising to his full height of six-feet-two inches.

"Okay, let's go." He said, his voice still a little bit shaky. He could feel a wet stickiness in the crotch of his underwear. He did not want to make it known, nor did he have time to fret over a clean pair of underwear, and pants. As he pulled his leather coat over his shoulders, he thought about what had just happened. He had never been bitten by a vampire before and did not know what to expect. He certainly did not expect to feel the indescribable pleasure he felt as Darian feasted on him. He knew at that moment, a vampire's life was truly one hedonistic experience after another.

"If I'm going to ride in *that* car…" Darian said as he pointed to the black squad car "I'm going to ride in the front with one of you." He stood by the passenger side of the car looking between Warren and Matthew. The two detectives glanced at each other and nodded. Matthew climbed in the back seat, as Warren took to the driver's seat. Darian was satisfied with the arrangement and opened the passenger side door, to climb into the hard leather covered seats.

"Not very comfortable, is it." Darian commented on the comfort level of the car seats.

"Good." Warren said as he started the engine. He glanced at Darian and smirked. "Put on your seat belt, you know the law!" He joked sarcastically. Darian rolled his eyes, but remained unbuckled. He did not like restraints, not in any form. Warren pulled the car out of the long, winding driveway and onto the main road. He reached the city's downtown party district and parked on the street. The three men had been silent on the way there, all mentally preparing themselves for the long night's search and pursuit. Darian had emerged from the car first. Matthew and Warren followed, Warren watched as Darian seemed to concentrate his powers.

"What are you doing?" Warren asked.

"I'm trying to locate her using my powers to search out her brain waves." Darian said. As he stood on the sidewalk, eyes closed, head tilted upward.

"I did not know vampires could do that!" Matthew said inquisitively, hoping Darian would elaborate. He received his wish.

"Only the old ones can. She is attempting block the mental connection." Darian said distractedly. "She is not in this area, perhaps we should try another." He looked at Warren, "any ideas?"

"Well, when I spoke with the victim earlier, he said something about the killers wanting to make a point to the mortal world." He paused to ponder the statement. "Now that I think about it, I think she might be in the human only district. Which can be dangerous grounds, even for one as strong as you." He said nodding his head at Darian. "We'll have to play it safe, come on, let's go." Warren said as they walked towards the car and climbed in. They drove on the expressway heading towards the human only district. It was a section of the city that did not open it's doors to the supernaturals. All of the businesses in that area reserved the right to deny service to vampires and shape-shifters.

Warren called into the precinct, "hey Billy?"

"Yeah Warren, what's up?" A husky male voice responded over the dispatch radio.

"I need a list of all the human owned nightclubs in the city and I needed it yesterday!" Warren urged.

"Okay, okay, shit! Give me a min! Alright, I'm in the computer now… yeah, okay, I have the list, you ready?" Billy asked.

"Yeah, I'm ready." Warren handed Darian a pen and paper to jot down the information. Darian frowned but took the stationary and listened to the addresses.

"Okay, it's four human only clubs in the city and the first one is, *The Sunlit Lounge* on Ontario. The next one is, The *Slayer's Lair*, actually, they're all pretty much in the same area. Ok, here's the other two, *Obsession* and *The Hit*. Is there anything else that you want?" He asked

"Nope that's all, thanks." Warren ended the connection. He looked at the list Darian held in his hands.

"So, If we go to that district, will you be able to sense which club she'll be at?" He asked the vampire.

"Yes, if she is there." Darian looked out of the window, exasperated. "There are a number of things I could be doing on this night instead of head hunting with you two." He looked at Warren. "There are some things we could do together, actually…" He turned to face Matthew and smiled. "The three of us could really enjoy ourselves." Darian said seductively. Mutual desire filled the car making the air thick with lust. Darian eyed Matthew a little longer before turning back in his seat to look at Warren.

"Look, I like to thank you for doing this we really appreciate it." Warren said as he turned the car onto Ontario street.

"I see there's no tempting the two of you when you're on the job." Darian let out a long breath, "very well, why don't you pull in over there." He pointed to a space in front of a clothing store. The three men climbed out of the car, Darian closed his eyes to focus his powers. His eyebrows creased then he slowly opened his eyes.

"She's near," Darian looked towards the *Slayer's Lair* night club. "She's there." He pointed at the club.

"How did she get in?" Warren asked perplexed.

"Yeah, all the entrances are protected by an ultraviolet lighting system. Which isn't controlled by the door bouncers, so they can't be mesmerized to turn it off for a vampire to enter." Matthew said perplexed.

"I believe she is waiting outside for her victim gentlemen." Darian said as he walked towards the club.

Warren turned to face Matthew. "Before you put up an argument listen to me." Warren said placing his hands on Matthews' shoulders.

Matthew knew what Warren was going to say and he wanted to protest. "Warren, I…I don't want to leave your side, I'm your back up…your partner." Matthew said, he felt exhausted, wounded and confused. He was unsure of himself, he did not feel confident enough in his abilities to be an asset to Warren, the painkillers he had taken were making him sluggish and the pain in his back was throbbing. His entire body felt stiff and soar, not to mention he was *mentally* exhausted. But he did not want to let Warren down.

"You're not letting me down, so don't feel that way." Warren stated, correctly guessing his partners feelings. "But in the vision that Natasha told me about, you were not in it. It was only Darian and me. I don't want you to be…" he paused and took a deep breath. "You are already injured, tired, hungry the list goes on. No my friend, stay here." Warren said.

Matthew looked defeated as much as he would hate to have to admit it, Warren was right, he was not up to fighting the vampire. He did not know how to explain to Warren that he felt like he let him down the night before. He knew Warren would not want to hear it and would say something to ease his conscience. Matthew nodded his head sadly and climbed back into the back seat of the squad car without another word.

Darian watched the two men from a few paces away. He noted Matthew's sad and defeated compliance. He concluded that Matthew would stay behind. Warren started walking towards him and Darian waited patiently for Warren to catch up.

"So tell me, will she know you're coming?" Warren asked

"Not if I do not want her to, I can shield my aura." He looked at Warren's questioning expression and smiled. "A vampire's aura is a lot like your wolf's howl. It can be used skillfully to gather vampires together or to warn them off."

"Ah, I understand now." Warren said, nodding his head. Both men stood outside of the boisterous nightclub. The big sign with the clubs name on it glowed bright green over the door. There was a long line of people waiting to get in, all dressed in brightly colored clothes. The bouncers watched over the door holding six inch silver stamping wands in their hands. They stamped the back of hands of all of the people that entered the club.

Darian wanted to laugh, he found it humorous that these mortals thought that wearing brightly colored clothes would repel a vampire. It also amused him how mortals would automatically assume that all vampires would wear dark colors at all times. He himself owned plenty of brightly colored clothes. There was only one thing that would keep him out of the club and that was the ultraviolet lighting that was installed at all the entrances as well as the interior itself. The closer the two men approached the club, the stronger the mental connection sharpened that Darian received from the female vampire.

"Around the back, let's split up!" Darian whispered to Warren urgently. Warren nodded and without hesitation he went in the opposite direction along the side of the club. Darian took to the other side to close her in. As they rounded the corner, both men spotted the female vampire, she was wearing a black latex catsuit. The outfit was so tight it looked as though she had poured herself into it. The latex fabric hugged every curve, leaving nothing to the imagination. She huddled over a man in the back alley of the club beside a dumpster. When she caught the scent of Warren, she looked up, her lips bloody from feeding. She let the unconscious human slip from her slender fingers and smiled.

"I've been waiting for you, wolf." She said seductively, then she turned to face Darian, "and you…Master."

Warren looked at Darian, he allowed a quick expression of shock to flash across of his face before regaining his composure. Darian leaned against the brick wall of the club, his arms folded across his chest. A sinister smiled crept across his face and he cocked his head.

"You've disappointed me Eliana. When I gave you my blood on that fateful night in Italy, I did not expect you to repay me in this fashion. You have come to my territory unannounced and have caused nothing but trouble." His lips forming the words as if they were a kiss.

"I paid you back in blood my dear master. How else should a fledgling repay their maker." She began to back herself against the wall centering herself between the two men. She stood legs parted, back facing the wall, marking her ground. Her arms dangled at her side, both index fingers tracing circular patterns on her thighs. Warren looked at Darian, this had turned into a matter between master and fledgling. Warren looked at the female vampire again and felt his anger rise.

"You had no right to kill all of those people because you have a grudge against your maker!" Warren said venomously as he balled his hands into fists. The female vampire disregarded him and kept her eyes focused on Darian. It angered Warren that she thought he should be ignored. He decided right then that he would not attempt to take her in to stand trial. He removed his 9mm with silencer from his holster and aimed it at her heart. Without hesitation he fired the first shot. He watched in amazement as she remain standing, unharmed. The bullet was lodged in the brick wall behind her still smoking, ultraviolet gel oozed from the bullet. He fired off two more shots only to realize that some how the vampire dodged each one.

Her eyes slowly left Darian's to glare at Warren. "You impudent little fool! Your weapons can not affect me and how stupid of you to think so. You, who have traded sides, tell me, does it make you feel superior to kill your own kind…for them!" She growled.

"You are not my kind! You are a murder, the same as any other murder. There is nothing about you that should warrant my respect!" Warren said, the barrel of his gun still pointed at her. He removed his custom automatic from his other holster, the one that contained the explosive metal bullets.

"You are stupid and stubborn. I will kill you slowly, I shall savor your blood before I grind your bones in my hands." She held her hands palm up, outstretched in front of her. To add emphases, she slowly curled her hand into a fist, one finger after another. A sinister smile played across her lips. "Then maybe I'll feed on your partner." She laughed wickedly.

"You touch him and I'll-"

"You'll do what wolf? You'll do nothing, because that is all you can do, puppet!" She said arrogantly, then turned to face Darian, who had been watching the battle of insults with a certain amusement. He did have to admit the last two nights held plenty of spontaneity . It was nights like this that Darian was reminded just how wonderful immortality was. He pushed himself off of the wall and walked towards Eliana . He stood in front of her, his long black trench coat flapping in the cold breeze behind him. His leather clad hands resting at his side.

"Is this a challenge to me, my darling?" Darian asked pointedly.

"Yes." Eliana responded, mimicking his calm.

"I spared you last night to teach you a lesson, I mentally warned you to cease this behavior." He exhaled deeply. "It did not have to be this way, if you were cross, you should have come to me on my terms. We could have worked this out." He began to remove his leather gloves from his hands, one then the other "You still make the most undesirable decisions, it's a pity that this will be the last time we will speak to each other. Tonight, I will end your existence being that is the one choice that you leave me with." He said, his eyes never leaving her intense glare.

"You underestimate me Darian, you always did. For if you had only given me what I asked, if you had increased my power, I would have been happy and it would not have come to this. You are so selfish, however, I found someone who would share power with me. This city…" She raised her hands and looked around the area. "…will be mine, as will your life!" She smiled at him.

"The only thing I underestimated was your common sense. But there is an easy way to remedy that. Now enough hot wind, I have matters to tend to before the sun rises." Darian said. He watched as Eliana's jaw tightened. It was the response he hoped for, anger, fury, all the emotions needed to make a fight worth his while. As he looked at Eliana and smiled, she was the second woman in twenty-four hours to have attacked him, though entertaining, he hoped it was not going to be a pattern. He braced himself as Eliana charged him, moving faster than Warren could see, but Darian could see her every move. In a move quicker than lightening, his hand shot out before him and caught Eliana by her throat. His fingers tightened around her slender throat. A guttural growl spat forth from her as she clawed at his hand. Darian braced himself and tossed her body upwards, sending her crashing against the brick wall with a bone-crushing impact.

Darian appeared under her and caught her in midair. His grip returning to her neck like a vice. Her clawed nails scratching his flesh, drawing blood. Darian's own nails began to extend sharp, strong and pointed. Then in one quick movement, he ripped her throat tearing flesh apart. Blood gushed from the torn wound spraying Darian's face and shirt. Eliana gaped at Darian, hands instinctively going to her throat closing over the bloody wound. Her mouth open wide, gasping, unable to scream in horror. Darian's hand rested at his side, pieces of her flesh clinging to his finger nails as drops of blood pooled under his hand.

Warren stood speechless as he watched the fight between the two vampires. He had never seen a fight between two vampires, witnessing the stronger over take the weaker in such a manner, it had amazed him. He had seen fights within his pack take place in spite of Xander's strict rules of the household. They had been bloody, vicious and always left both participants wounded, sometimes unto death. But never had he seen a fight were one member was left virtually untouched. He found himself truly astonished by Darian. He watched Eliana choke on her own blood as her body fought to restore itself. She backed away from Darian cautiously, her eyes held fear and resentment.

Darian began to move forward, like a stalking predator. Then in a movement too fast for Warren to see with his superhuman vision, Darian was upon the frightened vampire once again. His fangs buried deep into the bloody wound, drinking. Warren could see his throat swallow every drop of blood he took. Warren was relieved that they were in the back of the building away from the public's eye. He would hate to have to explain all that was taking place to the media or his official superiors. He watched Darian pull back from the wound. Darian released his hold on her limp body then he looked at Warren, mouth bloody, eyes glazed.

"She is yours to deal with now." Darian said simply.

"Is she dead?" Warren asked.

"No. I do not want to be wrapped up in this case of yours, not any more than I already am. It's easier for you to end her life," He looked down at her limp body. "You could even say it would be more humane." He said thoughtfully. His eyes gradually looked up at Warren. "I'll leave you, now." And with that, he vanished as if he was never there. Warren stared at the open air where Darian once stood only a second ago. It seemed that he would have to learn a lot more about vampires himself if he was going to continue to hunt them down. He gathered himself out of his deep thought and walked over to Eliana's prone body. He looked down into her face. Her dark wavy locks framed her head like a fan on the cement. Her eyes were half lidded, mouth parted slightly. The wound in her throat was healing still, but dramatically slower than before. Her hands fluttered weakly at her sides, her body began to turn pale. He pointed the barrel of his gun to her head and pulled the trigger.

He watched as a single ultraviolet bullet entered her flesh, embedding the thick skull. Blood oozed thinly from the wound then the flow began to turn thick, black and sticky, like tar. The surface of her skin began to dry and turn brittle and flake away, like ash in the wind. Her eyes paled till they lost all color and began to dry and shrivel inside their sockets. The muscles, bones and sinew had melted away to a thick greasy tar like substance in the shape of her form on the cement. Warren felt a chill ripple through his body, he did not know quite how to feel at this point. He was relieved that it was all over. He looked at the man she had been feeding on when they had come upon her. The man lay in a crumpled heap beside the dumpster but he was alive. Warren could hear his heart beat, smell his blood flow. He walked over to the man and checked him over, monitoring his pulse and breathing. He then called Matthew and informed him of the situation.

"I called for the ambulance." Matthew said as he walked into the alley. He stood over Warren's kneeling form.

"Thank you," Warren said, staring forward thoughtfully. "All this was done as a challenge to Darian, it was her plan to throw insult to him and have a thrill at the same time."

"Where's Darian..don't answer that, it doesn't matter. The only thing that matters is, it's all over." Matthew said, patting Warren reassuringly on the shoulder. They both looked up to see the approaching emergency vehicles. The flashing lights flickered over their faces. Two paramedics rushed over to them and immediately began checking over the injured victim. Warren and Matthew answered all of their questions, then watched as the paramedics placed the victim in the ambulance and drove away. The two detectives walked shoulder to shoulder to the squad car. Warren looked at the night sky and smiled. He pondered what a life as a vampire must be like to never be able to experience such a vision as dawn or high noon. To never be able to feel the suns rays on their skin. He concluded that vampires probably found the night to be as beautiful as any sunlit day.. He and Matthew climbed into the car. Warren turned on the engine and drove back to the precinct to wrap up the paperwork and close the case.

Chapter 22

Natasha awoke the next morning, the sun's warming rays shining on her smooth caramel-toned skin. She stretched, flexing both fingers and toes. She gradually looked over on her beside table glancing at the little black digital alarm clock. The time was 7:05am. She groaned softly, not wanting to get out of bed. She laid there in the bed staring at the ceiling, attempting to think of excuses to avoid going to work. Then after glancing once more at the clock and seeing five minutes had past, she decided to climb out of the bed before she would be late for work. When she reached the bathroom, she glanced at the counter behind the sink, remembering she had taken her medicine to block her visions. She did not want to see what would happen between Warren, Darian and the female vampire. She wanted to rest easy for the first time in five days. It felt good for a while, she had forgotten just how good a full nights rest felt.

Natasha climbed into the hot shower and soaped her body, enjoying the sensation of the tingling foaming bubbles of her shower gel. She rinsed off and stepped out of the shower, wrapping a towel around her body as she headed towards her closet. She slid the articles of clothing back and forth along the steel rod looking for an appropriate ensemble. Even as she looked for clothes her mind drifted to Darian, and Warren. She knew if she was going to have any peace of mind she would have to talk to Warren. She walked to her bed and sat down on the edge and reached over picking up her telephone. She dialed the cell phone number Warren gave her and waited for an answer.

A groggy deep voice came over the phone. "Hello?"

Natasha did not recognize the voice and checked the little green digital screen on her phone that allowed one to view the numbers dialed as well as caller ID. It was the right number.

"Hello, um, is this Detective Warren Davis?" She asked

"No, he's asleep right now, do you want me to wake him? Is it an emergency?" Asked the voice. Natasha wondered what he looked like, she enjoyed talking to people with sexy voices. She also derived a little guilty pleasure imagining the physical appearance of a person over the telephone who's voice was appealing.

"Um, I really hate to wake him I can imagine how exhausted he must be but I really do need to ask him something. Do you mind?" She asked politely.

"Not at all, one minute." Said the voice pleasantly, more clearer. Natasha listened as the voice called to Warren to wake up and to answer his phone. She could hear Warren groan loudly, but after a few seconds she heard his voice.

"Hello?" Warren asked groggily. Natasha giggled, she thought his sleepy voice was a far cry from his sexy awake and alert voice.

"Warren, this is Natasha, I'm really sorry to bother you I know how tired you must be. I just wanted to know what happened last night?" She asked steadily.

There was a long pause over the phone and Natasha began to suspect that Warren had drifted back to sleep. But then he answered her.

"First off, I want to thank you once again for everything you've done for us Natasha. I really mean that with all my heart." Warren said empathetically. "I can't imagine what you've had to see just to tell us what you knew and we couldn't have wrapped up this case without you." Natasha felt herself blushing over the telephone, tears began to well up in her eyes. She was always the sensitive type, a sentimental commercial for mother's day would often set her to crying. Warren's kind words were hitting home with Natasha and she had to reach over to her bedside table for a tissue to blow her nose and wipe her eyes.

"Oh, Warren...I..I don't know what to say. I'm just glad I could help. But more importantly, what happened last night? Are you okay!?" She asked concerned.

"Well, I went to Darian's home to ask him to help us," he paused, remembering the events of last night.

"Did he help? Or did he give you shit!?" Natasha asked annoyed.

"No, actually he was a hell of a lot more pleasant than the first time we asked for his help. He was willing to do it." Warren said, reflecting on Darian's obliging attitude. He did wonder why Darian did not refuse as he had before.

"Oh, okay. What else." Natasha asked, obviously surprised to hear how compliant Darian was. She did not know Darian well, but her first impression of him left her uncertain about his true intentions and personality.

"Well, we tracked her to the human only district. She was in the alley of the *Slayer's Lair* night club. She had taken a victim and was feeding on him when Darian and I interrupted her. It turns out that she was Darian's fledgling and wanted revenge." Warren said thoughtfully.

"You're kidding me right? She and that werewolf murdered all of those people just for her bitter revenge against Darian!!?" Natasha was furious. She did not like the fact that people died for selfish, hateful revenge.

"Yeah, I know just how you feel. Darian seemed a bit...well, I don't know. He just seemed a little sad after he left her for me to deal with." Warren said as he remembered the expression on Darian's face and his manner as he looked down at his own dying fledgling.

"Sad? So he fought with her and almost killed her?" She asked.

"Yeah and it was an amazing battle, I've never seen anyone move as fast as he does!" Warren said still amazed.

"All this is new to me and it's going to take some getting used to. Okay, I'm going to let you go I just wanted to know how things went last night. I wanted to make sure both of you were alright."Natasha said, finding a successful way to end the conversation.

"Yeah, we're alright. I'll be keeping in contact with you. Take care Natasha," Warren said.

"You do the same," she hung up the phone. She thought about what Warren had said about Darian. She could not figure Darian out, she found him to be arrogant, yet charming. Natasha looked at her little digital clock again, ten minutes had past since she first phoned Warren. If she did not get ready fast, she would be late for work. She walked back to her closet, picking a simple black tapered pant suit. Then located her black suede two inch heels and tied her long dark brown hair into a tight ponytail. Natasha gave herself a look over.

"Well, it's not elegant, but it will do." She said to herself, approving her attire. She grabbed her purse, coat and keys and left the apartment.

Her day at work was tiring, but not boring. She was still in the new employee training phase and needed to learn the ropes. There was a reporter working on a story about a school on the north side that was under investigation for violating the sanitation guidelines. Students had reported seeing rat droppings in their food as well as in their classrooms. Natasha had to accompany the reporter to the site of the school and take photographs of the condition of the school. It had angered her that a school would be in that condition. She felt sorry for the children that had to attend the school. She hoped the reporters efforts to expose the school would not go in vain.

After work, she went to the hospital to bring Annette home. Annette had been quite a popular patient. When Natasha walked into Annette's hospital room there were two male nurses with her both of the men were wrapped up in Annette's feminine wiles. One fluffed her pillow while the other joked with her. Natasha shook her head as she leaned against the door frame.

"Alright queen Annette time to go." Natasha said. The two male nurses smiled and left the room. Natasha watched both men as they walked past her glancing sinfully at their buttocks.

"Well I'm ready to go!" Annette said enthusiastically.

"You sure? I mean it looked like you were having fun. Don't let me interrupt you." Natasha said sarcastically.

"Girl please. I had to persuade someone to bring me some real food. I couldn't deal with hospital food three times a day I had to have some good food, the kind that won't make you sick." She said, eyebrows raised for emphases.

"Okay, let's go. You know how I feel about hospitals." Natasha said.

Annette looked at her." Come here, what happen to you?" She asked as she noted Natasha's blemish free skin.

"Oh, long story and I'll tell you when we get home okay? Come on! I'm tired I want to go home. Plus the cab's waiting." She urged Annette. Annette agreed to wait till they got home to ask more questions. She climbed out of her hospital bed slowly, with Natasha's aide. Annette was already dressed in a pair of blue jeans and blue knitted sweater. Natasha helped her put on her sneakers and coat.

"Okay, we're outta here!" Annette exclaimed. Both women walked out of the hospital. The stars shined brightly in the indigo blue nighttime sky. The winter air was cold and both women had to close their coats to keep warm. They climbed into the waiting yellow and black taxi cab. As they settled into the cab, they looked at each other knowingly.

"Remember what happened the last time we took a cab together. I don't know which one of us is bad luck, you...or me." Annette joked.

"Oh stop that, neither. Goofy ass woman!" Natasha said as she chuckled. It amazed her how Annette always had an optimistic approach to life. Natasha told the cab driver their address and within thirty minutes they were in front of their apartment. Natasha paid the driver and she and Annette went inside.

"Well, at least it's still clean. I figured you'd go insane throwing all sorts of parties without me here to monitor you." Annette joked.

"Oh shut up, I liked it better when you were at the hospital. Everything was peaceful." Natasha said playfully.

"Girl please, you know you missed me!" Annette said as she hugged Natasha with her good arm. Natasha smiled and nodded.

"You know I did. You know…" Natasha said as she looked at a corner in the living room, "we should get a Christmas tree before it's too late." She walked into the kitchen to make dinner, when she opened the refrigerator, she heard the door bell ring. "Annette, can you get that?" She called.

"Yeah, yeah, I'll get it." Annette said as she walked to the door. She peeked through the peep hole. And gasped. "It's Darian Alexander, my boss!" She squealed, a multitude of thoughts rushed into her mind. She calmed herself and opened the door, smiling. Darian stood in front her. His long black trench coat brushing his ankles, he was wearing a light grey ribbed sweater and smoke grey knit pants. His black leather shoes were shined perfectly. He held two sets of floral bouquets, one in each hand. He smiled his charming smile, revealing his dimples on both sides of his cheeks. His long jet black wavy hair was combed back and tied in a ponytail.

"May I come in?" He asked, traces of his Greek accent penetrated the words. His voice made Annette legs tremble slightly. She nodded, still smiling. Darian walked gracefully into the modest living room. He looked around and smiled. He turned to face Annette and handed her a bouquet of purple lilies.

"For you my dear. I am sorry that I was unable to visit you while you rested in the hospital. My most sincere apologies." He said, with his customary charm. Annette blushed and took the flowers. She held them under her nose and inhaled deeply. She looked up and smiled at Darian.

"These are beautiful, I love them. Thank you." She said coyly.

"You are most welcomed." Darian, the debonair gentleman, looked around the apartment then set his gaze towards the kitchen. "Is Natasha in there? Do you mind if I give her these?" He asked. Annette looked at him, confused.

"How do you know about Natasha?" Annette asked guardedly.

"We became acquainted two nights ago. With her assistance and my own, we aided the police in their investigation of the serial killings of the past week." He said matter of factly. "May I…" He raised the flowers to his nose and inhaled seductively, eyes focusing on Annette's. "…give these to her?" He asked once again. Annette looked at Darian and nodded. Darian smiled and

234

walked into the kitchen. He saw Natasha standing by the stove stirring a pot of pasta.

"Annette who was that at the door?" Natasha asked. She became concern when she heard Annette talking to someone.

"It is I," said Darian smoothly. Natasha turned around surprised. "I wanted to speak with you and bring you these. Although, they can't begin to convey my feelings for you." Darian said, extending the bouquet of red roses to Natasha.

She took the flowers and smelled them. She smiled. "Thank you. I heard what you did last night and I want to thank you for helping us, you did not have to." She said, she could feel herself blushing.

"I helped your police friends because I'm interested in you. It has been a long time since I've met a woman like you. You intrigue me, your gift..." He raised his hand now, to caress the left side of Natasha face. He brushed the back of his fingertips lightly over her soft skin. "You have an extraordinary gift. I want to help you control it, master it." He said in a hushed seductive voice.

"I...I don't know what to say. All this is new to me and I'm still trying to get use to the fact that you're a vampire and Xavier's a vampire, Warren's a werewolf and well, it's going to take some getting used to." Natasha turned, she placed the flowers on the counter and took the spatula to stirred the pasta. She opened a can of pasta meat sauce and poured the contents of the can into a separate pot. Darian watched her prepare the meal with a keen fascination. Natasha looked over her shoulder and caught him peeking over her shoulder at the pots on the stove.

"What?" She asked perplexed. He's eyes moved from the pots to hers.

"It's been a long time since I've seen anyone prepare a meal." He said honestly.

"It's been a long time for a lot of things for you hasn't it? Perhaps you should get out more." She suggested. Darian laughed, his dimples giving his features a boyish charm.

"So it seems. Why don't you show me all that I've been missing." He said softly. He step closer to Natasha, pressing his chest against her back. Natasha felt the alarms go off in her head. She was powerfully attracted to Darian as well as Xavier. Though, she did not know how she felt about Darian's advances.

"Darian listen, you are handsome, I'm sure you are aware of that. But I'm with Xavier...well, Xavier and I are talking, getting to know one another. It wouldn't be right if I started something with you. Not to mention it might be too overwhelming." Natasha said, she stepped away from Darian. His gaze still locked on her. He reached over and took her hand in his and leaning forward he pressed his lips in a gentle kiss on the back of her hand.

"Xavier hasn't told you, has he?" Darian asked looking up at her.

"Told me what?" Natasha asked. She did not like the way that sounded. What was it that Xavier had not told her?

"Natasha-" Darian started but the sound of the doorbell interrupted him. He glanced over his shoulder when he heard Annette open the door. He recognized the male voice as the voice charmed Annette. "Well, it looks like Xavier will tell you first hand what he decided to keep from you." Darian said. He turned off the pots on the stove, then took hold of Natasha's hand and led her into the living room.

Xavier stood in the middle of the room, fashionably dressed. He was wearing a long calf length black leather trench coat. His brown hair was cropped short and was neatly combed back and parted on the side. He was wearing brown silk slacks and cream cashmere turtle neck sweater. He was breathtaking. He turned and his eyes sparkled when he saw Natasha. Xavier's gaze then fixed on Darian and a hint of lust spread across his face.

"Hello Natasha." Xavier said as he walked towards her. He took her hand in his and performed the same act that Darian had done. He gently kissed the back of her hand. "You're looking gorgeous this evening." He said. He straightened himself and smiled at Darian. It was as if the two vampires were sharing a secret joke. Natasha did not like it.

"Annette, can you give us a few minutes?" Natasha asked, as she looked at the two beautiful vampires standing in front of her.

"Sure. I'll just finish dinner." Annette said. She wanted an excuse to leave the room anyway. She could feel the tension in the air. But she also wanted to stay, curious to see what was going on. She would have to ask Natasha later for all the juicy details. She walked past Darian into the kitchen to finish preparing the meal.

Natasha looked at the two men, her arms folded across her chest. "Okay Xavier, what is it that you need to tell me?" She asked sternly.

Xavier threw a glance at Darian who shrugged one shoulder. Xavier then turn to face Natasha. "I was going to tell you, we just haven't had a whole lot of time to be alone to talk. That's why I came over tonight." He looked at Darian. "I wasn't expecting to find you here."

"And I wasn't expecting to be interrupted by you once again. This is a pattern you're going to have to put an end to." Darian said playfully. Natasha glared at both men.

"Okay, so spill it, what is it!?" She asked, losing her patience. Xavier's eyes traced back to her and he sat down on the sofa gracefully. Darian followed suit, sitting next to him, their shoulders touching. Natasha looked at both of them sitting side by side and felt herself blush. They were both so beautiful to her, she did not want to have to choose but she was more interested in this secret that the two of them seemed to share.

"Natasha, Darian and I are lovers." Xavier said suddenly. He drew her out of her fantasy. Her eyes bulged as she stared at them.

"We've been lovers for over 70 years. I don't know how you feel about that. But I'd like to find out what you are thinking?" Xavier said.

"Think about it this way, you won't have to choose after all." Darian said, reading her mind. Natasha frowned, she did not like being violated in any way.

"Look you," she pointed to Darian. "Stay out of my mind, don't read my thoughts unless I want you to. Got that!?" She said forcefully.

"Ohh, though she be little, she is fierce." Darian said with a coy grin.

"You haven't seen fierce! I don't like you reading my thoughts, you said you were going to help me, and that's fine, but that's as far as it goes." Natasha said.

Darian nodded. "As you wish." He rose from the sofa and stood next to her. "Really Natasha, I am quite fond of you as is Xavier. Before you decide anything," in a movement to fast for her to see, she found herself in Darian's arms. His lips pressed to hers, his tongue exploring her mouth. She felt her knees grow weak. She wondered how many years he had to perfect his techniques. She felt her body respond to Darian advances and blushed. He released her, she opened her eyes only to find that Xavier had taken her into his arms. He pressed his lips to hers, mimicking Darian's kiss. Natasha had never been kissed the way they were kissing her. She had never known a man who could weaken her knees with such a simple intimacy. Xavier released her and sat her down on the chair. Both men looked down at her. After she regained her composure, she stared at them.

"I think both of you should leave." She said steadily. Both men glanced at each other.

"Remember, I am here if you need me my darling. I will be keeping contact with you." Darian said as he bowed. He turned and left the apartment. Xavier watched him leave. Then he turned to face Natasha.

"I did not want it to go like this. But I suppose there's no better way to reveal such a thing." Xavier said solemnly. "I love Darian, we are in a, what you may call, an open relationship." He kneeled down in front of Natasha keeping his gazed locked on hers.

"I know this is all alien to you and thoughts are running through your head right now. I do want to say this before I leave." He took her hands into his. "I want you to be with us, before you protest, think about the advantages of what we offer. I'm completely enamored with you and Darian's bewitched. Besides, once he sets his sights on something he goes after it. Just think about it." He said, releasing her hands. He rose to his full height and left her apartment.

Annette emerged from the kitchen carrying a hot bowl of spaghetti. She looked at Natasha and frowned. She did not like her friend looking so bewildered. She sat on the couch resting the bowl on the armrest. She folded her legs on the sofa for more comfort.

"Wanna tell me what's gong on?" Annette asked Natasha.

Natasha looked at her friend then exhaled deeply. She felt like she had been holding her breath the whole time. "Xavier and Darian are lovers." She said.

Annette smiled. "I suspected as much...go on."

"And you did not tell me!?"

"I *said* I *suspected*, meaning I was not sure..now finish telling me the juicy details.

"Fine, they want me to be with them." Natasha said flatly, uncertain and still in shock.

"A threesome? Wow, that's really kinky. In a way it's like having your own harem." Annette said. She was beginning to like the idea. Natasha looked at her.

"You're corrupt, you know that." Natasha said blatantly.

Annette pressed her good hand to her heart, mockingly. "Why I'm appalled. Here you have two of the most gorgeous men walking the earth drooling over you and you accuse me of being corrupt just cause I see the potential."

"Annette, I don't think so. I mean, yeah, they are gorgeous and mysterious and Xavier's really funny and laid back. Darian's charming and sexy...well, they're both insanely sexy. But Darian has something that's dark and intriguing about him. I feel like I'm drawn to it. I don't know. Maybe because I've drank his blood-"

"Wait, hold up! You drank his blood? When did this happen!?" Annette asked, shocked. She wanted to know all the details.

238

"Well, two nights ago I helped the police track down one of the killers I told you about. Well I was injured." She proceeded to tell Annette everything about the werewolf attacking them almost killing her and how Darian gave her his blood to save her life. Annette had listened to her with wide eyes. To Annette, it was like a movie.

"So can you do any vampire type stuff? What did it taste like?" Annette asked curiously.

"It…well…there's no way for me to tell you this without blushing, so here goes." She took a deep breath, and let it out. "It was amazing!!! It was like sex, only a thousand times better. It was also like the worlds most healing medicine. I could feel my body healing as I drank it. But it is something I want to avoid in the future." She said seriously.

"Why?" Annette asked. "anything that good needs to be bottled and sold retail!" She joked.

"Well Darian told me it was addictive and I just don't want to turn into a blood junky or whatever you call those people who hang out in vampire bars looking for a hit." Natasha said shaking her head.

"Yeah, I understand you. I guess I would not want to be addicted to that either. But then when you think about it, it' s not a bad addiction to have." Annette said cheerfully.

"If you say so." Natasha said doubtfully as she turned on the television. Both women watched the news at nine. Natasha smiled when she saw Warren's face on the news. Natasha informed Annette that he and his partner were the two detectives she helped. Annette told her how proud she was of her. As they ate their dinner and watched the news. After enjoying their dinner, both women went to their bedrooms. Natasha decided to pass on taking her pill this night, just in case someone needed help. She then climbed into her bed as she laid there looking at the ceiling she thought about the two vampires. Could she be in that kind of relationship? Would she like it? She felt the sleep blanket her…she closed her eyes, and drifted off.

The Guilty Innocent

By

D.N.Simmons

Due 2005

   I continued to watch their table the entire time as Elise translated, I could see the fear in Nikolai's eyes as he stared at the coldness of Dmitri's gaze. Nikolai put the briefcase on the table and opened it up, a smiled spread across his face and he nodded approvingly, then closed the briefcase. Dmtri finished his coffee, then rose from his seat, he said something else to Nikolai as he prepared to leave. I did not want him to get away, I looked towards Sergio, who seemed to know my intentions and he rose from his chair followed by Devin and then myself. Before we could walked towards them, Elise called out to us, we turned and looked at her, then I heard an eruption of screaming and saw hysterical people running towards the exit. Sergio leaped high in the air over four tables and landed in front of Dmitri, grabbing hold of his coat. Dmitri swung the leather briefcase, attempting to hit Sergio in the face, but Devin snatched the case from his hands. I looked back towards Nikolai and found him slumped over the table, a puddle of blood forming beneath him. I never heard a gun shot, Dmitri must have used a silencer and someone saw the assassination and started this chaos. Dmitri struggled in Sergio's vice-like grip. He pulled his gun from his inside pocket and Elise caught his hand and began to crush the bones, I could hear the crunching sound of his bones breaking. He cried out in agonizing pain and dropped the gun.

Elise began to speak to him in Russian softly, he shook his head wildly showing stubbornness. Sergio grabbed his chin in a powerful grip and forced his eyes to meet Elise's, Devin stood beside them, still holding the briefcase. Elise spoke to the man again and this time when he tried to refuse, Sergio's grip tightened as if he were trying to crush the man's jaw. Dmitri cried out and began to speak rapidly to Elise as she asked him more questions, this time, he answered. I began to hear police sirens approaching, I looked towards the door and saw another man dressed in all black, wearing a matching face mask. He entered through the door, holding an automatic machine gun. I dropped to the floor and yelled to the others to do the same. Instantly they were on the floor as the gunman sprayed the restaurant with bullets. Dmitri's body was shot through and through, blood splattered the floor around him as his lifeless body danced erratically as the bullets entered him. The man aimed the gun towards the floor, trying to kill us as well, Sergio positioned himself in front of the rest of us, as we crawled towards the kitchen.

About the Author

D. N. Simmons lives in Chicago IL., hobbies include; the martial arts as well as reading, biking, swimming and movie-going. To learn more, and have the opportunity to speak with the author personally, please visit the official website and forum at: www.dnsimmons.com Thank You.

Printed in the United States
58844LVS00003B/133

9 781418 481155